HOLDING ON TO CHAOS

BLUE MOON #5

LUCY SCORE

Bloom books

Holding on to Chaos

The book is a work of fiction. The characters and events in this book are fictitious. Any similarity to real persons, living or dead, is purely coincidental and not intended by the author.

Cover by Kari March

ISBN: 978-1-945631-11-5 (ebook)
ISBN: 978-1-7282-8266-4 (paperback)

Published by Bloom Books, an imprint of Sourcebooks
P.O. Box 4410, Naperville, Illinois 60567-4410
(630) 961-3900
sourcebooks.com

lucyscore.com

090722

To Dawn. Thanks to your eagle eyes, readers can enjoy my books without 70,000 typos.

1

Evangelina Merill was suffocating under a purple paisley wrap sweater that she couldn't get over her head. Autumn had descended on Blue Moon Bend, rendering her South Carolina work-from-home wardrobe of yoga shorts and tank tops ineffective against the chill.

At the time, a visit to the town's thrift shop had seemed like a good idea. But that was before she rapped her elbow on the dressing room wall hard enough to see stars. And before she got this sweater wedged firmly over her face.

And before the fire alarm went off.

"Everybody out!" The shopkeeper, a soft, grandmotherly type with a funny name—Meara? Morra? —pounded on Eva's dressing room door.

"I'm stuck!" Eva told her, her voice muffled through the fabric.

The woman yanked open the door, grabbed Eva's elbow and dragged her toward the door.

"Is this just a drill?" Eva asked through an armhole.

"I wish," the woman puffed. "Forgot the grilled cheese was

on the hot plate in the back. Caught a whole rack of hemp blouses and vintage leather vests on fire!"

That explains the beef jerky smell, Eva thought.

She felt a wave of heat at her back as the door of the shop closed behind her. And then a draft.

Oh. Shit. Her pants were on the floor of the dressing room.

Eva wrestled the sweater off her head in time to see the police cruiser pull up, lights flashing.

"Oh, no, no, no," she whispered. "Not him. Not now." Why did the response time in Blue Moon have to be thirty seconds? And why, dear God *why,* had she left the house in her navy pinstripe push-up bra and her Let's Do This cheeky bikinis?

"Oh, boy." The woman next to her gazed at her with sympathy. Another dressing room victim, she had long dark hair and was wearing nothing but a bodysuit and Chucks. The woman jumped in front of Eva and stood in a Superman stance.

"What are you doing?" Eva had to yell the question to be heard over the sirens of the approaching fire trucks.

"I'm blocking you. You're new in town. You don't need your Facebook gossip group debut to be this. I'm Eden, by the way."

Eva reached over Eden's shoulder and offered her hand. "I'm Eva, and I hardly ever go out in public without pants... or a shirt." They shook awkwardly.

Sheriff Donovan Cardona, all six-feet-four-inches of sublime male perfection, jumped out of the cruiser. "Everyone out, Mayva?"

Mayva! That was it.

It took Donovan all of half a second to zero in on her. She could tell without looking at him because her skin heated to approximately one thousand degrees. Her blush was visible from her hairline to her toes. Silently she cursed her redheadedness.

Donovan was still looking at her, staring really, Eva realized when she peered over Eden's shoulder. Six firefighters rushed past them and into the store.

"Eva." His voice, that delicious gravelly rasp, scraped over her bare skin like a razor.

"Morning, Sheriff," she said, attempting cheerful and casual. The man only caught her in embarrassing moments. She had a crush on him the size of North America, and every time he saw her, she was doing something stupid. Falling out of a tree that her nephew Evan dared her to climb, walking into screen doors, appearing practically naked in the middle of town.

She blinked when a camera shoved its way into her face. "Ladies, can you comment on what happened here?" A scrawny man with wire-rimmed glasses and a digital camera demanded answers.

"Oh great. *The Monthly Moon* is here," Eden groaned.

"What were you two doing when the fire broke out? Did you set the fire? Was anyone hurt? Are you going to buy those clothes?" He rattled off questions like a journalist at a press briefing, getting extreme close-ups of their pores.

"Anthony Berkowicz! You snap one more picture, and I'll shove that damn camera up your damn ass," Eden threatened.

"I'm not taking pictures," he claimed. "I'm shooting video."

"Anthony!" Eva and Eden shouted together.

Eden took a threatening step toward Mr. Nose for News, leaving Eva exposed. Donovan stared, then swore, and stalked back to his car. Eva promised herself right then and there that she wouldn't leave her house ever again.

"I have a right to bring Blue Moon the news," Anthony yelped as Eden made a swipe at his camera.

The sheriff, without a hint of humor, clapped a hand on the shoulder of Blue Moon's poor excuse for a journalist. He towered over Anthony, his broad shoulders blocking out the rest of the world. "Count of three, Anthony. If you're still taking pictures or video or painting a damn picture, I'm cuffing you."

Anthony lowered his camera reluctantly. "Can I at least shoot the fire?" he asked, dejected.

"Fire only. You swing that thing at these two one more time and you won't like the consequences," Donovan promised.

Anthony scampered off to get a better view of the smoke that was pouring from the back of the shop.

Donovan closed the gap between them and Eva tried to cover her chest and crotch regions. *Why were her hands so damn small?*

"Here." His voice was gruff, but the cotton t-shirt he dragged over her head was oh so soft. It smelled incredible.

"Thanks," Eva said, crossing her arms in front of her chest to ward off the chill. He had a good foot on her, and the t-shirt hit her at the knee, covering every bit that needed covered. She wanted to pull the shirt up over her nose and take a deep breath, but that would be weird and creepy with witnesses.

"You two all right?" he asked.

Tongue-tied Eva nodded.

"We're fine, Sheriff," Eden answered for the both of them.

"I gotta go do some traffic control before some idiot drives into a house," Donovan announced.

Eva nodded again.

"When do you think we can get our stuff, Sheriff?" Eden asked. Obviously, the woman was immune to sexy, Eva decided.

Donovan squinted at the building. Flames were visible in the windows now. "Not sure. I'll check with the chief and let you both know."

Mayva was shouting orders at the firefighters. "Forget the

clearance rack! Save the leathers! Oh, and there's this really cute tunic I had my eye on! No, not that one!"

Satisfied that everyone was alive and staying a reasonable distance from the flames, Donovan jogged off into the street leaving Eva to enjoy the view of his well-toned ass in his uniform pants.

"Well, I don't know about you, but I could use a drink and some pants," Eden announced.

"My place is two blocks over. I have a six-pack of John Pierce Brew in my fridge and at least four clean pairs of yoga pants," Eva offered.

"Winner!"

2

Eva had just popped the top on Eden's beer when the front door of the cottage burst open. "I can't leave you alone for two seconds without you nearly dying naked in a fire!" Eva's sister Gia, all long red curls and yoga wear, stormed into the house dragging her husband behind her. "Why didn't you call me?"

"My phone is in my pants, which are on the floor of the dressing room of Second Chances." At least she wouldn't have to deal with the dozens of texts and calls from nosy family and neighbors checking in to make sure she was okay, made it home, and put on some clothes.

"Hi, Eden," Beckett said, offering a wave. "How's the B&B?"

"Business is booming. How's the lawyer/mayor biz?"

"Small talk later!" Gia shoved her phone in Eva's face. "Explain!"

"I'm going to kill that Anthony guy," Eva gasped, yanking the phone out of her sister's grip. Eden crowded in to study the image on the screen. Eva, in her mismatched bra and underwear, was cowering behind the pantless Eden. Sheriff Cardona was staring at them both as if they were a zoo exhibit.

"At least we look pretty good," Eden sighed. "Toned. Right?"

Gia snatched her phone back. "You both look great. Now, how did you start the fire?"

Eva rolled her eyes. As the youngest in the family, she had a reputation for finding trouble. Her oldest sister Emma was a disciplined adult with schedules and spreadsheets. Gia was a multi-tasking forgetful yoga warrior. And Eva was the misunderstood dreamer. Their father insisted it was her natural sense of adventure that got her into trouble. Her sisters felt it was her disdain for responsibility. Eva thought both theories carried merit.

"I swear, this time I didn't do anything. I was trying on clothes when Mayva's grilled cheese on the hot plate set some inventory on fire."

"So, you don't need a lawyer?" Beckett clarified. He was one of Blue Moon's infamous Pierces. A trio of brothers so attractive that a magazine had once tried to offer them all modeling contracts. They'd been more embarrassed than flattered.

"No lawyering necessary," Eva winked at her brother-in-law. "But I appreciate the familial panic."

"I guess we can get back to that *thing*..." Beckett said, looking hopefully at Gia. The look on his face left no doubt as to what "that thing" was.

Gia flushed and grinned. "If you'll excuse us, my husband and I have a... uh, lunch... meeting." And just as she'd towed him inside, Gia dragged Beckett back out. "Glad you're alive," she called over her shoulder. "Bye, Eden!"

"Afternoon delight?" Eden mused.

"They look forward to the school year all summer long."

Watching her sisters and their husbands enjoy their marital benefits made Eva feel the thinnest edge of jealousy.

Not that she begrudged them their happiness. As far as she was concerned, her sisters were the best people in the world next to her father. It was just that she wouldn't mind ending the dry spell that had plagued her since her move to the hippie town in upstate New York. In her case, a dry spell not only affected her personal life but also her professional life.

She sighed, and Eden joined her at the kitchen island. They lifted their beers simultaneously.

"Please tell me all the good men in town aren't taken," Eva groaned.

"I'm sure there are a handful left," Eden predicted. She didn't sound confident.

"So, you run a B&B?" Eva asked, changing the subject

"Yep," Eden said, studying the beer bottle. "It's just south of town. Big, rambling Victorian. Pond. Couple of fluffy dogs."

"Oh! Right next to the winery!" Eva had seen the place. Three stories high with turrets, attic rooms, and an incredible navy, purple, and yellow paint scheme that somehow paid charming homage to both the architecture and the town. A burly pair of curly blonde dogs romped the grounds.

Eden grimaced at the mention of the winery and changed the subject. "What do you do for a living?"

"Oh, I'm a technical writer. Manuals and instructions mostly. Things like that." The fib rolled off Eva's tongue as glibly as the truth. Technically, up until a year ago, it had been the truth.

"That sounds..."

"Boring? Coma-inducing?" Eva supplied.

Eden laughed. "Hey, scrubbing guest toilets and baking muffins every day isn't exactly glamorous. It's like being a housewife to a bunch of strangers."

"It's amazing neither one of us has a drinking problem," Eva joked. She raised her beer in a silent toast.

"How long do you think it will be before Sheriff Sexy lets us get our stuff out of the shop?" Eden asked.

"So, it's not just me? He's really that gorgeous?"

"Blindingly beautiful," Eden agreed.

"He's caught me in every embarrassing situation known to single women since I moved here. I think he thinks I'm an idiot."

"It can't be that bad."

"He's pulled me over for speeding the day after I moved in. I fell out of a tree almost on top of him at a picnic, and then I walked into a screen door carrying a cherry pie, and I just know he was watching."

"Maybe he's watching because he's interested?" Eden suggested.

"Maybe he was watching because he considers me a menace to society."

"At least he's watching," Eden pointed out, sliding onto a barstool.

Eva huffed out a breath.

Just once in her life she wanted to get *the* guy. Not the online loser who lied about being divorced or the meet-cute-turned-weirdo who still lived in his mother's basement and insisted on "no crusts" through the intercom. The sheriff was the perfect representation of the kind of man who was her ideal and completely out of her league. Sexy as hell, built like a professional athlete, kind-hearted, even-tempered, responsible, carried a gun for a living—which was seriously hot—and probably also carried some nice equipment beneath those uniform pants...

Eva wanted a man like Donovan Cardona to take one look at her and fall madly, hopelessly in lust with her. And then rip her clothes off and take her to bed for two weeks straight.

But that was a fantasy, and she knew fantasy from reality.

In reality, it wasn't so much about the man as it was being seen as the kind of woman she'd always wanted to be. Smart, beautiful, witty, graceful, interesting, sexy. She was tired of being the screw up, the baby, the only Merill to need a tutor just to scrape by in geometry.

She had goals. She promised herself that she would become that woman once she'd conquered her demons and finally put the past in the past.

Eva sighed and pushed it all aside. She was in Blue Moon to be close to her family and focus on what came next in life. She'd have plenty of time to moon over Sheriff Sexy later.

"Let's see what else our pal Anthony said about the fire." Eva grabbed her laptop off the dining table and opened it on the counter. She navigated to Blue Moon's Facebook group and scowled at the screen. She had to scroll past seven pictures of herself prancing around downtown like an underwear model before she found the story. "According to Anthony's attempt at journalism, the fire is out. 'No injuries unless the two nearly naked customers—whose names have been withheld for privacy reasons—caught cold.'"

"That skinny little asshole," Eden grumbled. "As if everyone in the county doesn't know everyone else. We don't even need to run names with obituaries. Everyone already knows who's dead and who their second cousins are."

Eva had been warned about the gossip group but had dismissed it as small town exaggeration. She hadn't considered the possibility that she'd make her debut in the group in her underwear. Her father would be so proud. Next thing she knew, the Beautification Committee would come knocking trying to marry her off to a bellbottom-wearing hippie... who probably insisted that his mother cut the crusts off his PB&Js.

3

Eva, feeling neighborly, lent Eden her car so her new friend could get back to the B&B in time to set up for afternoon tea. Working from home and living in Gia and Beckett's backyard in the middle of town meant she did most of her traveling on foot.

With no word on when it would be safe to retrieve her things from the smoky dressing room, Eva changed into her work uniform, cropped leggings, a tank top, and her glasses. Donovan's gray t-shirt, folded neatly at the foot of her bed caught her eye. She picked it up, smoothing a hand over the fabric worn by countless washings. Sneaking a peek over her shoulder—she never knew when a niece or a nephew would appear—Eva brought the t-shirt to her nose and snuck a sniff.

She caught a glimpse of herself in the dresser mirror and saw a desperate, shirt-sniffing woman with eyes half-closed in dark fantasy. "Crap. I'm pathetic," she muttered, dumping the shirt back on the bed.

This dry spell needed to end immediately if the scent of laundry detergent and dryer sheets was putting her over the edge.

She bit her lip. Technically she lived alone. There was no one else in the house to judge her for wearing a crush's t-shirt. Maybe it would help her focus? She strutted downstairs cloaked in Cardona and felt inspired. She'd put in a few hours of work and forget about the whole half-naked in town thing for a while.

Eva fired up her coffee maker, slid on her headphones, and settled in to work.

And, as it happened on good days, she got completely sucked in.

She wasn't sure how long she'd been at it. Long enough that her knees buckled under her when she jumped out of her chair when a hand settled on her shoulder. She spun around, hands in the only karate position she could remember from the intro classes she'd taken in college.

Sheriff Cardona was standing in her kitchen, his hand hovering instinctively over his stun gun as his eyes scanned the room for the threat.

"Holy mother of God!" Eva screeched, her heart trying to claw its way out of her throat.

His lips moved, but she couldn't hear the words.

"What?"

He pointed at his ear and then at her. Her headphones. The Black-Eyed Peas were still rocking out in her ears. Eva swept them off her head and tossed them on the table next to her laptop. *Shit. Her laptop.* She slammed the lid shut on it.

"Uh, hi," she said, pretending that she hadn't just freaked out on him.

"'Uh, hi?' That's what you have to say for rupturing my ear drums?" Donovan demanded, righting the chair she'd knocked over in her haste.

"You're the one who broke into my house and scared the hell out of me!"

"I tried calling. You didn't answer. And when I got here, I knocked hard enough to rattle the glass." He was using his law and order voice on her as if she was some outraged citizen in need of talking down.

"My phone is back at the store. I left in a bit of a hurry *because of the fire*," she reminded him. "And I was listening to music," she sniffed.

"I'm amazed you can hear anything at all. You should be deaf from those decibels."

"Why are you in my kitchen?" she demanded. The man was taking up half the space in her house and making her feel defensive. But at least her tongue was no longer tied.

"Why are you in my t-shirt?" he countered.

Ah, crap. She'd forgotten what she was wearing.

"I, uh. What makes you think this is yours? It's my ex-boyfriend's," she insisted. She was nothing if not creative on her feet.

Donovan grabbed her by the shoulders, his hands a warm shock through the cotton. He spun her around. "Your ex-boyfriend is part of the Blue Moon PD?" he asked, reading the type across her back.

"I need coffee," Eva said, wiggling out of his grip. She couldn't think when she was being manhandled by Sheriff Sexy and his big, sexy hands. "Do you want coffee?"

She skirted the tiny island, grateful to have a barrier between them, and sniffed the still-full pot. She'd gotten sucked into work and never bothered to pour the first cup.

"Sure," he drawled.

Eva looked over her shoulder to shoot him a frown at the tolerant amusement she heard. Unfortunately, she misjudged her distance from the cabinet and opened the door into her face.

"Ouch." She rubbed absently at her eye and reached for

the mugs. But those big hands appeared above her, fishing two mugs out of the cabinet.

"Sit before you dump a full pot of hot coffee all over yourself," he ordered, hip checking her out of the way.

The good sheriff clearly knew nothing about women. The order to sit made standing a much more appealing position.

Donovan must have read the rebellion in her eyes. "Sit or no coffee," he said sternly.

"It's my coffee," she pointed out.

"And I'll be happy to share it with you if you sit your ass down and stop making me nervous."

"*I* make *you* nervous?" She laughed at the irony and slid onto a barstool.

"I feel like you're one second away from swinging a frying pan at me or falling through a window." He set a mug down in front of her, and she reached for the sugar bowl—a whimsical mermaid—she kept on the island.

While she dumped sugar into her cup, he opened the freezer and plucked out a handful of ice cubes which he wrapped up in her purple dish towel. "Here. Ice your face."

She did what she was told only because her face did hurt.

"Do you want to file a police report against the cabinet?" he asked, picking up his coffee.

She gave a small laugh. "No. I think I can work things out with it. It didn't mean it."

"That's what all cabinet doors say," Donovan said, a hint of a smile playing on his gorgeous lips. He looked like a Ken doll come to life. Dirty blond hair cut short for convenience, sharp blue eyes that told her they could peel away lies to get to the truth, and shoulders that would make a linebacker weep. He was big, solid, and oh-so-sexy.

Usually, the guys she ended up dating were leaner, more of the medium height and medium build type. Then again, the guys she usually dated were also usually assholes. Donovan—the opposite of an asshole—was taking up her entire kitchen just standing with his feet planted apart. His uniform fit him so well she wondered if he had it tailored to show off those pecs, those biceps.

Great. Now she was drooling.

Eva cleared her throat. "You may have said it when you came in, but I was busy screaming. Why are you here?" she asked.

He gave her a half smile that had her underwear combusting when the dimple appeared at the side of his mouth. She put her coffee down. She didn't need a warm up. She needed a cold shower.

"I brought your stuff from the store." He nodded toward a plastic bag on the floor just inside the door.

On cue, Eva's phone rang from the depths of the bag.

"Aren't you gonna get that?" he asked.

"It's just someone who wants to tell me they saw me almost naked on Facebook today." He looked away from her and became engrossed studying the pictures plastered all over the front of her fridge. "Please tell me this isn't the most embarrassing gossip group post in town history."

"I shouldn't have to tell you. You've lived here long enough to know what catches the eye of Mooners."

He was right. She was forgetting about Fitz's unfortunate face-first skid down Lavender Street after the ice cream truck last month.

"Is Mayva okay? Was there much damage to the store?" Eva asked, changing the subject.

"Everyone's okay," Donovan assured her. "Mayva's already planning a cruise when the insurance money comes in and Calvin Finestra and his crew start the reno."

Eva breathed out a sigh. "I'm glad it wasn't worse. I can't believe all that happened over a grilled cheese."

"I don't know what got into her. Mayva's been a vegan for thirty years, and today of all days, she gets a hankering for a grilled cheese."

"I imagine weird things happen a lot in this town," Eva predicted.

"You have no idea," Donovan grinned.

The full wattage nearly killed her. Blinded, she reached for her mug to give her hands something to do and succeeded in sloshing it all over the counter.

Wordlessly, Donovan ripped a paper towel off the roll and mopped up her spill. He looked like he wanted to say something, but his phone rang.

"Cardona," he answered briskly. She listened to his side of the conversation, a short series of "uh-huhs" and "yeahs."

"Okay. Thanks, Minnie. I'm on my way."

"Duty calls?" Eva asked, sliding off her stool and hoping for flirty and casual. It was hard to pull it off with a dishtowel of ice stuck to her head, but she gave it her best shot.

"Yeah, Garcia's ferrets got out again. Snuck into Mrs. Duphraine's house and terrorized her pitbull."

"Poor Willoughby. Thanks for dropping off my things," she said, escorting Donovan to the door.

He looked down at her, and her toes curled into the floor boards as she looked way, way up to meet his gaze.

"My pleasure," he said, his voice husky.

He reached for the doorknob.

"Oh! Wait. Your shirt!" Eva grabbed the hem and pulled it over her head.

Donovan was staring at her like she'd just made a repeat performance of this morning. *Geez. Hadn't he ever seen a tank top before? Oh, shit.*

She was topless again. The tank top came off with the t-shirt.

She clapped her hands over the lacey pink bralette that hid absolutely nothing from his cop eyes.

"Aunt Eva, why do I hafta wear clothes if you don't?" Aurora, her niece and seven-year-old wannabe nudist, was standing on her doorstep.

Eva wrestled the tank out of Donovan's shirt and yanked it over her head. He started to say something, but Eva knew there was nothing he could say that would make this situation less humiliating.

"Just go," she said, hanging her head and pointing to the door. "Go before my pants fall off and my kitchen sink erupts in a geyser."

The wise sheriff took his leave.

"Bye, Donovan," Aurora yelled cheerfully after him.

4

Donovan wanted a beer. And a curvy redhead to accompany him into a steaming hot shower. Only one of those things was going to happen tonight. Leaving the October afternoon behind him, he pushed open the station's front door and breathed in the familiar scent. Stale coffee and new carpet.

His mother wouldn't recognize the place, he thought, pouring himself a cup of hours-old coffee. The new coat of paint squeezed out of the budget had toned down the lavender walls—a color that some jokester a few decades ago decided would be soothing to prisoners. Not that Blue Moon ever really dealt with prisoners.

Hazel Cardona had put in her time as Blue Moon's sheriff and never batted an eye at the feminine color that had clashed horrifically with the mossy green and yellow carpeting. Now the walls were a nice, plain beige and looked just fine with the slightly darker beige carpet. Donovan considered it a victory that the issue hadn't been put up to a vote at a town meeting. His shoes would be cruising over some rainbow shag right now had the town had their say.

"There you are," said his right-hand woman, Minnie Murkle, as she bustled out of the file room. "You've been MIA all day. Did you have lunch?" she asked sternly.

He'd been running since the fire that morning, and part of him was grateful for the action so he couldn't keep thinking about Eva and her nearly naked appearances today. Great. Now he was thinking about it again. Minnie pulled triple duty as non-emergency dispatch, records clerk, and desk jockey. He dreaded the day she announced her retirement. But since she was sixty, he figured he could tempt her into a few more years.

"One crisis after another. I haven't seen a day like this in... ever," he admitted, avoiding the lunch question. Of course he'd forgotten. In the midst of the fire, the cleanup, the two fender benders between lookie-loos, and scaring the hell out of Eva Merill, food had slipped his mind.

"Something's got this town stirred up," Minnie agreed, leading the way into his office where she dumped a stack of files on his desk. "I sent Colby out on two calls today."

Colby was one of Donovan's two part-time deputies. Blue Moon had neither the budget nor the need for three full-time officers, which worked out fine for them all. Colby picked up the slack on Donovan's days off and spent the rest of his time helping out around Pierce Acres.

If Donovan ever could offer Colby full-time employment, his friend Carter Pierce would hunt him down.

Donovan's other deputy, Layla, had a few years on Colby and an edge that connoisseurs of her pretty, sunny exterior didn't notice until it was too late. Between the three of them, law and order was generally upheld in the sleepy little town.

Minnie walked him through his messages and gave him a running commentary on a few pieces of town gossip. "Saw that new Merill girl ended up naked in town square," Minnie commented.

"Her name is Eva, and she wasn't naked. And it was two blocks back from the square," Donovan corrected with the pertinent facts.

Minnie grinned. There was nothing the woman loved more than gossip. It was one of the main reasons the job fit her so well. "Poor girl looked a little chilly. Preliminary report from the fire chief is in that stack," she said, pointing to a pile of folders. "And tomorrow you have a meeting with Beckett and Elvira Eustace to nail down the details for the Halloween Carnival."

Donovan glanced at his watch. "Why don't you go on home, Minnie? I have a feeling we're looking at a busy week. Might as well take a break when you can."

"Sure thing, boss. Don't stay here all night," she said, pointing a finger at him. She paused in the doorway. "Say, you don't think we're looking at another planetary crossing, do you?"

Donovan sank down in his chair and rubbed the back of his neck. "Planetary whating?"

"Don't you remember back in the '80s? There was some kind of astrological thing that only happens once every thirty years or so? It had everyone acting like it was a full moon at an all-you-can-drink asshole reunion."

Something tickled at the back of Donovan's memory. Something he didn't like.

In any other geographical location on the face of this earth, he'd put zero stock in an entire town being affected by some planet spinning through some section of space. But in Blue Moon, anything was possible. "I don't know, Minnie. I'll have to give my mom a call. See if she recalls."

Minnie, a lapsed Catholic, made the sign of the cross and knocked on Donovan's desk. "Oh, she'll recall. Let's hope this isn't a repeat."

Minnie packed it in, leaving Donovan with his first peace and quiet of the day. He sat back in his chair and closed his eyes. The image of Eva popped crystal clear into his mind.

It was bad enough that he'd thought of her fully clothed about fifty times a day since she moved to Blue Moon—doubling the number of times she crossed his mind since first seeing her at his friend Beckett's wedding. Now that he'd seen her nearly naked twice? He wasn't going to be able to use his brain for anything but fantasizing.

He loved his job. His town. And he took his job serving the citizens of Blue Moon seriously. But Donovan wasn't used to serving under constant distraction. He'd seen beautiful women before. Seen them and forgotten them just as quickly. There was something about Evangelina that drew him in and hooked him.

He could have just drawn that pink lacy strap down one of her milky white shoulders and—

The bell on the station's front door broke him from his fantasy. Abashed, he realized he was going to need a minute before greeting any visitors so he could get rid of the evidence of his train of thought. Donovan was on his second deep breath, mentally reciting baseball stats when Carter Pierce wandered into the office, his son Jonathan on his hip and a box from Peace of Pizza in his free hand.

"Thought we might tempt you with early man dinner," Carter said, letting Jonathan slide to the floor.

The toddler waved at Donovan and scampered over to the file cabinet drawer that held among other things, a stuffed police teddy bear that the kid had made at Build a Bear and a bunch of plastic tools. While Jonathan giggled to himself trying to make the bear hold a bright yellow chisel, Carter slid the pizza onto Donovan's desk and planted himself in one of the visitor's chairs.

"Got beer?"

"The owner of a brewery asks me for beer." Donovan shook his head at the irony. He reached into the mini fridge behind him and fished out a beer, a water, and one juice box.

"You've got this honorary uncle thing down," Carter said, tearing off two paper towels and using them to plate slices of pepperoni pizza.

"When you end up with forty-seven nieces and nephews over the span of a year, you adapt quickly."

"What can I say?" He shrugged. "All the Pierces jumped on the marriage and kid train. When are you joining us?"

Eyes narrowed, Donovan took a bite of pizza. "You join the Beautification Committee?"

Carter snickered and combed a hand through his dark beard. "No, but I did see the pics of Eva today. You looked like the Big Bad Wolf ready to swallow Little Red whole."

"Did not," Donovan argued.

"Too. Jonathan, you want pizza, or do you want to wait?" Carter asked, turning his attention to his son who was making drill noises and pretending to stab holes into the wall of file cabinets.

"I wait," Jonathan announced without taking his attention away from his work.

"Hard worker that one. Where are your ladies today?" Donovan asked, hoping to steer the conversation away from Eva and the things he looked like he wanted to do to her.

"Summer and Meadow are doing a Facebook Live thing for the magazine with Gia and her girls. Something on parenting girls to be awesome instead of nice."

"Good topic," Donovan said, reaching for a second slice.

"Back to the original topic. Why haven't you made a move on Little Red yet?"

Carter was not one to be deterred or distracted and

Donovan should have known better, having known the man his entire life. He didn't bother pretending he wasn't interested. The entire town saw him mooning over her like a teenager at Phoebe and Franklin's wedding earlier that year. "It's a big transition moving to Blue Moon. I wanted to give her some space so she could settle in."

Carter chomped on a piece of crust. "Commendable bullshit. What's the real reason?"

Donovan ran a hand absently over the back of his neck. "Ah, hell."

"Boooolshif," Jonathan said in a sing-song voice.

Carter grimaced. "I'll fix that later. Talk."

"She scares the hell out of me," Donovan said, giving his confession in a rush. "I saw her and from that moment on I was hooked. I don't know if I'm ready for those kinds of feelings. I'm not an intense kind of guy, and yet one look at her and something punched me in the gut, and I still haven't caught my breath."

Carter combed a hand through his beard. "Are we talking love at first sight here?"

Donovan shook his head. "Man, I don't know what it is. It was just like 'there you are.' Like I was waiting for her or something."

"And that makes you avoid her at all costs?"

Donovan shrugged, wiping his hands on his pants. "Like I said, she scares the shit out of me. If I ask her out, I feel like that puts me directly on the marriage-kid train."

"Shif!" Jonathan said cheerfully as he began to hammer the carpet into place, the police bear tucked under his arm.

"Look, one punch in the gut isn't going to force you down the aisle," Carter argued. "Get to know her. Otherwise you're just oozing all this sexual tension and eventually the B.C. will take aim."

Donovan shook his head. “Uh-uh. I told them if they ever make a move in my direction, I’m arresting them all for assaulting an officer.”

“They’ve gotten a lot sneakier in their ways. You won’t even see it coming,” Carter predicted. “It’s better to jump in of your own free will and see what happens.”

Jonathan appeared at Donovan’s chair, his little arms waving in the universal signal for up.

Donovan picked him up and settled him on his lap.

“Peeza, peez!” Jonathan said, clapping his hands together.

“See? The kid knows what he wants, and he goes out and gets it,” Carter said ripping a few bite-sized pieces off a slice and putting them in front of Jonathan. “So, go find out if Eva’s what you want.”

5

It was after seven, and the sun had set by the time Donovan left the station with his paperwork mostly complete and feeling thankful that no new crises had erupted. His parents didn't answer his call, so he found himself steering his cruiser toward Pierce Acres. Phoebe Pierce—Merill now—had been tight with his parents. Maybe she'd remember something about this planet bullshit.

He was just crossing his t's and dotting his i's, Donovan assured himself. Being thorough enough to investigate threats, no matter how farfetched they seemed, was part of the job.

He turned onto the dirt and gravel lane of the farm where he'd spent as much time as a kid as his own home. He waved to Summer and Gia who were juggling kids and three dogs on their way out of the little red barn that served as headquarters for their online magazine.

He spared Gia an extra glance in the rearview mirror. Though the family resemblance was strong and the looks striking among the sisters, neither Gia nor Emma had ever stirred him the way Eva had.

He'd spent the better part of a year wondering if—sometimes hoping—that pull would go away. But Carter was right. He was going to have to make a decision one way or another. He followed the drive over a short crest and to the west. He could see the lights of Phoebe and Franklin's house ahead.

He drummed his fingers against the wheel when he eased in next to the dark blue Mini Cooper. If Eva's flashy little ride was here, odds were the woman was as well. He thought about her goodbye and grinned. She'd been embarrassed. He'd been turned on. He wasn't sure if the next time he saw her he wanted it to be with her parents present. He debated for another thirty seconds and released his seatbelt.

Hazel and Michael Cardona didn't raise him to run scared from anything. Not even a tiny redhead with bewitching eyes... and an incredible body.

His knock on the front door was met with frantic barking and the skittering of dog paws on hardwood. "I'll get it!" He heard the call from the back of the house and knew before she opened the door who it would be.

"Oh!" Eva stared up at him, her mouth gaping open. A snot-nosed pug shoved its flat face out the door and romped over to his feet to sniff him.

"Hi," he said to Eva, looping his thumbs into his pockets and letting Mr. Snuffles get a good whiff of cop shoes. "Are your parents home?"

"I'm having flashbacks to high school," Eva breathed, her eyes wide. "Tell me this isn't about my senior class prank." The way she shoved a bare foot behind the door made him think she was considering slamming it in his face if the answer was yes.

He laughed. "That's not at the top of my list, and neither is arresting Phoebe or Franklin. Just have some questions."

"In that case, come on in." She opened the door with a

flourish, and when he stepped into the foyer's light, he spotted the bruise. He took her chin in his hand and held her face to the light. "Doesn't look too bad," he commented.

Eva wrinkled her nose. "You should see the other guy."

"Don't tell me your landlord is going to make me arrest you for abuse of a kitchen."

"Who is it, Eva?" Phoebe called from the back of the house.

"The cops," Eva yelled over her shoulder. She grinned up at him, and his blood stirred. Bewitched and bewildered. That was his current status.

"You said you didn't have anything to do with the fire," Franklin yelled over the blender.

"Very funny!" Eva yelled back. "Come on back," Eva told Donovan, gesturing over her shoulder. "You're just in time for dinner."

He followed her and the sway of those hips as she padded barefoot down the hallway. She wore slim black pants that accented all the right curves. Her oversized denim shirt was tucked into the front, and the sleeves were rolled up. Her hair was up in a riotous ponytail of strawberry blonde curls that begged for him to fist his hands in them.

"Donovan!" Phoebe greeted him as if he was one of her sons with a kiss on the cheek and a studious look. Her short brown hair was streaked with silver. But it didn't make her look old. She'd never be old in his eyes. She peered at him over her wire rimmed glasses. "Tell me you're off duty and you can stay for dinner."

He thought about the two slices of pizza he'd gotten out of Carter and then about the cold cuts sitting in his fridge. The air in the main living space smelled of something delicious and Italian, and his stomach pleaded with him.

"If it's no trouble."

"I made enough for a family of ten," Franklin promised from the stove. He was a burly man with silver hair and a warm, ever-present smile. With the onset of fall, he'd traded in his Hawaiian shirts for colorful checkered long sleeve Oxfords.

"Here," Phoebe shoved bowls into his hands and then pointed Eva to the plates on the counter. "You two set. We'll finish up in here. Dinner in five. And Eva, get our sheriff here a drink, please."

Phoebe had practically run Donovan's campaign for town sheriff. And she'd been just as thrilled, just as proud as his own mother, when he'd won in a landslide. Whenever he got to missing his own parents, who'd moved to New Mexico a few years ago, he'd visit Phoebe. He was always welcome in her home, at her table. And there he could always find the family he needed.

Donovan followed Eva around the table, placing a bowl on each plate she lay down.

She stopped short at the head of the farmhouse table, and he bumped into her. She turned slowly to face him, and Donovan felt his breath catch. He gritted his teeth, careful not to show any outward reaction. If this was a crush, he never wanted to feel the full-blown thing. He could barely function around her as it was.

"What would you like to drink? Beer or wine?"

"How about wine?" he decided, feeling festive.

"Red or white?" she asked, her lips curving up at him. She was too close. He liked it too much.

"Surprise me," he said, his voice low and husky as if they were sharing secrets. His fingers twitched at his side wanting to reach out to her. To touch that slim, ivory neck.

When Eva stepped away, he could breathe again.

Franklin lugged a huge pot to the table and settled it on an owl shaped trivet. "Italian wedding soup," he announced.

Phoebe appeared behind him with a basket of bread in one hand and a large wooden salad bowl in the other. "Fresh garlic bread and beet and arugula salad," she said, putting them down on the table.

Eva appeared with two glasses of red wine and handed one to Donovan. He didn't think it was his imagination that her fingers lingered under his for just a second too long.

They took their seats, Phoebe pointing him to the seat on Eva's left, and the food dishing and passing commenced. If dinner was half as good as it smelled, Donovan decided he was going to owe Franklin and Phoebe a nice bottle of wine. Franklin owned and operated Villa Harvest, Blue Moon's Italian restaurant. *The man knew his way around a kitchen, that was for sure*, Donovan decided, spooning up another bit of hot, flavorful soup.

"Now that you're here, Donovan, you can help us interrogate Eva on how she got that black eye," Phoebe said, nodding at her stepdaughter. "She's being awfully cagey."

"Something about a kitchen accident," Franklin said. "Sounds suspicious to me."

Eva pointed a finger in Donovan's face. "You, keep quiet. You're bound by sheriff-citizen confidentiality."

He laughed. "That's definitely not a thing."

She screwed up her nose and frowned at him. "Fine. How about this?" Eva took his hand in hers and stared up at him, her green eyes wide and guileless. "Donovan, are you my friend?" she breathed each word as if she were imparting a secret.

He nodded, heart in his throat. Damn if that woman didn't get his blood flowing from one wide-eyed look.

"Good," she said brightly. "Because friends don't snitch!"

Vixen. Eva Merill was a sneaky, sexy, manipulative...

"Donovan was with you when it happened? Did you walk into a glass door during the fire?" Franklin asked.

Donovan snorted. "No, but that does sound like something Eva might do."

"Not nice, Cardona." Eva glared at him. She sniffed, haughty as a queen. "I clearly need better foundation if you can still see it. It's tiny. Practically invisible. Phoebe, what kind of cover-up do you use? I think I'm ready to graduate from drugstore makeup."

The conversation shifted from bruises and makeup and then on to Franklin's fall specials at the restaurant. Donovan realized Eva had successfully maneuvered interest away from her face and onto other topics without anyone but him catching on.

The woman had depths, devious ones.

"So, what brings you out our way, Donovan?" Franklin asked. "Nothing to do with the fire, I hope?" He shot his daughter a look.

Donovan shook his head. "No, that was a pretty straightforward investigation. Accidental and—believe it or not—not caused by Eva." Phoebe and Franklin laughed while Eva stuck her tongue out at him.

He shouldn't have gone rock hard at that, but he did anyway. He cleared his throat, tried to focus.

"Actually, it was something Minnie mentioned. We had a lot of strange calls today, and she mentioned something about some kind of planetary crossing?"

Phoebe dropped her spoon in her bowl, drawing Donovan's attention. "Are you sure that's what she said?" Phoebe asked before taking a gulp of wine.

He nodded, forcing himself to focus on the conversation.

"She said it happened back in the eighties. Something about the whole town going nuts."

"And they never recovered?" Eva asked with a wink.

Phoebe ripped off a piece of bread and threw it in her stepdaughter's direction. "Very funny." She grinned at her step daughter.

"I don't remember Mom ever talking about it, and she didn't answer my call today. I thought maybe you'd remember something about it," Donovan continued, dipping a piece of crusty bread into the soup.

It was Phoebe's turn to clear her throat. "Those were very dark days for Blue Moon," she began. "It was like the full moon lasted an entire month. People were just going crazy."

"Wait! Are you serious?" Eva interrupted, picking up her wine glass.

"Deadly serious." Phoebe nodded. "Hazel didn't sleep for the entire month. People were doing things so out of character. Vegetarians were stealing cold cuts from the butcher. Couples who had been cohabitating for decades were suddenly deciding they needed to get married and then filing for divorce the next day. Grown men were pulling fire alarms in the movie theater and the grocery store. There were more than twenty arrests for public nudity."

Donovan felt it, that cloud of dread as it grew over his head. "What caused it?"

"No one was ever sure. Charisma Champion, you know her?"

"Sure. I had her for American history and wool dying in high school," Donovan nodded.

Eva sputtered in her wine glass and clamped a napkin over her mouth. "Sorry," she said. "Wool dying got me."

Mr. Snuffles let out a loud snore from under the table.

"Well, she's also an astrology hobbyist," Phoebe continued.

"And I think she had a theory about something with a planet traveling through some system and wreaking havoc."

Donovan reached for his wine. No sheriff wanted to hear that there was a potential town-wide meltdown in the works.

"Let's hope that, this time around, a theory is just a theory."

6

Eva could barely concentrate on the bowl of heaven in front of her. Dinner—and the man next to her—demanded her full attention. The idea that some astrological apocalypse could be heading for town? It was fascinating like finding out that witches or vampires were real. And speaking of fascinating, there was Donovan Cardona. Still in uniform, still sexy as hell. She couldn't put her finger on exactly what it was about him that was so appealing. Sure, he was gorgeous. And manly. And had the whole do-right thing going on. But there was something else. Something steady and reliable and so solidly good about him.

And when she spelled it out like that, it didn't sound sexy, she thought, mentally editing her description of him. Eva didn't like it when things couldn't be defined by words.

Donovan's knee brushed hers under the table and derailed her thoughts. He fumbled his wine glass and shot her a heated look that Phoebe and Franklin missed.

Her heart tripped, and Eva straightened in her chair. There was no way in hell it was possible. There wasn't a shred of possibility that Sheriff Sexy was attracted to her. Granted, he'd seen her boobs, and they were pretty fantastic. But the rest of the package? She was a walking, falling down disaster. Donovan would go for someone tall and lithe and infinitely graceful. Like Taneisha, the marathon-running model of sweetness and perfection that Eva wanted to hate but couldn't.

God, they would have beautiful children.

"Pathetic," Eva muttered under her breath. Even in her own fantasies she was marrying off her heartthrob to other people.

"What's pathetic?" Donovan asked quietly, leaning in.

"Uhhhh, oh politics today. I mean can't we all just agree we want everyone to be healthy, safe, educated, and not poor?" Eva shoved a forkful of salad into her mouth to prevent the necessity of answering any follow up questions.

She was generally an excellent liar. After all, she was the only sister never to be caught sneaking home after curfew. But a few run-ins with the good sheriff, and she couldn't even string a plausible fib together.

"Forgive Eva, Donovan. She lives in her own little world half the time," Franklin said with an indulgent wink in her direction.

"My world is lovely. Thank you very much," Eva said, snagging her wine glass, grateful that no one actually knew where her little world had led her.

"We were discussing the Halloween Carnival," Phoebe told her.

"Ooh! A carnival! That sounds like fun. Unless of course the whole planetary alignment thing turns out to be true. Then it would probably be a nightmare."

Donovan gripped his spoon like it was a weapon. "I guess I'll have to make sure that doesn't happen."

A man cocky enough to think he could realign planets? Eva liked that.

~

Eva begged off dessert, already thinking about the time she'd need to spend in Gia's yoga studio burning off her dad's damn bread. Plus, she didn't want to have an awkward exit with Donovan. She'd had enough of those encounters today and didn't need to add fumbling with her car keys and accidentally backing into the big oak tree in the front yard to the list.

He'd been a nice addition to dinner, the handsome sheriff. He was clearly close with Phoebe, and his presence had added a sense of history to the cozy scene. Eva was still getting used to seeing her father happy, deliriously so.

When her mother had abandoned their family, Franklin had done his best to hide his pain from Eva and her sisters. He shopped for prom dresses and tampons. He made every parent-teacher conference and soccer game. He'd consoled them when boys had broken their hearts and cheered with them at graduations and weddings.

He had found a solid, loving partner in Phoebe, and there were few things in the world that gave Eva more pleasure than listening to her father's new wife laugh until she couldn't breathe at one of his admittedly corny jokes.

She dug her keys out of her bag and—in juggling the plastic container of leftovers and her oversized purse—dropped them on the ground.

"Crap," she muttered. Stacking purse and leftovers on the roof of her car, she blindly felt around on the ground until her fingers brushed her oversized keyring.

"Aha!" She rose triumphantly and smacked her elbow off her side mirror. "Son of a—"

"Car trouble, ma'am?" Donovan's shadow, cast from the porch light, fell over her.

"No, officer. Everything is just fine." Nerves played over her skin as he took another step closer.

"Have you been drinking, ma'am?"

"You sat next to me and watched me drink exactly one point five glasses of wine, Sheriff. And it's dark out here, so let me verbalize the fact that I'm rolling my eyes at you in case you missed it."

"I'm going to need you to walk over and back to that tree. Straight line, please." The serious sheriff was playing with her. And that only made Eva want to play right back. She sauntered first, then strutted, and when she reached the tree, she got a running start and landed a perfect one-handed cartwheel followed by a curtsy.

"Smartass," he teased.

"Shameful. Wasting the taxpayers' money interrogating poor little old me," Eva tsked, tugging her ponytail back into place.

"I get the feeling that an interrogation with you would get me nowhere," he predicted.

"I have no idea what you mean by that." She knew exactly what he meant by that.

"You're sneaky. You're distracting. I bet you lie really well."

"And you can tell all this from dinner with my parents?" Eva asked.

"I like that you call Phoebe your parent," he said, switching gears, his voice softer.

"If I could have handpicked a wife for my dad, it's that woman in there," Eva said pointing back at the house.

"They seem happy together. I haven't seen her this happy in a long time."

She smiled up at him. "I was just thinking the same thing about my dad. I love seeing him like this. It's like all his dreams finally came true."

"It's a shame that you don't feel like you can open up to them," Donovan said casually.

"What's that supposed to mean?" Eva's guard came up with her chin.

"Can't even admit that you got taken out by a cabinet door."

"Oh, that." She breathed a sigh of relief. "And, hey! Who's the sneaky one now?" Eva crossed her arms.

He grinned at her, and even in the dark, it was blinding.

"Fine. It's just yet another oops in a long line of distracted accidents that only serves to reinforce their opinion that I'm the klutzy baby of the family."

"You *are* the baby," he reminded her.

"I'm the youngest. There's a difference. I'm still an adult. I just don't pay as much attention as I should. I'm in my own head too much."

"So they think you need a keeper." His tone made it clear that he agreed with her family.

"If anyone needs a keeper, it's Gia. She can't find Lydia's diaper bag or her car keys on any given day of the week."

"Gia has a keeper. Beckett. Who do you have?" Donovan's voice had that rough edge to it that sent delicious chills up her spine.

"I'm still interviewing for the position," she told him, looking up through her lashes. They were closer than she realized. She could just reach out and touch him...

He leaned in, stopping just inches from her face. Her breath caught and her body revved in anticipation.

"Good to know," he said quietly. And just when she thought he was going to kiss her, Donovan reached for the door handle and opened her car door. "Drive safely. Good night, Evangelina."

Oh, sweet Jesus. Her full name from those sinfully perfect

lips? She was pretty sure her underwear had just incinerated. She was just going to melt into a puddle of lust right here in her parents' front yard. She let out the breath she was holding and carefully slid under his arm and into the driver's seat. "Good night, Sheriff."

He shut the door once she was in place and watched her pull down the drive. Eva waited until she was sure he couldn't see her before smacking her head against the back of the seat. "That. Was. Hot."

It was only nine, she thought, looking at the dashboard clock. With inspiration like this she should probably put in a few more hours of work.

7

Charisma Champion breezed into the police station in a cloud of eucalyptus and thick, black hair. Bangles jingled on her wrist as she waved at Minnie. She wore a linen poncho in pale purple over a long skirt, managing to look both ethereal and disheveled. She hadn't aged a day since Donovan had graduated high school.

"Ms. Champion," Donovan said, switching his coffee to his left hand to greet her.

"Please, it's been more than a decade since I was grading your papers. Call me Charisma," she insisted with a grand gesture.

"Charisma then," Donovan agreed, waving toward his office. "Thanks for coming in. I could have come to you."

"But then I wouldn't have been able to get a substitute for my Intro to Wool class and stop for a latte at Overly Caffeinated, now would I?" she said wiggling her coffee cup, eyes sparkling.

And since she'd walked past half the businesses in town to get to the police station, tongues would be buzzing with speculation.

"Well, thanks for making time for me," Donovan said, settling in behind his desk. "I appreciate it."

"I must say. A fire yesterday, and you calling me in for questioning? It's rather exciting!"

"It's related to the fire," Donovan began.

Her eyes lit up. "Am I a suspect? How thrilling!"

Donovan shook his head. "Not at all, unless you have something you'd like to confess." He was joking but cut her off when Charisma tapped her finger to her chin and began to think back on whatever mysterious transgressions she'd committed. "I just wanted to ask you a few questions as a consultant."

He wondered if he was the first sheriff to use an astrologist to prevent calamity.

Charisma interlaced her fingers over her knee and leaned forward. "Do tell."

"Do you recall anything strange happening in town back in the late eighties?"

"My dear sheriff, strange things happen here every day," she laughed.

"True. But I'm thinking of several strange things. Around the same time?" he prompted.

"Oh, you mean when Uranus and Pluto crossed? That was quite the debacle, wasn't it?"

"Was it?"

Charisma rose from her seat and approached his whiteboard, the lower portion of which was covered with stick drawings and crudely scrawled words like "fart" and "booger" from Aurora's last visit.

"May I?" Charisma asked, gesturing with the eraser.

"By all means."

She wiped part of the board clean and picked up the marker, slipping into teacher mode. "Here we have our solar system," she said, drawing a series of circles. "And here are our planets."

"Question. I thought Pluto was reclassified as a dwarf planet?"

Charisma snorted. "Science and astrology may share certain characteristics, but in the astrology community, Pluto is still Pluto, and its characteristics are still its characteristics. May I continue?"

"By all means."

She turned back to the board. "Each planet affects or 'rules' specific aspects of our lives. Hence why people born under different 'signs' have different personality traits."

Donovan was following her so far. *The Monthly Moon* dedicated an entire page to astrological signs every month.

"These planets are obviously not static. They're constantly moving. Some slower than others." Charisma began drawing arrows for motion. "The further out the planet, the slower it travels."

So far so good, Donovan thought, picking up his coffee.

"In 1987, we experienced some seismic spiritual shifts, shall we say, when Uranus crossed Pluto." She scribbled more circles and added a few x's. The board was starting to look like an offensive line play.

Donovan rubbed the back of his neck. "Okay. What do Uranus and Pluto rule?"

She grinned at him like a prize student. "Very good question. Uranus rules qualities of change and originality. Whereas, Pluto rules power and transformation. When they crossed in 1987, the angle of the earth was perfectly aligned for a direct hit on Blue Moon"

That sounded implausible and very, very bad.

"So, what exactly happens when these planets cross?"

Charisma scribbled three blobs within circles and a triangle. "They magnify the effects of each other. Change and transformation becomes monumental rather than small shifts. Add in originality and power? That's a big time strong, creative push to change."

"So, it's possible people might feel compelled to do things that are generally out of character?"

"Exactly!" She jabbed the marker in his direction.

"How often does this crossing happen?" Donovan asked.

"Every fifteen years," she said.

"Why didn't we experience the same thing fifteen years ago?"

Charisma went back to the board. "I'd have to check some resources, but my guess is the planets crossed at another time of year when the angle of the earth to the sun was different. Someplace else in the southern hemisphere probably went crazy that time."

"So, it's possible that we could be looking at another 1987?" Donovan clarified.

"More than possible. Highly probable." Charisma didn't look scared. She looked like she was thrilled at the possibility. "Let me do some research in the school's meteorology/astrology lab so I can tell you definitively whether that's what we're looking at."

DONOVAN DIDN'T NEED Charisma's chipper "it's happening" email that afternoon to tell him what he already knew. Chaos, or at least the beginning edges of its stormy presence, had officially taken up residence in Blue Moon.

His mother had called him back and effectively scared the shit out of him. Hazel had pointed him in the direction of a locked file drawer in the station's storage room. When he'd opened it with the key he hadn't known was taped under one of his desk drawers, he'd felt the first tickles of panic.

The drawer was full of neatly typed and filed police reports all centering around October 1987. At one point, the doorless cells had become so overcrowded, Hazel had to start remanding prisoners into the custody of the head librarian who opened the doors of the library to accept detainees until they could bond themselves out.

"Do you want us to come home?" Hazel had offered.

"No, Mom. I know you guys have another camping trip planned. I've got two deputies and Minnie. How bad could it be?" he'd insisted.

If he had half a brain, he should have called her back and begged her to come home. The rest of his morning was spent fielding a series of bizarre calls. He was on his way back to the station after helping old man Carson find the lawnmower he swore had been stolen when he dialed Minnie.

"Find the mower?" Minnie answered.

"Under a tarp next to his back porch. Carson swears he never parks it there."

"Vandals or old age?" Minnie asked.

Judging by the years-old tire ruts the tractor was parked in, Donovan's best guess was old age.

"This is just the beginning of it, isn't it?" he asked.

Minnie gave a mirthless laugh. "Oh, honey. Ain't seen nothing yet."

Donovan sighed. "We'd better put a call out to the team."

Over hoagies from Righteous Subs, Donovan did his best to go over Charisma's scribblings with his team in the conference room. True to Blue Moon standards, the station's conference and mediation room was five times the size of the "prisoner holding area," which was basically two glorified cubicles with cots instead of desks. The town's founding mothers and fathers felt that mediation and education would be more effective than jail. And in most cases, their theory held true.

Layla pointed at the board with the remaining stump of her loaded veggie sub. "I get all the planetary circle crap, but where do the farts and boogers come in?" she asked.

"If you're not going to take this seriously—" Donovan began, erasing Aurora's artwork.

"We take farts and boogers very seriously," Colby assured him. Colby, shaggy and blond, often reminded Donovan of a scarecrow in the field. Big smile, fuzzy tufts of hair, and a scrawny build usually hidden under flannel and denim.

"Ha," Donovan said humorlessly. "Now, can we get back to figuring out how we're going to ride this thing out without any loss of life or serious maiming?"

"Yes, boss," they both nodded.

Minnie rolled her eyes. "Exactly how long is this thing supposed to last?" she asked.

"One month. It should come to a head on Halloween night and then dissipate or stop or whatever the hell planets do."

That shut them all up. Colby dropped his bacon back onto the wrapper. "Well, hell."

Donovan nodded. "My sentiments exactly. Halloween is one of the busiest nights for our department normally. With this thrown in, we could be looking at some serious trouble. Which is why we're deputizing Minnie and working out two-man shift coverage until this nightmare is over."

Minnie clapped her hands together. "Do I get a badge and a gun?"

"You can have a badge and pepper spray," he told her.

"How about a stun gun? I can test it on my husband to make sure it works."

"No stun gun. And don't test the pepper spray on Mr. Murkle either," Donovan clarified.

Layla swore under her breath. "Come on guys. No planets are gonna break us," she said, rallying their little team.

Donovan liked her delusional confidence.

"So, what's the next step?" Colby asked.

"We call a town meeting and educate everyone on the fact they're about to turn into certifiable idiots."

8

"This is so much better than the movies," Emma Merill-Vulkov sighed, happily mowing down her carrot and celery hummus snack from the movie theater's concession stand.

Eva laughed at her sister. They had commandeered worn seats in the Art-Deco theater's middle section to make sure they wouldn't miss any of the action. The screen was hidden behind dusty, crushed velvet curtains guaranteeing all attention would be on the podium front and center.

Emma's husband Niko was down front in the theater, his camera at the ready. The fashion photographer and reformed ladies' man had fallen hard for Emma and her adopted town and documented their time spent here in their gorgeous home. As a side hobby, he also fed human interest shots to Summer Pierce for her Blue Moon blog on Thrive's website. Outsiders loved the blog.

"I freaking love this town so hard," Eva told her sister.

"Isn't it a thousand times better than bumming around the east coast?" Emma agreed.

Eva winced thinking about her last shitty apartment in the

last crappy town she'd hidden away in. No matter how carefully she'd covered her tracks, her past had always come knocking. She only hoped that the past would be smart enough to stay far away from Blue Moon.

Gia flopped into the seat next to Eva. "Sorry I'm late. Evan weaseled an extra ten bucks out of me for babysitting duty for Aurora and Lydia, even though Lydia's already asleep. 'Negotiating' he called it. I had to find and raid Beckett's petty cash."

"You're so lucky you have an Evan," Summer groaned as she and Carter filed into the aisle behind them. Carter slung an arm around his wife's shoulders as they took their seats. "We had to piggyback on Jax and Joey's bribe for Reva. She's watching the twins and Caleb at our house," Summer said, biting into an apple.

"Speak of the devil," Emma said as the youngest Pierce brother and his wife ducked in beside Summer and Carter.

"Where were you guys? You left before us," Carter asked, leaning over and helping himself to some of his brother's popcorn.

Jax slapped at his hand. "Dude, we had an empty house for the first time all week. We weren't going to waste it."

Joey, a leggy brunette who took exactly zero crap from anyone, kicked her husband in the shin. "Jesus, Jax. Keep it down."

"That's what she said ten minutes ago," Eva quipped.

"Ohhhh!" Gia offered her an enthusiastic high five.

Joey gave Eva's hair a playful tug. "You're just jealous."

"Yes, yes I am."

The house lights flickered, signaling everyone to take their seats and wrap up their conversations. A minute later, Beckett and Donovan took the stage followed by deputies Colby and Layla in uniform.

The crowd buzzed with excitement, and Eva felt her pulse

quicken when Donovan's eyes scanned the theater. He saw her, his gaze lingering a moment, before moving on. Mr. All Business. She wondered what went on beneath that stoic surface?

It was crowded. Everyone was undoubtedly curious about what prompted the emergency town meeting, and the town had turned out in full force. Rainbow Berkowicz, bank president and wife of a hapless hippie, was live streaming the meeting to the Blue Moon Facebook group from the front row.

Beckett put his hands on the lectern and leaned in to the mic.

"Okay, everyone. We're going to get started here. I'd like to thank Sheriff Cardona for bringing this issue to our attention, and I expect you'll be interested in what he has to say."

Beckett backed away as the applause started and motioned Donovan up to the mic.

"Thanks, everyone, for coming out. I won't keep you long. Who here remembers the summer of 1987?"

Eva looked around at the scattered hands that rose.

Donovan looked around. "How about who remembers everybody going crazy and acting like the Higgenworth Communal Alternative Education Day Care kids?"

Hands flew up everywhere. It looked to Eva as though everyone over the age of forty had a recollection. Eva leaned over to Gia. "Someone's going to have to explain that one to me."

Summer poked her head between their seats, her blonde hair falling over her face like a curtain. "HCAEDC is a free-range daycare that doesn't believe in discipline. The kids are little monsters who never hear the word no. Don't ask Carter about them. He's still scarred for life."

Carter shuddered convincingly behind her.

"Oh, my God. I love this town so damn much," Eva sighed.

"I don't want to alarm anyone," Donovan said. "But we're looking at a similar situation now."

Soap opera-worthy gasps went up around them.

"Now, astrology isn't my strong suit. So, I've invited Charisma Champion to give you a little overview on what we might be facing."

A woman with black hair that curled to her waist took the stage to enthusiastic applause. "Thank you, Sheriff," she said grandly before addressing the crowd. She jumped into a description of the solar system, planetary alignments, and astrological signs.

"I'm only catching every other word," Eva whispered to Emma.

"I'm on every third word. Moon! There. I know that one," Emma whispered back. "I can't believe I worked the lunch shift for this."

Emma managed John Pierce Brews, the Pierce's brewery and business was booming... or brewing.

"Totally worth it," Eva predicted. "Just you wait."

Charisma was finishing up her technical description. She scanned the audience. "Are there any questions?"

Every person present raised a hand, and Eva had the pleasure of seeing the crack in Donovan's façade as sweat broke out on his forehead.

"Hang on," he said, leaning into the mic, to quiet the crowd. "This is what you need to know. You might be tempted to do something out of character. You might feel compelled to act out in some way or to make a big decision this month. All we're asking is that you don't do anything at all."

Willa, owner of Blue Moon Boots and a self-proclaimed psychic, raised her hand from the third row. "I can't stop thinking about getting a perm. Is that because of Uranus?"

Eva couldn't quite stifle her laugh, and Joey leaned over

her shoulder. "I think Willa just said Donovan's anus talked her into getting a perm."

Tears pricked Eva's eyes as she struggled to hold in the laughter.

Willa's blonde hair was straight as a stick and hung to her waist in the same style she'd worn since she was eight years old and told her mother to stop giving her bowl cuts. The idea of the woman getting a perm was laughable. The idea of the woman getting a perm because Donovan's muscled ass told her to? Priceless.

Emma elbowed her in the ribs. "Stop snorting. I can't hear what they're saying."

"Sorry," Eva snickered. "I'm just so glad I moved here." God, this town and its Ken doll sheriff were just the inspiration she needed. *Maybe Donovan could unwittingly help her along by playing a starring role,* she thought. She just needed to spend some time with him.

"Why are you smiling like an evil genius?" Gia demanded.

"I'm just thinking about Uranus."

THE MEETING WRAPPED but not before Donovan assured everyone that his department would distribute a PDF on the signs of the coming astrological apocalypse and step-by-step instructions on how to fight the urge to do illegal and/or immoral things. Wading through the crowd, he spotted Eva standing on one of the theater chairs waving at him.

He started toward her when she slid off the cushion and landed hard on the armrest.

Donovan shook his head. The woman should be wearing bubble wrap.

Of course, in Blue Moon, navigating the crowd after a town

meeting took the same amount of time it took to make it three city blocks in Manhattan after five. A dozen greetings and required personal reassurances that would be rehashed on Facebook for the next twenty-four hours stood between him and the woman who was smiling at him like he was her personal hero.

He could have been a cop in a city. He could have been a sheriff in any other small town in the country, yet he'd chosen this life. For the most part, his job was peacekeeping and reassuring Blue Moon's citizens of their safety. He'd rescued ferrets, dried tears, bought candy for lost kids at carnivals, pulled over the occasional speeder—Phoebe at least twice a year. He spoke at town meetings, attended ribbon cuttings, and visited the schools. He talked about the dangers of drugs with teenagers and stranger danger with kindergartners. He taught self-defense classes, spearheaded food drives, triple checked car seats. He did whatever it was that his neighbors needed.

The Blue Moon Police Department was more outreach than crime-fighting, and he'd like to keep it that way. So he stood and listened while Mrs. Nordemann explained how just this week she'd felt compelled to buy a murder mystery novel instead of her usual contemporary erotica. And he nodded thoughtfully when the flannel-clad Fincher brothers who ran the campground outside of town told him how "wild" the wildlife had been acting recently.

He made his way methodically through the crowd until he spotted her again. He'd seen her, eyes laughing, hand clamped over her mouth, when Willa had brought up Uranus. Evangelina Merill was already nothing but trouble. He could only imagine what the alignment of planets would do to her. She'd need a full-time babysitter just to make sure she didn't blow up Beckett's guest house making popcorn.

She stood in a loose circle with the Pierces, laughing at a shot her brother-in-law Nikolai was showing her on the screen of his camera.

"There's our fearless leader," Summer said, patting him on the shoulder. "You realize this all sounds completely insane to people who haven't lived here their whole lives."

Niko looked up and grinned. "I think it might sound the same to a handful of others," he said, turning the camera screen to Donovan. It was a picture of him, standing behind Charisma in the middle of her explanation. He was mid-eye roll.

"It's nice to know you're just a little bit human," Eva said at his elbow as she peered at the screen.

"You expect someone to say Uranus that many times, and I won't have a reaction to it?"

"How seriously do we need to take this?" Jax demanded. "And is this going to do anything to stir up livestock? We've got a stable full of prime horse flesh that doesn't need any encouragement to get uppity."

"Oh, geez. Apollo with a bigger attitude?" Joey shook her head. "That narcissistic bastard can barely fit his head through the stall door as it is. No way. We're all packing up and moving away for a month."

"You try creating perfect equine gods and goddesses and see how big your head gets," Carter teased her.

"Oh, hell. What's this going to mean for kids?" Gia asked. "We've got babies on up through teenagers. What kind of a living hell is this month going to be?"

Good. Donovan would rather they be scared. Scared meant vigilant. And vigilant meant at least some of them some of the time would maintain their hold on their marbles. He'd die for these people. Any one of them. But he'd prefer it to be over something big, something meaningful, not being poisoned by perm chemicals or run down in the street by an irate farmer in his combine.

Eva put her hand on his arm, and all heroic thoughts vanished.

"Do you want to get a drink?" she asked.

"More than anything in this world."

She grinned up at him, and he felt six stories tall.

He let Eva pull him toward the door.

"Hey! Where are you guys going?" Jax called after them.

"Getting a drink," Eva said.

"I could go for a drink," Jax said, tugging Joey to her feet.

"No, you can't." Carter shoved his brother down in an empty seat and sent Donovan a wink and pistol fingers. *Message received.* Donovan was officially on his own with Eva.

~

To: Blue Moon Citizens

From: Blue Moon Police Department

Subject: Planetary Crossing Signs & Symptoms

Dear Citizen of Blue Moon,

In light of recent information, the Blue Moon Police Department has compiled this list of signs and symptoms that you may be affected by during the Pluto-Uranus crossing. This is not an exhaustive list. Should you feel a strong desire to do anything out of character, we in the police department ask that you refrain from making any important decisions until November.

1. Beginning or ending a relationship.

2. Eating foods that you have a known allergy to.

3. Altering your physical appearance by any semi-permanent or permanent means.

4. Anything with fire.

5. Making any large purchases that haven't been planned prior to now (tiny house, time share, new farming equipment, etc.)

Together, by applying caution and careful logic, we will look out for each other and survive this trying time.

Sincerely,

Sheriff Cardona and the Blue Moon Police Department

9

This was a date. It had to be. Didn't it? Why else would she have asked him and not everyone else? Donovan's mind chugged through the possibilities for a third time as he followed Eva's curvy hips to a cozy two-top at John Pierce Brews. The host tucked them into the corner with windows on two sides. Donovan took the chair facing the room so he could ward off any planetary dangers that materialized or any bamboozled Blue Mooners.

He tried to calm his date nerves by looking around. The building rehab had been a tedious process but worth it in Donovan's mind. The Pierces had revitalized the old barn after decades of neglect. It was hard to recognize that livestock had once lived in this very spot. Impressive beam work held up the roof two stories above them. Industrial lighting and fans gave the place an eclectic, loft-like feel. The hardwood floors were scarred with age. The windows, built into thick walls, overlooked pastures and fields. There was a patio behind them and someone had started up the fireplace for the handful of customers who weren't yet ready to face the transition to fall.

The bar, a long L-shape, was rustic, beefy. There was a

comfortable dining room with more seating to the right of the kitchen and a loft above that overlooked the action in the bar.

Eva slid onto the high-backed stool and picked up the beer list.

She was pretty, he thought, studying her. No, not just pretty. Fresh and bright and bold. There was an energy beneath her exterior that buzzed just loud enough to alert him to the fact that she was walking, talking trouble. And that made her beautiful.

She wore her hair loose tonight. Curls tumbling over each other to her slim shoulders. She had a gloss on her lips that she must have put on in the car on the way over. Her sweater, a rich, deep green, looked soft to the touch.

"Well, well. The sheriff and Emma Jr. Isn't this interesting?" Lila, the server raised her newly pierced eyebrow at them.

"Emma Jr.? Is that the best you can do?" Eva feigned pain.

"You're right," Lila grinned wickedly. "What can I get you, Naked in Town?"

"I think you should have stuck with Emma Jr.," Donovan said to Eva.

"I'm going to kill that Anthony," Eva grumbled. "I'll have the Belgian triple please."

"Stout for me," Donovan said, handing Lila the menu.

"Any snacks?" she asked. "It's been a slow night because of the meeting you called, so you should probably order food so you have to tip me more."

Eva laughed and eyed Donovan. "I know it's late, but I wouldn't say no to nachos."

"Nachos and the beer cheese soup," he ordered. "Two spoons, please."

Lila winked at them. "You got it. Be right back with your drinks."

They sat staring at each other in silence for a moment.

"Sooo," Eva began, propping her chin on her hand.

"Sooo." He was nervous, and that was ridiculous. It was just a casual date. He could do this and not end up marrying the girl if he didn't want to.

"What made you decide to be a cop?" she asked.

Okay. They were playing getting to know you. He could do that. *Keep it casual*, he reminded himself. Don't mention marriage and white picket fences. *Don't do it.*

"My mom was sheriff here for twenty years."

"No, kidding? Really?" Eva's eyes danced. They were lighter than her sisters', more hazel than green. He couldn't seem to look away from them.

"Yeah. Mom was sheriff, and Dad was fire chief."

"Wow. So, public service is in the blood?"

He nodded. "How about you? A technical writer, right? How did you get into that?"

Eva waved a hand. "It's what happens when a creative writing major can't land a six-figure book deal right out of college. We take whatever job that comes along involving writing words. It's nothing like what you do. I mean, you would put your life on the line to stand between your town and whatever danger is out there, right?"

Donovan ran a hand through his hair. "Yeah. I mean, that's part of the job."

"Part of the job?" she grinned. "You realize to us civilians that sounds insanely heroic. Your job requires you to put yourself in danger."

"There's not a lot of danger in Blue Moon," he pointed out. He didn't want Eva thinking he was something he wasn't.

"Still. Bad things happen everywhere, and you're one of the people who stops those bad things. What is it in a person's character that makes that an acceptable risk? Are you less selfish than the rest of us?"

"Are you saying you wouldn't take a bullet for someone?" Donovan asked, skirting her question.

"Sure, I would. But it's a select few on the bullet-taking-for list."

Lila returned with the drinks and napkins and then bustled off again into the thickening crowd.

"What about a stranger?" he pressed.

"I'd like to think I'd be brave and selfless and heroic, but how can anyone know how they'd react in a dangerous situation? That's what training is for, right?"

Donovan picked up his beer, sipped. "Yeah. The training is so ingrained that it becomes reflex. You don't have to fight your instincts. You just act."

"Wow." She took a contemplative taste of her beer and then switched glasses with him. "Mind sharing?"

"I don't mind." He drank from her glass, watching her. She closed her eyes and made an "mmm" noise. When they switched back, his fingers lingered over hers, or hers under his, and their gazes met.

She was the first to pull her hand away. "So, you got into this line of work because it's what your family does. What do you think you'd be doing if your mom hadn't been sheriff?"

"I don't ever remember not wanting to be a cop," he admitted. "And I always wanted to be one here. This place is home. These are the people I care most about. It's an honor to protect and serve here."

"Damn," Eva shook her head slowly. "You're a really good guy, Cardona."

He laughed. "I don't know about that. I'm sure there are some tarnished spots on this armor," he joked.

"We all have our secrets, I suppose."

The way she said it made him wonder exactly what her secrets were and how long it would take before he could find out.

Their food arrived, and they talked between bites. He watched her closely, finding it interesting that she seemed determined to get to know him while keeping him in the dark about her.

"Why do you do that?" he asked when she brushed off a question about childhood.

"Do what?" This time, he could tell she wasn't pretending to misunderstand.

"Why are you so interested in learning about me but dodge all questions about you?"

She flushed, light pink high on her cheeks, and picked up a soup spoon.

"Old habit, I suppose."

"See, like that. What's that supposed to mean?"

"Why do you want to know, Sheriff? Am I under investigation?"

"Say my name." He gave the order quietly.

"What?"

"I want to hear you say my name. Not Sheriff. Not Cardona. My name."

"Donovan." Her voice was silky soft.

The blush on her cheeks deepened. But her eyes. Oh, those eyes. They delivered a message. Interest, trust, heat. That had been a mistake, but he wasn't going to waste time regretting it.

"How old were you when your mother left?" He shifted gears fast enough that she didn't have time to put her walls up.

"Eight." She blinked as if surprised that she'd answered the question.

"I bet you got tired of having everyone ask you if you were okay all the time back then."

She was studying him now. "You're an interesting man, Donovan."

"You interest me, Eva."

"I do? In what way? Am I a puzzle to solve? A victim to save?"

He sidestepped her questions. He wasn't sure how she'd react to the blunt honest answer. That he wanted to take her to bed and then learn everything there was to know about her before potentially marching her down the aisle. There was something here. Something in her that called to him. Despite her evasive answers, despite her veneer of mystery, he recognized something inside her. And he wanted it. He just needed to find the key.

"I want to know what goes on in that dizzying mind of yours," he confessed.

She grinned at him and lit up the room with the smile. Honest, genuine, sweet. "You wouldn't survive an hour in there," she predicted.

He leaned in. "Try me."

She bit her lower lip, considering. And he felt his eyes narrow. Despite the food on the table in front of him, Donovan Cardona was hungry.

10

Eva was enjoying herself and not just because of the background she was collecting. Donovan was charming, smart, and his heart of gold—as shiny as that sheriff's badge—shone through in the stories he shared.

The man had climbed into the sewer to rescue Mr. Garcia's ferrets for God's sake. If that didn't say "good guy" Eva didn't know what did. With a few hours of work in front of her, she'd switched to water, and he'd done the same. Responsible, sensible, practical. It shouldn't be sexy, but damn it, everything Donovan Cardona did was hot.

She did her best to dance around his dogged attempts to draw her out. She couldn't understand them. Usually when she told people she was a technical writer who lived in her sister's backyard, they immediately changed the subject. Not Donovan. He worked every subject back around to her, and she found herself revealing more than she usually did.

He was the fascinating one and unexpectedly candid, too. He spoke of his parents with affection and admitted he never felt like an only child growing up. Not with the Pierces just down the road.

"Blue Moon must have been an interesting place with all four of you single," Eva smiled at the idea. She could just imagine the women fanning themselves when the infamous Pierces and their sheriff friend walked in the door. "Were you surprised that they all settled down and got married?"

The corner of his mouth lifted. "Not with knowing their parents. Phoebe and John and my parents, too. They had something. They made marriage look not just easy but fun. I think we all grew up expecting to find that."

"Three for four," Eva said, tapping his ring finger. "Are you lining up a Mrs. Sheriff?"

When he lifted his gaze to hers, she felt something sweep through her like a hot summer breeze. She swallowed hard and sat up a little straighter. "I mean, is the Beautification Committee chomping at the bit to get you married off?"

"I'm off limits to the B.C. It's a long-standing understanding. They can't mess with town officials."

She laughed. "I hate to point this out to you, but Beckett Pierce is mayor... and married off."

"Yeah, but I have a gun and handcuffs. I'm much scarier than Mr. Mayor."

Now that he mentioned it, she was feeling a few nerves with him looking at her like that.

"Donovan!"

Eva leaned back, breaking their gaze as Ellery rushed up to their table.

Her usually pale face flushed with rage. Her black cardigan had batwing buttons and a scythe embroidered onto the chest. She wore a checked, pleated miniskirt and black lace tights. Her lips were painted a deep purple. "I need you to arrest someone," she announced breathlessly.

"What's wrong? What happened?" Donovan asked, laying a hand on her shoulder.

Ellery closed her eyes and took a deep breath. "I need you to arrest the Beautification Committee," she said.

"The entire committee?" Donovan clarified.

"They kicked me off the committee!" Her voice rose two octaves.

"Oh, boy," Lila said, coming onto the scene. "Sounds like you could use a drink."

"Can you bring me the usual, Li?" Ellery asked, her dark eyes watering now. Eva patted Ellery's shoulder.

"One corpse reviver coming up," Lila said.

"You can put that on my check," Eva told her. "I'll take care of it when you come back."

"Hang on," Donovan argued. "You're not paying."

"I asked you here, remember?" Eva reminded him.

"Guys, can we please talk about who we're going to arrest first?"

"Why don't we talk about why you want them arrested first?" Donovan suggested amicably.

Eva loved seeing him slide into his sheriff's pants—though she'd prefer to see him slide out of them...

Ellery grabbed Eva's napkin and dabbed at the corners of her eyes.

When Donovan looked at her, Eva mouthed "Uranus?"

He shrugged and sighed.

"Let's start at the beginning. Did you have a meeting tonight?" he asked.

"Yeah. And they kicked me off the committee! I am the literal mastermind behind every match we've made since I joined, and they think they can do better without me?" She sniffled dramatically.

"Why would they kick you out?" Eva asked.

"Because of some dumb rule about single B.C. members needing their marital partners to be fully vetted."

"Wait. What?" Donovan asked.

Lila arrived with a dark purple drink and the bill. Ellery snatched the drink off her tray while Eva jumped on the check.

"No, hang on a second—" Donovan reached for the check.

Ellery knocked back the drink and slammed the glass on the table, narrowly missing Donovan's hand.

That's when Eva spotted it. The black diamond twinkling on Ellery's left hand. "Oh, my God!" She grabbed her hand to examine the ring. "You're engaged!"

"That's what I've been *trying* to tell you," Ellery wailed. "Mason proposed, and we're getting married on Halloween. And when I told my *friends* tonight, they said I could either postpone the wedding until they made sure we were compatible or I could resign."

Eva slipped her arm around Ellery's shoulders. "That doesn't seem fair." She wondered what Emma would say about finding out that her ex-boyfriend, the nice, normal accountant from California, was marrying Ellery, Blue Moon's sweet queen of goth.

"That's what *I* said. So, I told them the wedding is on and I'm staying on the committee. And then they took a vote and *kicked me out*!"

Lila appeared at her side with a fresh drink. "This one's on me, honey. If you want to hang out until after my shift, we can go throw goat shit at their houses—"

"There will be no throwing goat shit at anyone's house," Donovan sighed, pinching the bridge of his nose.

Ellery's purple lower lip protruded in a pout. "What's wrong with them all of the sudden? Why would they go crazy like this? I thought they were my friends."

Donovan took a slow breath. "Were any of you at the town meeting tonight?"

Ellery shook her head, her pigtails dancing. "No, we were at the library in our meeting."

"There might be a reason why everyone is acting out of character," Donovan began.

"Excuse me, Cardona," Bill Fitzsimmons, in all his skinny, hippie glory wiggled in next to Ellery. "Do you think I need to stock my bunker with more than a month's worth of supplies? I'm worried that someone might set fire to the whole town and I'd need to be underground for longer than this Uranus thing."

"Fitz, we're going to need a minute here," Donovan said, trying to be polite.

Eva grinned across the table at him. She pushed her stool back. "I don't want to take you away from town business," she told him. He reached out and grabbed her wrist, holding her in place. "Uh-uh. You're staying. Fitz, you don't need to lock yourself in a bunker. We're going to be just fine."

"Maybe *you* are," Ellery said, draining her second drink. "My life is ruined. My friends abandoned me. I'm getting married to the man of my dreams, and they kick me off the Beautification Committee."

"They kicked you out?" Fitz gasped, bringing his skinny fingers to his mouth. "It's starting," he whispered.

"What's starting?" Ellery demanded.

"The apocalypse! It's happening!" Fitz was shouting now. "Everyone get in your bunkers! The apocalypse is starting!"

The din in the bar quieted for a second and then exploded as people started shouting questions.

"Will the liquor store stay open during the apocalypse?"

"How much toilet paper should I stockpile?"

"What's happening with Uranus?"

"Ah, hell, Fitz," Donovan muttered. He held up his hands to address the crowd. "Everyone calm down."

Ellery slammed her empty glass down on the table and stared out the dark windows. "This means war," she murmured. Eva was the only one who heard her. She slapped cash on the table over the bill and wiggled her way through the crowd that was gathering around the fearless sheriff. As she headed toward the door, Eva felt the weight of his gaze on her. She turned and mouthed "thank you" over her shoulder. His eyes narrowed, and he shook his head.

She was in trouble with Sheriff Sexy. And she didn't mind one bit.

Eva dialed her sister the second she was in her car. Emma had moved to Blue Moon a year and a half ago, ending things with her boyfriend Mason and leaving him on the west coast. She'd never given him a second thought until he'd shown up in town with an out-of-the-blue marriage proposal orchestrated entirely by the Beautification Committee. Mason's proposal finally made Emma confront what she really wanted.

And what her heart had demanded was Nikolai Vulkov. He wasn't the 401(k) and mortgage kind of man. No, he was a whisk a woman away for a week of shopping and sinfully hot sex in Paris kind of man.

They'd eloped—to Paris, of course—just a few months before and Eva was thrilled to note she'd never seen her sister happier.

"Mason and Ellery are getting married," Eva said, cutting off Emma's greeting.

Emma laughed. "I know. They came to me this afternoon at the brewery. It was very sweet and completely unnecessary. I'm happy for them, and we're all invited to the wedding."

"Well, here's something you probably didn't know. Ellery broke the news to the B.C., and they kicked her out."

"What? Shut up!" Emma screeched. Her screech turned into a giggle and a whispered "Stop it!"

"Oh, geez. Is Niko there?"

"I'm here, and I'm distracting your sister, Eva," Niko said into the phone. "If you want to call back in an hour, you can have her all to yourself."

"Gross. Carry on. Em, I'll talk to you tomorrow."

"Yoga with Gia?" Emma offered.

"Sounds good. Bye, Niko."

"Bye, Eva."

She hung up before she had to hear more naughty bedtime giggles out of her sister and pulled into Beckett and Gia's driveway. She jogged around to the backyard, shoved her keys in her front door, and hurried inside. She didn't bother with the lights and, instead, went straight to her laptop.

She'd been itching to take notes at the brewery. The man was walking, talking inspiration. She was afraid she'd forget a piece of the Donovan Cardona puzzle, and then, when she recreated the man, he'd fall flat on the page. But if she pulled out her notebook, he'd make her explain what it was for. And she wasn't willing to go that far with him... at least not honesty-wise.

Coming here, meeting him. It was fate. He was exactly what she needed professionally. And, if she stared into those denim blue eyes a second longer, it would be personally too. It was embarrassing to think that she couldn't look at him without launching into a thousand fantasies while he probably saw her as just another citizen to protect. She didn't want to be protected. Her sisters and father had done enough of that in the years after their mother left.

No, Eva didn't need another protector. She needed a man

who would forget to be careful with her. One who made her feel lusted after, loved, craved, adored.

Unfortunately, no matter how many times she waded into the dating pool, she waded right back out feeling alone and unsatisfied.

Maybe that's why romance novels had appealed to her. That heat, that knowing, when heart and body recognizes what they've been waiting for. She had written her first love story in college, and was embarrassed at the thought of her dual business management and finance major roommate finding it, hiding it in a folder on her hard drive labeled Warranties and Manuals.

Then she'd written another. And another.

By the time she'd graduated with her freshly minted creative writing degree, she'd had a few dozen short stories and a sketchy outline for a novel. She'd written it, poorly, and told no one as she'd queried agent after agent, imagining the moment she would finally find her own book on a shelf somewhere.

After her twenty-first rejection, Eva scrapped the book and vowed to become a disillusioned adult. She landed a job as a technical writer, a "good" job in terms of money and benefits. But it was sucking the soul out of her.

One night, after too many glasses of wine out with friends, Eva had walked past a book store that drew her in with its glossy book covers and exciting titles on display. She'd decided then and there that she wasn't done with writing regardless of what any gatekeeper told her. Eva knew in her blood that this is what she wanted to do.

At night, between disastrous dates, she started fiddling with a new story. She worked on it for a year and between working and writing, she researched every tiny detail of indie publishing. If the big publishers didn't want to give her a chance, then she'd make her own.

To pay for a cover designer and professional editing, Eva saved every penny she could, living in crappy apartments with lukewarm water and stained ceilings. And in that year, she'd moved three times trying to outrun the past. But the past wasn't done with her yet. When her sisters asked about her vagabond lifestyle, she told them she was experiencing wanderlust. They applauded her independence... and then offered her money.

She knew they were coming from a place of sisterly love, but Eva was going to solve her problems and run down her goals on her own. She'd prove to everyone—herself included—that she was good enough. And then she would finally be the woman she'd always planned to be.

Her first novel, written under a pen name, found a tiny following that had grown with each successive release. Her modest living began to inch its way toward respectable, and when her monthly sales report hit the number she was looking for, she'd given her two-week's notice at the firm where she worked.

Her last book had caught fire, slowly at first and then each passing week drew more readers to her. She'd been inspired by Blue Moon when she arrived for Gia's wedding to Beckett. The zany antics of well-meaning gossip mongers? It was irresistible. As were the delectable Pierce brothers and, of course, Sheriff Sexy.

Her E-book sales had exploded as had her Facebook following and newsletter list. She was finally making it happen. Readers were begging for more. They wanted a series, and Eva felt she could make that happen. Here in Blue Moon, she was practically smothered in inspiration.

And once she'd nailed her next goal—a bestseller—she'd

break the news to her family. There'd be champagne and cake, and she'd give each one of them a signed copy. And everyone would finally know that she was okay, better than okay. She would be whole and worthy and pretty damn awesome.

Eva stared at the soft glow of her screen and flexed her fingers over the keyboard.

Her phone signaled a new text. She spotted Donovan's name and frowned. She hadn't given him her number, and she certainly hadn't programmed him into her phone.

Donovan: "You abandoned me to a mob."

She chewed on her lip and typed out a response.

Eva: "I know better than to get between a rock star and his rabid fans."

Donovan: "Very funny."

Eva: "How did you get in my phone?"

Donovan: "I found it in your pants."

His follow-up message came a second later.

Donovan: "After the fire. You really should have a security code on it."

Eva laughed.

Eva: "Thanks for clarifying. I couldn't remember you being in my pants."

She bit her lip and waited. Had she gone too far flirting with Sheriff Do Right? Donovan had pushed the limits by adding himself as a contact in her phone, but he hadn't gone as far as she would have by giving himself a cutesy nickname. And now she'd pushed them into full-on sexting.

Her screen dimmed and then turned off. Another ten seconds passed before her text alert dinged.

Donovan: "Guess I'll have to make sure to be extra memorable next time."

Eva blew out a breath and then kicked her feet against the floor in delight. He was flirting with her! *Did that mean... Wait, what did that mean?* Did he flirt with everyone? Or was there a slim chance that Donovan Cardona, god among men, was interested in actually getting into her pants?

Donovan: "Good night, Evangelina."

Eva squealed in giddy, feminine delight. The popular boy liked her. Maybe.

Eva: "Good night, Sheriff."

She thought back on her recent dating failures. None of them had made her feel this heady rush from just a text. None of them had made her feel much of anything.

She turned back to her screen, energized and let her fingers fly over the keys.

When her phone dinged again, she was still smiling. Until she looked at the screen and saw the text from an unknown number.

Unknown: "I think it's time we have another talk."

Anger flashed white hot. "Not this time," Eva whispered to herself.

She blocked the number and deleted the text without responding.

"Not here. Not ever again."

11

Eva dragged her ass into Gia's yoga studio at the ungodly hour of nine. She'd been up most of the night writing, feeling butterflies about Donovan, and worrying about the text. It hadn't led to any real sleep when she'd finally crawled into bed at four.

"You look like hell," Emma, in shorts and a cropped tank top, observed.

Eva hadn't bothered with makeup and had dragged on the first workout clothes she could find. "Why are you dressed for summer? Damn it! Did you con me into hot power yoga again?"

"There's my other favorite sister!" Gia danced over, all grace and smiles.

"I hate you guys."

"Come on. It'll be good for you. It'll help your coordination." Gia tsked when she looked at Eva's bruised face. "I didn't notice this with your hair down last night. Car door?" she asked.

"Kitchen cabinet." They all turned at the sound of Donovan's amused voice.

"Tattle tale," Eva grumbled.

"Eva, you're going to sweat to death if you take class in that," Gia interrupted, eyeing up Eva's loose sweatpants and long sleeve tee.

"You're right, I probably shouldn't take class—"

She shut up when she saw Donovan roll out a mat and strip out of his sweatpants.

"You were saying," Gia grinned.

"Gah. Shut up. What?"

"Don't start without us!" Summer—dragging Jax and Joey's foster daughter, Reva, behind her—bounced into the studio. "Sorry! The twins... Well, that's it. I have twins."

"You're going to be using that excuse for the next eighteen or so years," Joey rolled her eyes.

"We've got a minute before we start," Gia promised. "You three set up while I get Eva some sweat appropriate gear."

Before Eva could come up with a good excuse to go home and go back to bed, Gia had her shoved into a pair of tiny shorts and a two-sizes-too-small crop top that Eva's boobs were trying to explode out of.

There were twelve of them all together, which was impressive considering Gia's power class was a vicious, sweat fest that challenged even the most seasoned athletes. Including the gorgeous Taneisha who had rolled out her pretty purple mat next to Donovan and begun stretching her dancer-like body.

Eva tip-toed between them and noticed when Donovan's gaze fastened onto her explosive cleavage. She set up in the back row next to Joey and Reva.

"Freaking Summer said this was the lazy class," Joey muttered.

"It's going to be fine," Reva promised with Joey-neutralizing optimism. She was slim and sweet. And since Jax and Joey had filed for legal guardianship, she'd really come out of her shell. Freckles danced over the bridge of her nose. Her long brown hair was tied back in a braid. At nearly eighteen, she was as pretty as the girl-next-door got.

Summer's head popped up from her hamstring stretch. "Quit whining. Brunch after. My treat."

"I'm getting extra bacon," Joey announced. "Nice rack, by the way, Eva. Couldn't you find a smaller shirt?"

"Hey, don't turn on a fellow captive. We have to stick together."

"Sorry, I'm weak with hunger, and it makes me angry."

Eva grinned and folded forward over her thighs and felt her skin burn. She peeked, knowing she shouldn't, and found Donovan watching her. Great. Not only was she about to humiliate herself in yoga class, she was going to do it in front of Sheriff Sexy.

"Okay, guys. Let's get those juices flowing," Gia announced, launching into an hour of torture.

"Let me die in peace," Eva groaned, holding a towel over her face. She didn't know whose towel it was, nor did she care. Someone was slapping her in the shoulder.

"Water," Joey rasped next to her. "Gimmie."

Eva pulled the towel off her face and rolled her water bottle over to Joey's mat. A foot appeared in her line of vision. It was attached to a hairy, muscled leg. She could see up those blue gym shorts. *Oh, my. She hadn't been wrong about the undercover equipment.*

Donovan grinned down at her. "Morning," he said, cheerfully. Droplets of sweat clung to his chest. When he'd stripped out of his shirt mid-class, Eva had been so distracted she'd fallen out of her attempt at crow pose, knocking into Joey and sending them both sprawling.

"Morning," Eva returned, pretending that she wasn't laying on her back in a puddle of her own sweat.

He reached down and hauled her to her feet. When her head spun, she wasn't sure if it was the dehydration or the magnificent torso in front of her. His *abs* had abs.

"What are you doing tonight?"

"Huh?" *Great, response Eva. You're a real sweaty intellectual.*

"Have dinner with me?"

"You want to have dinner?"

"Did you hit your head again this morning?" he teased.

Eva shook her head, trying to clear the cobwebs. "Sorry, I didn't get much sleep last night."

His quick smirk was filled with dark promises. "Good. Neither did I. And I figured, since our first date was a coincidence and you asked me out for a second date, it's my turn."

"Dates? We're dating?" Her voice was a squeak that hurt her own ears.

"Not only dating, but we've made it to the third date." Donovan winked. "I'll pick you up at seven. You can wear that if you want."

He ambled out, leaving half a dozen women staring after him.

"What. Was. That?" Summer demanded, slapping Eva's shoulder with every word.

"Oh, my God. I don't know! Did he just ask me out?"

"Yes!" Gia said, grabbing her by the arms and jumping up and down.

"Holy shit. So, I'm not hallucinating?"

"Nice job, Tits McGee," Joey chimed in.

"What did I say? Oh, my God. Am I going? Am I *dating* Donovan Cardona?"

~

In light of the new development, brunch plans were abandoned and everyone followed Eva home. Gia raided the fridge in the main house and returned with bacon, eggs, Aurora, and Lydia. Eva started a fresh pot of coffee while Aurora poured herself a bowl of fruity-o's into one of Eva's mixing bowls.

"Your mom is going to freak," Eva whispered to her niece.

The little redheaded pixie grinned. "She's distracted. I'll eat half before she even notices." To prove her point, Aurora carted her bowl off to the little sunroom next to the living room.

Emma and Summer, the born organizers, shuffled everyone into stations. Eva was relegated to drink pouring when no one wanted to let her near a knife or the stove. She was a good cook. Really good. But accidents did have a tendency to happen. And for every perfect London broil she served, she had a bandage covering a cut or a burn.

Seeing as she'd had the foresight to stock her fridge with orange juice and the bottle of champagne she usually saved for completing a manuscript, Eva decided the occasion called for mimosas. She doled out plastic cups to everyone and enjoyed the sounds of female companionship. In all her moves, she'd made dozens of acquaintances but few lasting friendships. Here in Blue Moon, she had family and friends always willing to drink mimosas and talk about men.

Summer, an absolute failure in the kitchen, called Lydia-sitting duty and crawled after the baby on her adventurous trek around Eva's living room. The little girl's belly laugh drew "awws" from everyone present.

A bark sounded at the front door, and Joey opened it. Diesel, Gia and Beckett's huge "puppy," stumbled inside. He had a silver coat, blue eyes, and feet that were still too big for his body. His tail wagged hard enough that it swiped the mail off the entry table and onto the floor.

"Hey, buddy," Eva said, squishing his doggie cheeks in her hands. Diesel liked to keep her company during the day when his family was out. He gave her a sloppy kiss and ran into the living room to slobber on the green-eyed Lydia under the coffee table.

"Sometimes I can't believe this is my life," Gia said, a little misty-eyed, next to Eva at the kitchen island.

"Just think back two or three years," Eva sighed. Gia had been a down-on-her-luck and newly divorced single mom.

"What if this is the beginning of your story?" Gia asked, squeezing Eva's hand.

Eva felt her heart stumble. "Don't be ridiculous. It's a date, not a marriage proposal."

"What would you say if Sheriff Hot Bod came in here right now and begged you to marry him?" Joey asked, expertly flipping an omelet in Eva's pan.

"Uh, hello. You saw him without his shirt on at class. Who says no to that?" Eva joked.

"Just remember there's more to a relationship than looks," Reva said, steadily slicing strawberries on a cutting board.

Joey tugged Reva's hair with affection. "Do you guys see what a good job I'm doing with this whole parenting thing?"

"To be fair, Jax was the one who told me to stay away from hot guys," Reva corrected her.

"Yeah, but that's just so you don't run out and have sex with a hot guy who doesn't treat you right."

"Jeez, Joey!" Eva laughed.

"Please. Don't go all prudish on me. Our husbands were raised by John and Phoebe Pierce. Experts in 'the talk.'"

"It's true," Gia piped up. "Beckett nailed it with Evan, and

Phoebe gave me pointers on tackling it with Little Miss Nudist Colony in there."

"Reva, give 'em the highlights," Joey ordered.

Reva started adding strawberry slices to each plate. "Sex is awesome as long as you do it with a good person that you care about and is more worried about making you feel good than getting his—or her—rocks off."

"Condoms?"

"Always. No excuses ever," Reva recited.

"If you're not feeling it?"

"Never feel guilty about saying no."

"What if someone gives you a hard time about saying no?"

"Then I text Jax, and he murders the guy."

"Boom!" Joey said, high-fiving Reva.

"Holy hell! That took me like ten years of sex-having to figure out on my own," Emma said, continuing the high-five train.

"I am totally using this when Meadow and Jonathan are older," Summer said, bouncing Lydia on her hip. "It's very progressive of you guys. We should think about doing this as a piece for Thrive," she told Gia.

"Should we tell them the secret rule?" Reva asked Joey with a small smile.

Joey nodded sagely. "It's the right thing to do. They're all going to need it in the future."

"When I do decide to have sex, never ever ever tell Jax."

They laughed loud enough that Diesel tried to hide under the barstools against the island. He'd knocked two of them over before Eva rescued him from himself.

"What's so funny, guys?" Aurora demanded from the doorway of the sunroom.

"Aurora! What's in that mixing bowl?" Gia asked, hands on hips.

Over omelets and coffee, they dissected every text and interaction between Eva and Donovan. The verdict: Eva was dating Blue Moon's sheriff.

"I can't for the life of me figure out why he's interested?" They had nothing in common as far as she could tell.

"I can think of two reasons that he got an eyeful of in yoga," Joey quipped, pointing at Eva's chest.

"I'm sure he likes you for more than just your chest," Reva said sympathetically.

"Of course he does," Emma said, tucking an arm around Eva. "You're smart, you're beautiful, you're the best damn technical writer the world has ever seen."

Eva pushed the twinge of guilt aside. She'd tell them. Soon. "Why are you pep-talking me?"

"Because I don't want any of your Mom-baggage holding you back like it did me. I could have ended up in Niko's bed—life," she corrected with a glance at Aurora, "a lot sooner had I not been so hung up on protecting myself."

Eva saw it when Reva's smile faltered. The girl's own mother had abandoned her and her younger brother, Caleb, and hadn't been heard from since summer. Eva patted Reva on the hand.

"I think you're projecting," Eva told Emma lightly.

Emma shook her head. "Trust me, little sister. We all carry the scars. I was afraid of anything that wasn't one-hundred percent secure. Gia over there is obsessive about her kids to make up for Mom ducking out on us."

"Am not!" Gia argued. She was squeezing Lydia and Aurora on her lap, making both kids squirm.

"Are too!" Aurora wheezed, trying to slip free under the table.

"I haven't figured out what your damage is yet." Emma

pointed her fork at Eva. "But when it rears its sticky, ugly, complicated head, you can count on us."

Eva smiled despite herself. For the first time in her adult life, she was putting down roots. She was surrounded by family and friends, by dogs and kids. Her career was climbing, and she had a date with a man so sexy he could have walked off the pages of one of her books. Her sisters were happy. Her father was happy.

She wasn't going to let anything ruin it.

"Okay. Thank you, Emma, for airing our family's dirty laundry in front of these innocent victims. Now, enough about me, please. What's going on with everyone else?"

Reva's eyes never left her plate. "I have a date for Homecoming," she said casually.

12

Donovan arrived promptly at 6:58 with a bouquet of orange and pink spray roses and eucalyptus. Liz at the flower shop called it "Colorful Chaos," and he couldn't think of a more appropriate gift for Eva.

He knocked on the cottage's front door, and through an open window, he heard footsteps hurrying across the upstairs floor. The footsteps hit the stairs too fast and something that sounded like a body hit a wall. He heard her curse, loudly, colorfully, and then she came into view sauntering down the stairs and crossing the kitchen to open the door.

"Hi."

Donovan felt like he'd had the wind knocked out of him. Eva was standing there looking up at him, beaming. Her hazel eyes bright with anticipation, her full rosy lips parted in a heart-rattling smile.

He didn't even notice what she was wearing. It didn't matter. All that mattered was the fact that he was inconveniently, irretrievably, nonsensically head over heels.

Still reeling from the face-first skid into realization, Donovan wordlessly held up the flowers.

"Wow. You are nailing the old-school date moves," Eva sighed, accepting the bouquet and bringing it to her face. "Come in, and I'll put these in water."

He followed her inside, rubbing a hand over the heart that seemed to have grown uncomfortably full in his chest.

"Would you like a drink?" Eva offered. "Or are you on call?"

"Colby and Layla have it covered tonight."

"Beer?" she offered.

He wished for something a little stronger, something that would take the edge off the realization that his life was never going to be the same. "Beer's good."

She opened a bottle for him and slid it across the island. When she reached for the glass vase above the sink, he was there pulling it down for her. He put the vase in the sink but stopped her when she reached for the faucet.

"Hang on a second. I just want to make it crystal clear that this is a date," he told her, his thumb tracing the edge of her jaw. They were so close in the confined space, he swore he could hear the beat of her heart. "You seemed a little confused last night and this morning. So just so there's no misunderstandings..."

She stole his damn move. He was getting ready to close in on her, to kiss her until she melted against him. But it was Eva who gripped him by the shirt and dragged him down to her hungry mouth.

If his thoughts had been of love a moment ago, they were now violently approaching lust. Her lips were so soft, so busy, against his. His skin burned beneath his clothes everywhere she touched him. He wanted to slow it down, to take his time and *taste* her.

And then she opened for him. And he lost his damn mind.

He lifted her up, dropping her on the kitchen island and

changing the angle of the kiss. His tongue swept into her mouth, and she moaned against him, into him. He needed to find his control before they went too far, before he was stripping her naked right here and—

"Hey, Aunt Eva can I borrow—" Evan's strangled cry tore them apart. Eva nearly fell off the island, but Donovan steadied her and helped her down.

"Sorry, Ev," Eva said, fanning her flushed cheeks.

"What is with all you adults? Everyone's always making out all the time. I'm starting to get emotionally scarred. Don't you have anything better to do?"

Donovan grinned at her nephew. "In another year or two, you won't be able to think of anything better to do," he promised.

"Oceana and I have an *intellectual* relationship," Evan lectured them on his junior high girlfriend. "Sure. We kiss and stuff, but man, not all the time and not where you make food."

Eva wrapped him in a headlock despite the two inches he had on her. "Awh, poor Evan being surrounded by people who like each other."

"You sound like my mom!"

"Not cool, man! Not cool," Eva said, tightening her grip on him. "I'm the fun, awesome aunt."

"Fine. If you're so fun and awesome, can I borrow your zombie apocalypse game?"

"Schooling Beckett tonight?" she guessed.

"Yeah, he's been stressed with all this planetary crossing crap and trying to find Reva and Caleb's mom. I thought I'd distract him with some blood and guts."

She ruffled his hair. "You're a good kid, Ev."

"Yeah. I know. I don't know why everyone feels like they need to keep reminding me all the time. Why doesn't anyone tell me I'm tall or I smell okay?"

"You're a thirteen-year-old boy. You don't smell okay."

"Ha. Game please."

Eva excused herself to dig through a stack of games and movies in the living room.

"So, you and my aunt," Evan said, trying to appear taller.

Donovan grinned and held up his hands. "I remember your ass-kicking talk with Niko when he started dating Emma. You don't have to warn me again."

Evan sighed. "I knew this was going to happen. You always got that sappy puppy-dog look when she was around."

"Yeah, but it was a manly sappy puppy-dog, right?"

"Oh, sure. Definitely. But you carry a gun, so that helps."

The kid was placating him. No wonder the whole town called him Mini Mayor. He may not have been Beckett's by blood, but they were destined to be father and son.

"Aha!" Eva wielded a case triumphantly. "Found it. Don't scratch it, and don't beat my high score or I'll—"

"Yeah, yeah. You'll pelt me with pumpkin pies. Got it." Evan snatched the game out of her hand. "Thanks Aunt Eva. Don't cross any lines tonight, Sheriff."

"You smell okay, Evan," Eva called after him.

He grinned and ducked out the door.

"I love that kid so much I want to hug him until his head pops off," Eva sighed. "Is that murder?"

"Where are we going?" Eva asked as Donovan eased down Beckett's driveway. He'd traded the cruiser for his SUV. Eva couldn't help but shoot a glance over her shoulder at the big backseat. Her blood was still pumping from that kiss. She wasn't sure what had come over her, but it had been worth it to feel that heat. And so much better than worrying about it until the end of the date.

After Evan's hasty entrance and exit, neither of them had mentioned the kiss or attempted to reenact it. But Eva was fairly certain she wasn't the only one thinking about it right now.

"I made us reservations at a restaurant in Cleary," Donovan told her, heading east.

"Fewer distractions in Cleary?" Eva asked.

He glanced at her, his smile crooked, dimple winking, and took her hand in his. "Maybe."

She was holding hands with Donovan Cardona. He brought her flowers, let her kiss the hell out of him, and now he was holding her hand. *What alternate universe had she stepped into?* Eva wondered.

"Oh, no," she breathed, her dreams and fantasies collapsing in on themselves in a black hole of reality.

"Oh, no, what?" Donovan asked, squeezing her hand.

"Uranus."

"Excuse me?"

"The crossing. The stupid stellar apocalypse. This is all because of that, isn't it? You asked me out because you're going crazy," Eva wailed, covering her face with her free hand. "I knew this was too good to be true."

"Eva."

But she was too busy lamenting her cruel fate. "Why does this always happen to me? I'm not a terrible person. I shouldn't have all this bad karma—"

"Eva. Shut up!" he ordered.

Eva snapped her mouth shut.

"This has nothing to do with any kind of planetary alignment. I've wanted you from the first second I laid eyes on you."

"Great. Now I know you're crazy."

He squeezed her hand hard, and Eva yelped.

"Don't tell me what I do or don't feel, Evangelina," he said evenly. "These feelings didn't start up just this week or last or even last month. They've been around for a while."

"You're being very... honest," Eva told him. *Honesty made her a bit squeamish.*

"It's the only way to be in a relationship."

"So, we're in a relationship?" her voice squeaked up an octave.

"We are if that's what you want. I want to give you what you want."

Her laugh was nervous and sounded borderline hysterical to her own ears. What she wanted at this exact moment was a naked Donovan Cardona cavorting around in her bed. "This is overwhelming... I thought we were just going to dinner. Not planning a future."

"I want to be upfront with you. No surprises, no secrets. I want you Eva. And I think you might be it for me."

She had definitely hit her head at some point today and was hallucinating all of this. The handsome sheriff that she'd lusted after from afar was telling her she was *it* for him? Concussion for sure. Possibly an aneurysm.

She opened her mouth, but no sound came out. And now she was mute. *Awesome. Mute and concussed.* She felt nervous and excited and horrified and—dare she think it? —hopeful.

Donovan's phone buzzed from the tray in the dashboard.

He swore darkly.

He grabbed it and stabbed a button. "I thought I told you not to call—"

Donovan stopped, listened. "Are you puking right now?" He pulled the phone away from his ear, and Eva could hear retching.

"Where's Layla?" Donovan demanded. "Fuck. Okay. I'll be there in ten."

He hung up and tossed the phone back in the tray. "A little rain delay," he told Eva.

"What's going on?"

"Layla's on a call, and Colby's got some kind of stomach bug or food poisoning and can't stop puking. I have to go check on Fitz at the bookstore. Some customer called 911."

Eva was not about to let the evening end like this. Not without another kiss and a concussion check. "Can I come with you?" she asked.

13

There was a crowd in front of the used book store when Donovan pulled into the parking lot. A ragtag band of hippies were pressing their faces against the front windows. Through the open front door, Eva could hear shouting and a sporadic thwacking noise.

"Stay here," Donovan said. He made it as far as getting his seatbelt off before he reconsidered. "On second thought, come with me. I want to keep an eye on you."

"I don't need a babysitter," she complained but got out of the SUV anyway. She was dying to know what was happening inside.

"Oh, thank goodness, Sheriff!" A woman in flared jeans with peace sign patches on both the knees flagged down Donovan. "I don't know what happened. One second Aretha was browsing the clearance section, and the next she and Fitz are screaming and throwing books at each other."

"Thanks, Xanna. I'll talk to them."

Eva wasn't sure if anyone else noticed it, but she caught the straightening of Donovan's broad shoulders, the tightening of his jaw. He was making the shift from friend and neighbor to authority figure. It was sexy as hell.

"You stay behind me. Don't touch anything. Don't say anything," he ordered. "Got it?"

"Yeah, I got it. Let's get in there before someone throws a chair or a body through the window."

Inside, Eva was met with the musty perfume of old books. The shop looked a lot bigger inside than it had from the exterior. Rows and rows of mismatched shelves ran the length of the store. They were neatly organized by genre and author. In the center of the shop was a seating area with a few ratty couches and some beat up tables and chairs. Behind the furniture was the empty register.

"It was in clearance!" A woman who Eva assumed was Aretha—though she'd pictured more of an Aretha Franklin than the skinny white lady in her fifties—popped out of an aisle jack-in-the-box style and hurled a paper back at the desk.

Fitz's head popped up like a prairie dog from behind the register. "I said it was an accident! It was a hardcover! Hardcovers don't go in the paperback clearance!"

He dodged the magazine that Aretha chucked in his direction.

"It was in clearance!"

"I'm not selling you a Sylvia Day book for a buck! The sex scenes alone are worth at least five! How would I survive on prices like that?"

"You don't expect me to believe you make a living off used books, do you?" Aretha sent two paperbacks flying at once. "The entire town knows you sell weed out the back door!"

"I haven't done that since the nineties," Fitz argued, ducking the next literary volley.

Books were piling up in front of the register in a discarded monument. Aretha sent a hardcover flying and it knocked over the register monitor.

Fitz's head popped up again. "Hey! Don't you dare break that!"

"Enough!" Donovan's voice cut through the screaming and book throwing, and there was one second of absolute silence. And then Harry Potter and the Deathly Hallows in hardcover flew out of the stacks and caught Donovan on the forehead.

"Oh, shit," Eva gasped, clapping a hand to her mouth. "Are you okay?"

He didn't answer her. "Aretha, you come out here right now," Donovan ordered.

Eva noticed he'd unclipped the clasp on his stun gun but wasn't making any moves toward it. He had more restraint than she did. That lady would have been flat on her back seizing on the floor if Eva had been in charge.

"Not until he gives me the sale price!" she hollered back.

"Goddammit," Donovan muttered to himself. He yanked the handcuffs off his belt. "Stay," he warned Eva and hustled back the aisle. There was a high-pitched scream, a thud, and then Donovan was marching Aretha out from the stacks with her hands cuffed behind her back.

She was swearing up a blue streak when Donovan shoved her down on one of the worn arm chairs. "Now, sit there and be quiet so I don't tase a Sunday school teacher in front of half the town," he told her. "I'll do it, and I won't feel bad about it, Aretha."

The woman shut up and sat, pouting.

"Fitz, what the hell is going on?" Donovan demanded.

"Dude, I don't know! It's the planets, man. I knew I should have gotten in my bunker! She was just in here shopping with the book club and all the sudden starts screaming about clearance prices."

"The book was in *clearance*!" Aretha shouted, kicking her feet against the floor.

"For the love of God, woman. Keep quiet until it's your turn." Donovan rubbed a hand over the goose egg that was rising on his forehead.

Sensing the primary danger was over, Eva busied herself with picking up the books that had fallen victim to Aretha's rant. She stacked them neatly on the counter, piling up the damaged ones in the corner.

She was just pulling a cart over when a paperback she'd missed caught her eye behind the couch. Eva bent to pick it up and gasped.

It had happened. The very first time she found one of her books in a bookstore, and it was in Blue Moon's used book shop, and someone had thrown it in a tirade. It was even better than seeing it in the window of a Barnes and Noble, she decided.

Although being in a second-hand store meant someone hadn't loved it enough to keep it. But at least they'd read it.

"What's wrong?" Donovan asked looking over her shoulder.

"Jesus. I need to put a cat collar on you," Eva gasped, clutching the book to her chest.

There was a knock at the front door. "Is it okay to come back in, Sheriff?" Mrs. Nordemann, the world's longest mourning widow and busiest busybody asked from the doorway.

"I could really use the money," Fitz whispered to Donovan. "The stripping has really slowed down this month."

Donovan rolled his eyes. "Everyone can come in if they help Fitz clean this up and answer my questions. One more outburst, and I'm dragging you all into the station."

Eva didn't know what to do with her book. She tried to

slide it onto a shelf, but Donovan was watching her. She smiled and waved.

She scuttled behind the desk to help pick up the book shrapnel that had made it over the counter, and when she put her book down for one second next to Fitz's ancient fax machine, Donovan snatched it up.

"What's this?" he asked.

She reached for it, but he held it over her head out of her reach.

"Fated Fools by Ava Franklin."

Eva stopped fighting and squeezed her eyes shut as Donovan turned the book over.

"Holy shit. This is *you*?"

Why in the ever-living hell had she put her picture on the back of her books when she revamped the covers last spring? Eva lamented. She wrote under a pen name. Why didn't she have a pen picture or whatever the hell it was called.

"Don't say—"

"*You're* Ava Franklin?" Mrs. Nordemann gasped.

When Donovan dropped his arm, the woman pounced, wrestling the book out of his grasp.

"I can't believe it!" she squealed.

Donovan's eyes widened. Eva knew Mrs. Nordemann was not a squealer. She was a schemer.

Mrs. Nordemann held up the book to Eva's face. "I can't believe Ava Franklin lives in my town!" She was drawing a crowd. "You need to speak at Book Club," she decided, yanking out her phone and opening her calendar.

"Now, we were Skyping with Thalia Price this month, but we can reschedule her."

The woman wanted to reschedule a *New York Times* best-selling author who had three of her books made into movies for *her*? Eva felt dizzy.

Donovan took the book back from Mrs. Nordemann. "Evidence," he explained.

"Oh, of course. I have a copy at home." She waved her friends over. "Ava Franklin is a Mooner, and she's going to speak this month!"

Amidst the excited chatter, Donovan leaned in. "If you have anyone who doesn't know, you'd better tell them immediately."

"Oh, for the love of—" Eva dug through her bag and pulled her phone out. She scrolled through her contacts frantically and pushed Call.

"Dad? Yeah. Hey, listen. I'm a romance novelist. I quit my job a year ago and have been writing books for a living. I gotta go. Bye!" She disconnected, scrolled, dialed.

"Emma? Where are you? Is Gia with you? Great. Put me on speaker. Can you guys hear me? Awesome. I'm a romance novelist, and I quit my job. Bye!"

She fired off a group text to Summer and Joey to fill them in and then silenced her phone and shoved it back in her bag.

"Eva—or should I say Ava?" Mrs. Nordemann asked coyly. "Can we get a picture with you? We're your biggest fans!"

Donovan was roped into taking a group picture with Eva sitting next to a handcuffed Aretha and a grinning group of Mooners. Approximately forty seconds after that, the picture and announcement of Blue Moon's famous author-in-residence was uploaded to Facebook. Within five minutes it had two dozen comments and Eva's phone hadn't stopped buzzing. She turned it off and went in search of her date.

Donovan was taking notes on property damage when she approached. She tapped him on the shoulder. "I think I'm going to take a raincheck on dinner tonight," she said, her smile wavering.

"Don't even think about sneaking off. We have some talking to do," he began. His radio cut him off.

"Hey Sheriff, we got a problem..."

He swore.

"I think we've given each other a lot to think about tonight. So I'm going to go home and... think," she said, pointing toward the door.

"Let me drive you."

She shook her head. "It's two blocks. I could use the fresh air and it looks like you're going to be a while."

They looked around the store. The dozen people in the store had doubled in number. Entire shelves had been swept clean, and Fitz was arguing with Aretha again.

"This isn't over, Eva," he warned her.

14

Eva snuck like a thief into the backyard. They'd be waiting to pounce and she was in no shape to answer the millions of questions they'd throw at her. And the novelist outing was only one of her worries. Donovan had kissed her until her heart needed a restart and then calmly announced that she was it for him. Was it some stupid planets wreaking havoc, or could there be a thread of legitimate love there?

Shouldn't a romance novelist be an expert on these things? she wondered.

Eva let herself into the cottage and locked the door behind her.

She'd just buy herself some time to think things through. Without turning on any lights, she grabbed her laptop and trudged upstairs. She'd write in bed, her phone off, until she fell asleep. A temporary escape from the chaos.

She changed into pajama pants and a tank, dug out her glasses, and wrote by the glow of her screen. Donovan had given her enough character material that it came pouring out in a spontaneous character sketch of her main character.

He was so *good*. In her experience, few people were *that*

solidly good and kind and trustworthy. And she'd already gone and screwed it up.

No secrets. No surprises, he'd told her.

And she'd been lying to him—not to mention her own family—since day one. Stupid Uranus was really fucking things up for her. But in her heart, she knew she'd done more of the fucking up than any planet.

~

"Hey. Wake up!" The cheerful order had Eva sitting straight up in bed and scurrying back against the headboard when she found Joey plopped on the foot of the bed.

"What the hell are you doing here?" Eva demanded, pulling a pillow over her face. "And how did you get in here?"

"I shimmied up the drainpipe. You left your window open." Joey jerked a thumb at the window behind her.

"Why are you in my bed?"

Joey, dressed for work in the stables, stretched out on the bed. "Well, I got this funny text from someone I considered a friend," she began.

Eva groaned and pulled the pillow tighter over her face. Of all the people to give her a hard time, she hadn't expected it to be Joey.

"At least, I thought we were friends. But it turns out she's a big, fat liar and thought she could clean it up with a text," Joey continued. "I was expecting some kind of a post-coital text about how amazing Cardona is in the sack. So, I texted you back. And you know what happened?"

"What?" Eva mumbled through her pillow.

"There was no response. In fact, everyone in town has been texting, calling, messaging you, and beating on your front door. I had to wait until Cardona left your porch before climbing up here."

"Shit." Eva heaved the pillow off her face. It hit the floor with a dull *whoomph*. "I panicked. Donovan and Mrs. Nordemann were staring at me like I was a freak, and I could hear the Blue Moon grapevine gearing up."

"Were you ever planning to tell us?" Joey asked, swinging her legs.

"Of course! I had a plan. I just wanted to finish this book. And release it. And hit a bestseller list."

"That's a lot of ands," Joey observed.

"I wanted to be really good at this so it would be this amazing surprise to everyone."

"God, you're an asshole," Joey told her with no heat to the words.

"Come on! It's not that bad!"

"You have a family that loves the shit out of you, and you think the nice thing to do is keep this huge part of your life a secret from them, so not only do you cut them out of the process, but you make them feel like you didn't trust them to be there for you."

"That's not true!"

"I wonder how your sisters feel?" Joey said, nodding her head toward Eva's phone. "Family is supposed to be there for the hard work, not just the payoff. You robbed them and you of that."

"Great pep talk. Thanks, Joey," Eva said with sarcasm.

Joey sat back up and heaved a grocery bag onto the bed. "You can redeem yourself in my eyes at least by signing these." She upended the bag on the quilt and every single one of Eva's books spilled out.

"My books. You have them all?"

"Romance is kind of my guilty pleasure," Joey admitted.

"Keeps me and Jax pretty creative in the sack if you know what I mean."

"You want me to sign my books?" Eva felt the warm rush of pride.

"Duh." Joey tossed a pen at her. "You can start with 'To my best friend, Joey…'"

Eva was on her fourth book when a voice louder than it should have been carried through the open window.

"Eva Merill, get your ass down here now."

Eva and Joey scrambled to her window and peered into the yard. Donovan Cardona was standing on the grass wielding a Blue Moon PD bullhorn.

Eva yelped and ducked.

"I can see you," Donovan shouted, his voice echoing around the neighborhood.

"Jesus, is he going to arrest me?" Eva wondered out loud.

"I bet Cardona can get pretty creative with those handcuffs," Joey said, looking down at him. "Here. Hand me that," she said, pointing at Eva's discarded bra from the night before.

"What are you going to do with it?" Eva asked crawling over to it.

Joey hung it out the window. "Eva surrenders. She'll be down in a minute," she yelled.

"Damn it! Now I have to talk to him!"

"Don't whine to me. You could have been an adult about this and answered your damn phone. You're just paying the price for being stupid."

"Gimmie those books back," Eva said, diving for the bag. "I'm changing the inscriptions!"

"No!" Joey pounced on her, flattening her to the mattress and moving the bag of books out of her reach.

"What's going on up there?" Donovan called through the megaphone.

"Aunt Joey is on top of Aunt Eva on the bed," Evan yelled.

"What?" Donovan squawked.

Eva lifted her head and saw Evan leaning out of an attic window with binoculars. "They look really mad right now," Evan continued his commentary.

"Evan! Get down from there and put those binoculars away," Gia's voice sounded shrilly from the backyard.

Eva pushed Joey off her and stomped downstairs. "I thought it would be *so* great having family nearby," she muttered under her breath.

She unlocked the front door and steamed out onto the porch.

"What is going on?" she demanded.

Gia, Beckett, and Aurora were standing next to Donovan on the lawn. Emma and Niko were sitting on the back porch holding coffees seemingly enjoying the view.

"Invite the whole neighborhood, why don't you?" she grumbled.

"There's our grumpy little liar," Donovan said into the bullhorn.

"If you don't put that thing down, I'm going to hit you with it," Eva threatened.

"That's assaulting an officer, Aunt Eva. You probably shouldn't do that," Evan yelled from the attic window.

"You should listen to the kid," Donovan announced to the entire neighborhood.

Eva stomped over to him and yanked the microphone out of his hand. "Did Uranus suddenly climb up your anus?" she demanded into the mic. "Because you're acting like someone you should arrest."

Emma and Niko applauded while Evan snort laughed and Beckett covered Aurora's ears.

"Okay. We probably don't need this anymore," Donovan decided, putting the megaphone down.

"Great. Maybe I can go back to sleep." She made a move for the door, but he stopped her with a big hand on her shoulder.

Joey ambled out the front door. "Morning, everyone."

"Morning, Joey," everyone replied.

"Good luck with this hot mess," Joey said, jerking her thumb in Eva's direction and tossing her bag over her shoulder.

"Ladies," Donovan turned to address Gia and Emma. "You're going to get your shot at the interrogation, but I call dibs. Okay?"

"Soften her up for us," Emma said sternly.

"You heard your sisters. Let's go," he said, hauling Eva up onto the porch and into her kitchen. He shut the door behind them and made himself at home fixing a pot of coffee.

Eva yanked the refrigerator open harder than necessary and, not finding anything that looked good, slammed it again.

"You've got some thinking to do," Donovan said conversationally as he poured the water into the reservoir.

"Oh, do I?" He looked up at her with a bland look, and she felt like a petulant six-year-old. "I'm sorry," she offered.

"I think you're probably going to need to clarify that apology. Lying. Ducking out on me last night. Ignoring my calls. What do you think that does to a guy who thinks he's in love with you?"

"Jesus, Donovan. We haven't even had a first date yet. Let me catch my breath!"

"I've been letting you breathe since I laid eyes on you." The coffeemaker sputtered to life. "You let me know when you've had enough oxygen."

He was hurt, and she'd done it to him. Her choices had

hurt him and even though it wasn't her intention, she still felt a heavy blanket of guilt. Eva walked around the island to face him. She stepped between his feet and leaned against him, running her hands up his chest to his shoulders.

The man wasn't ready to forgive her, but his body had other ideas. Donovan Cardona was stone hard against her.

"I'm sorry for lying to you about what I do for a living. Especially after you told me that you didn't want any lies or secrets between us. I'm sorry for running away last night. I got overwhelmed. I like you." She looked at his chest. "I really like you. And I'm sorry for hurting you and hiding from you."

His hands moved from the counter to her hips.

"I don't want to screw this up," she continued. "But to me that means taking things a little slow until I can wrap my head around the fact that Sheriff Sexy is into me."

His fingers squeezed into her flesh. "I think that's a reasonable request."

"You can't love me, yet," she told him. "Not without knowing me."

"Then let me get to know you."

"I guess we could give it a shot."

"Why is that so hard?" he asked her, inching her chin up so she would meet his gaze.

She wrestled with the answer, the vulnerability it would uncover.

"Ugh. Fine. I was eight-years-old when my mother left. And everyone was so worried about how I was handling it, worried I'd crack. When people ask you a thousand times a day how you're doing, you learn that 'fine' gets the job done. I didn't want anyone to be worried about me when we were all hurting."

"Honey," Donovan said, pulling her in closer. "That was a long time ago. I think you and your sisters can handle the real stuff. You don't have to worry about hurting them with the truth, and they don't have to worry about you breaking. You're all grown up now."

"Oh, hell. I'm so sorry, Donovan," she whispered. "Everything's happening so fast. I don't know how to catch up."

"We'll slow it down as long as you're in this with me. You're not just leading me on for plot research or something, are you?"

She stiffened against him. Now was not the time to tell the man he was the star of her new book. Rather than lie, she laughed and brought her arms around his neck and stood on his boots. "I find you *very* inspiring."

This time he kissed her. And this time, the world disappeared. His mouth moved over hers whispering dark promises that sounded both terrifying and tender. She could feel the energy of need racing just beneath his surface. The idea that she could feel something like this? It was dizzying. Eva molded herself to him and enjoyed his groan when her hips cuddled against his erection.

"You guys about done in there?" Beckett called.

"Who gave that guy a bullhorn?" Donovan murmured against Eva's mouth.

She laughed. "I really like you, Sheriff."

"I really like you, too, Eva."

His phone rang and he groaned. "I gotta take this."

"I'll get your coffee to go," Eva told him.

He kissed her once more, hard on the mouth, before answering his phone. "What?" His frown shifted into a grin. "A noise complaint on Beckett's block? That's weird. I'll check it out. Thanks, Minnie."

He hung up and took the travel mug Eva gave him. "Someone's complaining about some idiot with a bullhorn. I'd better go investigate."

She laughed. "Sure you don't want to stay and protect me from my sisters?" she asked.

"I don't think you need much protecting, Eva. Just don't maim them or I'll be back here for another noise complaint."

She didn't want him to leave. But there was a town out there that needed to be protected from itself.

"Be safe out there," she called after him when he opened the front door.

He tossed her a salute. "Will do. I'll call you. Don't get into any trouble."

15

"What in the ever-living hell, Eves?" Emma stared at her, hands on hips, lips pursed. "I don't even know where to start with you. 'Oh, hey! By the way I'm a giant liar, and I'm only confessing because I got busted!'"

Gia took a different route. The one Eva hated. She sat perched on a barstool at Eva's kitchen island, her green eyes wide and sad. "Can you tell me what I did that made you feel uncomfortable trusting me? I feel awful that you felt the need to keep this whole part of your life from us."

Eva shoved her hands through her hair. The guilt trip. Gia had mastered it as a mother and wielded it like a sword used to stab her in the heart.

"Look. I'm sorry. I'm *really* sorry. It wasn't that I thought you guys would judge me. I mean, maybe a little, but—"

"I'm judging you and your jerky liar face right now," Emma snipped.

"Damn it! It wasn't supposed to happen like this!" Eva paced the small space and wished Donovan was still here.

"How exactly did you envision it going?" Gia asked calmly.

"I was going to hit a bestseller list, and I was going to have you two and Dad and Phoebe over for dinner—with champagne—and give you all signed copies, and you'd finally know that I wasn't some daydreaming screw-up anymore."

"We don't think you're some daydreaming screw-up," Emma argued. "We think you're our little sister. We pick, all of us. I'm the control freak, Gia couldn't find her damn car keys if they were braided into her hair, and you can't be bothered to pay enough attention to not walk into cabinet doors."

"So, if I come to you with a bestselling book—"

"You're still our Eva. Dumbass."

Gia shot Emma a warning look. "Eva, we're already impressed with you. You graduated college. You travel. You're living your dream right now and not waiting until you're fifty to chase it down. You're amazing, and I'm sorry we ever gave you the impression you were anything but amazing."

"I just always thought you guys didn't think I could take care of myself."

"Where did you get that dumbass idea?" Emma asked, a little less heat behind her words.

"When Mom left, you guys and Dad hovered over me like I might shatter into pieces."

"When Mom left, you were the youngest. You were also the closest to her. Gia and I were going through our rebellious phases already."

"Besides, Dad smothered us *all* with 'Are you okay?' 'Do you miss your mom?'." Gia pointed out. "It wasn't a 'you're too weak to function' thing. It was a 'you can talk to me thing.'"

"Great. Now, I really feel like crap," Eva groaned. "Stupid Donovan being right all the time." She prayed the subject change would lighten the mood.

"What did our esteemed sheriff have to say once he put the bullhorn down?" Emma asked, picking up a banana from the fruit bowl.

"He said—to paraphrase—family wants to be there for messy parts, not just the celebrations."

"The mess is more important than the big wins," Gia nodded. "That's like if I wouldn't have introduced you guys to my kids before they were potty-trained and feeding themselves. Babies and toddlers are the mess, but you can't skip over the mess and just land at the good stuff. Most of the good stuff is in the mess."

"Our resident philosophical yogi," Emma said, golf clapping.

"I fucked this all up," Eva sighed, flopping down at her table.

"Not everything," Gia said. "You did just have a very attractive man shouting at you from your lawn."

"He thinks he might love me."

"What?" her sisters screeched in unison.

"Ouch! My ears," Eva complained.

"What did you say when he made this approximal proclamation?" Emma demanded.

"I told him I need time to get used to the idea of dating him." Eva threw up her hands. "Technically we haven't even had a real date yet."

"And yet he thinks that you're it for him?" Gia asked, hearts and flowers in her eyes.

"I know. It's insane."

"I think it's incredibly romantic, Eves. He doesn't date unless he does it very quietly. The fact that he's coming on this strong… well, I think he means it." Gia clasped her hands under her chin.

"Of *course* the romance novelist gets the romance," Emma teased. "Speaking of, when do we get to read your book? Books? How many do you have?"

"You can start right now," Eva said, grinning. She skipped

into the living room and opened the storage compartment of her ottoman. She returned with an armload of books. "I have five out, and I'm working on number six."

Emma snatched one off the stack and flipped it open. "That's What She Said Publishing?"

Eva grinned. "That's me, too."

"You're a publisher, too?" Gia squealed. "I'm getting more proud by the moment!"

"Don't get me started on the indie publishing industry and how being your own publisher both rocks and sucks," Eva laughed.

"Her hand trembled as he skimmed his lips over the curve of her hip—" Emma read. "I think Niko and I are going to read this in bed tonight."

"Don't leave those laying around for Aurora to find and take to school," Eva cautioned Gia. "They're... steamy."

"Like on a scale of one to, oh, I don't know... *fifty*?" Emma asked with a wink.

"A strong forty-eight."

Gia whistled and fanned herself. "I can't wait until naptime today! Aren't you going to sign them for us?"

"I'll sign them if you like them," Eva decided. "And don't sugar coat it. If you don't like a book, tell me."

"Now that the yelling portion of the day is done," Emma said, "Niko and I are hitting the farmer's market with Baxter."

"How is Mr. Adorable?" Eva asked. Niko had surprised Emma with a yellow lab puppy and house as part of his proposal.

"My husband is amazing as always," Emma said cheekily. "And Baxter is pretty great, too. At least, he would be if he could figure out how to stop peeing in the closet."

"We're still talking about the dog, right?" Eva grinned.

She helped her sisters load up their books.

Emma turned around at the door. "Merill recap. Talk to us about stuff. You don't have to protect us from the bad or hold on to the good until it's better."

"Yeah. What she said," Gia said, nodding in Emma's direction.

Eva tossed her sisters a salute. "Got it. Now get out of here so I can write another book."

Gia ducked her head back in the door. "Trust us, okay?" And then she was gone.

But she couldn't. Even now, Eva couldn't. There were just some things that you protected your family from.

Eva poured herself a second cup of coffee and retrieved her phone from the bedroom. She powered it up and winced at the number of missed calls and new text messages. She weeded through them quickly. Saving Donovan's to read last.

She'd have to return her dad and Phoebe's calls now, but the rest could wait.

There was another text from an unknown number. Eva debated not opening but decided it was better to know what was in it.

Unknown: "Don't play games with me. I know where you are."

16

By Thursday, Donovan felt like he'd been in uniform for a week straight. The entire town had lost its damn mind, and he, Colby, Layla, and Minnie were stretched thin trying to restore peace every five seconds.

Every time he lay down to sleep, every time he stepped in the shower, his phone went off with another crisis. Someone had stolen an entire rolling rack of turtlenecks from the Second Chances sidewalk fire sale. Aretha had come to her senses after trying to brain Fitz with hardbacks only to get into a shoving match with Amethyst Oakleigh in the canned goods section of Farm and Field Fresh over the last six cans of tofu tomato soup.

Colby had taken the night shift and ended up driving half a dozen teens home to their parents after they attempted to move the statues in front of the high school into a compromising position. Minnie was working overtime just to keep up with the avalanche of paperwork.

He had yet to make and keep a date with Eva. So he did the next best thing.

He'd snapped up the copy of her book she'd found at Fitz's

store and tucked it into his desk drawer. Between the peaks of crazy, Donovan read. A chapter here, a page there. And now was as good a time as any to take a break. He checked to make sure the door to his office was closed, slipped out of his shoes, and opened the drawer.

He'd read for ten or so and then see about tracking down some lunch, he decided.

Eva's writing was strong, her language straightforward. Donovan had never picked up a romance novel before in his life, but he could guess at the genre's appeal. She added layers to her characters, and he found himself thinking about the book, about the characters, even when he wasn't reading.

It wasn't just the story that interested him. It was what it told him about the author behind the words. The heroine, he'd discovered, had been abandoned early in life by her mother and had taken to hiding her feelings to protect the rest of her family.

It gave him a better idea of what was going on in the brain of the woman he couldn't get out of his mind or his heart.

He paged through the paperback to find his spot, too embarrassed to use a bookmark in case Minnie snooped through his things like he imagined she did when she got bored behind the desk. Donovan propped his socked feet up on his desk and dug in.

He'd managed a chapter and then the better part of another when things began to heat up on the page. The heroine and her hero were losing clothing faster than he lost money to Fitz at poker. Donovan tugged on his collar and glanced up to make sure his door was still closed.

He was just getting to the good part, the *really* good part when his door flew open. He wasn't sure if it was adrenaline or embarrassment that had him chucking the book across the room. It hit the window with a *thwack* and fell behind the worn couch that he'd been grabbing cat naps on since the planets had gone to hell.

"Everything all right, Cardona? You look a little feverish," Beckett asked from the doorway. His cocky ass smile made Donovan realize he wasn't fooling anyone with his pitching arm. It was a good thing he was wearing his daughter Lydia in a sling or Donovan would have considered taking a swing at him.

"To what do I owe the interruption?" The Pierce brothers —all three of them—plus Niko filed into his office with three kids and a dog. Donovan tried not to think about the scene he'd just been reading.

Jesus. Was that sweat on his brow? Was he sweating?

"Man, you're sweating. You coming down with Colby's food poisoning?" Carter asked.

"Nope. Just a warm day," Donovan said, wondering where he usually put his hands when he wasn't hiding something. Everywhere they went felt awkward and fake.

"It's forty-five degrees outside," Jax pointed out. "See, buddy. This is what happens when grown-ups lie. They get all red and sweaty," he said to his foster son, Caleb. Caleb, at six, was all big eyes, messy hair, and shy smiles. He nodded with the hint of a curious smile as if still stunned that he was invited to be part of the man crowd.

Niko let Baxter, his dopic teenage puppy, pull him further into the office. "I think Baxter wants me to look behind the couch," he announced. "He must sense a threat. Maybe you should use him as a police dog?"

Baxter's tail wagged so wildly that Donovan wondered how his ass end hadn't broken off yet.

"Touch that couch, and I'll throw you in the slammer," he threatened.

"There's no doors on our cells," Jax reported to Nikolai. "You sit in a cubicle until someone bails you out."

Niko frowned thoughtfully. "And I do have my attorney here." He jerked his thumb in Beckett's direction.

"Worth it," Carter nodded, juggling Meadow from arm to arm as the little girl giggled.

Niko handed the dog leash to Caleb. "Hold this, Cale."

Together he and Jax moved the couch away from the wall while Donovan tried to bite back every violent threat that he wanted to rain down on his stupid friends. Meadow's big blue eyes were the only thing that made him hold on to his temper.

"Aha! Apparently, the sheriff has succumbed to the same book club our wives have," Jax held the book over his head.

"Fine. I'm reading it. Let me have it," Donovan sighed, waiting for the torrent of torment.

Instead, Carter shrugged his shoulders. "Hey, man. No judgment. That book got me—" he glanced in Caleb's direction. "L-A-I-D once already today. I call dibs on it when you're done with it."

"Man, Cale's six," Jax snorted. "He can spell plenty. Caleb, spell hammock!"

Dutifully Caleb recited the correct spelling. "What's get laid mean, Uncle Carter?" he asked.

Carter grinned. "Oops."

Beckett flipped through the book, his eyes widening. "Wait. Is this physically possible?"

"What?" Jax asked, leaning in to peer at the page.

"If she's like, you know, bent like that..."

"Yeah, I think so. I mean if the angle is right," Jax frowned thoughtfully.

"Hey, Caleb," Donovan said to the kid. "Miss Minnie made cookies today. Why don't you go on out there and see if she'll give you a cookie and some juice?"

"Okay!" Caleb hauled ass out of the room with Baxter on his heels. Beckett and Jax continued to try to re-enact a particularly acrobatic pose.

"No, you're the woman," Jax said, elbowing his brother.

"I thought you were," Beckett argued.

"You two." Donovan pointed to the two stooges, "You go any farther and I'm going to tase you both."

"How far are you in the book?" Beckett asked, consulting the page again. "Did you get to the part where Carley's in the bath and—"

Donovan shoved his fingers in his ears. "I can't hear you! So, you might as well shut up!"

"Don't ruin it for him, ass—... hat." Carter said, punching his brother in the arm.

Meadow grinned up at him as if she knew her daddy shouldn't be saying those words.

"Don't punch me when I'm wearing my baby!" Beckett gave Carter a half-hearted shove back.

"Anyone feel like telling me why you're all in my office in the middle of some astrological apocalypse?" Donovan yelled over the din.

Baxter wandered back in licking his chops to get the last crumbs of Minnie's homemade dog treat off his nose. He strolled over and laid down under Donovan's desk.

Beckett pointed at him. "We do have a purpose. A couple of them."

"Beckett and I were wondering if there's been any progress tracking down Reva and Caleb's mom?" Jax said, his eyes on the door.

Damn it.

Jax and Joey had been granted emergency guardianship over Reva and Caleb when the kids' mother abandoned them that spring. The Pierces were ready to make it permanent. But without Sheila Flinchy signing away her parental rights, custody was temporary and tentative.

Donovan shook his head. "I had a hit on her in the system ten days ago. A speeding ticket and driving unregistered in Oklahoma but nothing since then. This week it kind of got away from me."

Everything this week had gotten away from him. And now he was letting friends down. He was the asshat.

"We know you've got your hands full right now. Which is why we were thinking it's time to hire a P.I." Jax told him.

"I'd be happy to work with an investigator in whatever capacity I can to help," Donovan said, still kicking himself.

"Joey and I know you would, and we appreciate it. We're ready to make this official, and the sooner, the better. Jojo woke up in the middle of the night from a nightmare thinking Sheila stole the kids back. I had to wrestle the Nerf gun away from her and talk her down."

"We'll get this figured out, and we'll make it legal, make it right," Donovan promised.

"Great. We'll put the investigator in touch with you," Beckett said, making a note on his cell phone.

Carter tickled Meadow. "Business concluded. Who's ready for lunch and interrogating Cardona about a certain redhead?"

Meadow's hands flew up in the air.

17

Donovan wasn't at the station when Eva stopped by. But the ever-helpful and all-knowing Minnie directed her to the high school where he was dealing with "an issue". She wasn't sure what the issue was, but Eva wanted to make sure he'd accepted her apology, and the best way to ensure that was with food.

She'd seen the police reports that had taken up the entire first two pages of *The Monthly Moon* and knew he was running himself ragged trying to keep up with town-wide mischief.

This particular police issue appeared to involve the entire Blue Moon High School marching band hosting a sit-in on the school's crosswalk. A beside-himself band director was flailing his arms with an invisible baton, and the band was ignoring him.

Donovan, tall, sexy, and weary, was consulting with teachers and parents on the sidewalk.

Eva spotted Evan with his trumpet sitting cross-legged next to the blue-eyed, blonde-haired junior high temptress, Oceana.

"Evan! What the hell's going on?" she demanded.

"Oh, hey, Aunt Eva!" he said cheerily. "We're protesting."

"Oh, sweet Jesus, this town got you too," Eva sighed under her breath. "What are you protesting?" she asked, picking her way through the students to kneel next to Evan.

"The band director is insisting that we play this stupid song that no one likes at the football game tonight."

"What do you want to play instead?" Eva asked.

"Anything but his song." Oceana rolled her pale blue eyes heavenward.

"Mr. Burke is getting a divorce, and he wrote this song about it. He calls it 'Getting Taken to the Cleaners by a Wench'. It's a lot of brass and drums, and everyone else is just supposed to march and frown."

"Oh boy," Eva muttered. "And when did he spring this divorce and angry man song on you guys?"

"Yesterday. He made us practice for four hours last night just so we'd get it exactly right because his wife is going to be at the game tonight. She already came to see Beckett about drawing up papers."

"If I get him to agree to let you play another song, will you stop blocking traffic?" Eva asked.

"Yes, please." Evan nodded. "But good luck. We tried being reasonable with him, and he was not open to it."

"Excuse me, Evan's aunt?" A boy with a tuba waved at her. "Could you make it quick? I really hafta pee, and I'm not going in the sewer drain like Willard did."

"Give me a minute," Eva said. "I'll see what I can do."

She stepped over kids and musical instruments and hurried to Donovan's side.

"Ma'am, I don't think arresting forty kids is going to help," he explained to a harried teacher dressed in a lavender jumpsuit.

"We need to set an example," she said, her shrill voice carrying far and wide.

"Excuse me, Sheriff. Do you have a moment?" Eva tugged on his sleeve.

She saw relief in his tired eyes. "Excuse me, Ms. Friendly."

"Ms. *Friendly* wants to arrest half the high school?" Eva whispered as Donovan led her a few steps away.

"Usually she's much more like her moniker," Donovan sighed. "Everyone is insane."

"You look exhausted. When's the last time you slept?" Eva asked.

"I don't know? Tuesday? What day is it?"

"My poor, handsome sheriff. It's Thursday, and I brought you dinner. Baked ziti from Villa Harvest. My dad sends his compliments."

"I love you, and I love your dad," Donovan said, shoving his face in the bag to sniff. "I know we're taking things slow and all, but I'm going to marry you, and we're going to serve baked ziti at our reception."

"I think Uranus is getting to you, too."

Donovan yawned mightily. "I don't care what Uranus does to me as long as you're with me. As soon as I get this situation cleaned up, we should have a date. You can watch me eat the dinner you brought me."

"What *is* the situation here?"

"I have no fucking clue. The band director is melting down and won't talk. Just keeps muttering about going to the cleaners. Every time I try to talk to the kids, some teacher freaks out on me and tells me to arrest someone."

"How about this? You sit down and eat some ziti. Give me a minute, and I'll see if I can broker a truce."

"Good luck," he said, his mouth already full of fresh baked roll.

Eva took her chances with the band director. "Mr. Burke?"

He cut off his silent symphony mid-slice. "What?"

"The band will play tonight if you let them play another song."

"No! Absolutely not! It must be that song!"

She patted his shoulder. He wore a worn tweed jacket with patches on the elbows. His hair hadn't been combed in about a week. "I understand you're going through a rough time, but the fastest, safest way to get these kids out of the street and stop them from using sewer drains as urinals is to let them play a different song."

"How else am I supposed to stick it to my wife so she knows she's being unreasonable?" Dejected now, Mr. Burke shoved his invisible baton inside his jacket.

"Have you considered the possibility that all of this is because of the planets crossing?" Eva suggested gently. "Maybe she doesn't mean anything she says right now."

He perked up. "Do you think that's true?"

How the hell was she supposed to know? "Yes," she said firmly.

Mr. Burke scuffed his toe on the sidewalk. "I don't know. She said some pretty mean things," he said, sending a pouty look over his shoulder at Ms. Friendly.

"Ms. Friendly is your wife?" she whispered.

"Yeah." He sighed heavily. "She's beautiful isn't she? She told me she could do better, and I know she's right."

"Crap," Eva breathed. She straightened her shoulders. "Mr. Burke. This is for you and your band and your marriage." She grabbed him by the face and pulled him in for a loud, smacking kiss. Some smart ass in the drum section gave her a riff.

"Hey! That's my husband!" Ms. Friendly fumed.

"We good?" Eva asked.

No noise came out of Mr. Burke's open mouth, but his eyes were wider than Frisbees.

"The kids can play what they want?" she confirmed.

He nodded again and made a gurgling noise.

Eva dodged the purse that Ms. Friendly swung at her. "Okay, kids. You get to play whatever you want tonight at the game."

They gave her a blaring crescendo… all except for the tuba kid who was making a beeline for the restroom.

"Get out of the street and get ready for the game," she said, shooing them in the direction of the school.

Ms. Friendly, her arm locked through Mr. Burke's, dragged him back into the building, promising that she was calling Beckett tonight to cancel the divorce papers.

"All in a day's work," Eva sighed. She turned to look for her exhausted sheriff, but another police cruiser pulled to a stop in front of her.

"Evening," Deputy Layla called through the open window. "Looks like the situation is under control." She got out of the car and watched the kids file into the school.

"It was just a misunderstanding. No harm, no blood," Eva assured her.

Layla cracked her gum. "Good. Good. We're seeing a little too much action around here these days."

"Donovan looks exhausted," Eva said.

Layla rolled her eyes. "Guy's been on for seventy-two hours straight. I think he's worried me and Colby are going to end up joining the rest of these Mooner zombies and burning down the super market or something. Where is he anyway?"

Eva bit her lip and pointed. Donovan was leaning against a mailbox, his long legs stretched out in front of him, the container of ziti in his lap. He was sound asleep.

"Ah, hell. Knew that was coming."

Layla pulled out her phone.

"Are you calling for backup?" Eva asked.

Layla snorted. "Nope. I'm taking video. This is the last time he makes fun of me for falling down the bleachers doing security at the field hockey game."

Donovan let out a soft snore and Eva clamped a hand over her mouth to hold back the laughter.

Layla pocketed her phone. "Okay, Sheriff. Rise and shine," she said, kicking his shoe.

He shot to attention. "Huh? Oh. Hey, Layla."

"You're officially relieved of duty," she said.

"Huh? Oh, right. Yeah. I'll take off as soon as I figure out how to get these kids out of the crosswalk."

Layla peered over her shoulder. "You mean the kids that are warming up for the big game?"

Donovan rubbed his eyes and then looked at Eva. "How'd you do that?"

"Made out with the band director. I hope you don't mind."

"You got forty kids off the street, made all those teachers stop yelling at me, and you brought me ziti. I don't mind. I'm in love."

Layla and Eva each took an arm and hauled Donovan to his feet.

"Okay, big guy. Eva here's gonna make sure you get home. I'm telling Minnie that under no circumstances are you to be called before 8 a.m. tomorrow. Now get your ass out of here."

Donovan took a stumbling step off the curb, and Eva held him up. "I don't think you're driving, Donovan."

"His keys are in the ignition," Layla said, jerking her chin toward his cruiser.

"I can't drive a police cruiser!"

Layla shrugged. "Desperate times. See ya tomorrow, Cardona."

Eva poured Donovan into the passenger seat and hurried around to the other side. She had to move the seat all the way up to accommodate her short legs. Eva turned the key and then realized she didn't know where he lived. And he was sound asleep already.

He'd professed his love for her, and she had no idea where he lived. Of course, it was Blue Moon. She could just roll down her window and ask literally anyone on the street. They'd be able to tell her what magazine subscriptions he had and where he hid his spare key. But maybe a change of scenery would do him some good.

She pointed the car in the direction of her place. "Guess we're having our first sleep over before our first date," she murmured under her breath.

Donovan snored in response.

18

Donovan woke in stages, easing into consciousness. He felt as if he was emerging from a coma, awareness slowly returning to his fingers and toes, his limbs. Before his eyes were open, he knew he wasn't in his own bed. There were cushions beneath him and a fuzzy blanket draped over him.

He cracked an eye open and realized there was a redhead sound asleep on his chest. His mind may not have been fully awake, but his body more than made up for it. His dick went stone hard in the span of a breath. Her hair tickled his nose as his mind raced back over the previous night. He remembered the exhaustion, the marching band, the ziti. And then hardly anything at all.

Eva had driven him home. He recalled that vaguely. And then settled him on the couch with his leftovers. That was the last thing he could pull. *Did they have sex?* he wondered. God, he hoped not. His first time with Eva was supposed to be memorable, monumental, for them both. Dammit.

He stroked a hand down her back and was relieved to find her wearing a tank top. He was shirtless, but a quick exploration beneath the blanket proved he was still wearing pants that covered his throbbing erection.

Blearily, he gazed around Eva's living room. His duty belt was coiled on the coffee table next to his cell phone. A dull, rosy glow peeked through her windows. The softly coming dawn.

"Mmmph," Eva murmured, her lips moving against the skin of his shoulder.

Her mouth on him did nothing to dull the painful, voracious hunger he was feeling for her. He winced when the leg she'd tossed over his thighs inched higher.

"Eva," he whispered.

"Mmm, Sheriff Sexy." Her long-lashed eyes remained closed. He could see the faint freckles that danced across the bridge of her nose.

Despite the agony, he grinned. This was one hell of a way to wake up. The woman of his dreams wrapped in his arms while the rest of the world was quiet. Yeah, he could get used to this.

"Eva," he said again.

She yawned and wiggled closer, incrementally increasing his torture.

"Baby. Wake up."

Her eyes fluttered open and focused slowly on his face. She sighed happily. "Oh, good. It wasn't a dream."

The realization hit him like a cartoon anvil. Donovan bolted upright, nearly flinging her to the floor. He'd fallen asleep on his watch, leaving his town unprotected. "I shouldn't have slept so long," he cursed, scrambling out from under the blanket.

"Where do you think you're going?" the sleepy Eva demanded, doing her best to shove him back down.

"Eva, I have an entire town collectively losing its damn mind. I don't have time for sleep or… other distractions."

She prodded him in the chest. "For your information, you fell asleep sitting against a mailbox last night. Layla and Colby took the shift that you were too big of a hero to give them."

"I'm sheriff. I have a responsibility to these people," he argued. The worry that he'd let everyone down circled through his gut. First, he'd dropped the ball with Jax's hunt for the kids' mom, and now he'd slept God knows how many hours while the town ran amuck.

"What is this?" Eva asked. Since he refused to lay back down, she slid into his lap. "What's going on right now? You look like you're panicking."

"It's not panic." *It totally was panic.* He'd let people down, people who were counting on him.

"Take a breath and text Colby or Layla. Check in. Make sure all is well." She handed him his phone and stayed put in his lap.

Grudgingly, he did as he was told and fired off a text demanding a status update from his deputies. He was scanning the room for his shoes when Colby responded.

Colby: Relax, boss. All is well. A relatively quiet night for the apocalypse.

Layla was more succinct.

Layla: Leave us alone. See you at 8.

Eva read the texts as they came in and smiled smugly. "Care to start the morning over, Sheriff Crabby Pants?"

A hot wave of relief coursed through him. He hadn't let the entire town down, and he had a beautiful woman on his lap.

He didn't need any more coaxing than that. He lay back down, letting Eva sprawl out on top of him.

"Good morning," he whispered, brushing a curl back from her face.

"Mmm, morning. Did you sleep well? I couldn't get you upstairs, so I figured the couch would have to do."

"This is good. Really good," he said, brushing a kiss over her hair. "And you stayed with me, which is even better."

She smiled shyly. "I hope you don't mind. But I didn't want you sneaking out in the middle of the night, second-guessing your deputies."

"You were babysitting me." The irony of Eva being responsible for him had Donovan shaking his head.

"Did the alarm go off yet?" Eva yawned as she snuggled closer.

"Not that I heard."

"It's not even seven yet. That means you get breakfast."

"This morning keeps getting better and better."

She moved over his rigid length. "I'll say."

He pinched her and made her laugh.

"We're doing this whole relationship backwards," he lamented.

"We'll get it figured out," Eva promised. She buried her face into his neck and breathed in. "You know, I've never had a platonic sleepover before."

"How much time do I have to make it un-platonic?" He groaned. "Scratch that. We're taking things slow." He just wished he could relay that message to his cock, which wasn't interested in slow.

"Glacier-like," Eva reminded him. Reluctantly, she sat up. "You go shower, and I'll start breakfast."

She directed him upstairs, and he performed some acrobatics to get himself under the showerhead that had to have been designed for dolls. After a shower with rose-scented shampoo, he felt better than he had in days. He had energy. His brain was fired up.

He'd cull out some time today to run follow-ups with the locals on Sheila Flinchy so Jax had more to give his P.I. Then he could make his rounds starting around the park and make sure peace was upheld. With some luck, he could get a head start on the tidal wave of paperwork that was swamping his desk before lunch. In the afternoon, he'd put his head together with Beckett and figure out what the hell they were going to do security-wise for the Halloween Carnival, the apex of the planetary bullshit.

He could use a shave, Donovan thought, staring in the mirror swiping a hand over the crop of stubble that had turned into the early stages of a beard. A shave and a haircut. Maybe he could squeeze a stop in at the Snip Shack tonight and take care of both and catch wind of any gossip that might need police attention.

With no spare toothbrush, he used Eva's pink one and wondered how long he'd have to wait before he woke up next to her again.

When he returned downstairs, the smell of bacon and coffee were thick in the air.

She was still in her tank and pajama pants, looking entirely too enchanting. Her hair was loose and wild, framing her bare face.

"It should be illegal," he decided.

"What?" she asked, handing over a mug of coffee.

"You looking like that after you wake up."

"You know what else should be illegal?"

"What?"

"You being you. Charming, heroic, *and* sexy as hell? It's just not fair to the rest of the male population." She batted her lashes at him.

She plated two breakfast sandwiches and directed him to the table.

He sat, sipping the coffee.

"You wanna talk about why you still look like you're worried?" she asked him.

Donovan sighed. "Are all writers as annoyingly observant?"

She grinned over the rim of her mug. "Probably."

"I hate letting people down," he admitted.

"Who did you let down?" She was asking out of curiosity and not to call him out on something, Donovan realized. She wanted to understand, and he liked that.

"When I woke up, I thought I'd destroyed an entire town with my selfish need for sleep."

She nudged his plate toward him. "And now that those fears have been laid to rest, you still look guilty."

"Jax and Beckett came to see me yesterday. Well, all of the Pierces and Niko came by."

"What did they want?" Eva asked, biting into her sandwich.

Donovan took her cue and did the same. "We've been trying to track down Sheila Flinchy so Beckett can convince her to sign over her parental rights to Reva and Caleb. And I dropped the ball. I had a hit on her a week and a half ago, but with everything happening, I didn't dig any deeper."

Eva laid a hand on his arm. "You've been a little busy," she reminded him.

"I know, but the Pierces are my best friends from birth. I should have made time."

"Donovan," she sighed. "You gave me a swift kick in the ass when I needed it. Now it's my turn. You don't have to do all this on your own. Your mom didn't do it by herself. You have deputies and Minnie and your friends and me. You can lean on us. We don't have to always be the ones leaning on you."

"I like being in charge."

"We'll see about that once I get you naked," Eva teased.

And just like that his blood left his head.

"But in the meantime," she continued, "trust us to pick up the slack. When you run yourself into the ground you're not helping anyone."

"My mom dealt with this with one part-time deputy," he argued.

"That was 1987. I bet the town has almost doubled in population since then. You're not failing, and you're not letting anyone down. Asking for help isn't going to dull the shine on that armor."

He grunted. "When did you get to be so wise?"

"When it's someone else's problem," she laughed. "How about we make a deal. I'll solve your problems if you solve mine?"

"Deal. Tell me all your problems," he demanded.

She didn't laugh, and Donovan was quick to pick up on the shadow in her eyes.

"Right now, my problem is that the conflict between my characters needs to bump up another notch to keep it exciting," she said finally. But he knew there was something else nagging at her.

"Remember our deal, Eva," he said quietly. "Honesty. No more secrets."

"I remember," she said, keeping her expression blank.

She could try to hide from him, but he'd figure out her secrets, and he'd fix whatever was scaring her.

"So how do you feel since everyone found out about your

secret profession?" he asked, changing the subject. Patience was his strong suit.

She grinned, and his heart gave a lopsided thump. "I can't believe everyone knows. It's so wild and terrifying and freeing. Did I mention terrifying?" she sighed.

He took another bite of his breakfast. "It sounds like everyone in town is reading your books." If she wasn't ready to confess whatever she was hiding, he wasn't ready to tell her he was a fan.

"Really?" She laughed.

"Everyone's saying how good they are. You better get ready to be famous."

"Thanks to living in a town of big mouths, I did see a nice uptick in sales," she admitted, taking his coffee mug and wandering back into the kitchen to refill it. "But I'm not convinced it's not Uranus at work."

She put the mug down in front of him, and Donovan used the opportunity to snake an arm around her waist and pull her into his lap.

"Just because you're not where you want to be yet doesn't mean you aren't who you need to be," he said, cupping her face.

"Now who's the wise one?" Eva asked softly. Eyes more yellow than green studying him.

"You're amazing, Evangelina."

"You're not just saying that because of Uranus, are you?"

"Baby, I'm immune to Uranus," he insisted. What he felt for her? It had started long before any planets crossed anything. This was real and good, and he wanted more of it.

Slowly, she wound her arms around his neck.

Yet again, his dick stirred to life against her. Eva gave a sexy little gasp when she felt him harden beneath her. She wet her lips. "I think I'm okay with going a little faster," she said softly.

His hands clamped onto her hips as their mouths closed the distance.

Eva's front door burst open, and Ellery stormed in. "There you are!" she said accusingly. "I've been all over this town looking for you." She pointed at Donovan.

"I'm a little busy right now, El. Can't you call Layla or Colby or literally anyone else in the world?" Donovan asked without looking away from Eva's flushed cheeks, the heat in her eyes.

"Donovan Cardona!" Ellery clapped her hands gaining his attention.

"What?" he demanded, exasperated.

"This!" Ellery shoved her phone in his face. "They put this sign in my lawn. That's trespassing and vandalism. I know, I already checked with Beckett."

"So is kicking in Eva's front door," he reminded her.

"Sorry, Eva," Ellery said. "But technically, this is Beckett's house, and he told me to drag you out of here if I had to."

"Did he now?" Donovan added Beckett Pierce to his people to beat the hell out of list. He took the phone from Ellery and blew up the picture.

There on Ellery's front lawn was a black sign post dug into the ground.

Match not approved by the Beautification Committee.

"Again, Ellery. Why don't you talk to a deputy? Please." He would beg if it got Eva naked underneath him.

"I tried! Colby said it wasn't an emergency and that he'd 'stop by sometime today' if he had time! In the meantime, I can't remove the evidence from my lawn and the wedding invitations already went out. They're making everyone choose between me and them, and I'm not going to let them ruin my wedding day!"

"When are you getting married?" Eva cut in, slipping off Donovan's lap.

Ellery pointed to the stack of mail on Eva's table to a black envelope with silver ink. "You didn't even open it yet? I worked so hard on my calligraphy!"

Eva dove for the envelope. "I'm sorry. There was this crisis and then—"

Ellery's trembling lip cut Eva off.

"I'm opening! Here we go! Oh, what a beautiful invitation," she said, showing off the silver cobweb design to Donovan. "It says here your big day is... Oh. Boy."

Donovan took the card from her. "Halloween." He swiped a hand over his face.

"What?" Ellery demanded. "It's only my favorite day of the year."

"It's also in the middle of some planetary shitstorm," Donovan reminded her.

Ellery's lip trembled. "I'm not letting you or some dumb planet or anyone else in this town rain on my parade!"

Eva jumped in to soothe. "We're not going to let anyone rain on your parade or ruin your day," she promised, sending Donovan a hard look. "It's going to be the best day of your life."

"We have to make sure Bruce Oakleigh and the rest of the Beautification Committee don't interfere with my wedding," Ellery announced.

"How do you propose we do that?" Donovan asked. From the look on his face, Eva could tell he was dreading the answer.

Ellery smiled. "I'm glad you asked."

19

"Why are you waving a piece of paper in my face like you're a matador? Do I look like a bull to you?" Gia snatched the paper out of Eva's grasp.

"I need a favor," Eva said, wrinkling her nose in anticipation of a big, fat no. "Donovan needs you. Blue Moon needs you."

Gia scanned the text. "This is an application to join the Beautification Committee."

"Surprise!" Eva spread her arms wide. "Our assignment is to go undercover and keep them under control until this apocalypse deal gets straightened out and Ellery is reinstated. Fun, right?"

Gia hugged the application to her chest. "You don't understand. I have been *dying* to join the B.C.! I mean what could bring greater joy than pairing up true loves?"

"Have you ever thought about writing romance novels?" Eva asked.

Gia skipped over to the desk in the kitchen and grabbed a pen. "I'm filling this out right now! Oh, my God. What if they don't want me? Do you think Beckett could use his influence?"

Eva rolled her eyes at her sister. "You're the first lady of Blue Moon, and you've had stars in your eyes since the B.C. shoved you at Beckett. I think you're a shoe-in."

"This is the most exciting thing that's happened since Lydia was born," Gia said, cooing at her daughter in her highchair.

Lydia, bald and beautiful, banged her spoon happily on the tray.

"Hey! Didn't finding out your sister is an excellent romance novelist rate up there?" Eva reminded her.

"That is a close third," Gia promised. "Okay. Let's see what they want from us. 'Do you believe in happily ever after?' Yes," she said, as she resoundingly checked the box. "'How opposed are you to involving yourself in the business of others? Definitely, slightly, or love is everyone's business?'"

Eva snorted.

"Not even the slightest challenge here," Gia announced working her way down the application.

"Oh, boy," Eva whispered to Lydia. "I think your mama is going to be part of the problem."

Lydia giggled and threw a glob of pureed carrots onto the floor. Diesel snarfed it up and then spit it back out. Tripod Jr., the three-legged cat, meandered over and rubbed against Gia's legs meowing.

"Not now, Tripod. Mama has to rank these movies in order of most romantic."

Eva texted Donovan on her way across the back yard.

Eva: Mission accomplished. The Merills will attempt a takeover of the B.C.

Her phone rang, and she got a little jolt at the picture of the winking Donovan Cardona that popped up on her screen.

"When did you find time to sneak a selfie and add a contact photo to my phone?" she asked in lieu of a greeting.

"A law enforcement officer never reveals his secrets," Donovan told her. She could hear the smile in his voice. "We're supposed to be sneaky. That's how we catch the bad guys."

"You sound like you're in a good mood," she teased.

"Waking up with a beautiful redhead snoring in my ear has that effect on me."

"I wasn't snoring!" She let herself in the door.

"Like a lumberjack. It's amazing I got any sleep at all."

"You slept for ten hours," Eva reminded him. "So, should I wear a wire for the Beautification Committee meeting tonight? Because I have this fantasy of you taping a microphone between my—"

"Stop right there, Evangelina, or I'll leave this town to fend for itself and drive through Beckett's yard to get to you." His voice was rusty, rough.

She blew out a breath. A hot rush of lust and something else, something softer, scarier, swept over her. "Don't say it if you don't mean it."

He growled and that made it even worse.

"Changing the subject before I get any harder and have to get out of my car in front of the entire town. Thank you for last night."

Eva picked up her laptop and wandered out to the skinny stretch of sunroom off her living room. She flopped down on the god-awful flower print couch that looked as though it had barely survived since its heyday in the seventies. "What exactly about last night was gratitude worthy? We both stayed mostly clothed," she said lightly.

"You knew I needed a break, and you took care of me. And when I felt guilty about taking a break, you told me I was being an idiot."

What was that warmth in her chest? Was it heart burn?

"That's not exactly how I remember it. I think I was much more delicate than calling you an idiot to your face."

"You took care of me, and I appreciate it."

"Any time, Sheriff. Just try not to push yourself so hard that you pass out on a mailbox again."

She heard the chirp of his radio on his end and the sigh that he bit back. "I have to go, Eva. I'll call you later."

"Bye, Donovan."

"Bye, beautiful."

Eva let her breath out in a rush when she disconnected. *What was it about that man that made her feel so damn much?*

He was so honest, putting things out there as if it were completely natural to share feelings and thoughts. To be fair, he'd grown up in Blue Moon, the small-town answer to talk therapy. She'd grown up in a family that tried to protect each other by not ever blabbing about their feelings. It wasn't that the Merills weren't close. It's just that, after the trauma her mother had caused, no one wanted to open old wounds. No one wanted to hurt anymore.

And that's why Eva hung on to her secrets.

She worked through the rest of the morning and well into the afternoon from the couch on the sunporch. When the story flowed, she abandoned all other distractions and went with it. Inspiration was a fickle bitch, and when she showed up to play, Eva knew better than to try to tame her. After stalling out while trying to find a synonym for "smirk" that didn't sound too dickish, she took a popcorn break. And while the house filled with the heavenly scent, she paused to roll out her shoulders.

She wondered if it was the subject matter that had her inspiration firing on all cylinders. Her small-town sheriff hero was admittedly modeled after Donovan, even before she'd started pumping him for information, before he'd admitted his feelings. Eva hadn't needed to be on the receiving end of his lips to know he was a genuine romantic hero, and she had a feeling her readers were going to fall hard for him.

She just hadn't had the opportunity to bring up the topic to Donovan that he was about to become a romance novel hero. Okay, that was a lie. She'd had the opportunity but not the right motivation yet.

"Oh, hey, there, sexy guy with a gun. I hope you don't mind that I'm using you in the nicest possible way," she said aloud to herself.

Eva shook her head. Yeah, she was going to have to come up with a better way to broach the subject. Maybe if they ever made it out to dinner? Somewhere cozy and dark. She'd lean forward and take his hand in hers. The candlelight... no. Scratch that. The firelight would glint off her hair. Yeah. That worked.

The microwave dinged, temporarily quieting her writer's imagination.

Eva had always known her brain worked differently than the organized, number-loving Emma. Gia, too. Her middle sister lived in a big picture kind of world where details often slipped through the cracks, but the plan was always still the plan.

Eva, on the other hand, spent her mental energy rearranging words to paint pictures in her mind. Her own little world, as her family had called it when she spaced out, had been a romantic fantasy since she'd discovered boys at thirteen. She'd penned embarrassing short stories about junior high true love that took place in the hallway between gym and biology.

And now she was living one, Eva thought, scooping a handful of popcorn out of the bag.

She had a handsome hero ready and willing to sweep her off her feet and profess his over-the-top instalove that her readers would swoon over. Her sisters and father had all found happiness here. And despite the present circumstances of being in the throes of an epic town-wide temper tantrum, she felt like maybe her happily ever after could be on the horizon.

If Donovan was willing to give her a little wiggle room in the truth and honesty department.

She took another handful of popcorn, sighed, and then choked when a kernel tried to sneak down her windpipe.

"Dang it," she coughed. She hoped that wasn't a warning from karma. She had her reasons for not dragging anyone else into her mess. She was going to fix it once and for all this time. And maybe once the shadow of shame that had followed her everywhere was finally vanquished, maybe then she could really think about a relationship with Donovan.

Her phone dinged, and she saw a new text from Donovan.

Donovan: "Did you make out with the band director or was that a dream?"

She smiled at the screen, feeling like a teenager with a crush all over again.

Eva: "Ask not what your town can do for you but what you can do for your town."

Another text popped up. This one stole her smile and her good mood.

Unknown: "I think it's time we talk face-to-face. You owe me."

Her reaction was visceral and instantaneous. Anger and hurt coiled together in a molten ball in her belly. Why couldn't this shadow stop following her? Maybe it was because she tried to escape the confrontation rather than face it. Over and over again. But she wasn't going to be chased out of Blue Moon. She'd stand her ground here. Her thumbs flew over the screen.

Eva: "If anyone owes anything. It's you. I'm not playing your games anymore."

Unknown: "You'll play any game I tell you to."

She shuddered at the response, then straightened her shoulders. No. It was far beyond time to put a stop to this. She had a future to think about, and there was no room for the person at the other end of the text in it.

Eva: "Not happening this time. Leave me alone. Permanently."

Eva tossed her phone on the couch and paced in front of it. She wouldn't break this time. Not here. Not now. She was finally living out her dream of being an author. She shared this lovely little town with everyone who mattered in her life. She wasn't letting anyone take this from her.

"Yeah," Eva nodded in agreement with her inner pep talk. She wanted to be here. She was earning her place, surrounded by family, getting to know Donovan, writing her books. Blue Moon was home, and she wasn't going to let anyone take that from her. Not this time.

She blocked the number and, feeling brave, went back to writing about love.

20

By mid-week, the entire town was in a variety of uproars, and Eva and Donovan still had failed to set and keep a date. There'd been the dinner plan for Monday. Eva had been knee-deep in a chapter rewrite that afternoon when Donovan had called to rain check. Someone had dumped an industrial size jug of organic dish soap into the fountain at the playground on the edge of town. Suds as big as SUVs were floating around the pocket-sized park.

Tuesday, Eva invited Donovan to meet her for an early yoga class and breakfast. He'd made it through one sun salutation before getting called away to deal with a vandalism emergency. Ernest Washington's neighbor had gotten sick of him raking his leaves onto their lawn. The neighbor had filled every single one of the VW buses on his car lot with dead leaves.

The evidence photos made their way to Blue Moon's Facebook group and the onslaught of finger pointing and social media feuding had Donovan pulling the plug on the Facebook group until further notice. Of course, that only spurred

Anthony Berkowicz to announce that *The Monthly Moon* would become a weekly paper to keep up with all the gossip.

Every time Donovan canceled or postponed or rain-checked, a new bouquet from Every Bloomin' Thing arrived on her doorstep. Eva was up to four arrangements and out of vases when he made the switch from flowers to food. A personal pie from Peace of Pizza arrived with her favorite toppings—black olives and green peppers—one afternoon after she'd unwittingly worked through breakfast and lunch. When she called in an order to Righteous Subs for herself and Gia's family one evening, she arrived to find it already paid for by the generous sheriff.

Even his apologies were perfect. *Was there nothing about this man that was human and flawed?*

Eva blinked at her screen, realizing she'd once again spaced out. She was in the middle of prime writing time and the words were halting, stalling on the page. It was as if her inspiration had dried up without consistent access to Donovan.

She kicked back in her chair and stretched. Diesel, her furry footrest, stirred beneath her desk and rolled over onto his back.

Eva didn't believe in writer's block, but she did believe in resistance, and she was facing a mountain of it at the moment. There was only one way through it. Chiseling through, word by word, until she smashed it. This was where her hard-headedness came in handy. Nothing would stand in her way of "The End."

She struggled, typing and deleting, cursing and complaining for another hour, until a knock at her door offered her a welcome distraction. Diesel gave a half-hearted bark and leisurely wandered to the door.

Julia from OJ's by Julia stood on her porch, a smile on her pretty face and a fresh juice the color of carrots in her hand.

"Delivery from one handsome sheriff," Julia chirped. She'd gotten rid of the summer's pink highlights and switched over to a fall-friendly burgundy streak. "He says he's sorry, but he can't meet you for coffee this afternoon."

Disappointed but not surprised, Eva sighed. "Tell me this tastes better than the Flu Fighter," she said, reaching for the jar.

"Hey, wellness sometimes has to come at the price of flavor," Julia snorted. "But this one doesn't taste like dead leaves."

Eva sipped and smiled. "Oh, that's a good one. This should go on your permanent menu." Julia's shop was on the square in town and featured a rotating selection of fresh juices and healthy smoothies. Most of them tasted great. Some of them—the really healthy ones drank only by hard core hippies—were worse than chewing lawn clippings.

Julia grinned. "Sheriff Cardona thought it reminded him of your hair, and here I am."

Of course, he did. The man would package the sunrise for her if he thought she'd like it. "Want to come in and keep me from punching my laptop in the keyboard for a few minutes?" Eva offered. It felt good that she didn't have to hide her occupation anymore. And her book sales had seen a pleasant little bump with a few hundred Mooners and their friends picking up her backlist titles.

"Scene giving you trouble?" Julia asked, strolling into Eva's kitchen and looking around.

"Scene, chapter, book. Want some coffee?"

"One of those days," Julia said in empathy. "I'd love a cup."

"How are the kids?" Eva asked, warming up her coffeemaker.

"The oldest started kindergarten this year," Julia sighed, dropping onto a barstool. "Five seconds ago, he was a tiny baby, and I was terrified of him. Now, he's practicing writing the alphabet and spelling 'poop' with the refrigerator magnets."

"Time flies," Eva agreed, thinking of how much Evan and Aurora and even Lydia had grown. "But the poop stage lasts a pretty long time if Aurora is any indication."

"I'd ask what's new with you, but I think I already know. A career as a novelist and hot pursuit by a man in uniform," Julia said, nodding at a particularly stunning arrangement of ranunculus.

"It's been a crazy month," Eva said, gesturing at the flowers.

"Well, for what it's worth, I've known Donovan for his entire life, and I've never seen him more into a woman before you."

Eva bit her lip. "That makes me nervous."

"What's to be nervous about? A gorgeous, single, heart-of-gold sheriff wants to date the hell out of you."

Another knock sounded at Eva's door.

"A gorgeous, single, heart-of-gold sheriff who didn't show any interest until Pluto and Uranus started dancing the tango," Eva said, setting the coffee in front of Julia and crossing to the door.

"Surprise!" Summer, her smile nearing crazed, shoved a toddler into Eva's arms. Meadow smiled up at her, her blue eyes bright and mischievous.

"Come on in," Eva said, mentally kissing her word count good-bye. Summer, holding Jonathan, strolled inside and greeted Julia. Valentina, the world's biggest dog, at least in Eva's experience, meandered in behind Summer. Her black and white coat and behemoth size made her look more like a cow than any dog.

Eva scratched Valentina behind the ears. Diesel, still sleepy from his nap half-heartedly nipped at the bigger dog's leg.

Meadow reached up and tugged on one of Eva's curls. "Hi!" she chirped.

"Hi, back," Eva said, bouncing the little girl on her hip. "Coffee?" Eva volunteered to Summer.

"I'd love some. I'm running on zero sleep," Summer said, putting Jonathan down on the floor and pulling a toy truck out of her suitcase-sized purse.

"Kids keeping you up?" Julia asked sympathetically.

"More like Ava Franklin's book," Summer announced, yanking a paperback and a Sharpie from her bag. "I started this yesterday afternoon and rescheduled a call with an advertiser just so I could keep reading. Then when these little hellions went to bed, Mama curled up on the couch to read one more chapter. Next thing I know it's four a.m., and I'm checking Amazon for the next one. Sign please." She shoved the book and marker at Eva.

"You liked it?" Eva asked, giddy with the face-to-face feedback from a woman with excellent taste. Summer ran a hip online magazine for women and was easily the most stylish woman in town. She'd hailed from New York, and a handful of years in Blue Moon and two toddlers hadn't dulled her taste one iota.

"Like doesn't even begin to cover it," Summer announced.

"Snack pweez!" Meadow sang to Summer.

"Me, too!" Jonathan announced, driving his truck up Summer's leg.

Summer dug back into her bag and pulled out a baggie of crackers.

"Sit at the table, and don't feed the dogs, please," she instructed.

She piled crackers in front of each kid and then produced two dog treats from her bag and sent Diesel and Valentina off to the living room rug to enjoy their snacks.

"There. That should buy us three whole minutes," she said, accepting the mug from Eva. She slid onto the stool next to Julia.

"God, you're organized," Eva sighed with envy.

"If I weren't, chaos would reign," Summer laughed. "So, what are we talking about?"

"Eva was just expressing her concern that Donovan Cardona's ardent feelings for her are because of the whole planetary disaster," Julia filled her in.

Summer sipped her coffee and considered. "Hmm."

"What if I go for it with him, and then Halloween is over, and he just wants to be *friends*?" Eva said, pacing behind the island. "*Or,* what if I go for it, and his feelings are real, and I screw it up somehow? My entire family finally lives in the same place at the same time. Do I really want to see an ex-boyfriend every day? What if it ends so badly that I have to move out of town? I really like it here."

Being pushed from town to town, new start to new start, Eva had never stuck around in one place long enough to deal with an ex-anything.

Summer hmm-ed again, and Julia drummed her fingers on the countertop.

"Well? Where's my married lady wisdom?" Eva demanded.

"We're trying not to shove it down your throat," Julia said cheerfully. "This town is kind of over the top with its free advice giving."

"Julia and I have a pact not to browbeat people with our sage knowledge," Summer told her.

"Well, I'm asking for it. So, shove and browbeat away."

Summer let out a breath of relief. "Thank God. I didn't think I could keep it bottled up much longer. Whew. Okay, if you're concerned that Donovan's feelings for you aren't real or are being influenced by the solar system—seriously, could this happen in any other town in the world? —just wait to have s-e-x until after Halloween. The planets will have uncrossed, and everyone will be back to normal."

"And, you can use the time of non-s-e-x-having to get to know each other," Julia suggested. "Flirt. Date. Talk. Sext. Figure out if this is a man you'd want to keep in your life."

The three of them shared a look and then burst into laughter. The dogs eyed them warily.

"As if there's a woman on the planet who wouldn't want to keep Donovan Cardona," Summer giggled, dabbing her eyes with a napkin.

Eva slapped her leg. "I mean, he's basically perfection," she gasped, trying to catch her breath.

"I knew it when I said it," Julia snickered.

"So, I should give him a chance to really get to know me, warts and all. And once Halloween is in the rearview mirror, I'll have my answer?" Eva sighed.

"As long as you can keep your pants on, I think it's a good plan," Julia nodded.

"It's only two weeks," Summer said with the cheer of a woman getting laid with obnoxious regularity.

Two weeks. Eva could manage to keep Donovan out of her pants for fourteen days. No. Back to two weeks, she decided. Fourteen days sounded too long.

21

Eva wasn't sure if Mr. Mayor had thrown his weight around or if the Beautification Committee couldn't see a setup coming. Whatever the reason, she and Gia were formally invited to attend Wednesday's top secret, emergency membership meeting.

She wrapped the loose cardigan around her a little tighter to ward off the chill on the walk over to the library with Gia. Eva had bought it, and half a dozen other sweaters, online to avoid another fire/naked dressing room situation. She wasn't putting anything past this whole Uranus Crossing fiasco. A trip to the grocery store might end with her being locked in a freezer with the goat milk ice cream.

Gia was practically skipping with glee on the sidewalk next to her. Her sister was providing a much needed distraction from the weighty issues Eva was trying to ignore. What little mental energy that was left after writing and obsessing over Donovan and his potential feelings was spent on that little nastiness that seemed determined to hunt her down. She was determined to finally put the shadow that had followed her, exploited her, and played upon her emotions for years behind her. This time the answer was "no" and that's what it would stay.

"Do you think they wear cool robes during meetings? Will there be a secret handshake?"

Eva poked Gia in the arm. "I can't believe you're this excited about it."

"Are you kidding me? We're about to join a secret society! Something I've always wanted to do. And we get to play Cupid with people's lives? I can't think of a better way to spend my free time."

"Just keep in mind our primary objective, okay? We're here to get in and make sure the B.C. doesn't go nuts and start pairing up married people with swingers or something."

Gia waved away Eva's concerns. "Please. You're still new here. You don't know these folks like I do. There's *nothing* they wouldn't do for true love."

"You are ridiculous," Eva told her sister.

She didn't hear Gia's response because Eva was too busy being yanked off the sidewalk behind a tree. She yelped, ready to defend herself against her attacker, when she realized her attacker was her very sexy, very warm, sort-of boyfriend.

"What are you doing?" She laughed as he backed her against the tree.

"I missed you," Donovan breathed. He ran his hands up and down her arms. "Where's your coat?"

"Forgot it. Maybe you have something that could warm me up?" She said it teasingly, but in that moment, there was nothing that she wanted more than a kiss from Donovan Cardona in the shadows on a chilly October night.

"It's my duty to serve," he told her. His lips branded her, crushing down on her mouth until she whimpered. She wasn't cold anymore. No, the chill was chased out by embers that sparked an inferno.

He went instantly hard against her, and this time when Eva shivered, it had nothing to do with the cold. She wanted him, *needed* him. Uranus and nerves and uncertainty be damned. If this was crazy, she wanted to embrace it as the rest of the town had.

"Excuse me. Can you two get your tongues out of each other's mouths, please?" Gia stood on the sidewalk tapping her foot and looking at her watch.

Eva shot her sister a dirty look. "Gia, do I interrupt you and Beckett when you're making out?"

"Of course not. We have three children that do that," Gia huffed. "But if you don't stop eating Donovan's face, we're going to be late."

Eva sighed, not ready to let go of him. She could feel his need humming under her hands. "Duty calls," she said softly.

"You could just blow off the meeting," Donovan whispered.

"Sheriff Cardona," Gia gasped, hands on hips. "I'm beginning to think you're under the influence of the planets. The sheriff I know would never shirk his responsibilities or ask anyone else to. We're doing this for you so there's one less group of citizens you have to watch."

"She's really excited about joining the B.C.," Eva explained.

"I can see that. But I'm not sure she knows how much I'm looking forward to being alone with you."

"I have eyes," Gia announced. "And *you* have a town full of people to protect from themselves. We'll report in after the meeting."

Donovan pressed one last kiss to Eva's lips, and it promised to get just as out of control as the last one until Gia dragged Eva out of his arms.

"Bye," Eva waved, tripping over a tree root.

"See you soon," Donovan said with enough heat to keep her warm for the rest of her life.

Gia linked arms with Eva and blew out a wolf whistle as they continued on toward the library. "That was one hell of a kiss."

Eva fanned her flushed cheeks. "Our sheriff should have his mouth registered as a weapon."

Gia released Eva and dug her phone out of her bag. "Excuse me. After seeing that live porn performance, I need to sext my husband."

"Tell me the truth," Eva said, putting a hand on her sister's arm. "Don't you think this whole thing with Donovan and me is moving a little fast?"

"What are you getting at?" Gia asked. "Are you looking for an excuse not to? Because that's more Emma's MO than yours. She almost missed out on Niko because she spent all her time coming up with excuses for why their relationship couldn't possibly work."

Eva shook her head. "That's definitely not what I'm doing. I'm just concerned that Donovan's feelings for me have something to do with this whole planetary thing. Everyone's going at least a little crazy. What if this isn't real?"

Gia's eyes widened. "Well, crap!"

"See?" Eva said triumphantly though she felt anything but victorious inside.

Her sister was shaking her head. "No. That's not what I meant! I know he has feelings for you, and they started long before Uranus stuck her nose in anything."

"A crush then," Eva argued. "But let's face it. He didn't act on it before. So, why now?"

"What I'm saying is, I know you can trust this. Sure, the timing is suspect, and I can understand why you'd have concerns there. But it's real. I know it is."

"How?" Eva grumbled.

"Aren't you the romance novelist? How do your heroines know when it's love?"

Eva ran a hand through her hair as they climbed the front steps of the library. "I guess they learn to trust their feelings and just go with it."

"Like with Olive in *Wild Desire*," Gia pointed out. "Olive didn't know if Alexander really loved her, but she knew how she felt and decided to love him anyway." She held the door for Eva and stepped inside.

"I can't believe you read my book," Eva said with glee, following Gia through the door.

"*Everyone* is reading your books," Gia laughed. "I saw Mrs. Nordemann devouring *Strings of Destiny* at Overly Caffeinated yesterday."

Eva grinned and took a deep breath. She loved the smell all libraries seemed to have. Old books, carpet cleaner, and a world of possibilities.

"Olive took a leap of faith," Gia continued.

Eva sighed. Her sister was using her own fictional characters to educate her.

"That's what love is," Gia insisted. "A giant, scary leap of faith because there's no guarantee that the other person will love you back. I don't believe for one second that you don't have feelings for Donovan. Not after that tongue wrestling back there. There's something strong and bright and exciting between you two."

"I've never felt this way about anyone before," Eva confessed as they headed toward the back of the building past shelf after shelf of books. "I just assumed it was the insanity that everyone else caught."

"Eves, frankly, he's exactly the kind of man I've been hoping you'd end up with," Gia said, squeezing her hand.

"You can be scared, but don't be paralyzed. Trust your feelings."

"Jeez. You were made for the Beautification Committee," Eva laughed.

They climbed the stairs to the second floor. The three-story brick building had once been a high school and while the first floor had been opened up for the book collections, the back half of the second floor maintained the original class-rooms. They were now used for conference rooms and storage.

"Which room is it again?" Gia asked.

Eva dug through her purse. "Let me look at the email."

An arm shot out of a darkened room and hooked through hers.

Eva yelped as she was dragged inside.

"What the hell, Ellery?" Eva demanded. "I'm going to start carrying pepper spray if I keep getting accosted on the mean streets of Blue Moon."

Ellery shushed her and dragged Gia inside before shutting the door. She flipped one of the switches on the wall, and an ancient fluorescent light flickered to life on the ceiling.

"What's with the cloak and dagger, El?" Gia asked, completely unconcerned by the abduction.

"I need to make sure you two are focused." She snapped her fingers in their faces like a hypnotist waking her victims. "The committee has some radical members who don't under-stand how relationships actually work. Their ideas are terri-ble... and dangerous. And since I'm no longer a calming influence in there, I need you two to protect the single people of Blue Moon from bad matchmaking."

"How will we know if it's a bad plan?" Eva asked. She assumed all plans from the Beautification Committee would be mostly awful.

"Think of it like your books. Just like a story, a good matchmaking scheme involves layers of psychology and physical attraction. You need to understand each party and dig into what they really want or need in life. The subconscious desires of the psyche."

"Damn, Ellery. I could use you as a beta reader on my new book," Eva grinned.

"Make sure those yahoos don't ruin my wedding day, and I'll read the heck out of your beta," Ellery promised.

"So is there going to be a test or something to see if we're fit for membership?" Gia asked nervously.

Ellery nodded solemnly. "There's a test."

"What kind of questions are there? Do you have the answers? Are there essays or multiple choice? Have you ever accepted anyone who didn't pass the test? Oh, my God! What if they don't let me in?" Gia's verbalized train of thought ran off the rails.

"I can't give you the answers because that would be unethical," Ellery said, taking Gia by the shoulders.

"But they screwed you over," Eva pointed out.

"Ah, but that's their karma, not mine. *I* still believe in the mission statement of the Beautification Committee and am sworn to uphold my dedication to promoting love."

Eva looked over her shoulder to see what was giving Ellery that far-away look in her eyes. It was either the dusty bust of Mozart or Ellery's own ideals.

"Together, we will conquer personal fears and anxieties and mold the foundations of relationships to form unbreakable bonds!" Ellery stood with hands on hips like a super hero.

"Okay. So, cool. Uh, we'll do that," Eva said.

"And if those pompous, rule-bound weirdos in there give you any crap, I'll take care of them," Ellery said darkly.

"When you say 'take care' of them..." Eva began.

"I'll make them sorry for crossing me and ignoring my contributions. My great-grandmother was a voodoo priestess, you know."

No, Eva didn't know that. *Great. Not only did they have to put the Beautification Committee on a leash, but they had to make sure that Ellery didn't start marching in a vengeance parade of one.*

"So, what are you going to do during the meeting?" Eva asked easing away from the subject.

"I'm going to climb into that air vent and eavesdrop." Ellery pointed at the wall above them. "If there's anything insane being discussed, I'll text you instructions."

22

Conference Room 204 was buzzing with enough activity that Eva barely heard the occasional clank and bump from the air duct. She probably should have suggested that Ellery lose the tiered chains she wore as a necklace before climbing into the metal tube. *Oh, well. Next time.*

The tables, decorated with bud vases of pink roses, were organized in a U-shape that faced a large white board framed with pink and red hearts.

"Welcome, potential members!" Bruce Oakleigh waved from the front of the room. His fluffy beard matched the gray sweater vest that hugged his ample belly. "Come in. Come in."

He ushered them over to the snack table where Eva chose a heart-shaped muffin top while Gia gushed her gratitude to Bruce.

"I'm just so excited that I would even be considered for this committee. It's really an honor," Gia said, clasping her hands together.

"Well, we're honored that you would consider joining our little team," Bruce beamed. "And a real-life romance novelist?"

he said, turning to Eva. "You're practically a professional matchmaker."

"Well, sure. If you count fictional people," Eva joked. Gia elbowed her in the stomach.

"So this is where the magic happens," Gia sighed happily as she took in the hustle and bustle of the room.

Bruce appeared to be a sort of ringleader and fluttered off to discuss something with his wife, Amethyst, a bony thing with a spectacular beehive hairdo and superior posture. Eva recognized Bobby, the owner of Peace of Pizza with her trademark silvery dreads and flowing tunic, arranging champagne flutes on a tray.

Rainbow and Gordon Berkowicz, the bank president and part-time garden center proprietor respectively, had their heads together over a pink binder. Willa, the owner of Blue Moon Boots, wore denim on denim with her long—still unpermed—blonde hair hanging loose to her waist. She was loading her plate up with cookies.

There was an older gentleman that Eva didn't recognize, which was unusual for Blue Moon. He had thinning hair and wore a carnation in the lapel of his suit jacket. "Who's that?" she asked Gia, nodding in the man's direction.

"Wilson Abramovich," Gia told her, flashing her wedding ring. "He's the jeweler on the square."

"He must have made a fortune off the Pierce family recently," Eva teased. Wilson waved at Gia from across the room and raised his glass of punch in a toast.

"If everyone could take their seats, we'll get started," Bruce said from the front of the room.

Everyone scrambled for seats like a daycare game of musical chairs.

Bobby proceeded to pass out glasses of champagne.

"For those of you who are new," Bruce said, as if there were dozens of newbies present rather than just the pair, "we start each meeting with a toast. Amethyst, my dear, if you'd be so kind."

Amethyst rose, glass held aloft. "To true love and our responsibility to mold it."

"Cheers," the residents around the table called out.

"Cheers," Eva and Gia echoed.

"Now, let's get down to business. I presume the committee has had a chance to review both Gia and Eva's membership applications?"

Heads nodded around the table.

"Wonderful. Let the interview and testing process begin," Bruce said, clapping his hands together.

"Gia, if you'll come with me, please?" Willa said, her voice breathy and sweet.

"You'll take the written exam while we interview your sister and then we'll swap," Bruce explained.

"Written exam?" Gia asked, her eyes wide like a deer in headlights.

"Nothing to worry about," Bruce assured her. "It's merely a formality. The interview is much more intense."

Oh goodie, Eva thought to herself. She pasted on a bright smile and waved her sister out of the room. They were being separated. That was never a good sign. This was starting to feel like an interrogation. While the rest of the committee opened their pink binders in front of them, she fired off a quick text from her lap.

Eva: "What the hell did you get me into, El?"

She heard the distinct "ding" of a cell phone in the air duct and a muffled *thunk.*

Bruce looked up and frowned at the committee members. "All cell phones should be silenced per B.C. Rule #319."

Dutifully, everyone around the table pulled out their phones and double checked them.

Eva's phone vibrated in her lap.

Ellery: "Don't panic. Just answer truthfully... unless they ask you if you're working with me to take them down. You can lie about that. Oh, and don't mention swinging, orgies, or open marriages."

"Eva, what we like to do here with potential members is really try to get to know them and make sure they're a good fit for our committee," Bruce explained. "If you're ready, we'll just start our interview. Anyone can ask a question at any time. If it's something you're not comfortable answering you are free to pass on answering it."

"Oh, good. Okay," Eva nodded, relieved.

"Of course, if you do that, we'll have no choice but to deny your application." Bruce chuckled, and the rest of the table joined him.

"Okaaaaay," Eva said through the gritted teeth of her terrified smile.

Amethyst raised her hand. "Eva, if you could, please tell us do you think happy relationships strengthen or weaken a community?"

Whew. Okay, a softball. Maybe they were all like this? "Happy relationships strengthen the communities they exist within," she said with confidence.

Everyone bent over their notebooks and began to scribble.

"When did you first realize the value of true love?" Wilson Abramovich asked, pointing his pen in her direction.

"How much time do I have for answers?" Eva asked, stalling.

"Take all the time you need," Bruce said jovially. "Of course, if you need more than say, thirty seconds to answer, we'll most likely be forced to deny your application."

"I guess it was at my father's wedding to Phoebe," Eva blurted out. "Here is a man I've loved my entire life who is finally happy. It's like Phoebe's love erased all those hard years for him or at least made them worthwhile."

The pens scratched over paper again, and Willa ducked back into the room. She paused to whisper in Bruce's ear and Eva thought she heard "essay."

Poor Gia.

"When did you lose your virginity, and what are your thoughts on premarital sex?" Bobby asked as if she was wondering what time it was.

"Uh, well, that's rather personal," Eva squeaked.

"You're more than welcome to pass," Bruce reminded her.

"I was seventeen, and I think people should do what works best for themselves and their relationships. Personally, I would find it hard to commit my life to a man when I didn't know how... uh, compatible we were in that specific area." She blurted the words out as her cheeks flamed.

"Has anyone ever told you to mind your own business, and what was your response?" Bruce asked.

She was doing this for Donovan and Ellery, Eva reminded herself. A Beautification Committee member had to be nosy by nature, but they prided themselves on their romantic ninja skills.

"No," she said. Everyone stopped writing and looked at her and then each other. "Because my prying is so stealthy people never know I'm doing it."

There was a collective sigh of relief that went up around the table and Bruce nodded his approval.

"Are you currently romantically involved with anyone?"

Rainbow demanded.

Uh-oh. They'd thrown Ellery out for getting engaged to someone they hadn't set her up with. Maybe they wouldn't let her in? But she wasn't going to lie. Not with half the town seeing Donovan's police cruiser parked overnight in Beckett's driveway. The rumors had to already be flying.

"I'm seeing Donovan Cardona," she said. They probably had a dossier on Donovan since he grew up here.

The committee members exchanged a look and then began to flip through their binders.

"Is that a problem?" Eva asked.

"Got it. Potential Match fifty-nine on page thirty-eight," Willa, announced triumphantly.

Everyone furiously turned pages.

"I guess technically we haven't had our first date yet," Eva said, her fingers digging into her knees under the table. "We've been trying, but he keeps getting called away. I mean, we've kissed. And wow, can that guy kiss. I mean, fireworks every time. But that's all. And really all this could just be because of the planetary crossing." She was blabbering like a raving lunatic and couldn't shut herself up.

She heard another *thunk* from the air vent, and her phone vibrated in her lap. Eva glanced down.

Ellery: "Stop talking!"

She did as she was told and bit her lip until everyone was done reading from their binders.

Bruce spoke first, pulling off his reading glasses. "Well, you and our esteemed sheriff are indeed on our list of approved matches."

"Oh good," Eva said, relieved. "Wait. What?"

"Yes, it says here that we were going to tackle you two in

the spring. That would give you a little more time to settle in here," Rainbow said through bites of a pink frosted pastry.

"Spring?"

"And it looks like the main area of concern we've identified is your potential abandonment issues caused by your mother leaving the family," Wilson noted.

"My abandonment issues?" Eva felt like an incredulous parrot.

"Yes, dear," Gordon, spoke up, wiping crumbs off his vintage Jerry Garcia t-shirt. "Your sister Emma gave us quite a headache with hers."

"I don't have abandonment issues," she squeaked.

The Beautification Committee chuckled as if she'd made a joke, and Eva's phone buzzed again.

Ellery: "You totally do."

"My, my. This is an interesting situation. We've never had a potential member claim her partner without our help before," Bruce said, twirling his glasses. "I think we're going to need to put some stipulations on this."

"I agree," Rainbow said, all business.

"Let's put it to a vote," Bobby announced. "Eva and Donovan are free to continue dating if she can make headway with her abandonment issues. If she isn't able to handle it on her own, she and the sheriff must wait until spring when we can give them our full attention."

"All in favor?" Bruce called out.

They raised their hands unanimously.

"Good. The matter is settled. Eva, you can get to work on your issues right away, and once we start to see a resolution, you'll be permitted to resume your relationship with Sheriff Cardona."

23

The exam was one-hundred questions long. All were multiple choice except for two essays at the end. Gia had looked shell-shocked when Bobby led her back into the conference room. But to Eva, the test was still better than facing the inquisition. She felt stripped bare and scrutinized. They'd grilled her on everything from family to birth control to favorite romantic couples of stage, screen, and page.

Eva dove into her test while cursing Ellery under her breath. She was on question forty-two when her phone buzzed on the table.

Donovan: "How's the meeting? Any bloodshed? Any weird rituals involving chickens?"

Eva: "I need you to steal a fire truck, drive it onto the library's sidewalk, and raise the ladder to Conference Room 203. I'll be the redhead hanging out of the window."

Donovan: "What kind of gratitude can I expect for such dangerous heroics?"

Eva: "Spaghetti dinner complete with antipasto, salad, and dessert."

Donovan: "Sold. Be there in five. I'll be the knight on the flashy red steed with sirens."

He made it so easy to like him, Eva thought. Donovan kept things simple. He liked her—a lot—and he told her so. There was no hiding feelings or keeping secrets, at least, not on his end. She hadn't realized just how much she wanted all of this to be real. Eva wanted him to like her and she wanted to loosen up and let herself like him back.

Donovan was a genuinely good man. Smart, kind, protective, solid, dependable. Not to mention gorgeous and sixty steps beyond sexy. And she wanted him with a fierceness that scared her.

What if it's real? What if it's all real? Eva wondered. *And why did that scare her more than the thought that it wasn't?*

She sighed and picked up her pencil again. She needed to get through the next thirty-eight questions and the rest of the meeting and then she could start thinking about the what ifs.

BY THE TIME Eva was led back into the meeting room, Gia looked as though she'd been steam cleaned and hung up to dry.

"They asked me about birth control," Gia hissed when Eva sank into the seat next to her.

Eva snorted and tried to cover it up with a cough.

Amethyst turned out half of the lights, throwing the room into shadows.

"We've come to a decision," Bruce said gravely from the

front of the room. "And unfortunately, we can only allow one of you to join our ranks."

Eva felt oddly disappointed, but Gia looked crestfallen.

"You two must choose," Bobby announced, her demeanor calm and distant like that of a priestess.

"*We* have to decide which one of us gets to stay?" Eva squeaked.

The committee members nodded.

"It should be you," Eva said to Gia. "You've wanted to be a member since you were matched. I think you'd be a wonderful, stable addition to the committee."

Gia squeezed Eva's hand. "I really want to join, but Eva I think you could benefit more from this."

"What?"

"I already found my happily ever after thanks to the B.C. It's your turn, and I think with this committee steering you, you'll end up happier than you ever imagined."

Eva felt her eyes go damp. "But you want it so much," she argued. "I want you to have this."

"I'd rather see you happy," Gia sniffled.

"I'm not taking something that you want away from you," Eva said. "It should be Gia."

"It should be Eva," Gia countered.

Amethyst flipped the light switches chasing away the shadows, and Bruce beamed at them.

"Excellent work, ladies. Allow me to be the first to welcome you both to the Beautification Committee."

The other members applauded. Someone pressed another glass of champagne into Eva's hand.

"I don't understand," Eva began.

"The most valuable quality a Beautification Committee member can have is selflessness," Willa explained grandly.

"We do what we do, not for personal gain or notoriety but to truly make the lives of our neighbors better."

"You two just proved that you would give up something important to you to make the other happy. That's exactly what we're looking for," Bobby told them.

Gia squealed and grabbed Eva in a hug that was closer to a headlock.

"Thank you all," Eva said through the strangulation.

"Let's get down to business," Bruce announced.

24

"I would like to propose to the committee that we revisit a declined pairing," Bruce announced to the room. "Since the *original resistance* to this pairing is no longer a decision maker, I would like to finally pair up Eden Moody and Davis Gates."

A collective gasp worked its way through the entire Beautification Committee except Eva. She had no idea what was gasp-able but had a feeling that Ellery was the "original resistance" to which Bruce was referring.

"Their feud has gone on for far too long, and it's clear to us all that they would make an ideal match," Bruce continued.

Eva blinked, remembering Eden flinch at the mention of Blue Moon Winery. Her phone buzzed quietly in her lap.

Ellery: No! No! No! Nope! Abort! Abort!

Eva nudged Gia under the table and turned her phone toward her sister. Gia read and frowned.

Gia cleared her throat. "Question. What was their feud about?"

Bruce waved both hands. “Oh, it was a tiny, practically insignificant misunderstanding.”

“How insignificant?” Eva pressed.

The other members around the table shared guilty glances.

“Technically it was a feud between their fathers,” Bobby said vaguely. “It carried through to the next generation.”

“Now, I know that *some* people felt that they needed more time to cool off,” Bruce began. There was a loud clang from the air duct. Eva refused to look in the direction of the vent. Her phone buzzed.

Ellery: “Sorry. Leg cramp.”

“However, I see this as an opportunity to really spread our wings,” Bruce pressed on. “Not only would we be matching up excellent candidates for soulmate-hood, but we’d also be ridding our town of the negativity their feud has caused.”

Eva: “Keep it together up there!”

A hand raised and Bruce pointed at his wife. “Yes, Amethyst, my pearl?”

Ellery: “If I don’t get out of here soon I’m going to enter the beginning stages of rigor mortis. Make them wrap it up!

Amethyst blushed prettily at her husband’s nickname for her. “What would we do with our Team Eden Team Davis signs?” She asked the question as if she was reading the question from a cue card.

Oh sweet Jesus, this town, Eva thought.

Bruce clapped his hands. “I’m so glad you asked. We could

have a celebratory bonfire when the engagement is announced and use the signs as kindling."

Eva's phone vibrated.

Ellery: "This is bad. Real bad."

Donovan: "Where should we go on our honeymoon?"

"All in favor of committing to Eden and Davis for our next match?" Bruce called for the vote.

Eva held Gia's hand down just in case her sister got swept up in the crowd mentality. Everyone else except Bobby raised their hands in favor.

"I don't feel comfortable voting when I don't have any background information on the couple," Eva said hastily when Bruce frowned in her direction.

"We still have a majority," he said, glaring at Bobby who remained unfazed under his scrutiny. "I suggest, before our next meeting, you review the couple biography in your binders and be prepared to offer suggestions on the best approach."

"I'm sure they'll make a lovely couple," Gia placated when Bruce handed over their pretty pink binders.

Eva wasn't so certain. If Ellery had been the brains behind the B.C.'s operations, they were practically flying blind without her.

"Now, I'll need you both to sign the nondisclosure agreements at the front of the binder and return them to me before the next meeting," Bruce announced, tapping a finger on the table.

Eva made a mental note to have Beckett review the NDAs before she signed anything. It wouldn't do to get sued by the

B.C. If she upset them, she could just imagine the chaos they could wreak on her life.

She breathed a sigh of relief when the meeting let out and towed Gia into the hallway. They ducked into the darkened conference room on the other side of the hall, and Gia held the desk while Eva climbed up to help unwedge Ellery.

She came out sneezing and swearing, platform boots first followed by black and white striped tights and then her corduroy romper.

They helped her down, and Gia offered Ellery a drink from her water bottle while Eva picked cobwebs and dust bunnies out of her dark hair.

They were so busy whispering none of them noticed when the door opened.

"Aha!" Bobby shut the door behind her and crossed her arms. "Who wants to go first?"

"Hello, Bobby," Ellery said coolly.

Eva tugged Gia out of the line of fire. They backed up against the conference table and tried to be as inconspicuous as possible.

"Hello, Ellery."

The women stared each other down for nearly a full minute.

"Girl, what the hell?" Bobby broke first. "You knew the rules. Why didn't you just tell us about Mason and let us do our thing?"

"I planned to!" Ellery said defensively. "I just got swept up in it. I mean we'd barely started dating, and then he was proposing and it was just magical. And I was so excited."

"You should have told us."

"I know. And you shouldn't have kicked me out."

"I know," Bobby agreed.

"What's happening?" Eva whispered to Gia.

"Shh," her sister shushed her. "They're communicating to solve their problem."

"That's weird," Eva hissed back.

"Shut up." Gia nudged her.

"I'm sorry," Ellery said offering her hand to Bobby.

"I'm sorry, too," Bobby said, shaking Ellery's hand.

"See? That's how grown-ups solve their problems," Gia said smugly.

"What are you trying to say, smarty pants?"

"You're asking everyone their advice on what you should do about Donovan. Why don't you just go talk to him about it?"

"Shut up," Eva sighed.

"Now, what are we going to do about this disaster with Eden and Davis?" Bobby asked.

25

Donovan stared through the open door of his office at the teenage tuba player sitting glumly in the cubicle cell. The kid had been caught red-handed with the empty vat of dish soap used in Monday's fountain sabotage under his bed. To teach him a lesson, his parents reported him to Donovan and were refusing to pay the kid's fifty-dollar bail.

It made Donovan's life just a shade worse than it already was.

Instead of sleeping in his own bed tonight or finding a way to wrangle another overnight invitation from Eva, he'd be hitting the lumpy couch and listening to this kid recap the entire storyline of *The Lord of the Rings*.

Sometimes his job just plain sucked.

He picked up Eva's book and found his place.

"Can I at least watch something on TV?" Tanbark whined.

The kid never had a chance at life. Not with a name like Tanbark.

"Man, you're lucky you're not in an actual cell. Do your homework if you're bored," Donovan told him.

Tanbark sighed heavily and pulled a book out of his backpack. "Are you any good at trig? My mom usually helps me with my homework."

"Tanbark, you're in jail. You can't ask the jailer for help with your homework."

"It's my first time. I'm not clear on all the prison etiquette."

Donovan silently cursed Tanbark's parents.

"Just sit there and be quiet."

Donovan picked up the book again. He was going to finish the damn sex scene this time if he had to lock his door and handcuff half the town. He kicked his feet up on his desk and paged through to find his spot.

Olive stared into Alexander's eyes as he tugged her panties down her milky white thighs. Those sleek thighs quivered as Alexander trailed one hot fingertip over her skin, climbing higher and higher until—

Jeez, it was hot in here. Had Minnie cranked the thermostat again? Donovan tugged at his collar and wished he was at home in sweats and a t-shirt instead of the uniform he'd been in for thirteen hours straight.

Three orgasms on the page later, Donovan was sweating. He stopped and re-read, counting as he went. Yep. Olive had just screamed and whimpered her way through three mind-blowing orgasms.

Shit. Exactly how high were Eva's expectations? Donovan wondered. He was no slouch in bed. Had never had a complaint, just the opposite if he were a bragger, which he wasn't. But those were regular women. Women who didn't *write sex scenes* for a living. What if he was too boring for Eva? How much excitement did she need to be impressed, and how far outside his comfort zone would he need to go?

Alexander used a vibrator on Olive. Would Eva want toys?

Despite regular handcuff jokes, he'd never felt the need or interest to delve into the world of toys and S&M and B&D and whatever the hell else had been in those books that Mrs. Nordemann had hosted book clubs and movie nights about.

He pulled up an incognito browser window and did a search for sex toys.

"What the hell is that for?" he wondered aloud, turning his head to the side.

"Is this what the townspeople pay you for?"

The figure in his open door scared the shit out of him. "Damn it, Tanbark. I told you—"

But it wasn't a pudgy teenager. It was Eva. Donovan wasn't sure which was worse.

He dropped the book and stabbed the button on his monitor to make it all go away. He stabbed a little too hard and the monitor flipped over backwards.

"I can explain!" He got to his feet, ready to give chase if Eva gave any indication that she was rabbiting.

But she was staring at him. And smiling.

It was moments like this, unexpected and spontaneous, when he realized just how much he wanted her.

"Hi," she said shyly.

"Hey. What are you doing here?" Guilty as sin, he swiped a hand over the back of his head.

She looked over her shoulder and back again. "I wanted to talk."

"I can explain about—" Donovan gestured at his now horizontal monitor.

"Don't mind me." Tanbark's whiny voice piped up behind Eva. "I'm in prison. Are you any good at trigonometry?"

"Jesus Christ, kid," Donovan groaned.

"First time in the big house?" Eva asked Tanbark with a grin.

The kid nodded. "Yeah. I thought it would be funny to put some soap in the park fountain. Only I got soap on my hands, and the whole bottle fell in."

"And that's a jail-able offense?" Eva asked, eyeing Donovan with amusement.

"Destruction of public property," Donovan reminded her.

"Ah. I didn't realize that carried jail time in Blue Moon."

"Only when your parents try to teach you a lesson by turning you in and not paying your bail," Donovan told her.

Her lips quirked. "What is bail for destruction of public property these days?"

"Fifty bucks."

"I've got forty on me. Would that buy my friend here some freedom tonight?" Eva asked, digging into her purse.

"Sold," Donovan breathed. "Let me get the form."

Three minutes later, Donovan was shoving Tanbark out the door on his way home with instructions to never deface anyone's property again. Eva waited in his office. When he returned, he found her sitting in his visitor's chair holding her book.

"My, Sheriff. What interesting reading habits you have."

"What kind of eventual fiancé would I be if I didn't support your talents?"

She laughed and shook her head. "You keep bowling me over, Donovan. How can you be so sure about your feelings for me? Aren't you the least bit concerned that this is your version of dumping a gallon of dish soap in a public fountain?"

"Eva." Her name caught in his throat with the rawness of what he felt for her. "The feelings are real, and the sooner you accept that, the faster we can enjoy each other." He sat on the edge of his desk, his legs stretching out on either side of her chair capturing her between them.

She chewed on her bottom lip, worrying a problem.

"Might as well spill it. What's going on in that very imaginative brain of yours?"

"I'm not sure if I'm allowed to tell you this, but since I haven't signed the non-disclosure agreement, oh well. The Beautification Committee says we have to wait until I either get over my abandonment issues leftover from my mother on my own or until spring, when we're up on the matchmaking docket, and then they will commit all committee resources to fixing me so I'm relationship-appropriate."

"Is that so?" Donovan asked. He took her by the hands and drew her up out of her chair to stand between his legs.

"And Summer and Julia suggested that I not have sex with you until after Halloween so I can be sure that your feelings are real and not heavily influenced by some celestial bodies."

"You're lucky I'm a mature man intent on listening to your concerns and not making a good celestial body joke right now," Donovan said, skimming his hands up her arms.

"From where I stand, I'm very lucky," Eva breathed.

Donovan threaded his fingers through her hair, brushing it back from her face. "The first time I saw you, you wore this short gold dress and these glittery shoes that no woman should be able to walk in. Your hair was down, like this," he said, smoothing her curls. "Your eyes were brighter than all the stars in the night sky. You were so happy for your sister. And you were laughing at something Beckett was saying."

Her lips parted like she wanted to say something, but no words came.

"I was standing there, in the middle of the happiest day of someone else's life. And it was like something punched me in the chest hard enough to knock the wind out of me," he admitted. "I've never felt anything like that before in my life. It was New Year's Eve, one of my best friend's weddings, and I felt like *my* future had just started."

"Wow." Eva's breath left her in a rush. "Do you have any idea how romantic you are? Also, do you mind if I take notes?"

"I'll write it down for you," he promised, tracing a thumb over her lower lip. "I tried to find you at midnight that night."

Eva breathed in. "I was with Evan and Aurora under the cake table."

"Lucky them," Donovan said. "You went home, back to your life in South Carolina, and I kept waiting for the day that I wouldn't think about you. For the time when I wouldn't try to pump Gia and then Emma for information about you. I kept waiting to get over you."

"Did it work?" Eva whispered.

He shook his head. "Not for a second. I've been thinking about you ever since I saw you that first time, Eva. Maybe the planets did have something to do with it. Something like fate. But the only thing that's going to keep us apart is one little word from you. I'm sure, and I'm all the way in. I don't care if you do or don't have abandonment issues or some crazy quirks or you want to wait for a year. I want to know every piece of you, and I'll be as patient as you need me to be."

"Why do you have to be so perfect?" Eva sighed. "I'm not ready for perfect yet. I have work to do on myself."

"I'm ready for you now. As is. No returns," he promised.

She looked at him hard, turning it all over in her mind. Fire lighting those green eyes that grabbed at him and held him captive.

"Oh, hell," she sighed out the words and dove for him. She pressed her lips to his in something close to violence.

Donovan welcomed the kiss as if he'd been waiting for it his entire life. Planets and fate and chaos be damned. This was the woman he was going to marry. The woman he was going to taste like this every day.

With her mouth eager against his and her fingers stumbling over the buttons on his shirt, Donovan nearly lost his mind. He could feel his heartbeat echoing in his aching cock.

"Baby, I'm trying to be a good guy here." When she didn't stop, he grabbed her by the shoulders. "Eva."

She smiled up at him dreamily, just as she had in every one of the thousand fantasies he'd had about her. "You *are* a good guy, Donovan," she said, her fingers toying with another button.

"You want to take things slow. I'm trying really, *really* hard to respect that. We haven't even been out on a real date yet."

She grinned. "Maybe this is the way it's supposed to be."

"Here? In a police station." It wasn't that he hadn't thought of taking her here on every flat surface his office provided. It was that he wanted this first time to be special, memorable, perfect.

"It sounds like something that would happen in one of my books."

"Speaking of your books, exactly how high are your expectations here?" He couldn't stop his hands from roaming her curves.

Her laugh sounded strangled. "I don't think you know how to disappoint," she told him.

"Are you one-hundred percent sure?"

She nodded, wide-eyed and honest. He cupped her chin in one hand. "It's okay if you're not ready. You're worth the wait, Evangelina."

She closed her eyes on her name. "God, Donovan. It's like you keep taking potshots at my heart."

"Join the club, beautiful." He kissed her again, softly, sweetly. She purred against him, and pleasure pulsed between them.

She opened the last button on his shirt and freed it from

his waistband. When Eva's small hands spread over his chest, resting over where his heart hammered, Donovan knew love and lust and everything in between.

"I thought there'd be candles, wine. Maybe a fire," he said, trailing kisses down her neck.

"I thought there'd be handcuffs."

He lifted her up, and she gamely locked her legs around his waist.

His desk was too low, but the counter behind it... With no finesse, he shoved two weeks' worth of files to the floor and settled her on the surface. He'd never be annoyed by paperwork that sat here again.

With one swift move, he shucked her sweater over her head and breathed a worshipful sigh over the curves of her breasts that spilled over her black bra. "I'm the luckiest man in the world," he breathed.

"You're about to get luckier," Eva whispered. She levered herself up, and he made swift work of her boots and leggings.

"Oh, God. You're not wearing underwear." Blackness creeped in on the edges of his vision.

Her laugh was a sigh. "Is that a problem?"

"I wasn't mentally prepared for—" He pressed her thighs apart and felt his world go black for just a second as every last ounce of blood left his head.

"Are you okay?" she asked. Her fingers danced over the skin of his chest, the flat of his abs, before finding his belt. "Why do you have so many clothes on?"

"I... I have no words..."

Reverently, Donovan ran his hands up her silky inner thighs. To torture them both, he let his fingers brush the damp strip of curls between her legs.

Her breath caught, and Eva's wrestling match with his belt

paused. "Oh, God. I'm not sure if I'm going to survive this," she confessed.

"At least we'll die together."

Eva's cheeks were flushed, her eyes bright. Those full lips were swollen from their kisses. Donovan had never seen anything sexier in his entire life.

"You've just ruined me for every other woman on the face of the planet."

She grinned. "We're just getting started. I plan to ruin you for all generations past, present, and future."

He took a breath, trying to find the air in the room that was suddenly in short supply. "I really want to take my time. Enjoy this..."

"But?" she asked.

"But I can't guarantee I'll stay in control once I'm inside you," he murmured.

She shook her head slowly. "I *really* wish you'd let me take notes."

"You can take them during the encore," he promised. He cupped her breasts through the black netting. "What kind of bra is this?"

"A lounge bra. It's like a sexy version of a sports bra," Eva said, closing her eyes as his hands worked their magic.

"Very sexy," he agreed. Everything about her was. Those auburn curls. Her thickly lashed eyes. God, those lips. And her skin, ivory dusted with freckles.

"Your pants," Eva said. "They need to come off."

"They're my last line of defense," he told her.

"Yeah? Well they're standing between me and my final frontier." Eva cupped his rigid shaft through his uniform pants.

"God, Eva." In a purely defensive move, he kissed her hard.

Pouring himself into the kiss, branding her like she'd branded his heart. When she melted into him, he slowly slipped a finger between her slick folds. Swallowing her gasp, he plunged inside her.

All teasing, all sweetness evaporated.

She was fire in his hand. Clinging to his open shirt, Eva chanted his name as she began to ride his fingers.

He was lost watching her, swamped with the need to give her what she begged for. Her pleasure was his desire.

"Donovan!" She gasped his name in surprise, in wonder, in pleasure, as she came for him and Donovan knew he'd remember this moment for the rest of his life.

She was still quaking around his fingers when she reached for his fly. "Now," she demanded.

Now was good. Donovan reached for his wallet in his back pocket. Freeing the condom, he flung the wallet to the floor.

While Eva shoved his pants and underwear down, he shredded the foil packet.

"Oh, boy," she whispered. Her eyes were wide when she stared down at him.

That look—hungry and anxious—nearly pushed him over the edge. He'd never been this hard before in his life. With fingers coated in Eva's arousal, Donovan rolled on the condom and guided himself to her opening. He'd just notched himself in place and was bracing for what could only be the most soul-shattering moment of his life to-date when Eva slapped a hand to his chest.

"Wait! There's something you need to know!"

Donovan's hands dug into her hips. "Baby. I'm going to literally die in the next four seconds if I'm not inside you."

"You're my next hero." Her words came out in a breathy whisper.

"I don't know what that means," he said, using every fiber of self-control not to drive himself into her. It was nearly impossible to hear her over the pounding of blood in his head. His dick throbbed with its demands.

"I wrote you. You're in my book."

"I can live with that. We good?"

"So good—" Eva's words were choked off by a gasp as he sheathed himself in her.

It was better than everything he'd ever imagined, better than every fantasy. The reality of her walls gripping him like a velvety vise destroyed him. He let himself go, pulling out only to lose himself in each swift thrust back inside her, back where he belonged.

She was speaking nonsense, chanting unintelligible words. He gripped her hips as he pistoned in and out of her. The pace was wild. His blood was singing in his veins. He'd been made for this. Made to pleasure her. Made to make her beg and come and love. He'd never take that responsibility lightly.

"Donovan." It was a breath, a sigh hot against his skin. He needed more, to give and to take.

He felt her quicken around him, a flutter that teased his cock as he slammed into her.

"I feel you, baby. Let go." *Please, for the love of God. He needed her to let go so he could follow her into the abyss.*

Eva opened her eyes, and her heavy-lidded gaze held him enthralled. He barely noticed her fingers digging into his shoulders. They were joined together in the most primitive of ways, carrying each other to perfection.

"Now." She whispered it, but his body obeyed as if she'd shouted it. They came together, one release milking the other. As he emptied himself into her, Donovan vowed that this would be his last first time.

"I love you, Evangelina." The words escaped him on waves of ecstasy.

"I'm starting to believe you," she whispered back, pressing her lips to his throat.

26

"I'm going to build a shrine right here. I'm going to need a naked picture of you, just like this," Donovan announced.

Eva laughed. She was sprawled on top of him on the floor behind his desk. Round two had seen the removal of her bra and his pants and shoes. She'd been too busy orgasming to take notes, but she was sure she would remember the highlights forever seeing as how they were branded into her brain.

"Tonight has been one surprise after another."

She traced a heart shape over the warm skin of his shoulder.

"Tell me about your night," Donovan said, tugging her fingers to his mouth to kiss them.

"Well, you were there for the best part of it."

"Both best parts," he reminded her in pure male conceit. "But I'm hoping to distract you from getting up and putting your clothes on. So, tell me about your meeting?"

"My legs aren't going to work for at least another ten minutes," she teased and then started at the top, filling him in on the meeting. "The B.C. is basically one never-ending head game," Eva said.

"Are you surprised? You've seen them in action."

"Nothing about this town should surprise me. Did I mention that Bobby caught us dragging Ellery out of the air duct?"

Donovan gave her a playful pinch. "No, you didn't mention that."

"I thought the jig was up," Eva said. "But it looks like Bobby is Team Ellery, so at least we've got three of us to stand up to any harebrained schemes the rest of them come up with."

"I appreciate you keeping an eye on them for me. It's one less group I need to worry about."

"I'm using it as writer's research. That committee is going to end up in a book someday," she predicted.

"I like your books," Donovan admitted.

"Books as in plural? As in you've read more than one?"

He grinned and Eva felt like the world got more beautiful.

"I had to order this one online since Fitz sold out of them."

"Really?" Eva grinned. "I have to admit. I'm surprised at how respectful Blue Moon is being. No one's approached me on the street or accosted me in my house, except for Joey who climbed up a drainpipe to demand autographs."

"Blue Moon's never dealt with a real celebrity before."

"So, what do you think of the books?" Eva prodded him in the chest.

"I think you're very good at what you do, and like the fans in your reader's group on Facebook, I think Shelly and Brandt deserve their own book."

"You take being supportive to a whole new level," Eva told him.

They fell into satisfied silence, and she listened to the

steady beat of his heart under her ear. She felt the sting of well-earned carpet burns on her knees and back, saw the dim glow of the town's street lights through the blinds covering the window.

"What are you thinking?" Donovan asked, stroking his hand through her hair.

"I'm trying not to ask you about your orgasm-induced proclamations or what all this means. I'm also choreographing this as a scene for my book, and trying to decide what I'm going to eat as a snack tonight."

"Your brain is a wonder."

"Did you mean it?" she asked, raising up to look at him.

"Every word, every time," he vowed. "And before you ask me how I can be so sure, ask yourself if you've ever felt this way with any man before. You were meant for me. So, you might as well start getting used to it."

"I think it's a lot to take in," Eva sighed.

"That's what she said."

"Donovan!"

"Sorry. I left my maturity in my pants."

"You're cute when you're not being Mr. Authority Figure."

"I'm cute then, too. Cute and bossy," he argued.

"I'm crazy about you, Sheriff Sexy."

"I know you are, Evangelina. And soon you're going to figure out that you're desperately in love with me."

"You're awfully confident for someone who imprisoned a tuba player."

"Right is right. There are rules that everyone needs to follow. Honesty, decency, not destroying public property. And then there are laws of nature. That's you and me. We're right, and you'll see."

"So, what do we do now?" Eva asked.

"Now? I take you home to my place, and we spend the

night together. And if my phone rings before morning, I'm locking the bastard up without bail."

If sex with Donovan was Eva's just dessert, his home was the icing on top. He lived a mile south of Blue Moon. Tucked into the woods by way of a long gravel drive, the house appeared in Donovan's headlights through a clearing. Cedar shingles covered the exterior of the two-story house. It had the rustic charm of a cabin but with a little more space and a lot more windows. The wide front porch glowed under the light of a single lantern next to the front door. The trees surrounding the house were a riot of autumnal colors of rusts and golds.

He ushered her in through the front door and flicked light switches on his way through to the kitchen. It was a bachelor's cabin, Eva thought, with its wood tones and stone fireplace. Few knickknacks to clutter up the space. There was a loft that overlooked the living room. A pristine dining room table occupied the space in front of a wall of windows overlooking the back of the property.

The kitchen. Oh, the kitchen. Eva trailed a finger over the white quartz that topped gray cabinets. She could cook here with a glass of wine and a view of the woods.

Donovan grabbed two bottles of water out of his refrigerator and handed one over. "I don't know about you, but I'm weak with dehydration and hunger."

"Do you cook?" Eva asked as her stomach growled.

"I cook all the time. Leftovers go in the microwave. I push important buttons and the food comes out hot."

"So, no then."

"You're welcome to these appliances that I don't know how to use anytime you want," Donovan offered grandly.

"Let's start with what leftovers you have," Eva suggested. He let her snoop through his cabinets and fridge, and she considered it a jackpot when she stumbled on containers of day-old Chinese food.

Donovan produced forks and paper towels, but when she made a move toward the table he guided her down a hallway and into the master. "Sorry in advance, but I should warn you we're going to be living out every fantasy I've ever had about you for the next few years."

Eva laughed as he took the containers from her and pulled her sweater over her head. "First up, naked leftover picnic," he insisted.

Donovan lit a fire in the gas fireplace, and they ate General Tso's and sweet and sour pork on the flannel quilt of his sleigh bed and watched the waxing moon through the windows. The room was comfortable and, like him, oh so masculine.

"This is quite the place you have here," Eva said, pointing with the fork.

"I'm glad you like it," Donovan said, stealing a forkful from her container. "It's not finished, yet, but it's home. Upstairs is two more bedrooms that need to be relieved of their popcorn ceilings and wood paneling. And I haven't done anything with the loft yet."

"I like your place," Eva said, admiring the thick beams in the cathedral ceiling. It wasn't a huge room, but it didn't need to be. The space was efficiently used, cozy even.

"I do, too. I have a shower I can stand up in," he bragged.

She laughed. "I can't believe I'm here having a naked midnight picnic with Donovan Cardona," Eva said. She was certain that no matter how long she spent staring at his naked body, eternity wouldn't be long enough to appreciate every millimeter of his fine male form.

He put a warm hand over her foot. "Neither can I. I'm glad you finally came to your senses."

"You're ridiculous. You spring this whole 'we're destined to be together' thing on me and expect me to jump right into bed with you—"

"Permanently," he cut in.

Incredulous, Eva shook her head. "I wish I could have your confidence. Even just for a day."

"Maybe your lack of confidence is a result of those abandonment issues the Beautification Committee accused you of having."

She pointed at him with her fork. "Not nice, Cardona."

He shrugged his massive shoulders. "You went through something traumatic with one of your parents while the other one had to pick up the pieces. It's bound to make you stop and think."

"It is, isn't it?" she nodded.

"It must be interesting in your head, crafting these romantic stories of true love and then struggling with the reality of relationships in your life."

"Are you using sneaky cop interrogation skills on me?" Eva asked, nudging him with her foot.

He grinned, and again she was struck by the boyish joy she saw in his gorgeous face.

"I'm just empathizing with you. My parents? After my dad wore down my mother, they were a team. Nothing could come between them, and that's what I grew up wanting."

"Not everyone's that lucky," Eva pointed out. "My parents were happy once. But people can change and in unexpected ways."

"How do you think your mother changed?" he asked, hefting a forkful of chicken.

Eva shrugged one shoulder and paid special attention to the carton of sweet and sour pork in her lap.

"We're having a romantic naked picnic, Eva. There can't be anything between us." His eyes, the color of worn denim, seemed to delve beneath the surface and into her.

"Drugs," she said. Letting loose a secret she'd kept for years made her feel panicky and maybe just a little relieved.

"Your mom was on drugs?"

"She'd had bouts of depression for as long as I can remember," Eva sighed, committing to the telling. "I didn't know until years later that it may have been postpartum depression. But after I came along, she started trying to find ways to feel something, anything. I was so young I didn't understand that when we visited her 'friend's' house she was taking me to see her dealer. It was prescription meds mostly. And once they got a hold on her, it was like I didn't have a mother anymore. Dad was at the restaurant trying to scratch out a living, and my sisters were in school. So, it was just her and me."

He took the Chinese food from her and stacked the containers on the nightstand before pulling her into his arms.

She rested the side of her face against his chest. "She'd wait until my sisters got on the bus, and then she'd go dig out her pills from whatever hiding place she'd stashed them in. She'd just lay there on the couch. Sometimes I couldn't tell if she was still alive. She called it naptime. It was such a relief to me when I was old enough to go to school, too."

It didn't hurt as much to tell it as she thought it would. But Donovan hadn't been there, hadn't missed the signs, hadn't assumed that Eva was safe at home with her mother. Eva knew her father and sisters wouldn't forgive themselves for not knowing. They also might not forgive her for choosing to carry the burden alone.

Donovan swore quietly against her hair. "Your sisters don't know. Do they?" he asked, reading her mind.

Eva shrugged again. "I never said anything to them about it. They were so upset when she left. To them, it seemed out of the blue. But for me? I was relieved."

"And you felt guilty for feeling relieved," Donovan guessed.

She nodded letting his hands soothe her. "I feel guilty for everything. It was my fault that she left. At least, that's what she told me."

Donovan's hands stilled on her skin and then began to move again. "When did she tell you that?" he asked. And Eva realized her mistake.

"It was just something she always said. That her life was so different after I came along. Worse," she said, correcting herself.

He wanted to ask more. She could feel him holding back the questions. She was done talking. Done facing the shadows. She wanted the light again, and Donovan could take her there.

Eva turned in his arms and brought her mouth to the rough texture of his jaw. "Show me again what you feel," she breathed against his hot skin. And then he was rolling over her, shielding her from the world with his body.

27

Eva dreamed of being chased through town square by the Beautification Committee and their pink binders. She tried to tell them that she was working on her issues, that once she took care of this last problem she could finally start to live a normal life. But no one could hear her over Bruce Oakleigh's shouts about true love and non-disclosure agreements.

When Donovan's phone rang at six, he told the caller he was going to put them under house arrest if this wasn't a real emergency. When they called back at 6:07, he reluctantly dragged himself out from under the covers. Eva yawned and burrowed further under the pillows.

She woke again minutes later when Donovan prodded her with a set of car keys. "You don't have to get up, baby. I'm just showing you the keys to my SUV are right here on the nightstand. If I can't stop the cold brew shitstorm at Overly Caffeinated and get back in bed with you, you can take my truck home whenever you want. Okay?"

"Mmm-kay."

"Eva, I need to know that you're at least partially awake and hearing me."

"Mmm-kay, Sheriff Sexy. I'm probably going to go through all your stuff while you're gone."

"That's fine. My secrets are your secrets." He slapped her on the butt, dropped a kiss on the back of her neck, and was gone.

The front door opened and then closed, and Eva pretended the words didn't bother her. He didn't mean it as a dig—he couldn't know—but it still got under her skin. Wide awake and now guilty, Eva decided to start her day by discovering where Donovan kept his coffee stash.

She crawled out of bed and dragged on one of the clean t-shirts she found neatly hanging in the walk-in closet off the bathroom. On her way back through the bedroom, the glitter of something on top of his dresser caught her eye. Her snooping instincts insisted she get a closer look.

She'd seen him put his wallet and gun on top of the dresser. An ingrained habit, it seemed. It was a spot he visited every day. A spot where his most important things went. On the back of the dresser was a framed photo of a couple—his parents, she assumed—mugging for the camera. Both had blond hair and the kind of tans that spoke of outdoor living. She wore a sheriff's uniform while he was dressed in a Blue Moon Fire Department t-shirt.

And in front of that frame was a comb. *Her* comb. She'd worn it in her hair at Gia's wedding. She'd loved the rose quartz stones and gold filigree. Aurora had wanted to play with it at the reception, so she'd taken it out. She hadn't realized until this second that she'd never gotten it back.

Donovan had found it and kept it. Not only that, but he'd put it in a place that he'd see it every day.

Eva sat cross-legged on the floor, holding the comb in her hands. Inexplicably, tears pricked her eyes.

"He means every damn word," she whispered to herself. Donovan Cardona loved her. The current her. The messy, distracted, hot mess of a woman that she was today.

She was sitting in the bedroom of a man who loved her without reason, without history. Where she'd spent her entire life trying to prove herself worthy of love, he'd simply loved. More than that, he trusted his heart without questioning whether or not it was right.

And just like that, the broken pieces of a little girl's heart knit together a little tighter.

She looked around the room where she'd spent a few hours of her life that she'd remember forever. The moody gray walls, the plush carpeting, the heavy, dark furniture. She wanted this. She wanted this with him. And she owed it to Donovan to try to be the person he saw her as. Honest, open, and head over heels for him.

She was loved.

Eva caught a glimpse of herself in the dresser mirror and saw happiness, bone-deep.

As CHEERFUL AS she'd ever been at seven a.m., Eva pulled up outside Overly Caffeinated and was disappointed to find that whatever ruckus had taken place at the café was now settled. Donovan was nowhere to be seen, and the usual morning rush was in full swing.

Well, since she was here it would be a shame to leave without indulging, she mused.

Eva slid out from behind the wheel and followed her nose in the direction of caffeine.

The crowd inside was a dapper blur of tie-dye, hand-knit cardigans, and varying desperation for coffee. Eva kept herself entertained in line by revisiting the highlights of last night with her writer's mind. Had she written it herself, it couldn't have been better. They'd connected on a level that, until now, only her characters had been able to find.

And that was only a little bit terrifying. Okay. A lot bit. Eva vacillated between enjoying the ultimate female satisfaction and the terror that she was about to step off solid ground into an abyss.

"What can I get you, Naked in Town?" The girl behind the counter, an ethereal third generation Woodstock-wannabe, asked with all the interest of a robot.

Her counterpart, a dark-haired guy with an eyebrow ring and about a quarter mile of ink visible on his skinny arm, snorted. "Naked in Town is old news. She's the sheriff's girlfriend," he said, elbowing the blonde out of the way.

"How did you—"

But he was shaking his head. "It's Blue Moon. We know everything. Plus, there was a special edition of *The Weekly Monthly Moon* this morning. You want your usual?"

Eva had no idea what her usual was since she had the tendency to try new things every other time she came in here. "Sure," she shrugged.

"You get the law enforcement girlfriend's discount," he said, taking five percent off her total.

"Uh, thanks?"

"If you guys get married, it goes up to ten percent," he promised. "Next."

Eva handed over the cash and slipped out of line to admire the glass case of sinful pastries and pretend the guy hadn't just mentioned marriage.

"Well, don't you look chipper today?" Ellery, clutching her

black matte thermal mug, eyed Eva from her seat by the pastries.

"Should I be seen talking to you?" Eva whispered. "Or will the B.C. run us both out of town?"

Ellery's black lips curved. "I work for your brother-in-law in your front yard. I think we can come up with an excuse for chatting."

"Here you go, sweetie." Ellery's fiancé swooped in with a flaky croissant drizzled with chocolate.

"Awh, thanks, hubby-to-be," Ellery grinned up at him.

"Hey, Mason," Eva greeted him. She still found the relationship fascinating. Goth princess Ellery was marrying number-cruncher Mason with his gray suits and his nerdy glasses. It was adorable, even if the match was completely incomprehensible.

"Oh, good morning, Eva," Mason smiled. "Will you and your sisters be attending the wedding?"

After dating Emma in L.A., Mason had been an instrument wielded by the diabolical Beautification Committee to cement her sister's decision to date Nikolai. In the midst of the subterfuge, Mason had fallen hard for Ellery.

"We wouldn't miss it, and I believe I'll be bringing a plus one if that's okay?"

Ellery's black lips stretched wider. "The sheriff is already on the guest list, but I'll make sure he's at your coffin."

Eva blinked. "Coffin?"

"We're using pine coffins as reception tables," Mason said as if it were the most natural thing in the world.

"Of course you are," Eva said.

"Hey, weren't you wearing that last night?" Ellery asked, frowning at Eva's outfit. "And isn't that Sheriff Cardona's SUV you drove up in?"

"I won't comment on your coffin tables if you don't comment on my walk of shame."

"Deal." Ellery beamed, slipping her arm through Mason's.

Eva waved the happy couple off and stole their table. It offered her a view of the hustle and bustle coming in through the door. Her drink turned out to be a soy cinnamon latte and good enough that she considered making it her official usual.

Everyone seemed to be sane today. A chorus of pleases and thank yous echoed from the cash register. There were smiles all around as caffeine surged through systems. It was as if the momentary insanity that had the town in its grip had passed and everyone was back to normal.

Eva waved to Rainbow Berkowicz as the woman picked up her decaf and loaded it with enough sugar to choke a horse. She smiled at Ernest Washington who was huddled at a table with the ancient Old Man Carson. The two eyed up every pretty girl who walked into the shop and then went back to arguing about football.

She *loved* it here. The vibrant community had accepted her with open arms. It was something she'd been seeking, subconsciously, since she was a child. That easy acceptance, that genuine interest. She belonged here, and she was starting to think that maybe she belonged here with Donovan.

The front door chimed again, and Eva grinned when she recognized her father and Phoebe. The delight on Franklin's face when he spotted her warmed her already full-to-bursting heart.

He hurried over and dropped a kiss on Eva's cheek. "There's my pretty girl," he said.

"Phoebe, don't you make this poor man coffee in the mornings?" Eva teased.

"We're treating each other after a late night," Phoebe announced, pretty in her cozy purple turtleneck. Her cheeks carried a flush that didn't have anything to do with the morning chill.

"Don't tell me you two are falling victim to the planetary crossing," Eva laughed.

"Oh, no! Not at all. This was just our normal Naked Wednesday," Phoebe said, smiling up at her husband.

Franklin cleared his throat guiltily. "I think I'll just go get our coffees," he said, all innocence.

Eva laughed when she watched him practically skip to the counter.

"You look happy," Eva told Phoebe.

"You're looking rather pleased yourself," Phoebe said, watching her shrewdly. "So pleased that your incredibly observant and intelligent stepmother would be willing to bet that you had a late night yourself."

Eva blushed scarlet and picked up her coffee to give her hands something to do. "There may have been a few late hours," she admitted.

Phoebe drummed her finger tips together like a diabolical mastermind. "I am so happy to hear that. Donovan I'm assuming. Oh, I just knew you two would find each other."

"You could have given me a head's up!"

"Sweetheart, I was one of the founding members of the Beautification Committee. Shoving romance into someone's face rarely works."

"You were?" This was news to Eva.

"Another story for another time," Phoebe promised. "Now, back to you and your front-page story on *The Weekly Monthly Moon*."

"I need to see this paper," Eva muttered, wondering exactly how much trouble she was going to be in when the Beautification Committee found out she'd jumped head first into relationship territory. "Anyway, as you so astutely guessed, it is

Donovan and we did have a late night, and he is just..." She trailed off, at a loss for words.

"Isn't he though?" Phoebe said, understanding exactly what Eva meant. "I've known that boy as long as my own, and he is one of the best this world has to offer. And you know what?"

Eva leaned forward. "What?"

"You're pretty spectacular yourself. Don't you forget that and get all caught up in comparing yourself to Donovan's perfection. He had a solid upbringing, the best parents, and there was no room for self-doubt. You took some lumps when you were younger and had to work for your confidence, your independence. Don't discount that work. You've earned every inch of where you are today."

"How did you know that I was..."

"Feeling a little insecure?" Phoebe grinned, her blue eyes lighting up behind her glasses. "I'm your stepmother, and I love you to the moon and back. And I would feel exactly the same way in your position. You're a wonderful, amazing, talented, smart woman, Eva. Don't forget that."

Eva leaned across the tiny table and squeezed Phoebe's hand. "You know I love you, right?"

Phoebe grinned. "As my boys used to say until it drove me insane and I threatened to cut the internet to the house, 'duh!'"

Franklin returned with two coffees and a kiss on the cheek for each of them. "Well, my lovely ladies, I hate to cut this short, but I need to get to the restaurant."

Phoebe rose. "And I need to get to Gia's so I can help her with her bookkeeping."

"Is she catching on yet?" Eva asked.

Phoebe laughed. "We really use it as an excuse to eat pie and play with Lydia. I don't think your sister is going to be interested in learning exactly what constitutes a business expense or when quarterly taxes are due."

"Well, enjoy your pie, your coffee, and your grandbaby," Eva said, wrapping her in a tight hug. "And you, my fine father, have a beautiful day."

"I don't see how it could get better," Franklin said, cheerfully. "Dinner soon. Or lunch. Come by the restaurant."

Eva waved them off and decided she might as well get home, shower, and test how unbelievable sex affected her writing. She gathered her things and headed out the door into the crisp autumn morning.

She was clutching her latte and navigating the sidewalk traffic when someone called her name. Ice formed in her belly, and every muscle tensed before she turned around to face the past.

"Hello, mother," Eva said evenly.

28

Agnes Merill, or whatever she went by these days, hadn't aged well. There was little left of the bright, beautiful woman from the family photo album in the too thin, too sharp woman before her. Her once red hair was dyed a shade of burnt blonde. Sallow skin sagged around her chin, and her cheeks were hollow. Her fingers were yellowed with nicotine stains, pink paint peeling from the nails.

In all the times Eva had seen Agnes since the woman found her, she'd never seen a hint of the woman her father had married, the woman who had baked her sisters fanciful birthday cakes and taught them silly songs. That woman had disappeared just as surely as if she'd died. And in her place was a scheming, angry shell.

"I've got some plans cooking, and I need that cash now," Agnes told her, lighting a cigarette with a cheap Bic that flickered in the autumn breeze. There was no greeting, no "How's it going, sweetie?" Everything with Agnes was about the bottom line.

Eva looked over her shoulder and breathed a sigh of relief that Franklin and Phoebe were no longer in sight.

Agnes rasped out a laugh and with it a cloud of blue smoke. "Yeah, I saw him. Looks like Frank got himself a new wife."

Eva's eyes narrowed. "Stay away from them," she said. She may be a lot of things, a push-over, a liar, a chicken shit. But *no one* messed with Eva's family.

"Oh, I will, but it'll cost you."

Eva was already shaking her head. "Not this time, Agnes. The ATM is closed."

Agnes gave another dry laugh, one that didn't reach her bloodshot green eyes. "You owe me, Eva. Because of you, I lost everything."

It was the line that had gotten Eva a hundred times before and the guilt, familiar as an old quilt, settled onto her shoulders. "If you'd just gotten help—"

"There was no help. You were born, and I was dropped into a black hole. I lost my husband, my family, my home," Agnes counted her losses on her stained fingers.

"You walked away from your husband, your family, your home," Eva countered.

"Well, well. Look who decided to grow a backbone," Agnes said, amused.

"Get out of Blue Moon now, and don't ever come back."

Agnes looked around them at the morning sidewalk bustle of a town waking up and starting its day. She shrugged rail thin shoulders. "I don't know. I kinda like it here. I might decide to stay."

"If you don't leave town and leave me alone, it'll be your turn to pay," Eva said, her voice shaking with the vehemence behind her words. It ended now. She was done paying for something that wasn't her fault.

"Now, you listen to me. I want ten grand, and I want it by next week. If you don't deliver, I'll do everything I can to ruin your pretty little life, just like you ruined mine. And when I'm done with you, I'll start on your sisters and your father," Agnes spat back.

Eva took a threatening step forward. She wasn't sure just how far she'd be willing to go on the sidewalk on Main Street, but Agnes didn't need to know that.

"You go anywhere near—"

"Everything okay, Eves?" Nikolai and Jax, handsome as devils and looking concerned appeared behind her.

Agnes's twisted face smoothed into a bright smile. "Thanks for the directions, sweetie. I'm sure I'll be seeing you around."

It was a threat plain as day but one Eva couldn't deal with right now. Not with family witnesses. She watched Agnes scurry off toward the park and then pasted a facsimile of a smile on her face.

"What brings you two handsome men out so early today?" she asked brightly.

"Who was that?" Niko demanded, his eyes still on Agnes's thin frame.

"Yeah, you looked like you were about to deck her on the street," Jax commented.

"She's no one. Just a stranger asking for directions."

Neither of them looked remotely convinced. "Eva, if you're in trouble—" Jax began.

"You give us names and social security numbers, and no one will ever find the bodies," Niko interjected, doing his best impression of a hitman from Jersey.

Eva laughed to reassure them though the pit in her stomach seemed to grow by miles. "Are you two doing some kind of overprotective street patrol for Donovan?" she joked, her voice tight in her throat.

"We're on our way to pay our pal the sheriff a visit. The PI turned up a trail for Reva and Caleb's mom. We want to move on it before it goes cold."

Christ on a freaking cracker, what was with mothers abandoning their children and being shit human beings? Eva wondered, her chest tightening. She hoped that Reva and Caleb's story would be a happier one than her own. Jax and Joey would stand between those kids and their mother just as she stood between hers and her family.

Eva bobbed her head. "Uh, well, good luck. Tell Donovan I said… never mind. I'll see you guys around."

She turned, but Jax stopped her.

"Hey, are you coming out to the farm Saturday? Apple butter boil day. You don't want to miss it."

"Uh, sure. Yeah. I'll be there," Eva nodded. "See ya."

This time she escaped, climbing behind the wheel of Donovan's SUV and locking the doors.

Nothing was going to dampen Donovan's mood today. He diffused the cold brew battle at Overly Caffeinated without even having threatened anyone with charges. Clayton, a teddy bear at heart that looked like a retired linebacker, graciously accepted Selma's apology for dumping her cold brew coffee on his crotch after an argument about whether the Giants' new quarterback was worth his $20 million contract.

Donovan even scored a free cup of truly excellent coffee for his troubles and was in the office, whistling, by seven.

"Someone's in a good mood," Minnie said, raising an eyebrow as he snatched a blueberry muffin out of the box she'd brought.

"The sun is shining. The birds are singing. And I didn't

have to arrest anyone before seven a.m." Donovan told her. "What's not to be happy about?"

She rolled her eyes. "Yeah. Right. The sun that's not even over the horizon yet," she snorted. "Did the sun also bail out Tanbark and send him home? Wait. Nope. That was Evangelina Merill according to this form." She waved the paper in his face.

"Eva has a big heart. She thought Tanbark should be home with his parents."

"Uh-huh. And did she also believe that two weeks of files should be tossed on the floor of your office and rolled around on?"

"Don't you have some filing or faxing or muffin-eating to do?" Donovan asked.

Minnie stuck her tongue out at him as he grabbed the new *Weekly Monthly Moon* off the counter and resumed his whistling on his way into his office.

He wasn't even shocked by the headline. But that didn't mean he didn't roll his eyes. That Anthony Berkowicz made small town journalism look more like a high school yearbook.

Sheriff Dating Fire Victim: Engagement announcement expected shortly.

He settled in behind his desk and sat for just a moment, enjoying the coffee and the sunshine that was just now peeking over the park and Main Street. He wondered what Eva's reaction to the paper would be. Her reluctance had certainly taken a backseat last night. He swiveled in his chair to stare fondly at the bare counter behind his desk. Everything had changed last night. Years of waiting, of wanting, of dreaming and fantasizing, had finally come to a head, and he couldn't have imagined it being more perfect.

The way Eva responded to him… hell, the way *he* responded to *her*. It was like coming home. No wonder he had a big, stupid smile on his face. The rest of his life had finally begun.

His phone vibrated on his desk.

It looked like his work day had begun too.

~

DONOVAN HELD up a finger when Jax and Nikolai strolled into his office.

"I appreciate it. Keep me apprised," he said into the phone.

"Keep me apprised," Jax mimicked in a falsetto to Niko.

Donovan raised a different finger in his friends' direction. "Uh-huh. Thanks, chief," he said and hung up the phone. He tossed the empty muffin wrapper at Jax. "You're going to feel like an asshole in a minute."

"You sound like my wife," Jax grinned. "We come bearing news that needs to be acted on ASAP, and we need your shiny little badge to get some shit done."

Donovan brought his fingers to his temples. "Let me guess. Your P.I. found Reva and Caleb's mom in Ocean City, Maryland, and we need to move now?"

Jax rushed Donovan's desk, his excitement palpable. "How'd you—"

"Your P.I. texted this morning. She got a hot tip thanks to a Facebook post. That was the chief of police in OC. He's having a car pick up Sheila at her motel now on a few outstandings."

"Hot damn!" Jax grabbed Donovan by his shoulders and laid a kiss on his forehead. He punched Nikolai in the shoulder and ran for the door.

"Where are you going?" Donovan yelled after him, wiping the back of his hand across his forehead.

Jax ran back. "I gotta tell Joey. We gotta tell the kids."

Donovan sighed. "Jeez, it's like someone just told you you were gonna be parents. Tell Joey, but wait on the kids until the cops pick her up. Have Beckett fax the papers to this number," he instructed, shoving a scrap of paper at Jax. "If she signs, drag the kids out of school and throw a damn party."

"Tell Joey. Fax papers. Have party. Got it!" Jax took off leaving the fax number on Donovan's desk.

Donovan sighed again. "You mind delivering this to your idiot friend?"

"Happy to help," Nikolai said. "You got a minute?" he asked, glancing toward the doorway.

"No one's burned anything down yet today," Donovan said. His interest piqued when Nikolai shut the door.

"Okay, first thing is kind of a formality. I hear you and Eva are... seeing each other."

Donovan steepled his fingertips. "Not that it's any of your business, but yes. We are."

"Technically, through marriage, Eva is my business," Niko argued amicably. "So, I wanted to give you the 'treat her well or else' spiel."

"Message received." Donovan could appreciate the protective vibe, but the only man Eva was going to need protecting her was him. Not some well-meaning brother-in-law.

"I also wanted to let you know that I think you two are a good thing. So, when I tell you this, I don't think I'm being disloyal. Their mother leaving them had an effect on each of them. They all seem to think that since Eva was the youngest, it was easier on her. I think she lets them think that. And I can tell by your expression I'm not telling you anything you don't know."

"I think Eva tends to cope by keeping things to herself," he admitted. "But I plan to make sure she understands that honesty is the only policy."

Nikolai looked relieved. "Just wanted to make sure you were aware. These Merill women are formidable, and I want you in the fight."

"Appreciate it," Donovan said. They shook over his desk. "Anything else?"

Niko shrugged his shoulders under his leather jacket. "We ran into her on our way here. Looked like she was arguing with someone."

"Who?"

"Don't know. Said the woman was a stranger. But that wasn't the vibe she was giving off. I didn't catch what they were saying, but it was tense."

"What did the woman look like?"

"Bleach blonde, older. Smoker. From the looks of her, she had some other unhealthy habits. I'm new here, but she definitely wasn't the type that usually hangs out around town. And the way they looked at each other?" Nikolai shook his head. "There's history there."

Donovan frowned. He had a hard time imagining Eva having an issue with anyone. She'd be more likely to pick someone apart and use them as an antagonist in a book than hate them.

"I'll ask her about it," he told Nikolai.

His friend nodded. "Good. Okay. I'm going to go find my wife and talk her into breakfast in bed."

"You do that. And thanks, Niko."

Donovan drummed his fingers on the desk when Nikolai left. He didn't want to jump to conclusions, but it sounded like Eva was keeping secrets.

~

To: Beautification Committee

From: Bruce Oakleigh

Subject: Privacy reminder

Hello, fellow B.C. members,

President Bruce Oakleigh here. Attached, please find the minutes of last night's meeting. I'd like to once again welcome our two new members and remind them that confidentiality and subtly are two of the Beautification Committee's hallmarks of operation.

Gia and Eva, if you have any concerns about your capability to keep our business secret, here are a few suggestions.

Only open B.C. emails on a private device in a private room (i.e. Linen closet, locked bathroom, etc). This ensures that no family member accidentally stumbles upon our confidential information.

Use only the operational codes for matches. This ensures that no matchee knows they are being matched.

Consider hiding your B.C. binder in a safe, secure place. Amethyst and I purchased a fire safe which is kept in a secure location within our home.

Should you have any questions, please don't hesitate to contact a senior member of the committee.

Yours in matching success,

Bruce Oakleigh

P.S. It is forbidden to discuss committee business with any past members, especially those who have been ousted.

29

Eva usually didn't mind keeping secrets. She was good at it. But this one wasn't sitting well. Not with how raw she felt over seeing her mother in the flesh standing on the picturesque Main Street of Blue Moon. And not with Donovan calling her up to mention how much he admired her honesty and appreciated her trusting him enough to talk about her childhood.

"So how was your morning?" Donovan asked sweet as pie through the phone.

"You mean my post-orgasmic bliss? It's going well," she joked.

He laughed softly, and Eva felt some of the ice in her belly thaw.

"Are you home?" he asked.

She could tell he was fishing for something. "I am," she said, pacing through her tiny living room and willing away the unsettled feeling. "Getting ready to write thanks to all of last night's inspiration."

"That was a lot of inspiration," he admitted amicably. "Enough to warrant a good strong cup of coffee this morning."

She couldn't tell if he was making a statement or outright asking, but the bottom line was Niko and Jax had sold her out.

"Let me guess, Jax and Niko blabbed to you."

"Eva." It was all the confirmation she needed before mentally adding their names to the running list of secondary characters to torture in future books. She frowned at the way Donovan said her name, oozing with patience. "Don't use your sheriff voice on me," she warned him.

"Jax and Niko said they ran into you outside the coffee shop."

"And invited me to the apple butter boil, whatever that is, on Saturday. Did they tell you that, too?"

"They mentioned it looked like you were having a confrontation." He was tenacious, sticking to the point with a stubbornness that was putting her in a tough spot.

"Did they now?"

"Eva. What happened?"

Frustrated, she blew out a breath. "I need to ask you a favor."

"Anything," he promised.

"I need space to handle something *before* I can talk to you about it. I need you to trust me to handle it on my own, and I promise you, once it's fixed I'll tell you anything you want to know."

He was silent, and she could hear his wheels turning. She was using his own goodness against him, but there was no way she was going to dump this mess on his lap. If she hadn't gone to her own family for help, she certainly wasn't going to drag her shiny new boyfriend into it. No, this was her journey. Her responsibility. She'd enabled her mother for her entire adult life. It stopped now, and it stopped with her.

"Please, Donovan? I need to do this on my own." He'd give

her anything she'd ask for within reason. And he only had to debate whether this was within reason.

He swore. "I don't like this Eva."

"I swear to you it's nothing to be worried about. It's just an old mess that I'm finally cleaning up. I know it's a lot to ask given your perpetual town-wide caregiver state, but I need to do this for me. I can't have someone else fix it for me."

"You'll tell me once it's done?"

"I'll tell you everything," she promised. "But there's one more thing."

"Eva," he rasped.

"You can't say anything to my family. They don't need to know about this."

"How can I say anything when you're not trusting me to tell me what's going on?"

"Donovan, I trust you. This is just something I need to do myself. Please understand. Please?"

He sighed, and she knew she'd won. But the victory wasn't sweet. She felt like she was letting him down.

"I know I'm asking you to take a leap of faith here. But I promise I'll make it up to you."

"You're not doing anything illegal?" he demanded.

"No. Nothing you'd have to arrest me for," she promised.

"That woman. You weren't married to her or something, and she's refusing to divorce you because you adopted five kids together?"

Eva laughed and felt the weight lift off her just a bit. "No, and where did you get that idea?"

"This cosmic bullshit that's happening right now makes anything possible."

"I promise to make this up to you as soon as the cosmic bullshit is over."

"Holding you to it. And Eva?"

"Yeah?"

"You know if you need me I'm there, right?"

She smiled, felt the truth of his words. "Yeah. I know that. And I love it."

"I love you, Eva."

She chewed on her lip. "I'm not sure if I'm ready for non-sexual declarations of love," she admitted.

"Yeah, well. Get used to it." He sounded down, and she hated knowing it was her fault. He was the hero type. He considered it his job to clean up messes for the people he cared about, and she wasn't letting him do that.

"I'm going to go write, but I'll be thinking about you," she promised.

"Please be safe, Eva."

~

EVA GLARED at the blinking cursor and willed the words to come. She'd expected a flood of romance to dance from her fingers after her night with Donovan.

And then her mother had shown up and ruined everything. And letting Donovan down didn't exactly help those creative juices flow either. She felt like a big, human-shaped pile of shit. And it was all Agnes's fault.

She'd hoped a simple, stalwart "no" would drive her mother out of her life. Taking the shame and self-doubt with her. But by showing up here, Agnes was threatening everything Eva held dear.

She pushed away from the table, abandoning the blinking cursor, and got up to make coffee. She found the pot was full with hot water. Apparently forgetting that she'd a) made coffee and b) forgotten to actually add the coffee.

"Get a hold of yourself," Eva cautioned herself. But the

worry was clawing at her throat. The woman who had single-handedly inflicted damage on every one of her family members was here and waiting to strike. And this time, she was close enough that she could hurt them all. They were all married and happy, working and living and loving in this tiny town. And Agnes Merill wanted to take that from them. *Why?*

"Because she's an empty shell of a human being. And a bitch," Eva reminded herself.

Her phone rang, and she welcomed the distraction when she saw Eden's name on the screen.

"Hey, what's up?" she answered.

"Uh. Hi," Eden said. She sounded stilted, and Eva heard the sound of a door closing. "Hey, listen. I have a woman here at the B&B who says she's a friend of yours."

Eva swallowed hard. "Oh, yeah?"

"Yeah," Eden said. "She said her name is Agnes and that you'd be paying for her room?" Eva could hear the edge of unasked questions in Eden's voice.

Mother fucker. "She did, did she?" Eva asked.

"She was pretty adamant about it," Eden admitted. "If she's not a friend like she says, I'd be happy to get rid of her."

Eva could only imagine the consequences. "No. It's fine. We're, uh, distant acquaintances. I'm just helping her out. Temporarily." Paying for a hotel room was different than shelling out ten grand, she rationalized. "Let me give you my credit card number."

"Are you sure?" Eden asked.

"Yeah. Yeah. But listen, if you don't mind, I'd really appreciate it if you didn't tell anyone about this. Like *anyone* at all."

"I'm an innkeeper. I keep everyone's dirt."

"Remind me to get you drunk sometime and dig into all that dirt," Eva joked.

"Ha."

Eva read off her card information.

Eden thanked her. "Okay. I gotta go. I just wanted to check that this was all kosher. And if you come visit your… acquaintance, stop by and say hi."

Oh, Eva would be stopping by all right. And she'd be dragging Agnes out of there and tossing her out on her skinny ass.

30

By Saturday, Donovan was tied up in knots. The planetary crossing was still wreaking havoc. Just that morning, Old Man Carson's cows had inexplicably busted out of the barn and stampeded into town where they proceeded to crap all over One Love Park and eat most of the landscaping. Cleanup was still ongoing.

And Eva still wasn't opening the vault on her secret. Donovan had a bad feeling about it, but she'd asked him to trust her. He'd been turning it over in his head, wondering exactly what this woman was to Eva and what trouble she could cause. When he'd picked her up to take her over to Pierce Acres for the apple butter boil, she looked pale, exhausted.

"Everything okay?" he asked, his tone easy.

"I'm fine," she announced with a bright, phony smile. "Excited about apple butter."

He gripped the steering wheel a little tighter. Even his monumental patience was finite. He'd asked her point blank, and she'd batted those hazel eyes at him, all innocence and sweetness, and then lied to his face.

He was in law enforcement. Sure, Blue Moon was a sleepy-ass town with hardly any trouble, but that didn't mean he couldn't spot a lie at ten paces. He didn't like that she didn't trust him with this secret, but he'd waited this long to win her. He could wait a little longer to earn that trust. She wasn't going to shake him. If either of them was going to do the changing, it was her.

It was with this determination that he took her hand in his as he steered his SUV toward Pierce Acres. Colby and Layla were splitting the shift this afternoon and into the night, leaving him free—barring any major emergencies—to enjoy the return of the Apple Butter Boil.

"I assume you've never been to an apple butter boil?" he asked Eva, his thumb stroking her hand under his.

She shook her head. "Apple butter boil virgin."

"I think you'll like it," he predicted.

"Well, with apples, sugar, and Phoebe's chicken corn soup, what's not to like?" Eva joked.

They pulled into the gravel drive and bumped their way toward the house and barn. Donovan pulled off into the front yard, which resembled more of a parking lot than a yard.

Kids and dogs wrestled and played chase. Men with beers and mugs of coffee stood around a huge kettle over a fire. Women, Eva's sisters included, juggled glasses of wine and babies. And right then, as Donovan took Eva's hand and led her into the fray, everything in his life felt just about perfect.

The Pierces greeted them with beverages and cookies and a tour of the apple butter setup. The witch's cauldron—as he and Beckett had called it all those years ago—hung over a crackling fire. The scents of apple and burning wood hung in the air. The trees had all turned here, too. Golds and rusty reds clung to the branches for one last hurrah before winter settled in.

It was beautiful. It was home.

"We were just discussing the madness around town," Summer said, opening a bottle of Chardonnay on the picnic table.

Jonathan, dressed in a tiny flannel shirt, ran over to Donovan arms raised. Donovan lifted the boy up over his head and spun him around delighting in the giggles.

"He just ate carrots," Summer warned. "That is not attractive vomit."

Donovan settled Jonathan on his hip and tuned into the conversation.

"It's like the entire town has PMS and a hangover," Joey said.

Donovan froze and stared at her. "Jesus. You got bangs."

Joey shrugged scraping her fingers through the choppy layers covering her forehead. "What's so weird about that?"

"You haven't changed your hair since you were seven," Beckett pointed out, burping Lydia on his shoulder.

"You grew a beard," Joey shot back.

"That's different. That was for a bet."

"You kept it. Maybe *you're* under Uranus's influence," Joey argued.

Carter slapped a hand on Donovan's shoulder. "I imagine you've been dealing with this kind of shit all over town."

"You hear about Clayton's crotch of cold brew the other day?" Donovan asked, handing Jonathan over when the little boy reached for his dad.

"That's all it was? I heard Selma dumped an entire pot of hot coffee on him," Carter said.

Donovan rolled his eyes, well used to the Blue Moon grapevine.

"I heard that Selma threw the pot at his head, and he

tossed her over the counter to protect himself," Franklin piped up.

"This is what happens when you disable the gossip group on Facebook," Joey muttered.

"What? You get bangs?"

"Stop talking about my hair!"

Donovan reached for Eva and reeled her in. "I can't believe you're related to all these weirdos," he teased.

"Blood and marriage. You *chose* to be here. So, who's the real weirdo?" she grinned.

He leaned down, intent to take her mouth with his own, before remembering that Eva's father was standing next to him.

"Soooo," Franklin drawled staring at them. "Anything you want to tell your father, Evangelina?"

Donovan looked at Eva, trying to telegraph his mental panic.

"Dad, Donovan and I are dating," Eva said, looping her arm through Donovan's.

Franklin nodded, considering. "I actually found out through that spot of investigative journalism Anthony wrote up in *The Weekly Monthly Moon*," he said amicably.

"Sorry, Dad," Eva grimaced. "I should have told you sooner. It's been a crazy few days."

"I'm used to getting the news on Facebook rather than hearing it from the mouths of my daughters. Donovan, you're a lucky man. Eva, try not to screw this up."

"Dad!"

It was as much of a blessing as he needed. With a grin, Donovan silenced Eva's protest with a smoldering kiss.

"Geez, guys. Can you do that somewhere else?" Evan asked. Donovan reluctantly pulled back from Eva's sweet mouth and caught the kid rolling his eyes.

Niko slapped a hand on Evan's shoulder. "Not too long from now, Evan, you're going to be finding things to do somewhere else, too," he predicted.

Gia appeared out of nowhere and covered Evan's ears. "Nikolai Vulkov, don't go putting ideas into his head!"

"Mom, I'm thirteen. The ideas were already there," Evan argued. "I'm just way more mature about it than all of you."

"He's not kidding," Gia sighed, letting her son wiggle out of her grasp. "He's so grown up. He's not going to need me anymore."

Phoebe put an arm around the lamenting Gia's shoulders. "Honey, they'll always need you," she predicted.

"Mom! How long should the soup simmer?" Beckett called from the porch.

"Mom, did you bring cornbread?" Jax demanded.

"See?" Phoebe said.

Donovan draped an arm over Eva's shoulder. "I feel like we're looking at our future," he predicted.

Wordlessly, she cuddled into his side, resting a hand over his heart, and everything felt just about perfect again.

It got even better ten seconds later when Clementine the goat, cool as a cucumber, ambled by and ducked behind a tree.

"Shouldn't we—" Eva gestured toward the camouflaged goat.

"Oh no," Donovan shook his head. "Let's just let nature take its course."

The damn goat had the patience of a four-star general and bided her time until Jax was inhaling a slice of cornbread the size of his forearm. He never saw it coming.

"Watch out, Uncle Jax," Aurora shouted with glee. But it was too late. Clementine head-butted him in the gut, and as he doubled over, she caught him in the face with a toss of her head.

"Ouch! What the fuck!"

Quick as a ninja, Clementine snatched the cornbread out of his hand and trotted over to Joey.

Jax, clutching a hand over one eye, glared at his wife. "You said you'd untrain her!"

"I've been busy! We have kids and horses and..."

"Your bodyguard goat just punched me in the face over cornbread!"

Whistling cheerfully, Carter slipped a halter over Clementine's beady-eyed head.

"And *you*! You insist on keeping this monster around." Jax pointed wildly at Carter.

Carter held up his hands. "Man, I can't help it if she hates you. She likes everyone else."

"Mom!" Jax yelled.

Phoebe sighed. "A mother's work is never done."

Joey, trying to hide her laughter, hustled into the house to get ice for her husband's face.

"If you're my friend, Cardona, I want you to shoot that stupid goat right now!

POST-GOAT ATTACK, the apple butter boil was everything Eva hoped it would be and more. Jax—with his new black eye blooming—orchestrated a football game with the kids, his brothers, and the ever-competitive Emma and Joey. More bottles of wine were opened, more food brought out, and the apples slowly cooked down under the heat into a soupy mixture.

Seeing her sisters and father relax and enjoy themselves reinforced Eva's decision to keep her current woes to herself. She could just imagine what dropping the Mom Bomb would do to their little festive picnic. It would be a disaster, ruining the day they were all enjoying.

She let Donovan distract her, and together they shared a steaming bowl of soup and the easy touches of a couple. He was attentive and sweet and so damn sexy. When he rolled up his sleeves to take a turn stirring the apple concoction with the long wooden paddle, she stared at him over the shoulders of her sisters and friends as she caught up with everyone. She cuddled her niece Lydia and let Meatball the beagle fall asleep with his droopy head in her lap.

When Donovan stretched out in the grass next to her, she fed him pieces of Phoebe's cornbread while they watched the sun sink lower on the horizon.

"I love it when we're all together like this," Eva admitted, leaning back against Donovan.

"How many kids do you think we'll have?" he asked, twirling a blade of grass between his fingers.

"Donovan! You are ridiculous. I'm still waiting on our first date."

"I'm only asking because I was an only child. I thought it would be fun to have more kids, like the Pierces." He nodded toward the brothers who were picking on each other, using the familiar arts of headlocks and name-calling.

"Fine. We can have two then," Eva laughed, going with the moment.

Donovan stiffened beneath her and then relaxed. "Talk like that is going to get you a ride straight to the justice of the peace, Evangelina," he warned.

She shivered at the heat in his tone.

"When can we get out of here? To have sex, I mean, not get married," she corrected herself.

"If you don't want any apple butter, we can go right fucking now," Donovan said, already rising to his feet.

Eva giggled and let him pull her off the ground. She felt giddy as if Donovan and the day had pushed away all of the bad that had been closing in on her. The bad that had sent her a note that said simply "Sunday." It was Agnes's deadline for Eva to cough up the ten thousand dollars. She didn't have a plan yet, but she would, and then the woman would be out of her life forever.

"Maybe we could just go find a nice quiet cornfield or a barn," she suggested, a new need revving her system with anticipation.

"Is this research, or do you really want to have sex in a barn?"

"Everything is research, and yes, I really want to have sex in a barn," she laughed.

He was dragging her across the drive to the little red barn when a candy apple red pick-up truck eased up the drive.

"Well, I'll be damned," Donovan breathed, stopping in the middle of the lane.

"Who is it?" Eva asked.

The horn tooted and the driver waved out his window.

"My parents."

The truck came to a stop and was immediately surrounded by the horde of Pierces.

"Surprise!" the woman in the passenger seat called through the open window.

Whoops and greetings were shouted out as the couple climbed out of the truck.

Donovan had the long-limbed blonde woman in a ball cap in his arms and dangling off the ground half a second after she stepped out of the cab of the truck.

The family resemblance was strong and got even stronger when the silver fox with a tan and well-fitting jeans ambled around the hood.

For the first time ever in Eva's experience, Donovan was speechless.

Phoebe was grinning maniacally, and Eva knew she had something to do with the surprise.

Donovan dropped his mother gently to the ground and embraced his father in a one-armed hug.

"What are you two doing here?" he asked, his voice gruff with emotion.

"You think we'd miss a planetary crossing in Blue Moon?" his mom laughed.

"You did *not* come back here to hold my hand while I do my job," Donovan said.

"No, you dope," she grinned up at him. "We came back because we missed you. And we heard the Apple Butter Boil was resurrected."

Donovan swung around to face Phoebe. "You?" he asked.

She shrugged innocently. "I missed them as much as you did. Plus, I figured you might have someone you'd want to introduce them to," she said, shooting a pointed look in Eva's direction.

He wrapped Phoebe in a one-armed hug and kissed her on the top of the head before releasing her.

He reached for Eva's hand. "Mom, Dad, there *is* someone I want you to meet."

"There's a lot of someones," his father said, scanning the crowd. "I'm only recognizing about fifty percent."

"Well, start here," Donovan said. "This is Eva, my girlfriend. Eva, these are my parents, Michael and Hazel."

Hazel's eyes widened marginally, but it was the woman's only outward sign of surprise that showed. She still had cop written all over her in her straight-as-a-lance posture, and the way she took in everything without reacting to it.

"It's great to meet you," Eva said.

"Real nice to meet you, Eva," Hazel said, offering a firm shake.

"Well, hello," Michael said, all wolfish charm.

"Dad," Donovan said warningly.

Hazel punched her husband in the shoulder. "Don't pick yet. Let her get to know you before she has to deal with your flirtations."

"Anything you say, my bride," Michael said, winking in his wife's direction.

Hazel opened her arms to Phoebe. "It's about damn time I see your face again," she said.

"It's about damn time you came back from the west coast," Phoebe countered, wrapping her friend in a bear hug.

"You got any wine around here? Where's Elvira?" The two women linked arms and wandered off.

"It's good to see you, Dad," Donovan said.

Michael slapped a hand on his son's back. "It's mighty good to see you, son. We're staying with you by the way. Hope you have clean sheets."

31

The banter between the Cardonas fascinated Eva. They had their own language interspersed with call codes and memories of Blue Moon past. She liked seeing him with his family, seeing how he'd become the man he had.

But it also gave her a little tickle of doubt. Donovan came from solid stock. A sheriff and a fire chief, heroes by profession and good citizens by practice. While Eva's father was above reproach and just about as perfect a human being as one could get, points were lost on her mother. A child-abandoning drug addict who repeatedly bilked her youngest daughter for money? That could be reason enough to make Donovan and his parents think twice about welcoming her with open arms.

She left them to their conversation, each taking turns at the kettle paddle, and wandered over to where Joey was drumming her fingers on the picnic table and staring at the front door.

Eva sat down next to her. "You look like you've got something on the brain."

"Don't try to mine me for novel plotlines," Joey said,

without taking her eyes off the front door. "Reva's in there getting ready for Homecoming. Emma's doing her hair."

"And why are you out here?"

"She said my pacing was making her nervous."

Eva grinned. "Are you nervous?"

Joey gave a sullen, one-shouldered shrug. "This is the first big thing for her since she moved in with us. I want it to be great, perfect even."

"What's there to worry about?"

Joey shot her a look. "How long has it been since you were a teenager? Or did you block out those years?"

"Right. I forgot. Unpopularity, parents who just don't get you, sweaty boys with roaming hands..."

"Exactly. Reev's had enough shit in her life. She deserves the good stuff now."

"Donovan said the P.I. tracked down Sheila," Eva prompted.

"Yeah, and you know what that fucking shitbag of a douche mother did?" Joey said.

Eva blinked. "I'm guessing it wasn't good."

"She said she'd sign the papers for twenty grand."

"Jesus." Eva blew out a breath. The situation hit just a little too close to home for her.

"I mean, can you imagine a mother extorting her kids for money?"

Eva shook her head. "No." *Yes. She could and without trying too hard either.*

"Anyway, Jax was reaching for his checkbook—I love that man. He'd do anything for anyone. But Cardona stepped in. He said if we pay her off this once, she'll just keep coming back. Even if she makes promises or signs papers. It won't be the last time. She'd always be in our life or worse, in theirs." She nodded toward where Caleb and Aurora were chasing

Waffles the tireless dog around a tree. "He says the only thing that's going to work is a no."

Damn it all to hell. Where had Donovan been the first time she'd scraped out the last forty bucks in her meager checking account in college so her mother could fill her tank to drive to Philadelphia? Agnes had come back every time, always needing more. And every damn time Eva had caved. Until now. Now was the time to finally clean up this mess. She just didn't know how.

"So, what did you do?" Eva asked, focusing on Joey.

Joey grinned. "Told her to fuck off and threatened her with prison for child neglect and abandonment. Papers were signed and are being overnighted. We told Reva today, and she got pretty choked up. In the good way... I think. We're going to look at colleges next weekend."

Eva grabbed Joey in a hard hug. "You, my friend, are a mom."

Joey shook her head slowly. "I know. I can't fucking believe it. And my daughter is in there getting ready for her first big thing, and I'm so nervous for her I might puke."

Eva slid down the bench putting a few inches between her and Joey. "You just give me fair warning if that happens."

Summer and Carter's front door opened, and Reva appeared on the porch. She did a slow turn in her midnight blue dress to the whistles and the applause of the crowd in the yard. The sequined bodice caught the sunlight, and the flirty tulle lifted as she spun. Her hair, that lovely doeskin brown, was swirled up in a sassy updo courtesy of Emma's competent fingers. Summer had outdone herself on Reva's makeup. It was perfection. Light and bright and highlighting her youth and natural glow.

Joey was damn near chewing through her lip to keep from

crying. "Shit. Why does it feel like my chest is caving in?" she muttered.

Eva patted her friend on the back. "I think it's just love."

Jax, on the other hand, was having an entirely different reaction.

He stormed up to the foot of the porch steps. "No. Oh, hell no. You're not going anywhere like that!"

For a moment, Eva thought he was joking. But one look at his panicked face, and she knew he was dead serious.

"Jackson," Joey said, standing up from the table. "Chill out. She's practically an adult."

"I can see that. The whole *world* can see that in that dress," Jax argued, pointing accusingly at Reva's dress. "It doesn't even have straps! You're not leaving this house dressed like that."

Two months ago, Eva thought, Reva would have hung her head and shuffled back into the house. But her time with Jax and Joey had rubbed off on her. She put her slim hands on her hips and stared Jax down. "Yes, I am," she said calmly.

Jax blinked at his daughter and then turned his rage on Joey. "You see this? This is your fault! She sounds just like you!"

"Me? You're the one acting like a fucking moron. Sorry, Cale," she said, tossing an apology at Reva's little brother.

"That's okay," he said, waving amicably at Joey.

"I'm not acting like a fucking moron. Do you have any idea what 17-year-old boys are like?"

"If you'll recall, I remember perfectly what they're like," Joey said, drilling a finger into his chest. "And from where I'm standing, late twenty-somethings aren't much better!"

"Reva, you look lovely," Phoebe said, stepping in to smooth it over. Caleb skipped over to her to get away from his shouting parents.

"Thanks, Gram. Joey helped me pick the dress," Reva said, smoothing her hands over the skirt.

"*You* put her in that?" Jax shouted at his wife.

"Excuse me, but last time I checked, you didn't want to go dress shopping because it was a 'chick thing.' So, if you don't like this gorgeous dress that our gorgeous daughter picked out, you can just shut your damn eyes and your mouth and give the rest of us a break."

Eva wasn't sure if anyone else had caught the "our daughter" remark. Their family was so new that they were all still trying to get used to the relationships. On the steps, Reva was standing open-mouthed, watching the argument unfold, a pretty flush on her cheeks. Eva wondered what it must feel like for the girl. Going from being discarded by her own mother to being welcomed into—and maybe a little smothered by—a new family as if she'd belonged there the whole time.

It made her eyes just a little glassy with happiness for the girl who was loved. It's what the Pierces and Blue Moon did. They welcomed people into the fold, blood or no blood, and made a place for them. They'd made a place for her, too, and in that place, she'd found Donovan.

And for the first time in her adult life, the pieces of a child's broken heart were starting to mend themselves.

Donovan appeared at Eva's side and sighed heavily.

"You gonna handle this situation, Sheriff?" Hazel asked, a hint of smile playing on her bare lips.

He sighed and turned to Eva. "Baby, listen. If he punches me, I'm cuffing him," he told Eva before strolling over to where Jax and Joey stood, steaming mad.

"Jax, my friend, you're outnumbered, and I think you should calm down before you ruin Reva's night."

"Calm down?" Jax spat the words out at Donovan. "Do you

remember what you were doing at Homecoming and prom and after just about every football game?"

Eva bit her lip when the blush reached the tips of Donovan's ears.

"I sure do. And I'm sure Reva has better judgement than any of us did back then."

"Did you go to Homecoming, Bucket?" Aurora asked, wrapping her arms around Beckett's legs.

He winced, presumably recalling memories of Moon Beam Parker, and lifted his daughter up to settle her on his hip. "I'm with Jax," he announced. "We can't let Reva go. Not with hormonal teenage boys oozing testosterone."

"It's about time you came to your senses," Jax approved.

"Hang on, now," Gia dipped a toe into the fight. "I'm not okay with you siding with Jax on this."

"Sorry, Gianna, but these are our daughters. We have to protect them from idiots like we were."

"Were?" Joey challenged.

"I hate to say it, but my stupid brothers might have a point," Carter butted in. Meadow was cradled against his chest yawning.

"Stupid's not a nice word, Uncle Carter," Caleb said.

"You're right. Sorry buddy," he said, ruffling the boy's hair. "My mentally deficient brothers," he corrected.

"Carter," Summer said. Her voice held a warning tone.

"What?" he challenged her. "We've all got girls, except for Niko, but I bet he'd agree with us." They all turned to look at Nikolai.

He muttered a curse. "Sorry, babe," he said, dropping a kiss on Emma's cheek. "But I've got to go where the testosterone goes." He stepped over the invisible line dividing the camps. A line that Eva noticed Donovan was straddling.

Franklin pulled up a couple of lawn chairs so he, Phoebe,

and Evan could sit and enjoy the entertainment. Caleb climbed into the safety of Franklin's lap, and Michael and Hazel stood behind them ready to act if necessary or at least capture the fight on video.

"Doesn't anyone care what I want?" Reva demanded from the front porch.

"No!" shouted the men.

"Yes!" the women announced.

"This is Uranus right here, isn't it?" Eva hissed at Donovan.

"Uranus and a couple of remorseful post-teenagers," he whispered back. "You want to help me out here?"

"Let me talk Jax down, and you take the ladies."

"They're more likely to take a swing at me," he grumbled. But he took Joey by the arm and dragged her a few feet away to listen to her complaints.

Eva slipped an arm through Jax's. "Jax, Jax, Jax. We're like step-brother and sister-in-law, right?"

He was still glaring at Reva's dress. "Huh? Yeah, I guess so."

"Good, because this would sting if it were coming from someone who wasn't family."

"What would—"

Eva slapped him upside the head. "Listen to me. You are this close to ruining what's got to be one of the happiest days of your daughter's life."

"It's fucking Homecoming, not her damn wedding day. Oh, God. She's going to get married—"

She smacked him again. "Stay with me. This is a girl who's been abandoned by her parents. Who probably didn't have a great life with her mother before she left. And now she's part of this big, amazing family, and you're making her feel like shit for her choices."

"No, I'm not!" he argued.

"The dress, the date. She chose those, and you're not trusting her decisions."

Jax sputtered, but Eva cut him off. "Listen to me. How did you feel the first time your dad handed you the keys to his car? Or let you stay out past curfew? Or talked to you like an adult?"

That shut him up.

She laid a hand on his shoulder. "You need to tell Reva that you trust her and her decisions. She's a great kid. An amazing one, and you're lucky enough to have her in your life. Don't take her special day and turn it into a guilt-fest for your idiocy when you were her age. Trust her to make better choices than you did."

"What if she doesn't? I was convincing as hell when I was her age. Ask Joey," he pointed at his wife who was staring stonily up at Donovan and possibly growling.

"And look how you two ended up," she pointed out.

"Yeah, but that's different. What are the odds of that happening? One in a trillion?"

"What are you trying to protect Reva from?"

"Guys like me!"

Carter and Beckett stepped in to flank him, still juggling their daughters.

"Guys like *us*," Beckett corrected him.

Eva looked heavenward and groaned. "Okay, listen to me. All of you. You are good men. You've grown up, you've married amazing, *patient* women—except for Joey—and you're raising awesome kids. All you can do is be good examples for your kids. Do you think Reva is going to settle for some loser jerk when she sees what you and Joey have?" she asked Jax. "Or what Beckett and Gia and Carter and Summer and my dad and Phoebe have? She sees all of this and knows that she can have this, too. You just need to trust her to make the right decisions."

Oh shit. She wasn't just talking about Reva anymore.

"Our step-sister-in-law makes sense," Beckett mused.

"I just want her to be happy and safe... and stay a virgin forever," Jax sighed.

"She will. Minus the virgin part," Eva promised.

"What's a virgin?" Aurora wanted to know.

"I get what you guys are trying to do. It's sweet, but so, *so* misguided. Trust her to be her. Okay?"

"You're a wise woman. Bring it in, Eves," Carter said. They surrounded her in a manly group hug. Aurora jumped from Beckett to Eva and wrapped her arms around her neck.

"Why isn't anyone telling me what a virgin is?" Aurora asked.

"It's a Madonna song, short cake," Beckett told her.

"Guys, I can't breathe," Eva said, her face smashed up against someone's chest. "And you should be hugging Reva."

They moved as one, a dozen-legged organism climbing the porch stairs and enfolding Reva into their ridiculousness. Waffles and Baxter danced around them, sensing a game.

"Guys, please don't mess up my makeup," Reva grumbled.

"Or her hair," Emma shouted from the yard.

Phoebe shot her fist into the air. "I finally feel like the Mother's Curse is kicking in. Now you all get to suffer through everything you put me through."

The men released Eva, Reva, and Aurora to jump off the porch and wrap Phoebe and then Franklin in a sloppy, testosterone-filled hug.

"We're so sorry, Mom," Jax lamented.

"We were horrible human beings," Carter added.

"You're a saint," Beckett decided.

"You're crushing me!" Phoebe yelped. "I don't think this chair can hold this much—"

The lawn chair gave way under her, and they all landed in a laughing pile on the ground.

"Nice work, deputy," Donovan said, slipping his arm around her waist.

"Are those scratch marks on your arm?" Eva asked.

"Joey's mean."

32

"I'm not sleeping with you with your parents in the house," Eva hissed at Donovan as he made another rather lewd and very tempting suggestion in her ear. The apple butter was jarred, the kettle scrubbed, and the fire burning low. Reva had left with her date, and Donovan hadn't had to handcuff Jax, even though he did shake Tobias' hand a little too hard.

Everyone was enjoying the peace of the country night and the warmth from the last of the flames. Donovan's parents and Phoebe had hit the wine and beer hard enough in their reminiscences that their sheriff son wasn't letting them drive themselves home.

"You're being ridiculous," Donovan argued. "We're adults. They're adults. Everyone under that roof is an adult. Plus, they're going to pass out as soon as they hit the sheets."

"I literally just met them. I'm not going to have sixty-five orgasms through the night and then just play it cool over coffee in the morning."

"Okay, sixty-five is high even for a romance novelist."

"I'm not going home with you, Donovan. You've been cock blocked by your parents."

"Parents ruin everything," he said with all the angst of a teenager.

Eva leaned up to give him a kiss on his cheek. "Something tells me you'll get over it."

"I wanted to be with you tonight," he murmured against her hair.

She shivered at his touch. "There'll be time for that. Spend some time catching up with your parents."

"Will you miss me?" he asked, his voice husky as he traced his fingertips over her jawline.

"Uh-huh." She nodded as her insides turned to molten lava.

"Breakfast tomorrow?" he asked. "I can meet you."

She nodded again, at a loss for words. She wanted this. She wanted a real shot with Donovan. A clean slate and no secrets. She'd find a way to make it happen.

Eva took Donovan's SUV home so he could drive his parents home in their truck. Once ensconced in her cozy cottage, Eva started to brainstorm. She had a person she needed to get rid of. Hiring a hit man wasn't an option. Asking her family for help was definitely not an option. She needed to find a solution that would get Agnes out of her life and away from her family without anyone being the wiser.

What would she do if this was a book plot? She paced as she plotted.

Distracted, her toe caught on the edge of the rug, and she hurtled forward, catching her shins on the viciously sharp edge of the coffee table. "Damn it all to hell!"

Rubbing her shins, she saw the lights on at Beckett and Gia's. She bit her lip, debating. Finally, Eva dug out her phone and sent off a text.

Eva: *"Can you meet me for a minute?"*

Five minutes later, Beckett showed up at her front door in cotton pajama pants and an NYU sweatshirt. "Drop your earring down the sink again?" he asked, wielding his rarely used toolbox.

Eva let him in. "Not exactly. I need some lawyerly advice... for a book I'm working on."

His face brightened. "That's way more fun than digging through plumbing."

She fetched him a beer and leaned against the kitchen island. "So, what kind of advice would a lawyer give someone who needs to get a bad person out of their life?"

Beckett settled on one of the stools. "A lawyer would ask for more background."

"Say my heroine has someone who periodically comes into her life unwelcomed and demands money."

"Blackmail?" Beckett asked, frowning.

"Eh. Not exactly. It's not like this person is threatening to release incriminating information or naked pictures. More like threatening to be a nuisance."

"And you want to know the best way to get rid of the nuisance?"

She nodded, toying with an apple she pulled from the bowl on the counter.

"I'd suggest a restraining order. If there's extortion involved, that shouldn't be an issue. Have your heroine go to the cops and file one. If the order is violated, it becomes a police matter."

Eva was already shaking her head. "What if the heroine can't go to the cops?"

"Why wouldn't she be able to go to the cops?" Beckett asked.

"Uh, plot twist?"

"Okaaay," he drawled. "How about a cease and desist letter from an attorney? They can be applied in cases of harassment."

"What happens if the person doesn't cease and desist?"

"Then it would be time to threaten legal action and get the police involved."

"How often does a cease and desist letter scare off a bad guy?"

"It depends. Some people aren't capable of making rational decisions."

"What about—and this of course is purely hypothetical—not exactly legal means?"

"An assassin?" Beckett speculated.

"Not exactly that not legal. What would you do if it was someone being a nuisance to your family."

Beckett's eyes went stony. "I'd find out what that person is afraid of."

"Interesting. Become the boogeyman."

"This *is* for a book, isn't it?" Beckett asked, eyes narrowing.

Eva laughed nervously. "Of course, it is!"

He was eyeing her up like a suspect on the stand. "Because if you're in trouble and you're trying to handle it on your own, I know several people who are going to be good and pissed. One of them carries a gun for a living, and I live with another. She's scarier."

"Beckett, would I lie to you?"

"Yes," he answered immediately and without hesitation.

Eva glowered at him. He'd spent too much time around her sisters. He knew her too well. "It's nothing I can't handle," she sighed.

"I do not like that answer. Are you putting yourself at risk? Because if you are, keep in mind that not only would that piss me the fuck off, but you live in my backyard twenty feet from my family."

Eva looked at her feet. "No one is in danger," she promised.

"I'm not leaving here until you tell me what's going on, and if you don't spill it, I'm texting your sister, and she'll pry it out of you with creative yoga poses."

"I have to tell Donovan first," Eva blurted out. "I owe him that."

Beckett swore ripely. "You have until tomorrow night, and then I'm siccing Gia on you." He downed the rest of his beer and put the empty bottle on the counter. "Don't pretend like you need to handle this alone. You have family. A big, sloppy, multi-generational one full of people who will be royally pissed at you if you try to play the martyr."

Eva blew out a breath between her teeth.

"Tell Cardona," Beckett pointed at her and walked out, slamming the door behind him.

Great. She now had twenty-four hours to fix this.

"SO, EVA, HUH?" Michael prodded, accepting the glass of water Donovan poured for him in the dark kitchen.

"Yep. I hope you like her because I'm going to marry her."

Michael hooted, his laugh booming off the high ceiling. "You've got a lot of your mother in you, you know?"

"What's that supposed to mean?"

"I had a crush on your mother for ten years before I finally got up the guts to be real with her."

"Ten *years*?"

"Oh, I noticed her all right my junior year and spent the rest of my high school career acting like an idiot to get her attention. She turned me down for prom our senior year."

"Is that the senior prom you took two dates to?"

"It would take more than one woman to replace your mother," Michael quipped.

"So she turned you down," Donovan prompted, familiar with the story.

"And I crawled off to lick my wounds and convince myself I was over that pretty blonde with the mean streak. It wasn't until years later when John caught me mooning over her and called me a chicken shit for not going for it again."

"Your romance began with chicken shit," Donovan grinned.

"My point is. I'm glad to see you didn't wait as long as I did. Your mom likes her. She likes the way she handled Jax's freak out. I still can't believe all those snot-nosed kids are adults and parents now. All except my boy."

"Give me time, Dad. I'll have you wearing World's Best Grandpa shirts eventually."

"Think Eva will stick?" Michael asked, grinning over his glass.

"If she can get out of her own way she can. But I, unlike you, am a patient man." Donovan pointed at his father.

"That you are, son. Well, you've got good taste anyway."

"She's a romance novelist," Donovan grinned.

"No shit?" Michael perked up. "I'll have to tell Hazel. She's a big fan of those Fifty Shades books."

"Jesus, Dad. I don't want to know that shit about Mom."

"Technically it's me *and* your mom. I watched the movies, and we found this website that sells—"

"I swear to God if you finish that sentence, you're going to be sleeping in the garage.

Michael laughed. "Ah, it's nice to be able to mess with you in person again, son."

"It's good to have you home," Donovan admitted. "As long as you can keep your mouth shut about your sex life."

33

It was after midnight, and Eva was wide awake staring into the pitch black of her bedroom. She couldn't figure out what would scare off her mother, and she felt the hours ticking down. There must be something?

She was rejecting her fifty-seventh terrible idea when she heard a commotion downstairs. Her front door opened and closed, and heavy footsteps crossed the kitchen and then stumbled over the laundry basket she'd left at the foot of the stairs so she'd remember to finally wash her damn clothes.

"Son of a bitch!" she heard a low male voice growl.

She snapped on the bedside lamp and padded the three steps down the hall. Donovan, in sweatpants and a long sleeve tee, was making his way up her stairs.

"Well hello there, Officer Breaking and Entering."

"Technically, I used one of the six hide-a-keys," he said, slipping his hands around her waist. "Also, there's this random 1985 town ordinance that states as a sheriff I can give anyone permission to enter a home if I suspect suspicious activity."

"What suspicious activity did you suspect?" Eva asked, leaning into him and sliding her hands under his sweatshirt.

"I suspected a beautiful woman was sleeping alone."

"Such a crime." She brought her palms around to skim over the ripple of his abs. "I thought you were spending time with your parents?" Eva said, stepping into his grasp.

"Those lightweights passed out as predicted. I snuck out," he said, pressing a kiss to the tip of her nose.

"Sneaking out to your girlfriend's house?" Eva tut-tutted. "You're going to be in so much trouble."

"I'm hoping you'll make it worth my while," he whispered, trailing his lips down her neck. "What are you wearing?" He stroked over the lace at her side.

"It's just a slip thing."

"I like it. I'll try not to rip it when I take it off you." He picked her up and followed the light to her bedroom. Eva unwound her legs from his hips and gasped as they fell on the bed together. He was already hard for her, and the sweatpants were easy for her to shove down his legs using her heels.

Donovan groaned when he discovered there was nothing underneath the slip. "Jesus. You were made to drive me crazy." He pushed her higher against the pillows and gently pressed her knees apart.

"Lose the shirt," Eva breathed, yanking on the back of his t-shirt.

He yanked it overhead and threw it blindly. Fully naked now, Donovan put his hands behind her thighs and lowered his mouth to her bared center. The brush of lips and tongue had Eva drawing in air through clenched teeth, hissing against the pleasure he sparked.

"You taste like perfection," he murmured against her folds.

Eva fisted her hands into the sheets. "Oh, g-g-god."

He fed on her, using leisurely strokes of his tongue to drive Eva wild. Her knees fell open, and she begged him for more with shallow thrusts of her hips. In the soft lamp light, she looked down and decided she'd never seen anything sexier than Donovan's head between her legs, a devilish gleam in his eyes.

She took that gleam as a challenge and shoved him backwards. Surprise lit those blue eyes now. Surprise and need. Eva pushed him onto his back, and when she positioned herself over his head and leaned down to take his thick cock into her mouth, he groaned.

"Marry me," Donovan rasped.

She didn't have to answer. Her mouth was full of him. Eva slid her lips over his crown and smiled to herself when she heard his sharp intake of breath. His hands dug into her arms harder than he probably intended. She used the flat of her tongue to slide up his shaft and heard Donovan murmuring something like a prayer behind her.

She was feeling full of herself when she added her hand and worked him with mouth and fingers. His muscles were so tense beneath hers. She felt powerful. His body was perfection. Big and muscled. So hard. She just wanted to bite those muscular thighs.

God, she had a thing for Donovan's thighs.

It was then that he remembered what he had access to. She cried out when he slid two fingers home and flexed them just enough, skimming over exactly the right spot. "I want to die doing this," he whispered, bringing his mouth to her slit.

Eva gasped at the magic of his mouth. "Just not right now, okay?" she breathed out.

His reply was lost as he buried his face against her. His tongue and fingers worked to bring her to a frenzy. Through the haze of lust blinding her, Eva did her best to keep up, to drive him insane. He was achingly hard, and she was so eager to please.

His free hand clamped onto her hip, holding her in place

whenever she tried to wriggle free. It was building. She could feel the need taking her higher and higher out of her body as if she were cresting a wave.

"Donovan?" She said his name to ground herself. She didn't want to get lost. But it was too late for that.

He slipped his fingers into her again, and she came, clutching and begging. She saw fireworks behind her closed lids. Pops of color that shimmered and glowed as she rode out her release.

"There is nothing sexier in the world than you coming for me," Donovan said, twisting under her. He tossed her to the mattress facedown and closed her hands over the rungs in her headboard. "Hold on for me, baby."

"Hurry, Donovan," she breathed.

He stroked his hand over her shoulder, down the arch of her back and across the curve of her hip. He pushed the lace and silk of her slip up until she was exposed. "You're my every fantasy come true, Evangelina," he told her.

She bit her lip to keep from blurting out the words that were clogging her throat. There was too much to fix before she could say them.

"Now, Donovan. Please!"

With great care, he lined himself up to her entrance and pushed into her. Eva felt the words she longed to say replaced with an uncontrollable whimper as he finally filled her. Her knuckles went white from her grip on the spindles.

Donovan's shout of triumph was cut off. "Shit. Damn it, Eva." He stilled in her. "I wasn't thinking."

"What?" she hissed the word out, not caring what the problem was as long as he didn't leave her.

"I forgot the condom."

"Birth control."

"Yes. That's what a condom is," Donovan growled, his fingers digging painfully into her hips.

"No. I'm on birth control."

"You're okay with—"

"God, yes. Donovan, if you don't start moving right now, I'm going to die, and this moment will be your life-long regret."

"Yes, ma'am. I live to serve."

And serve he did.

Bare, with nothing between them, Donovan stroked in and out of her. Eva dropped her face into the pillow because breathing no longer mattered. Nothing did but the feel of the man inside her, behind her, above her. She felt raw, vulnerable, exposed. But she didn't feel scared. She felt... free.

He pushed her to her knees, and her spine bowed.

"I can't get enough of you," he said in staccato bursts between his powerful thrusts. "Eva." He gritted her name out through his teeth.

In response, Eva rose on her hands and looked over her shoulder. His face was tight, the cords in his neck standing out as he fought for control. She'd taken him here. Let him take her with him.

Her muscles clenched and closed over him, and she knew he felt it, felt *her*.

He groaned, beads of sweat making their way down his expanse of chest. She couldn't look away. She wanted to watch him as they went off together. She wanted to see him the first time he lost himself in her with nothing keeping them apart.

Her muscles quickened around his shaft. "I feel you, baby. I know you're ready. Touch yourself," he commanded.

Eva would have done anything the man asked in that moment. She brought her fingers to the apex of her thighs, and as Donovan pumped into her she stroked herself to a blinding orgasm. She felt him tense on the first explosion. He levered his hips into her and held firm with a half-shout. She came like that, with him buried inside her, pouring his own release into her.

Hot, pulsing need was finally fulfilled. He was moving again, more gently now as he drew out both their orgasms with a slow, smooth ride.

Eva flopped face down with a satisfied moan and Donovan collapsed on top of her.

"I'm so glad you snuck out," she said into the pillow.

He grabbed her by the hair, lifting her face out of the bedding. "Huh?"

"Glad you snuck out," she repeated.

He let her face fall back into the pillow and laughed softly as he gathered her to him. "Me, too. You're worth getting grounded over."

Eva giggled. "I bet you were a Boy Scout of a teenager. Probably never got in trouble. Never came home after curfew. I'd even wager that when your parents left you home alone, you never threw a wild party. You were a good boy who grew into a good man."

"You make that sound like a bad thing."

"On the contrary, there's something awfully sexy about a white knight with a heart of gold. Makes me want to dirty you up a bit."

He bit her ear lobe and made her gasp.

"Baby, you dirty me up a lot," he promised. "I bet you were grounded all the time. Weren't you?"

She shook her head. "Nope. Never."

"How did you manage that?" he asked, biting her on the shoulder.

"You're saying you don't believe I was a sweet little angel?"

"You're going to try to sell me on that after you shoved my

face between your legs and begged me to make you come? I think you were a bad girl who grew up to be a badass woman."

"Heat of the moment," she argued. "You can't take conversation during sex seriously."

Donovan buried his nose in her hair. "You can with me. I love you. We're getting married. And you're so fucking hot."

"You're insane. Uranus has blinded you," Eva murmured as her heart did a cartwheel in her chest.

"Your incredible body has blinded me. Now, back to how you never got grounded."

"I was sneakier than my sisters."

"That doesn't surprise me in the least. Example?"

"I'd go to bed, wait until everything was quiet, and sneak out the back door. I'd stash my pajamas in the shrubs behind the house so when I got home I could change in the yard. If Dad ever caught me—which he did once or twice—I just told him I heard a noise outside."

"Franklin believed you were going all scary movie heroine instead of being a bad party girl?"

"I think he wanted to believe it. And I was convincing. I'd mess up my hair. I even had my retainer out there. No one would believe I went to Tammie Germanski's party with my retainer."

"You are a natural sneak. Why is that? I'd think, as the baby, you'd be allowed to get away with everything."

She yawned. "I didn't want to worry everyone." She snuggled in a little closer to his chest. "They already thought I'd fall apart over Mom leaving so I tried not be too much trouble."

"That's a big burden to carry," Donovan said. He was stroking his hand up and down her arm, and it felt so good. Every cell in her body felt good.

"Small price to pay to keep my family safe."

"Safe?" Donovan prodded.

"I mean happy. They deserve to be happy. And so do you."

"And you're going to make that happen?"

Eva yawned again. She was going to sleep for a million years in these arms.

"Whatever it takes. I'll make sure no one ruins it."

"Who's trying to ruin it?"

"Parents ruin everything..." Eva's voice trailed off as she fell asleep wrapped in the safety of Donovan's arms.

~

To: Beautification Committee
From: Bruce Oakleigh
Subject: Banquet

Hello, fellow B.C. members,

Bruce Oakleigh, president, here. As you are aware, one of our founding members, Hazel Cardona, has returned to town. Some of you have expressed an interest in hosting a Beautification Committee Past and Present banquet. I feel such an occasion would call for an exciting interactive presentation on every match in our history.

Personally, I feel that if we are to do justice to all of our happy matches, we should spend a minimum of five minutes on each couple. Who in our little group is adept at PowerPoint and available to conduct interviews by say next Tuesday?

Yours in matching success,
Bruce Oakleigh

34

Eva kissed Donovan good-bye after a naked breakfast of cold cereal while the world was still dark. It was barely five a.m., but he wanted to sneak home before his parents got up, and she had plotting to do. She'd slept without dreams, which was unusual for her. Even in sleep, her imagination usually worked in overdrive.

But in the cold dark of morning, her mind was clear. Today was the day she was getting rid of Agnes for good. She channeled her nervous energy into two hours of writing, and by the time the sun came up, she was stalling out. She got up to pace, mindful of the coffee table this time. The picture on the mantel caught her eye.

It was her graduation day. She and her father were grinning like fools at Emma who was behind the camera. Gia stood next to her, wielding the dozen roses they'd chipped in to buy her. She remembered that day vividly. Eva had always wanted them to be proud of her like she was of them. And that was the first time she'd felt like she'd really caught a glimpse of that pride.

She traced a finger over the frame. She'd do anything for her family. Eva guessed that made them her Achilles' heel.

Her lips curved in a slow, fierce smile as an idea formed. It was more satisfying than figuring out the perfect plot twist. She was clearing the path to her own happily ever after.

Eva dressed quickly and applied make-up as if it were war paint. Satisfied, she gave her reflection a final nod and then marched out the door.

"You're leaving today, *mother*. And you're never coming back," she rehearsed in the car. "No. Too personal. You're leaving today, Agnes. Yeah. A little disinterested like she's an annoying gnat."

The B&B was just minutes from Donovan's house, she noted, turning down the tree-lined drive. At the Y in the road, she followed the signs left toward the Blue Moon B&B. The right appeared to lead to the neighboring winery and the mysterious Davis Gates that the Beautification Committee was so enthusiastic about.

Interesting.

Eva's Mini cruised up the paved path, and she brought it to a stop to gawk at the oddball splendor. The structure rose three-stories and sprawled over half the manicured lawn. Turrets, adorned with jewel-toned shingles squatted on the peaked roof. The porch, a wide avenue of stained wood, wrapped around both sides of the house. Stained glass, ivy, and a comical crescent moon weather vane were the icing on the sugary sweet cake.

She refused to be distracted by the whimsy of the place. Nope. Not even the fluffy dogs romping in the side yard were going to dull her temper. Her mother was inside this hippie fantasy, and one of them was leaving today and never coming back.

Eva strode onto the porch and pushed open the front door. A fairy bell tinkled above her head.

A door on the far side of the front desk swung open. "Oh, hey, Eva!" Eden's bright greeting came from behind a mound of steaming biscuits. She wore a ruby red apron over slim black pants and a white button down. *What kind of woman baked in a white shirt?* Eva wondered.

Eva's stomach growled, distracted by the heavenly scent of fresh baked carbs. She'd burned off the cereal hours ago thanks to her writing sprint and furious plotting.

"Hi, Eden. Is Agnes around?" she asked, staring at the platter of cloud-like biscuits.

"Sure. Follow me. She's in the dining room. You can join us for breakfast."

Eva, a sneaky observer of human behavior, detected the slight edge in Eden's tone. Agnes had that effect on people.

"Okay. Sure," Eva decided. She'd have to postpone the smack down until she could get Agnes somewhere more private. But at least she could eat one of those gorgeous biscuits.

She found Agnes sneering at *The Weekly Monthly Moon* at the far end of the dining table. She was dressed in a ratty off-the-shoulder sweater. Her denim-clad leg was jiggling, fingers were tapping a distracting beat on the hardwood. The rest of the guests seemed to pick up on the unfriendly vibe and hovered around the opposite end of the massive table.

Eva flashed an apologetic smile at them and took the chair next to her mother.

"About damn time," Agnes rasped without looking at her. "You bring my money?"

"Why don't we talk about this somewhere more private?" Eva suggested.

"What? You don't want an audience," Agnes sneered in the

direction of the guests at the other end of the table. They studiously avoided eye contact, and Eden cheerfully distracted them by launching into the day's weather report.

Eva rolled her eyes at Agnes and rose. "You know what? I don't have time for this today. Or ever." She grabbed a biscuit off the platter, hefted it in her palm. "I'm going to go talk to Eden about settling your bill, and then you can hit the road." She headed for the door.

Damn if it didn't feel good to be the one walking away for once. She took a victorious bite of the biscuit. It was hot and flaky on her tongue.

She made it as far as the front desk.

"That's quite a mansion Emmaline got for herself," she said casually. "Looks like she's done well for herself," Agnes said from behind her.

Eva said nothing. Usually, a vague threat like that would have her jumping for her checkbook. But not this time.

Agnes's eyes narrowed. "I'm thinking about hanging around here. There's this little yoga place in town. Maybe I should drop in?" Agnes let the comment hang there.

Eva casually took a bite of biscuit. "So, you're into yoga now? Better than prescription drugs, I guess."

The woman that gave her life scowled at Eva. "I saw that fancy husband of Gianna's walking the kids to school. Maybe they'd like a visit from Grandma?" Her smile was mirthless. "They look like they got money."

Eva laughed, a short sharp bark.

The woman didn't even know the names of her grandchildren. Had no idea how many she had. To Eva's way of thinking, it was a good thing. Those kids didn't need to be tainted by this woman ever calling their name on the street, laying any sort of claim on them.

"Oh really?" she asked coolly. "What exactly are you going

to do? Demand their lunch money? Because I don't think Gianna raised any pushovers."

Agnes gave a sullen shrug. "I'm family. Families take care of each other."

Eva saw it clearly for the first time, in the moment. Agnes knew what her buttons were. Family. Responsibility. Guilt. Well, her mother wasn't the only one who could push.

"You know, *Mom*. I couldn't agree more," Eva smiled sweetly, even though the word stuck in her throat. "That's why instead of enabling you with another ten grand, I decided to do something even better."

"Where's my money?" Agnes demanded.

"Oh, you'll get it. But this time you're going to earn it." Eva smiled sweetly, almost enjoying herself. Growing a pair felt pretty damn amazing after a lifetime of guilt-ridden people pleasing.

"What the fuck are you talking about?" Agnes spat out the words.

"Well, family takes care of each other. So when I told Grandma and Grandpa that you were in trouble and needed help, well they drove straight down from Connecticut. We've lined up a sixty-day stay in rehab for you. Once you complete that and pass a weekly drug test for six months in a halfway house, then we'll put you up in an apartment here in town. Maybe you can work part-time at Dad's restaurant or with Emma? You'll be surrounded by family, clean and sober, and enjoying your grandchildren."

"I want my money!"

"You'll get it as an investment in your healthy future," Eva chirped. "We'll cover rehab and your costs in the half-way house afterward. We'll even help with the security deposit for your apartment. You'll finally be part of the family again, a productive member of society."

Agnes reached out, quick as a flash, gripping Eva's wrist. "Just give me the money, and I'm gone. I won't come back. Out of your life forever."

"Oh, but Mom. We're *family*," Eva replied. "We're going to get you the help you need. So, let's get in my car, and we'll drive to Dad and Phoebe's. She's really looking forward to meeting you by the way. Grandma and Grandpa are waiting. Let's go."

"I'm not going anywhere with you! I want my money!" Agnes howled. Her nails dug into Eva's wrist.

Eva used the woman's grip on her to start dragging her toward the door. "Now, I know a life of sobriety sounds pretty scary," she said conversationally. "But I think you'll find in the end it's so rewarding."

Agnes released her grip and took a step backward. "I want my money, and you're going to regret it if you don't give it to me."

Eva plowed on as if she hadn't heard her and opened the front door. "Naturally with your parents in town, I had to tell everyone about our 'relationship' for the past few years. And Grandpa thinks it's only fair that you pay me back for all the loans I gave you. We can work that out later. But, just a head's up, Emma and Gia have a lot of questions for you. Like a *lot*. So it's probably best if we head over there now."

Agnes's crepey skin flushed an angry pink. "You're going to regret this, Evangelina."

"Oh, not as much as you," Eva promised. "But life is full of regrets, isn't it? I think I'm done regretting things."

"Is everything okay?" Eden asked. She was standing in front of the now closed door to the dining room.

Eva winced. She hadn't meant to have her showdown so publicly in Eden's place of business. "Everything's great," Eva said, trying to telegraph an apology to Eden. "My friend Agnes here is checking out today."

"We're sorry to see you go, Agnes," Eden said without a hint of sincerity.

"Now, go pack your things. Everyone is going to be so excited to see you," Eva promised.

"You're going to be sorry," Agnes said, pointing a jagged fingernail in Eva's direction as she backed away from her. She turned and stormed toward the stairs.

"What. Was. That?" Eden asked, her eyes wide.

"I'm so sorry," Eva whispered. "I can't explain it yet, or possibly ever, but I'm so, so sorry for putting you in the middle of this."

"Hey, everyone's got shit, right?" Eden shrugged. "I'm not saying I won't be throwing an internal party when that woman leaves. But I'm also not going to charge you the $500 penalty for her smoking in a non-smoking room."

Eva winced. "I owe you so big for all of this."

"Yeah, pretty much," Eden agreed, leading the way to the desk. "I'm just glad I didn't have to call the cops on the two of you or hose you down."

Eva was glad too. Especially about the cop part. "Thank you for your restraint."

"Well, I figured if you wanted the cops to be involved, there would be a very tall, very broad-chested sheriff already with you. Plus, your makeup is seriously flawless today. Hosing you down would have been a travesty."

Eva laughed. "Thank you on the makeup. The rest of it is this planetary crossing. Everyone is insane," Eva explained.

Eden printed out the room invoice, and Eva gaped at it. "Christ. This woman ate like a high school football team. Corn nuggets?"

"Yeah, I had to barter with Shorty's to get them for her. She was *very* insistent. Traded him my Belgian waffle recipe for an emergency delivery."

"I think I owe you at the very least a really nice purse. This definitely feels like a purse-level apology," Eva mused.

"How 'really nice'?" Eden asked, swiping Eva's credit card.

"I think we're looking at a Michael Kors level."

"I knew we'd be friends," Eden laughed.

They both turned toward the front windows at the sound of tires screeching.

"There she goes," Eden observed as a rusted out blue coupe careened around the first turn of the winding drive.

Eva grinned as she watched the little car disappear. She felt lighter than she had in years. She'd done it. Vanquished the enemy. Now the only thing to do was to come clean to Donovan. And if she could scare her mother out of her life, then she could be brave enough to give Donovan a real shot.

Eva scrawled her signature across the receipt. "We should go out for drinks to celebrate that thing that I can't tell you about."

"We definitely should. I've had a stressful day. A hard-to-please guest left under mysterious circumstances."

Eva glanced around at the lobby's soaring ceiling and thick molding. The staircase was a spectacular combination of ornately carved wood and plush carpet. "Can I have a tour while I'm here?"

"You going to write about an innkeeper?" Eden asked.

"Depends. How sexy is your life?"

"Well, I don't bake biscuits naked. If that's what you're asking."

Eva grinned. "I don't know. You look like you've got some smolder in you."

"The smolder died a long time ago," Eden quipped. "It's mostly smoke and cobwebs at this point.

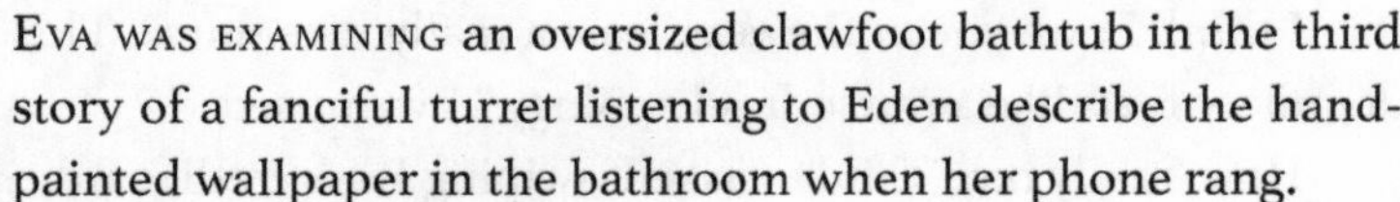

EVA WAS EXAMINING an oversized clawfoot bathtub in the third story of a fanciful turret listening to Eden describe the hand-painted wallpaper in the bathroom when her phone rang.

"Aunt Eva?"

"Yeah, Evan. What's up?"

"There's someone in your house."

Eva's stomach dropped. She held the phone in a white knuckled grip. "What do you mean 'someone'?"

"There's some weird lady. Frizzy hair. I heard glass break, and she went inside, and I don't think she used a key. Roar's at a sleepover and Mom and Beckett are out with Lydia and I—"

"Evan lock your doors. Right now."

"Okay." She heard the snick of a lock and Diesel's big dog bark.

"All of them, okay, bud? I'm on my way." She'd pushed too hard. She thought she finally had the situation under control, and she'd only made it worse. And now Agnes was striking back.

"Should I call the sheriff?"

Damn it all to hell.

"I'm calling him right now, and then I'm going to call you back. Don't open the door for anyone, okay? And keep Diesel with you."

"Geez. Okay. Okay. Is she crazy?"

"She's not nice," Eva said quickly. "And I don't want you anywhere near her."

With a rushed promise that she'd call him right back, Eva hung up and dialed Donovan.

"I need your help," she said, choking on a sob. "Someone broke into my house, and Evan's at home alone."

"Eva—" he began.

But there was no time for explanations. Not with Agnes just steps from Evan. "Just please, Donovan, get there fast. I'm on my way now."

"Eva, stay where you are—"

But she was already hanging up on his order as she pushed the accelerator down. She dialed Beckett and Gia's house, but the line was busy. She alternated calling the house phone and Evan's cell. The minutes dragged on, achingly slow. Even as she whipped the wheel around One Love Park, Eva felt as if everything was in slow motion. She couldn't get there fast enough. She'd pay for this. That's what Agnes told her.

Eva beat Donovan's police cruiser into the driveway by half a second. She jumped out and sprinted for the back door of the house. "Evan!"

Donovan caught her around the waist, lifting her feet off the ground and spinning her around. "Stop." He gave the order with a steely calm that had the fight leaving her.

He put her back on her feet, one strong arm still holding her around the waist.

"Trust me, Eva." He started for the backyard, hand on his gun.

"I'm coming with you," she announced, shadowing his long-legged gait.

He swore quietly. "Stay behind me."

She heard more car doors slam in the driveway, felt her heart clutch when she saw the broken glass on her front porch, the door now ajar.

"Oh, hey guys." Evan appeared on the back porch a cereal bowl and phone in hand. Diesel, fur still bristled, pranced down the porch steps to sniff Donovan's pant leg and roll over on his back.

"Where is she?" Eva asked.

Evan shrugged. "She left about two minutes ago. Carrying

a buncha stuff. She tried to get in the back door, but it was locked, and Diesel jumped at the window and scared the heck out of her." He took a bite of cereal, milk dribbling down his chin.

"Oh, my God, Evan. I'm so sorry," Eva said, wrapping him in a hug and spilling milk and cereal all over them both.

"Evan!" Gia and Beckett rushed around the side of the house with Lydia squalling on Beckett's hip. Gia tossed her phone to the ground and hit them at a dead run knocking them to the porch boards.

"Everything under control?" Deputy Layla jogged around the side of the house.

"Clear the cottage," Donovan said briskly, nodding in the direction of Eva's house. He waded into the pile and pulled Evan to his feet.

"You're going to interview me, right?" Evan asked. "Cause I'm a witness."

"That's right."

"Who would do this?" Gia demanded as Beckett plucked her off the porch before he wrapped Evan in a tight hug.

Donovan stared down at Eva, slowly pulling her to her feet. Guilt had her knees buckling. He held her up, but she could see the hurt, the anger.

"Eva, you'd better tell me right now whether this had anything to do with your hypothetical bullshit last night," Beckett growled, taking a step toward her.

She opened her mouth but found herself facing Donovan's back.

"You're gonna want to calm down, Pierce," Donovan said, slapping a hand on Beckett's chest.

"What's going on?" an out-of-breath Emma demanded as she and Niko ran into the yard.

"Is everyone okay?" Niko asked, scanning the tense faces.

"Eva knows who did this," Beckett said coldly.

"That may be," Donovan said evenly. "But taking a swipe at her now isn't helping me find whoever did this."

Gia grabbed Beckett's arm. "I know this was terrifying, but I can't see how yelling at my sister is helping anything!"

"Eva, start talking," Beckett demanded.

"Stop yelling!" Gia yelled.

"Back off," Donovan warned him. There was no hint of the decades-long friendship between them in that order.

"If you all can sideline the pissing contest, the house is clear but wrecked," Layla announced hopping off the cottage's front porch and crossing the yard. She took an easy stance next to Donovan. But Eva noticed she kept her hand near her cuffs.

"This is all my fault," Eva said, scrubbing her hand over her face.

"Eva, what are you talking about?" Emma asked, climbing the steps of the already overcrowded porch. "Do you know why someone would break in?"

Donovan, careful to keep himself between Beckett and Eva, turned to look at her.

"I know why, and I know who," she admitted, her eyes welling with tears. She willed them away, but there was nothing she could do about the lump in her throat, the ice in her belly.

"Let's go inside and talk," Donovan said quietly.

35

They filed into Beckett's kitchen, and while Gia fussed with bottles of water and glasses of iced tea, Eva sat, face pale, lips tight. Donovan made sure to keep Beckett on the other side of the room. His friend had no idea how close Donovan had come to losing his cool. He was furious with Eva, but that didn't mean he wouldn't stand between her and any threat.

"Who was it, Eva?" Donovan asked, keeping his tone calm, his voice quiet. Layla readied her notebook. It was highly unusual to interview a victim with so many other people present. But this way, Eva would only have to go through it once.

"Agnes." Eva answered quietly.

"Agnes who?" Emma demanded.

"Is this some crazy fan?" Gia asked, sliding a glass of tea in front of Eva.

Eva shook her head. "Agnes Merill."

Gia and Emma froze.

"Mom?"

"Our *mother*?"

Donovan nodded subtly at Layla who scratched the name down on the pad and quietly left the room to call it in to Minnie.

"Why don't you start at the beginning?" he suggested. He could see that his all-business tone hurt her. But that was something that would have to wait until later.

She began with what he knew. The depression, the drugs, Agnes's downward spiral.

Emma and Gia, to their credit, sat quietly, flanked by their husbands, and listened as the story unfolded.

Emma shook her head slowly. "I knew something had changed in her. She'd just... I don't know. Disconnected from us."

Gia nodded, remembering. "I wonder if Dad suspected. He started making us spend our time after school at the restaurant instead of at home with her."

"It explains a lot. I always assumed she'd been unhappy and met someone else," Emma added. Niko laid a hand on her shoulder. Emma reached up to hold it.

"I thought I had done something to make her want to leave," Gia confessed. "She was so angry leading up to her leaving. I hated even having a conversation with her."

Eva was shaking her head. "No. Not you. It was me."

Emma rolled her eyes. "You were eight years old. What did you do that was so horrible she couldn't live with us anymore?"

"I was born," Eva said matter-of-factly.

"Don't be an idiot," Beckett muttered. Donovan shot him a look. The man was skating on very thin ice, even if Donovan agreed with the sentiment.

"She told me, off and on, that I'd ruined her life. That there was an Agnes before me and a different one after me."

"You have zero responsibility for postpartum depression," Gia argued.

"I know that. At least I do now. But I didn't for a long time. The first time she came to me asking for money, she reminded me that she'd left because of me. Because I'd ruined her life."

"That's bullshit," Emma snapped.

"Yeah, well, I was nineteen and naïve."

"So, you paid her," Niko filled in.

Eva nodded. "She always came back. And if I balked or didn't have enough, she'd threaten to come back."

"What do you mean?" Beckett asked.

"She'd make promises about stirring up trouble. Things like paying you all a visit. She'd make comments about how well it looked like Emma was doing for herself in L.A., and she was sure you had some to spare for your poor mother."

"And I would have told her to go fuck herself," Emma snapped. Donovan saw Niko squeeze her shoulder in approval.

"That's why she went after me," Eva whispered. "I was the weak one."

"Now you're starting to piss me off," Gia announced.

Eva shook her head. "You don't understand. I grew up thinking I ruined my own mother's life. I was young enough, dumb enough, to believe what she was telling me. For a long time."

"Why did she show up here?" Beckett asked.

"Because I told her no."

"That's who Jax and I saw you on the street with," Niko guessed.

Eva nodded. "She surprised me seconds after Dad and Phoebe walked out of the coffee shop. Told me she was going to make trouble for all of you if I didn't pay out this time."

"What could she have done?" Emma asked, getting up to pace.

"I can't explain what it's like to have the shadow of this woman hanging over me at all times. Every text, every phone call. Is it her? How much does she need now? Why won't she leave me alone?"

"That's why you moved so much," Gia said quietly.

"She always found me."

"How much money did you give her?" Emma asked.

Eva shrugged.

"Eva," Donovan said.

Her sad hazel eyes met his gaze.

"No more lies," he told her.

"Twenty-six thousand dollars." Anger, hot and fierce, raced through his system, and Donovan wished he could shoot something or at least beat the hell out of someone.

"Why in the hell didn't you tell us?" Gia demanded.

"At first I believed her. That you would blame me if you knew that I was the reason she left. Then I just wanted to keep her far away from all of you."

Gia took a cleansing breath and then another one. And when that one didn't work, she gave up. "I honestly don't know who I'm more mad at right now."

Beckett ran a hand down his wife's hair, a steadying stroke, and Donovan wished he could do the same for Eva. But she needed to finish it.

"Explain what happened today," Donovan told her.

"She put herself up in Eden's B&B. And I had to either get her the money tonight or fess up to Donovan," she said shooting a look at Beckett. "So, I came up with a plan to get her to leave without the money. I figured she kept threatening me with my family, and maybe I could do the same thing."

"How?" Donovan asked.

"I told her that I'd come clean with everyone about everything and that her parents were here and ready to take her to rehab. We were all going to support her recovery and help her get clean so she could be brought back into the fold, so to speak."

"Grandma and Grandpa?" Gia asked. "We haven't seen them in years."

Eva shrugged. "I thought it worked. She panicked and took off."

"That's how you became the monster?" Beckett asked, swiping a hand through his hair. Donovan shot the man a long cold look. If his friend had known anything about the trouble Eva was in and didn't tell him? There wasn't much room for forgiving him.

"Yeah," Eva continued. "And I thought it worked. She ran out of the inn like she had Batman and the cops on her heels. She was so angry at the idea that she'd have to face everyone she abandoned. She doesn't care about any of us. She just pushes buttons until she gets cash."

"So she left the inn, and she came straight here," Donovan said.

"Yes. Evan called me and told me someone had broken in. And I called you, and here we are."

"When you catch her," Emma said, looking at Donovan. "I want ten minutes alone with her."

36

Donovan left the family in the kitchen to talk while he followed Layla through Eva's house. Agnes hadn't had much time inside, but she'd used it to do the maximum amount of damage.

Furniture was over turned, drawers were dumped, and papers were scattered everywhere. Eva's laptop was missing from its habitual spot on the table, Donovan noted.

Satisfied there were no existing threats inside, he instructed Layla to take Eva through her house to start a list of missing items while he interviewed Evan.

He found the boy in the front parlor of the house. It was Gia's space and generally off-limits to the kids. The wainscoting was a dark navy that complimented the fleur-de-lis wallpaper. Antique tables and contemporary, overstuffed couches were arranged around the fireplace. There were candles and color everywhere, reminding Donovan of the woman who had decorated the space.

Evan was sipping hot chocolate on one of the floor pillows in front of the fireplace. Diesel was snoring next to him, and Beckett was pacing the length of the room.

Donovan sat down on the couch closest to Evan.

"Some excitement today," he commented.

The boy nodded enthusiastically. "Sure was."

"How about we start with when you noticed something wasn't right?" Donovan suggested, taking his notebook out.

"Well, I was in the kitchen because I wanted a snack, and Diesel started barking at the back door. I almost let him out, but I saw someone standing on Aunt Eva's porch. Sometimes Diesel scares people when he runs up to them because he's so enthusiastic. So I took a second look."

"Can you describe who you saw for me?"

Evan smirked. "I can do better than that." He held up his cell phone. The one he'd argued for for three months straight before Beckett and Gia had caved.

"Okay, here she is on the porch," he said, opening his photos folder.

Donovan took the phone and scrolled through the pictures. The kid had captured the entire breaking and entering and even shot video of her coming out of Gia's house with her haul of stolen goods. The video cut off abruptly when Agnes climbed the steps to Beckett's back porch but not without catching a full-on of her face.

"Nice work, kid," Donovan said. "I'm gonna need to borrow this, okay?"

Evan nodded. "Would she have hurt Aunt Eva?" he asked.

Beckett cleared his throat, but Donovan ignored him.

"What do you think?"

Evan shrugged. "I mean, she looked kinda frail and rickety. So Aunt Eva could have taken her down pretty easy if she wanted to. But..."

"But there's other ways to hurt people," Donovan finished for him.

"Yeah. How can a mom do that to her own kid?" Evan asked.

"Evan—" Beckett began.

"You guys think a kitchen door is like a cone of silence. I heard everything," he admitted without shame, rolling his eyes.

"I think you already know the answer, right?" Donovan asked him.

"I guess blood doesn't make family," Evan said. "I mean, Gia's not my biological mom, but she's my real mom, right?"

Donovan nodded. "That's right. And just because your mom and aunts' mother wasn't there for them doesn't mean they don't have a real mom."

"Phoebe's their real mom now," Evan decided.

"Exactly."

"But how much does blood have a say in who you are?" he asked.

Donovan blew out a breath and glanced in Beckett's direction. His friend put his hands up in an "all yours" gesture.

"Well, from what I can tell, everyone's got blood and choices. You can come from someone who isn't a good person, but I think it's your choices that determine who you turn out to be."

"Mom and Aunt Eva and Aunt Emma are good people," Evan said.

"Yes, they are."

"And just because my dad's kind of a flake doesn't mean I'm going to turn into him, right?"

"Right. You can still go out and be a lawyer like Beckett. Although, with your work here today, I think you should consider law enforcement."

Evan grinned. "Chicks dig guys in uniform. That's what Oceana tells me."

Donovan cracked a smile. “Again, in my experience, that does seem to be the case.”

“I’ll consider it,” Evan said wisely.

“Did you happen to get a look at the suspect’s car?” Donovan asked.

Evan snorted. “I’m not an amateur.” He pointed at the phone in Donovan’s hand.

Donovan scrolled again and found a picture of an ancient blue Ford Escort and a close up of its license plate. He grinned and ruffled Evan’s hair. “You did good. You kept your head and gathered evidence that’s going to help us catch her.”

“Is Aunt Eva going to be okay? I mean, does she get she’s not going to turn into her mom?”

“I think so,” Donovan said. He hoped so.

“You’ll take care of her? Make her feel better?”

“I will,” Donovan vowed. “But first I gotta yell at her a little bit for not telling us about all this.”

Evan nodded. “It’s only fair. Just maybe don’t yell too loud. Or do it when you’re holding her hand or something so she knows that you still like her even though you’re mad.”

“You’re a smart kid, Evan.”

“Yeah. I’m pretty awesome. Beckett, can I have some more hot chocolate? Maybe pizza, too? Aunt Eva spilled my cereal, and I’m getting real hungry.”

“You can have ten pizzas, Ev,” Beckett promised.

Donovan headed out the door to give them some time, but Beckett caught him.

“We’re gonna need to talk,” Beckett reminded him. “Settle things.”

Donovan gave him a cool look. “I think we might need to do more than talking.”

“You let me know where and when.”

"Go get your kid some pizza," Donovan said and strode down the hallway to the kitchen.

He found Layla, Gia, and Emma in the backyard.

"Where's Eva?" he demanded. The panic from earlier at her strangled voice begging for help resurfaced.

Emma jerked her thumb over her shoulder toward the garden shed in the corner of the yard. The door was ajar and there was a steady thumping noise coming from within.

"She's pissed and scared and guilty and upset. So she's doing a little therapy," Gia told him.

He sighed, handed his notes over to Layla. "Evan got everything on picture and video, including the car's license plate. Get the BOLO issued."

"I'm on it," Layla announced, pulling out her radio and calling Minnie.

"Maybe go easy on her," Gia said, worrying her lower lip. "She's been through a lot."

Donovan shook his head. "Gia, I appreciate the concern, but maybe it's time you stopped worrying about your baby sister so much. She's an adult. A smart one."

"A smart one who made a really stupid choice over and over again," Emma pointed out.

"That's the truth. But there's a difference between supporting her and babying her. And quite frankly, I really need to yell at her because she scared the hell out of me."

"Noted. Yell away," Emma said, slinging an arm over Gia's shoulders.

With a nod, Donovan crossed the yard to the shed. He ducked to get through the door and watched as Eva slammed her fists into the heavy bag hanging from a groaning bracket mounted to a rafter. She saw him but kept hitting. A sheen of sweat glistened on her brow. She was barefoot and pissed, and despite how angry and disappointed he was with her, he was still swamped with a swift rush of love.

He fought the urge to hold her, to wrap her in his arms and never let go. Instead, he leaned against the stud wall and watched her.

She was ablaze. Anger crackled off her, electric in the confined space. *Anger was good*, he thought. It was stronger than defeat, more formidable than fear.

Eva was exhausting herself, fighting through the mad. Her strikes on the bag were weakening, but she kept going. He saw blood and bruising on her knuckles. *Damn it.* Donovan stepped between her and the bag, crowding her against the wall.

She growled, and he took her hands, both as a precaution and to examine her knuckles.

"Why do I want to be mad at you right now?" she grumbled as he stroked a thumb over her abused hands.

"I have no idea, but I'm pretty pissed at you, so we might as well be mad together."

Her shoulders slumped, and he saw her eyes go glassy with tears. *Ah, shit. If she cried he'd be done for.*

"You've done nothing for me to be mad at. I'm the asshole here," she sniffled.

"You'll get no argument from me."

She didn't pull away. Instead, she took her lumps and leaned her forehead against his chest. He gave in for the briefest of seconds and dropped a kiss to the top of her head before pushing her back a step.

"I'm so sorry, Donovan. So sorry. I thought I could handle this on my own. Thought it was better that way. And I screwed it all up."

"And then you went to Beckett."

She winced. "I don't want you to think that I trusted him

over you. I thought he'd fall for my 'hypothetical' situation. But he was sharper than I gave him credit for. I didn't tell him anything either, but he guessed I was in trouble and gave me until tonight to come clean to you."

"And Agnes forced your hand."

Eva shook her head. "I was going to tell you—"

"But you didn't. I find out when the woman who has been blackmailing you for years breaks into your house to collect the payout you denied her this time."

"I suck. I know. Believe me I know. She took my laptop. My grandmother's diamond earrings. Hell, she took all the wine I had in the house."

He cut her off. "Eva, I've put myself out there at every turn. You know how I feel about you." He couldn't quite bring himself to say the words, afraid he'd crumble and sweep her up in his arms. But she needed to know. Needed to get it. "You asked me to trust you, and I did."

A single tear escaped from the corner of her eye, and he wiped it away gently with his thumb.

"I don't know how to tell you how sorry I am, Donovan. You've been nothing but honest with me, and I've been everything but."

"Figure it out."

"What?" she asked, rubbing her cheek against his palm. It killed him just a little to pull his hand back.

"You made this mess. Figure out how to clean it up."

He made a move for the door, but she stopped him. She gripped his wrist in both hands. "Wait. Do you still feel... do you think you still love me?"

He faced her, looked her square in the eyes. "Until the day I die, Evangelina. But that doesn't mean I can't be hurt and disappointed."

She absorbed the words like the blow he'd meant them to be, closing her eyes against them.

"You can't stay at your place tonight," he told her. Back to business. "So, I'd make other arrangements if I were you." And with those words, he turned and exited the shed.

He heard the barrage of fists on the bag as he crossed the yard. He just wanted to go back, to hold her and promise her he'd take care of everything. Vow that no one would ever hurt her again. That Agnes Merill would never get close to her for the rest of her life. But that wasn't what Eva needed. She didn't need blows softened or messes cleaned up. She needed the painful yet invaluable experience of solving her own problems and fixing her own mistakes.

At least he could handle the legal side of things. And nothing would give him a greater sense of satisfaction than locking that woman up. He poked his head into the cottage and shook his head at the destruction. Someone with the intent to do harm had gotten this close to the woman he loved. Mother or not, Agnes would pay.

"We were thinking—"

He spun around and found Gia and Emma standing on the grass, brooms and trash bags in hand. He was already shaking his head. "No. Absolutely not. You can help her clean up the mess *if* she asks you for help. Don't offer, don't do it for her, or I swear to fucking God I will throw you all in jail."

"We just want to help," Emma began.

"Listen to me. Eva's spent her entire life thinking that you wanted to protect her from everything. She thinks she's finally found a way to pay you back by keeping Agnes out of your lives and focused on her, and it blows up in her face. You don't need to fix this for her. *She* needs to fix this for her. She needs to understand that asking for help isn't a weakness and being part of a team means being all in."

Dejected, they muttered their agreement and started carting their cleaning supplies back into the house.

Beckett appeared on his back porch, cup of coffee in hand. "You got time for that talk now?"

"Yeah. Might as well get it over with now." Donovan noticed Niko come out on the porch, but the man made no move to intervene.

Beckett put his mug down on the railing and crossed to Donovan.

Donovan's fist caught him just under the eye, snapping his friend's head back. "Fuck!" Beckett grimaced. "I knew it was going to hurt. But Jesus, do you have steel hands?"

"Don't ever talk to Eva that way again," Donovan said, shaking his hand out.

"Yeah. I know. I think this Uranus shit is getting to all of us. I'll apologize to her. But I was pissed."

"She put herself and your family at risk by keeping secrets," Donovan said. "I get that."

"And if you talked to Gia the way I talked to Eva, I'd be breaking your nose."

"Settled?" Donovan asked, offering his hand.

"Settled." Beckett agreed, shaking it. "Want some ice?"

"God, yes. Your face felt like a cinder block."

"What the hell, Cardona?" Eva ran up, gaping at them.

Beckett, his eye rapidly swelling shut, looped an arm around Eva's shoulders.

"I'm sorry for yelling at you and accusing you of being unconcerned for my family's well-being. I know that's not true and you were just doing your best even though your best sucked."

She was shaking her head at him. "I deserve it. I made mistake after mistake, and I'm so sorry that Evan could have been hurt."

"No one was hurt—besides me," Beckett grinned. "Now maybe we can all team up and make sure this never fucking happens again."

She nodded. "I'm sorry."

"Me, too. Do you want to hit me too?"

Eva shook her head. "No, but maybe a hug would help."

Beckett swept her off her feet and squeezed.

"Okay, that's enough," Donovan said, breaking up the embrace and dragging Eva out of Beckett's arms.

"What the hell is going on out here?" Gia demanded from the porch.

"Beckett walked into Donovan's fist, and everyone is friends again," Niko reported.

"Imbeciles," Emma muttered.

"Next time go for a body shot. I have two consults tomorrow," Beckett groaned touching the swelling under his eye.

"So, how are we going to figure out how to keep Dad from finding out about this," Gia asked. "It's going to be all over town that Eva's house was broken into."

"Shit," Emma said succinctly.

"Maybe we can say that it was just a random act of planetary crossing?" Eva wondered.

Niko closed his eyes and pinched the bridge of his nose. "I'm sorry. Are you guys saying you don't think your father needs to know about Agnes?"

"Of *course* he doesn't need to know," Emma argued, gesturing wildly with her hands. "Things are so good for him right now; if we spring this on him—"

Donovan slapped the handcuffs on her before she could even finish her sentence. "I'm gonna take a raincheck on that ice," he told Beckett.

"What the hell, Cardona?" Emma growled in her best manager voice.

"Donovan! Stop it!" Eva reached for his arm. But he caught her wrists easily enough and slid the zip ties over her hands. Gia took a step toward them as if she was going to help but changed her mind and ducked behind Beckett.

Beckett dragged her out. "Baby, you know that I love you more than anything in this world, but you were enraged at Eva for keeping this from you. Now, you want to do the same thing to your father."

"Beckett Pierce! You and your hulking bodyguard can release me right now because I'm going to murder you both!"

Beckett kissed Gia on the cheek and handed her over. "Good luck, Sheriff."

37

Eva watched Niko waving from the curb as Donovan pulled out of the driveway with the three Merill sisters in the backseat. Emma flicked off her husband despite her bound wrists. Immediately they exploded as one. They were loud and angry and half Italian. Donovan did the only thing he could. He turned the stereo up.

"Where are you taking us?" Eva demanded. If Donovan Cardona thought that he could just arrest her and take her to jail, he had another thing coming.

"Your boyfriend is going to be in so much trouble when these cuffs come off," Emma snarled.

"He's clearly lost his damn mind," Gia muttered. "Maybe we should wave something out the window so everyone will know we're in distress."

"Good idea," Eva rolled into Emma's lap and tried to raise her foot up to the crack in the window.

Donovan, smiling to himself, closed the windows. The yelling in the backseat increased.

"Who's got a cell phone on them?" Eva asked. "Maybe we can call someone?"

"Who can we call? Donovan is the law. Who's going to rescue us from an insane sheriff?" Emma groaned.

"You can't arrest us," Eva tried again, leaning up against the divider between the front and back seats. "We didn't do anything illegal."

"You all are behaving in a manner so stupid it should be illegal," he argued, heading toward the western edge of town.

"Oh, my God. You're not taking us to..." Gia trailed off, her words filled with dread.

"Oh, hell. He's taking us to Dad," Eva whispered.

Emma slumped against the seat. "I'd rather go to jail."

"Donovan, I'm starting to get legitimately pissed at you," Eva warned him.

"Back at ya, baby," he said cheerfully.

He pulled into the parking lot of Villa Harvest, Franklin's charming Italian bistro and parked right outside the front door. "Now don't go anywhere, ladies," Donovan said with a wink and a grin at Eva in the rearview mirror.

"I hate your boyfriend," Emma muttered when he slammed the door and sauntered into the restaurant.

"Is it wrong that I'm the tiniest bit turned on?" Eva wondered out loud.

"Yes!" Emma said.

"Not at all," Gia disagreed. "A hot law enforcement officer handcuffed you and manhandled you into the backseat of a car."

"Fine. You can be mad and turned on," Emma decided. "Just be more mad."

Five minutes passed before Donovan reappeared. He had a large to-go lemonade in one hand and a breadstick in the other. Franklin bustled out behind him.

"They're all yours, Franklin," Donovan said, juggling the

breadstick over to his other hand so he could open the back door.

"Girls, I expected this out of you when you were in high school. Not now that you're all adults," Franklin said, looking more amused than upset.

One by one, Donovan removed their restraints. Eva rubbed her sore wrists. Between her wrists and her knuckles, she was going to be typing with a limp.

And then she remembered she no longer had a laptop because her own mother had stolen it.

She was mentally overwrought, she decided. It was the only explanation for why she burst into tears. She hated heroines that cried at the drop of a hat. She wrote women with steel spines and big balls. Not the quivering, whimpering victim type.

Strong hands cupped her face.

"Everything is going to be just fine, Eva. I promise you," Donovan said, staring down at her. His blue eyes were serious. "Now be a good girl and tell your dad why you made so many boneheaded decisions."

He kissed her lightly on the nose and turned her toward Franklin.

His radio squawked. "Sheriff, you anywhere near the liquor store? We got an unsub riding a tricycle through the aisles."

Donovan swore. "If you need any help with these three hellions, you call me," he told Franklin and climbed back into his car.

Eva watched him leave.

"So, who wants to explain to me why my daughters got arrested today?"

~

It appeared that Phoebe was taking the news harder than Franklin. "Back up a minute," she demanded, pointing a pink-polished nail in Eva's face. "Your mother has been taking money from you for years, following you around the country, and when you said no, she broke into your home and stole from you... *and you told no one?*"

Franklin had given them all a ride to his house so they could yell it out Merill style without witnesses.

Mr. Snuffles waddled out from under the dining room table, gave everyone a good glare, and sneezed his way upstairs away from the noise.

"That pretty much sums it up," Eva admitted with a nod. There was no use hiding or lying now.

"Phoebe, my dear," Franklin said, reaching for his wife's arm as she paced behind his chair. "Why don't you make it clear who you're angry at before Eva gets the wrong idea."

"Your mother." Phoebe spat out the words. "If I could just get five minutes alone with her and a pitchfork, I'd feel much better about all of this. But you're not off the hook either, Eva. You have a responsibility to your family. So I'm mad at Agnes and disappointed in you."

Ouch. That stung just a bit.

"And the rest of you? Thinking you could hide this from your father? I'm very disappointed. He is a wonderful, understanding man. But he also has quite the spine in case you didn't notice when he was raising the three of you! Conspiring to hide something from him that affects the entire family is not just disappointing, it's disrespectful."

Emma and Gia hung their heads.

Franklin kissed Phoebe's hand. "Thank you, my beautiful wife. Now how about you take these two into the kitchen and open a few bottles of wine?"

Phoebe nodded curtly. "Let's go, ladies. You can start practicing your apologies."

"Yes, ma'am," they murmured, rising from the table.

"I could go for some wine," Eva said hopefully.

"You have other business to attend to first," her father said, patting her hand. "Come on."

He led her into his study, a cozy room at the front of the house with all the trappings of both an office and a man cave. It was a chaotic sketch of disorganization with piles of papers, books, and knickknacks jostling for space on every flat surface. Franklin closed the glass doors behind him and gestured for her to take a seat in a chair in front of his desk.

He scooted his desk chair out of the way and fiddled with the combination on the floor safe behind it. He got the combination right on the second try, mumbling the entire time, and triumphantly pulled four envelopes, creased with age from the depths.

Franklin sat down behind the desk, envelopes in hand. "Now, I promised myself that I would never show you what was in these envelopes. And I'm not saying that I regret that decision. But today seems to have made the promise void."

"What's in them? Love letters? Is Agnes not our mom? Do you have other kids somewhere?" The questions spilled out of her mouth, each faster than the last.

Franklin laughed, a big, booming chuckle. "You always did have an excellent imagination. I'm very proud that you're doing something wonderful with it."

"Thank you, Dad. You haven't read any of them, have you?" She wasn't sure she was mentally prepared to hear about her father reading her sex scenes.

"Four so far. I'm waiting for Phoebe to finish the fifth." He grinned.

"Dad you don't have to—"

He raised his hands. "I read the first one to be supportive. I read the next three because you're damn good at what you do, Eva."

"I'm flattered… and a little disturbed."

He chuckled and then sighed. "Enough small talk. I owe you an apology. Possibly more than one."

"Dad, I'm the one who kept this—"

He held up his hands. "I met your mother in the early eighties. She was somewhat of a free spirit. She'd made a few, let's say questionable, life choices, including what I thought were recreational drugs." Eva leaned forward.

"So, she was—"

"Dabbling well before you or I were in the picture."

Eva sat back in her chair to absorb the information. "I had no idea."

"At first, I felt like it was her choice, that she'd grow out of it eventually. But as I got more involved in the restaurant industry, started saving for my own place, she seemed to be clinging to the party lifestyle. So I asked her to make a decision. And she chose me."

Franklin pushed an empty coffee mug around the calendar on his desk that still claimed it was May.

"Things were good for a while. She was clean, working. I was manager at a place in New Haven. And along came Emmaline, and Gianna, and you.

"I was working sixty-hour weeks trying to get my restaurant off the ground. Your mother was left with the rest of our life to manage. Even then I knew that wasn't fair to her. But we had decided together. I didn't see it. I didn't notice the signs."

"Dad, you were providing for us," Eva cut in.

He nodded. "I was. But being a father requires more than bringing home a paycheck. I leaned too heavily on your mother. And I didn't see that she'd returned to familiar coping mechanisms. You knew. At five years old you knew."

"I didn't know exactly what it was. I just knew that when she saw certain 'friends' or took certain pills, she was different," Eva admitted. "I didn't want to tell on her or to make you guys fight."

Her father's shoulders slumped a little lower. "We were fighting a lot towards the end. I know it. I wasn't home enough. She wasn't present enough. It doesn't make me feel good to know that's the kind of home we had created for you. I'm ashamed to admit that when she left, I was relieved."

"That makes two of us," Eva admitted.

Franklin sighed. "I'm sorry for not seeing. I would have fixed it, ended it. I wouldn't have let things go on the way they did."

"I know, Dad. And you have nothing to apologize for. You did the best you could. And for the record, your best is pretty amazing."

He tapped the envelopes on the desk. "There's one more thing. Agnes didn't just disappear."

He turned the envelopes over, fanned them out. And Eva saw the names of her sisters and her father scrawled across them.

"She left notes?"

Franklin nodded. "They're not pleasant. She didn't write them to comfort anyone in her absence. She wrote them to hurt and point fingers. I never gave them to you."

"Can I read them?" Eva asked.

Wordlessly, he pushed them across the desk to her.

Eva opened the one addressed to Franklin.

Frank,

Well, you win. You got your way. Since I can't do anything right in your eyes, I'm leaving. I deserve to have a life, too. One that doesn't revolve around taking care of ungrateful, demanding kids who never see their absent father.

You don't like the way I'm raising them? They're your responsibility now. Have fun with that. Let's see what kind of a father you'll be now that you don't have a choice.

You never were the man I thought you'd be. You're weak and boring. No therapy or counseling is going to fix that. I deserve better. I'm going to have better now that I'm done wasting my time. Don't try to find me. I'm done with you and this joke of a life.

Agnes

Eva blew out a breath and stuffed the paper back in the envelope. "I don't think I need to read the others."

"A wise choice," her father said softly.

"She blamed you."

He nodded. "Yes, she did."

"But she's been telling me all along that I'm the reason she left."

Franklin waved Emma and Gia's letters. "She blamed everyone except herself. Never took an ounce of responsibility. No, I wasn't home enough. No, I didn't help out enough around the house, and maybe I was boring, but that doesn't mean that she was without blame."

"Dad, you were never boring," Eva smiled. "And you were a better father and mother than she could have ever hoped to be."

"I wish I would have told you sooner. If you'd read the letters before she came after you for money—"

She waved a hand. "I probably still would have given it to her. She played me that first time. 'Trying to get her life together. Therapy is expensive.' She said she was entering a counseling program in Pennsylvania and needed money. I'd have fallen for that part of it no matter what. I wanted it to be true."

"And now? What if she comes back to you sometime in the future?" Franklin pressed.

"Never again. I wish I wouldn't have had to learn the lesson so painfully... or so publicly. But Agnes will never see another dime from me."

"And you won't feel the need to keep things from the rest of us?"

"I promise, Dad. And next time, it won't take a ride in a cop car for me to come clean, okay?"

He beamed at her. The man who had loved her unconditionally since birth. The man who had made her favorite meal when she was sad, the one who had made emergency runs to the drug store for tampons and chocolate. The man who would someday walk her down the aisle. She saw a flash of the day. Of Donovan, steadfast and patient waiting for her. His blue eyes gleaming. The faces of her family and friends.

Her mother wouldn't be there. But Eva didn't need her. That spot had long since been filled by her sisters and Phoebe and by friends and neighbors.

"Dad, I'm in love with Donovan." She admitted it in a rush.

His silvery eyebrows winged up. "Well," he said. "What does he say about all this?"

"I haven't told him yet. He thinks he's head over heels for me."

"Well, of course he is, Eva," Franklin sighed.

"Don't go all 'of course he is.' You're biased," she pointed out.

"With good reason," he argued. "And you're going to add a whole new layer of disappointment to how I'm feeling if you actually believe that you're not worthy. It's long past time you got your mother's voice out of your head, Eva."

Is that what it was? That doubt that Donovan might not really *love her?*

"I wouldn't say she's the voice in my head. But I'm willing to admit I might hear her whisper occasionally."

"Do you doubt that you love him?"

She felt the smile, blindingly bright, spread across her face. She shook her head. "Nope. I think this is the real deal. We've been moving so fast. I'd like to slow it down a little bit."

"Sometimes fast doesn't mean wrong," Franklin said with a wink. "Not when happiness is on the line."

"My own father quoting my writing back to me," Eva laughed.

"Maybe you should start listening to yourself. Or at least your characters," he suggested.

Eva blew out a breath. "I feel like today was one really long, painful therapy session."

"Then let's go take our medicine." Franklin pointed behind her. Eva turned. Phoebe was standing on the other side of the doors wiggling two empty glasses and a bottle of wine. They met her at the door. Phoebe poured, and Eva sipped as they headed back to the kitchen.

"Just to recap," Phoebe said, gesturing with the bottle. "I'm a lot mad at Agnes and only a tiny bit mad at you, but that doesn't mean that I don't love you."

Eva wrapped an arm around Phoebe's shoulders. "Thanks, Mom." She gave her a smacking kiss on the cheek.

"Now, come on and help me figure out why Emma turned down a glass of wine."

Eva's gaze flew to her sister's face. Emma, stylish as ever with her swing of red hair and designer clothes, was sipping ice water and laughing at a story about Aurora that Gia was telling.

"Holy. Shit. You're glowing," Eva gasped.

Emma flushed scarlet to the roots of her hair. "No. I'm not."

"You're glowing, and you're drinking ice water instead of day drinking with the rest of us," Eva pointed out.

"Oh, my God!" Gia squealed. "You're—"

"Don't you dare say it," Emma shrieked, holding her hands up. "No one say the word."

"What word?" Franklin asked, baffled.

"Okay, no one is saying the 'p' word. But are you?" Eva asked, bouncing on her toes.

"If I am, I want to tell Niko first."

"Tell him what?" Franklin asked.

"That he's going to be a daddy," Emma said, promptly bursting into tears.

38

Eva juggled grocery bags and her overnight tote as she climbed the steps of Donovan's porch. The sky was already going to dusk, and the lights were on inside, casting a soft glow through the windows. He wasn't home. She'd seen him talking to a group of kids who were inexplicably painted blue in One Love Park. She'd made a mental note to get the story out of him or out of Evan.

But for now, she had important business. Food was love in the Merill family, and she was going to cook the hell out of some pasta for Donovan tonight. But first, she had to get past the gatekeeper. She took a deep breath and rang the doorbell.

Hazel Cardona answered the door in jeans, a crisp button down, and vest. Even retired, everything about her said "law enforcement."

"Eva, this is a nice surprise. I hope you don't think you have to ring the bell just because we're here."

"I knew Donovan wasn't here, and I didn't want to interrupt...anything..."

Hazel laughed. "Michael told me he was ribbing Donovan about our sex life. But, of course, that wouldn't embarrass you being a romance novelist and all. If it wouldn't give Donovan a heart attack, I could tell you a few stories. Come on in." She stepped back from the door and took two of the bags from Eva. "Cooking for an army tonight?"

"It's an apology dinner," Eva said, pushing a strand of hair out of her face. "I screwed up. Pretty big. I'm hoping the spaghetti will soften him up."

"The boy never could turn down a home-cooked meal," Hazel winked. "Wanna talk about the screw up?" she asked over her shoulder as she carried the bags back to the kitchen.

The Eva of yesterday would have side-stepped the question and turned the attention on someone else. But a whole hell of a lot had happened in twenty-four hours, and if she was really turning over a new leaf, then she might as well turn it with Donovan's mother. "Let me give you the background since the Facebook group is out of commission and you may not have heard the whole story yet," Eva offered.

"Your mother has been coming after you for money for years. She followed you here looking for a handout, and when you said no, she got nasty," Hazel summarized.

"Well, that's the backstory I guess." Eva dumped her bags on the counter and started stashing ingredients in the fridge.

"My son gave me the bare bones, and Phoebe filled in the rest. I like you, Eva. And I *really* like your books. My husband is quite the fan too, if you know what I mean," she grinned. "Anyway, let me give you a couple of what kids today would call 'cheat codes' when it comes to my son."

"Please do."

"He is a good man through and through. He stands between his people and danger."

"It's his hero complex," Eva sighed.

Hazel shook her head. "Oh, no. It's bone deep. He's a fixer. He sees a problem, an injustice, a hurt? Well, he's going to do everything in his power to right the wrong. Depriving him of that? Of at least letting him in on the problem? It cuts deep. It says to him that you don't trust him."

"I do. I really do. I just wanted to solve it on my own."

"I get it," Hazel said, crossing her arms. "I really do. You're independent. You stand on your own two feet, solve your own problems. Only maybe you haven't been solving them real well alone? Maybe you could take advantage of your resources and find a better solution."

"And maybe you're in town because Donovan needs help."

The corner of Hazel's mouth quirked. "He hasn't asked. Yet."

"But you'll be there when he does."

"As long as he's not as damn stubborn as his girlfriend," Hazel grinned.

"Well, let's hope that's not the case." Eva plucked ripe tomatoes out of one of the bags and began to slice.

Hazel peered into the bags. "You're making me sorry we're missing dinner."

"You won't be here?" Eva asked. "I brought enough for a small army."

"An apology will go over better without me and Michael slurping up noodles. Besides, Michael just landed four tickets to an eighties revival concert at a winery in the Finger Lakes. Last minute, but we're taking Phoebe and Franklin with us overnight."

"Oh, they'll love that," Eva said. "I think you'll like my dad. He's pretty much the best human being I know. Ranks right up there with your son… if he's smart enough to accept my apology."

Hazel gave her that crooked grin. "He'll make you work for it. But you'll do okay, Eva. You and Donovan will be just fine," she predicted.

DONOVAN NOTED the smoke coming from his chimney as he pulled into the garage. It was dark, and there was a bite to the night air. There was a frost warning tonight, and his parents must have lit the fire to warm up the house.

Maybe there was a small benefit to having his parents crash with him. He might even be lucky enough to find dinner on the table.

He sighed and ducked under the garage door as it closed. Damn if he didn't need something to go his way today. The mess with Eva weighed heavy. She hadn't texted or called after he'd dropped her unceremoniously in her father's lap. Not that he'd expected her to. He needed her to work through this on her own, and he hoped she'd find her way back to him.

In the meantime, he'd personally made sure that every station in a five-hundred-mile radius was on the lookout for one Agnes Merill. He'd find her, and when he did, she'd never go near his Eva again. Between spreading the word, he'd taken half a dozen calls and plowed through a fraction of the backlog of reports that his desk was buckling under.

He checked his phone as he trudged up the porch steps.

Still no messages from her. God, he needed her tonight. Wanted her naked in his bed or curled up against him on the couch. Any way he could get her, Donovan needed Eva. It killed him to think that she could have asked him for help. That she'd gone to Beckett with hypotheticals rather than trusting him to help her.

He got it. He did. It was important to her to stand on her own two feet. But dammit, she'd put herself in danger. He didn't know what Agnes was capable of, but it wasn't the upstanding citizen that bilked their own daughter out of $26,000. He could—and would—take care of the legal end of things, ensure that Agnes was out of Eva's life forever. But he'd have to wait for Eva to do her best to clean up the situation on her end. She needed to solve it herself. And he needed to let her.

He opened the front door and wondered when the hell he was going to get a dog. He'd meant to. As much as he enjoyed the privacy and solitude of his cabin, sometimes it was downright lonely. The property was perfect for a dog, and he wouldn't mind a four-legged pal to take to the station with him. Maybe after this cosmic shitstorm was over and everything went back to normal he'd visit the shelter and see who looked like a cop dog. He'd take the Pierces with him. After all, they had experience adopting every single homeless animal in Blue Moon.

His house smelled like garlic and basil and a dozen other scents that had his stomach growling.

"I'm home," he called, not wanting to catch his parents in an embarrassingly intimate moment in his kitchen as he had so often growing up.

His heart rolled over in his chest when Eva appeared, barefoot in leggings and an off-the-shoulder t-shirt. A cheery red apron covered most of her except for the lacy bra strap peeking out from under her shirt. He itched to touch it.

She was holding a beer.

"Hi."

"Hi," he repeated. He clenched his hands at his sides so he wouldn't grab her and hold her.

She wet her lips, and despite his best intentions he went rock hard, his dick straining against the zipper of his uniform pants.

"I made you an apology dinner," she said, offering a shy smile. "Spaghetti." She held the beer out to him.

"You're apologizing with food?" Their fingers brushed

when he took the beer from her, and the contact jolted him as it always did.

"Among other things," she said lightly. "I hope you don't mind if I stay tonight. I'm not supposed to stay at my place."

If Donovan had his way she'd never go back there again. She'd stay here, write, cook, play with their future dog, let him rub her feet. Hell, whatever she wanted to do. But she had to choose him, choose them.

"Do I have time for a shower?" he asked, still careful not to touch her.

She nodded. "I need a few minutes for the garlic bread. I laid out some comfy clothes for you on the bed. I hope you don't mind."

Her hesitancy cut at him. *All he wanted was for her to be happy and safe... and here with him.*

"I love you, Eva. Don't think that just because I'm supremely pissed at you that I don't mean that anymore."

She closed her eyes and took a shaky breath. "I'll make it up to you," she promised.

"It better be one hell of a dinner," he said lightly.

She smiled softly. "Cardona, you have no idea. Go shower and change," she ordered, slapping him on the ass. And damn if that didn't make him even harder.

One cold as fuck shower and a pair of sweatpants later, Donovan wandered back into the kitchen pulling a t-shirt on over his head. Eva bobbled the bowl of pasta that she was carrying, and he smirked.

"Like what you see, Evangelina?"

She walked smack into an open cabinet door before he caught her.

"Oh, my God. It should be illegal to smell that good," she breathed.

He took the bowl from her. "Table?" he asked.

She nodded, nervously fingering the tie to the apron.

She'd already set the table, he noted. And the fire in the living room was crackling away. There were lit candles dotting window sills and table tops.

"Where are my parents?" he asked, realizing they weren't in residence.

"They're doing an overnight at Seneca Lake with my parents," Eva called from the kitchen where she wrestled the sauce pan off the stove.

Envisioning a night in the ER with second degree burns, he took it from her and placed it on the hot pad on the table.

"I had a long talk with Phoebe and my dad today," she said, taking the garlic bread sprinkled with—dear God, was that real mozzarella? —cheese out of the oven. "And then I had another one with your mother when I showed up here."

Donovan's eyebrows winged up. "How did those talks go?"

She took a deep breath as she quickly transferred bread to basket blowing on her finger tips.

"Baby, please use tongs," Donovan said, slapping a pair down next to her.

"You can take the salad in," she said, jutting her chin in the direction of the fresh greens on the counter.

He did as he was told and waited patiently for her to fill him in.

They sat and dished out the food, Eva handing him shaved Parmesan before he could even scan the table for it. "My father, being the perfect human being he is, was incredibly supportive and forgiving. Phoebe, on the other hand, nailed my ass to the wall for being 'selfishly and unnecessarily independent.'"

Donovan, convinced his mouth was about to meet heaven, twirled his fork into the obscene pile of spaghetti on his plate. "She did, did she?"

"You're not going to give her a black eye, are you?" Eva asked, sipping her wine.

"I hit Beckett for a different reason," Donovan argued. He put the fork in his mouth and let his eyes roll back in his head. "My god, woman."

"Told you," she said smugly. "Now, back to you punching Beckett. You hit him because he yelled at your woman?" Eva guessed.

"He kicked you when you were down. Granted, he was scared, and you did endanger his family, but—" he caught her wince, "you thought you were keeping everyone safe by putting yourself between Agnes and them." Donovan snuck another bite of literally the best spaghetti he'd ever had in his life.

"I really did. It seems stupid now, but I thought she'd ruin everyone else's lives like she'd ruined mine."

He covered her hand with his. "She didn't ruin anything. You're here now. Aren't you?"

"If you'll accept my apology and let me stay tonight."

Tonight wasn't enough in Donovan's book. He wanted forever. "Well, let's try it out. See how good your apology is. And just so you know, you're important to me, Eva. And I'm not going to let anyone, even one of my lifelong best friends, kick you when you're down."

"I'm sorry you and Beckett fought because of me. And I'm beyond sorry that I didn't come clean with you. I never told anyone about Agnes. She taints everything she touches. I've dreaded the sound of my text alerts since I was nineteen years old and she found me the first time."

She played with her pasta on her plate rather than eating it.

"She showed up on campus with some down-on-her-luck story about trying to get enough money to get away from the drugs and the bad people in her life, get into a program. I gave her everything I had. Forty-two dollars. And as she was leaving, she told me I'd done the right thing since it was my fault she left anyway."

Donovan's hand tightened on his fork. "It wasn't the first time she'd said that to you," he said recalling the retelling at Beckett's.

Shamefully, Eva shook her head. "She used to tell me when I was a little kid that I'd ruined her life. Every time she'd cry or yell, it was because of me. My fault. I couldn't behave or I couldn't be what she needed."

Donovan swore and pushed his chair back from the table. "Come here," he ordered.

Eva abandoned her chair and slid a slim leg over his lap to straddle him on his chair. He threaded his fingers through her hair, pushing it back from her face. "Baby, tell me you know that's not true."

She melted into his touch, needing to accept it as much as he needed to give it.

"I know it's not true in the way she meant it. But the facts are the facts. She was a different woman after I was born."

He started to argue, but she placed her hand over his mouth. "Wait," she said softly. "Dad told me today that she'd experimented with drugs before. He'd caught her once or twice and put his foot down. It was him or the drugs, and she got clean. But she had that history. It didn't all start with me."

"It wasn't you, Eva. It was never you."

"I know, but try telling that to the five-year-old inside me. This helped. Knowing that I wasn't the beginning of it. But that doesn't change the fact that I royally screwed up with you."

"No, it doesn't," he agreed.

"Not going to make it easy for me, are you?"

"Why didn't you tell me, Eva?"

"I didn't want you judging me based on what I came from. Your parents are wonderful and giving and kind. And so is my father, but doesn't it give you pause at all to know that I come from Agnes? That I have that in me?"

"Sweetheart, what decision in your life have you ever made that lined up with Agnes?"

"Maybe I've been pushing you away because part of me believed what she said. And maybe I'm done thinking like that. I'm sorry. I'm so sorry for hurting you. I can't imagine how it felt to find out this way and to know that I didn't come to you with this."

"It killed me, Eva. I need you to trust me, believe in me. I don't need to fix things for you—though I might be inclined to be consulted—I just need you to trust me enough to let me in. You can't spend your whole life keeping secrets from people, from me."

She took a deep breath and closed her eyes. "Are you ready for one more?"

"A secret? Good god, woman, how many do you have in that vault of yours?"

"I love you, Donovan Cardona."

39

He gripped her hips hard. He hadn't known he'd needed the words so very badly until he'd heard them.

"That's some apology, Eva."

"That's an addendum to the apology. I'm sorry. I love you. Two separate statements," she said. Her eyes were cloudy with tears.

"Don't you dare cry. It'll tear me up inside," he warned her.

"Dammit. I never cry!" A tear escaped, and she swiped at it nervously. "Shit. Okay. I love you Donovan for everything that you are and everything that you see in me. And I don't care if it is the whole planetary crossing or not. I'm all in."

"I'm going to want marriage, Eva," he warned. "Definitely a dog. Some kids."

"That sounds pretty good to me. In time," she clarified, laughing through the tears. "I promise I won't lie to you again unless it's about a surprise party or a Christmas present."

"What about withholding? You seem to do that more often than outright lie."

"I won't do that either. Unless absolutely necessary for happy surprise purposes."

He pinched her, and she laughed.

"Apology accepted," he said, bringing his mouth to hers.

"You didn't even try the garlic bread. That was supposed to be the clincher."

"You're the clincher, baby. We'll eat later."

He kissed her hard and let the fire spark to life inside them. She shifted against him, rocking into his hard-on, and he saw stars behind his eyes. When she breathed out that soft little moan against him, he knew love.

Holding her by the hips, he ground his cock against her.

"Please, Donovan. God, *please*."

"All you have to do is ask, Eva."

"Oh my God. Here? Please?" she breathed.

"Here first," he said darkly. "Another fantasy."

Her hands streaked under his shirt pushing it up his chest.

He grabbed the cotton behind his neck and dragged it off his head before diving down to capture her mouth. When she accepted the thrust of his tongue into her mouth, Donovan felt beyond possessive, beyond hungry.

He abandoned her lips only long enough to pull her t-shirt over her head.

She was wearing another one of those lacy lounge bras that drove him insane. So delicate, tempting him with what was visible beneath. "Jesus, woman. You drive me over the edge."

"I haven't even done anything. Yet," she laughed, her voice low. She wiggled off his lap, and as he reached for her to bring her back, she dropped to her knees between his legs. His breath left him in a hiss when she worked the drawstring of his sweatpants loose.

There was already a wet dot visible at the front of his

pants. This is what she did to him, made him want beyond anything he'd ever felt before.

"Do you see what you do to me?" he rasped.

Eva's gaze found his and held as she stripped him of his pants. He watched her as she eagerly gripped him by the root. "Go slow, baby," he warned. But Eva didn't listen. She never did.

Every muscle in his body tensed as her lips parted over his already wet crown. He fisted his hand in her hair, drawing a squeak from her when he pulled just a little too hard.

He wanted to apologize, but the words wouldn't come. All that existed was her hot little mouth on his cock. She worked him with hand and mouth, dragging him toward the edge faster than any fantasy.

"Shit. Eva, you need to stop."

But still her lips flowed over him, tasting, sucking. He felt the release build in the tightening of his balls. "Eva!"

"Come for me, Donovan. Let me taste you," she demanded before taking him to the back of her throat.

He came, shouting her name and pulling that red hair. Every muscle tensed with an orgasm that blazed through his system, lighting him on fire.

"Fuck. Baby, I told you to stop," he admonished, his breath coming in gasps.

She released him from her mouth, a cocky smile playing on her lips. "Oops. Guess I didn't hear you over all the prayers and you screaming my name."

"If that was part of your apology, I can't wait 'til you fuck up again," Donovan said.

"How are you still hard after that?" Eva demanded, staring at his half-mast dick.

"Super power," he said, not bothering to pull his pants

back up. He liked the way she was eyeing him. "Now let me show you another of mine."

He pulled her to her feet and shoved her leggings down with more enthusiasm than finesse. He lifted her from the waist and settled her ass on the dining room table, spreading her thighs wide.

"Oh, shit," she breathed.

"Lay down," he ordered her, shoving plates and dishes further down the table. "Lay down and spread yourself open."

She honest-to-God whimpered as she complied, and he went from half hard to all the way on that breathy noise alone. He knelt on the floor and slid his hands under the sweet curves of her ass. "The things I'm going to do to you," he murmured just before sliding his tongue through her folds.

Eva hissed. She was rainforest wet, slick and hot and ready for him. And she'd gotten that way by touching him, tasting him. He growled. Using his shoulders, he braced her knees apart so she was spread before him. Donovan lifted her higher so he could feed. He sampled her flesh, teasing and tasting. Using his tongue to make her writhe against him on the table.

He plunged into her, using shallow thrusts of his tongue to make her say his name over and over again. Then, when he felt her coiling around him, he sheathed two fingers into her and brushed his lips and tongue over that tight bundle of nerves.

Every muscle in her body tightened and froze. Her breath stilled as she went stiff as a board, and then those beautiful tremors exploded, closing around the fingers he crooked inside her.

"Yes, Eva. My beautiful girl." He breathed the words against her, licking at her with measured strokes as she trembled beneath him.

He ached for her. His cock throbbed as if he hadn't had an

axis-shifting orgasm minutes ago. It was never enough. He always wanted more from her, with her.

She was loose and limp in front of him, a secret smile of satisfaction blooming on her beautiful face.

"Do you want more, Eva?" he asked, his voice gravelly with desire.

She opened those hazel eyes slowly, smiled lazily, and nodded.

"Tell me." He stroked his palms over the smooth skin of her stomach.

"I want to feel you inside me. I want you to ride me here until we use each other up." Her whispered confession had his head spinning.

He was wild when he stood, rough when he yanked her to him. She stared greedily at his cock splayed across her belly as he lowered himself to take her mouth with his.

"Donovan," she moaned under his lips.

"I love it when you beg me, Eva. You're better than every fantasy." He stroked eager hands over the lush curves of her breasts, pausing to nuzzle at the peaks.

She bucked her hips against him. "I want you so much it hurts," she confessed.

"Now you know how I've felt since I first saw you."

Waiting was torture, but he wanted—needed—this to last. Fisting his erection he stroked, priming himself.

"Jesus, Cardona. Hurry the hell up," Eva demanded, her voice ragged.

He couldn't say no to that. Notching the broad head of his cock against her opening, he hinged forward to grip her chin. He wanted Eva to watch him take her. Watch what being inside her did to him.

With every ounce of control he had left, he eased into her until he was fully sheathed inside her. Their gazes connected, held, and Donovan swore he could see her thoughts. "You're mine, Eva. You can't feel this and question it." It was truth, plain and simple. There would be a ring, and a home, a family, and a lifetime of nights just like this one.

She tightened around him, a velvet vise, as her body reacted to his words. "Donovan! I'm—" Her words cut off, and he felt her shatter around him, her orgasm taking them both by surprise. She bowed up as her body ran with the release. It nearly carried him with it, those tremors milking him as he stroked in and out of her. But he held on, gritting his teeth.

"You're so beautiful when you come, baby."

"I need you closer," she murmured, reaching for him.

Donovan rested a knee on the table and leaned over her. The change in angle brought a gasp to her lips. Eva brought her hands to his face, her soft palms rubbing across the stubble on his jaw.

It was exquisite torture taking his time. She stared into him, her full lips parted as he began to move. Slowly, slowly, he eased out of her before sliding back in to the hilt. It wasn't a race. They had a lifetime ahead of them. He stared down at her, this spectacular creature naked in the candlelight, her eyes glassy with desire.

She moved her hands to his shoulders and dug in with her fingernails. He liked it, that little bite of pain. It made him impossibly harder, and he knew when he came, he might die.

"Say the words, Eva." He gritted out his demand.

"I love you, Donovan! I love you!" She chanted it over and over again. Every thrust. He couldn't keep it slow, not with his orgasm building. He was getting rougher, and Eva liked it.

"I need you to come again, baby."

"I don't know if I—"

He shifted, slamming his cock into her. Her eyes glazed over.

"Oh, shit."

Donovan braced himself on one hand and used his thumb to work her toward the edge as his balls tightened. "Come now."

She dug her fingers into his shoulders, eyes wide. He couldn't hold back anymore. His release erupted out of him. Grunting, he pushed into her and felt that wet vise close around him. She screamed, her nails tearing at his skin. He was grunting, thrusting, completely lost in the pleasure that burst like an inferno between them.

They used each other, riding out their orgasms until there was nothing but weak tremors left. Donovan's knees buckled, but he didn't want to leave her. So he dragged her to the floor with him. They lay on the rug, half under the table in a tangle of limbs and not-quite discarded clothing. Her hair spilled over his shoulder. His hand splayed between her breasts.

"Put that in your book," he challenged, miming a mic drop.

She laughed. "I have a feeling I left an ass print on your table."

"God, I hope so." He traced a finger over the curve of her breast.

"Am I forgiven?" she asked, lacing her fingers with his.

"You're probably the best apologizer I've ever seen in action. You could have stolen my truck and driven through half of the businesses on the square in town, and I'd still have forgiven you."

Eva lolled her head to the side to look at him. "You know, if this is how you accept apologies, I can't wait to have something new to apologize for."

~

To: Beautification Committee
From: Bruce Oakleigh
Subject: Current business

Hello, fellow B.C. members,

Bruce Oakleigh here, your faithful president. We've got a few housekeeping details to take care of before our next meeting.

Everyone can stop sending me instigation scenarios for the Eden-Davis match, hereafter known as Operation Inebriated Chinchilla. We've had a doozy of a suggestion from yours truly that I can't wait to share with you. It's guaranteed to spark friendly feelings between our matchees. Does anyone have any experience with stink bombs?

Our next regularly scheduled meeting falls on Halloween, and I know we'd all like to attend the Halloween Carnival. I am fine with rescheduling for the following evening as long as everyone is willing to picket She Who Shall Not Be Named's wedding as planned. To be respectful, we won't chant during the vows, but we will be waving our signs and frowning fiercely.

Amethyst and I are looking forward to seeing everyone's costumes!

Yours in matching success,
Bruce Oakleigh

40

Donovan scrolled through the electronic record of one Agnes Merill—or Agnes Miller, depending on the alias and the woman's mood. She'd been picked up for shoplifting in Buffalo and had two DUIs, one in Allentown, Pennsylvania, and another one in New Haven, Connecticut. She hadn't shown in court for either of those.

Then there was the string of bad checks scattered across four states, two counts of breaking and entering in New Jersey, and three counts of possession, two with intent to sell.

She'd skipped out on every warrant, bailed on every court date. Donovan was well aware of how overtaxed the court system was, but it was still frustrating that criminals like Agnes Merill walked the streets, wreaking havoc until they got busted for something they couldn't post bail for.

And if he didn't find her fast, that's exactly what would happen here. He felt helpless sitting here waiting. But it was only a matter of time before she was picked up.

Minnie poked her head into his office. "Quite the rap sheet isn't it?"

Donovan rubbed the back of his neck. "Now, Minnie. I don't need to tell you this is all confidential, do I?"

She rolled her eyes at him like a teenager, meaning she'd already told the entire town. "Everyone's worried about Eva. We don't like when someone comes in here and messes with one of our own. We're all watching out for her," she sniffed.

Donovan sighed. All of Eva's secrets had gone from vault to public in a matter of days. And as glad as he was that she wasn't keeping them to herself anymore, he didn't want her to feel the scrutiny of the public's opinion.

"When we find her, just please keep it under your hat until I've had the chance to talk to Eva, okay?"

"Sure, Sheriff. Hope you catch the bitch," Minnie said with uncharacteristic venom.

He would, and when he was done with her, Agnes would regret ever coming to Blue Moon.

CHARISMA CHAMPION TOOK the chair across from Eva in a bizarre yet pleasing cloud of patchouli and homemade bread.

Eva bit back a sigh and tugged the headphones off her ears. She'd borrowed an old laptop from the black-eyed Beckett and set up shop at Overly Caffeinated to pour herself into writing. No thieving mother or public shame was going to derail this book. Certainly not while she tried to transcribe everything Donovan said to her last night while working her body into one human-sized orgasm. With inspiration like that, nothing was going to keep her away from her online backups.

"Eva," Charisma breathed as if she was fogging up a crystal ball. "So lovely to finally meet you. I'm Charisma." She held out a hand decorated with moonstone and amethyst rings.

"It's nice to meet you as well," Eva commented, shaking

the offered hand. "What brings you out in the middle of a school day?"

"Oh, I have the meditation class right now. It's basically naptime for eighth graders. I usually sneak out. And when I saw you here, I felt like it was fate."

"Hmm, fate. Okay."

"This trouble with your mother," Charisma began.

In her head, Eva heard the sound of the figurative shoe dropping. She'd purposely chosen to show her face in town today. Dealing with the public fallout of her choices was one reason. The other possibly more prevalent one was the fact that she just wasn't ready to return to her house yet.

"Is this typical behavior for her?" Charisma asked.

Eva tilted her head. "Why do you ask?"

"Well, I'm concerned that this planetary event that we're experiencing may be affecting more than just Blue Moon. I understand you've been estranged from your mother, but I wasn't certain that she has shown a history of criminal behavior. If this is bigger than Blue Moon, we could be looking at a multi-state disaster next week."

Next week. Halloween and Ellery's wedding.

Charisma pressed on in true small-town gossip fashion. "Now, I've heard from a few sources that your mother has a long history with, shall we say *disagreeable* behavior. Then there's the story that she left your family to join a convent, and that's where she's been for all these years and just suddenly decided to renounce her vows, reconnect with you, and break into your home. Which could indicate that the radius of this planetary crossing is increasing. Which would mean that my calculations were incorrect, and that's never happened before."

Charisma's voice got higher and shriller with every

sentence. She was a woman who took her calculations seriously.

"I think your calculations are intact," Eva said, taking pity on the woman's crisis of self-confidence. "My mother hasn't been a pillar of society for a very long time."

"Thank goodness! You had me worried there for a moment. Whew!" Charisma wiped her brow in relief.

"I'm glad to alleviate your fears," Eva said dryly.

"Yerba mate with a side of wheat grass," the eyebrow-ringed barista called from the counter.

"Oh, that's me! I'd better be getting back to my class. So glad your mother's a criminal!"

"Uh, me too?" Eva watched Charisma grab her drink and head for the door.

"I'll see you tonight, Eva!" Charisma called cheerily as she exited.

"Tonight?" Eva asked no one in particular.

The barista shrugged and went back to his graphic novel.

Eva shook her head and put her headphones back on.

She dug back into her backlog of social media and email correspondence first. She didn't like going too long without talking to her fans. The days of sending handwritten fan letters to a publisher who may or may not forward your sentiments on to your favorite author were long gone. Now, she could speak directly with her readers and get instant feedback on titles, covers, and plots.

And torture them with sneak peeks at her work in progress.

She replied to comments and emails, trying not to let her head get too big when one reader compared her to *the* Nora Roberts.

She felt her table jostle and looked up to find Rainbow and Gordon Berkowicz crowding a third chair around it. They settled and stared at her expectantly until she removed her headphones.

"Hello, Berkowiczs," she said. Gordon was in his usual uniform of dirty, decades-old cargo pants and a t-shirt that fit him a bit better when he graduated high school. Rainbow was in her traditional bank attire in a neat-as-a-pin pantsuit.

"We're here on official you-know-what business," Gordon said in a hushed whisper. In the perusal of her pink heart binder, Eva had noted that discussing the Beautification Committee and its business was strictly forbidden in public.

"Shouldn't we be discussing this in private?" Eva asked, glancing around them at the quiet café.

"Subsection 2C allows for public discussion in the event of an emergency." Rainbow rattled off what Eva could only assume was B.C. procedural code.

"What's the emergency?" Her curiosity was piqued.

They shared a glance and Rainbow nodded at Gordon. "We heard about your mother," he told her.

Dang small towns.

"Yes, my mother broke into my home after blackmailing me for years. No, she did not escape a convent. And I don't think it's related to the planetary crossing. Anything else?"

"Well, how are you feeling, dear?" Gordon asked, patting her hand.

"We can only imagine the upheaval this has been for you. And if you feel at any time that you think it's negatively affecting your abandonment issues, we're prepared to drop all current projects and focus on you," Rainbow jumped in.

"All current projects, including picketing Ellery's wedding?" Eva asked.

"Of course. But only if you feel that this unfortunate run-in with your mother is going to have a detrimental effect on your relationship with Sheriff Cardona," Rainbow said.

"Yes," Gordon said. "We were surprised to find you two were getting so serious despite the B.C's request that you work on yourself first. But that's young love for you."

Eva rubbed her eyes and debated just exactly how much she cared for Ellery. *Hell.* Her little goth pal, a woman who had been nothing but absolutely lovely to her, was getting married. And here was Eva's chance to ensure her perfect day.

"You know, now that you mention it, I've been feeling a little..." she glanced at the two of them. "Unhinged?"

Rainbow slapped Gordon on the shoulder. "We had a feeling," she said knowingly. "We'll work out a treatment plan immediately."

Eva cleared her throat. "And will this treatment be *confidential*?" she asked, wondering what further damage Beautification Committee interference would do to her already dingy reputation.

"Of course. Everything we do is confidential," Rainbow reminded her.

That word did not mean to Blue Moon what it meant to the rest of the world.

They rose and Rainbow patted Eva awkwardly on the shoulder. "You don't have to worry about a thing. We'll take care of everything. I'll contact Donovan directly about his role."

Eva opened her mouth and managed a strangled "Uhhhh?" before they hit the door.

"See you tonight." Rainbow waved cheerily.

Eva walked herself through her usual coping mechanisms and discarded them immediately. Nope. Keeping this one to herself wasn't going to do any good.

She dialed Donovan. "How good of a mood did last night put you in?" she asked.

"I'm skipping down the street leaving puppies and rainbows in my wake."

"Oh good. Because I just did something you're going to hate."

~

BY THE TIME Eva left the café, it was getting dark, and she was worn out. She managed to convince Donovan that going to whatever couples counseling options the Beautification Committee provided would keep them from stink bombing someone's house and ruining Ellery's wedding. He wasn't happy, but she'd promised to fix that too with another stellar apology. That had cheered him up considerably.

She'd debated calling Ellery but decided the bride didn't need anything else to freak out over. She'd already gone into a tailspin over red velvet coffin runners.

Eva took a deep breath and hugged the borrowed laptop to her chest. She'd finally hit her word count goal. The third latte had really given her brain the boost she needed to block out her surroundings. Of course, the caffeine tremors had slowed down her typing, but overall, Eva was freaking thrilled with how the book was coming together. It almost made up for everything else.

Earlier in the day Deputy Layla, picking up to-go caffeine, had reported that Eva was clear to return home again. But Eva still wasn't ready to revisit the wreckage the careless Agnes had inflicted. Not tonight.

Tonight, she'd be in Donovan's bed again. And that was something she could look forward to.

She was dreamily fantasizing about exploring Donovan's shower with him when a minivan pulled up beside her.

"There you are!" Mrs. Nordemann yelled out the window from behind the wheel.

The rear passenger door slid open, and Aretha, the book-throwing, fit-haver from Fitz's bookstore hopped out. "Come along, dear. We're going to be late." She dragged Eva to the van with an astonishing strength for her small frame. Throwing hardbacks around must have added some lean muscle mass.

Eva resisted.

"Oh, now. Don't be shy!" Another woman poked her head out and latched on to Eva's wrist. "Places to be! People to see!"

Eva started to struggle. "Hang on a minute. Are you going to kidnap me and dump my body in the middle of some field?"

They giggled until Ellery rolled down the passenger window.

"You, too?" Eva demanded.

"Get in the van, Eva." Ellery's voice was serious, almost scary.

Four against one. She could probably have taken the first three, but Ellery was the wild card. Beneath her skull sweaters and pleated skirts, she had a wiry build.

"Where are we going?" Eva demanded as she climbed into the middle row of seats.

Mrs. Nordemann looked at her in the rearview mirror. "This is the shuttle to Book Club," she said cheerily. She cranked up the Abba song that was playing and they rolled away.

41

Eva: "*I've literally been kidnapped.*"

Donovan: "*Your kidnapper can't be very good if you still have your phone.*"

Eva: "*Excuse me, sheriff. Your girlfriend was just dragged off the sidewalk in the middle of town by four whackjobs and you don't sound very concerned!*"

Donovan: "*Your sheriff boyfriend is busy trying to shoo an entire flock of fucking Canadian geese off Mervin Lauter's front porch that some asshole coated with peanut butter and bird seed. Where are your kidnappers taking you?*"

Eva: "*Book Club???*"

Donovan: "*Just got bit by one of these fuckers. If I don't die an Alfred Hitchcockian death by goose I'll swing by and pick you up when it lets out.*"

~

The minivan picked Bobby up in front of Peace of Pizza and then headed a few blocks west. The women around her chattered on about anything and everything while Eva wondered how she'd ended up in a town where kidnapping was acceptable.

They pulled up in front of a large brick home. Cars lined the street, and it looked as though every light in the home was blazing. They poured out of the minivan like a clown act.

"Welcome to my home," Mrs. Nordemann said grandly, toddling up the walkway.

It didn't really look like the sort of place neighbors were murdered. The architecture of the home was quite traditional, but the personal touches pushed it into Blue Moon territory. A pair of turquoise papasans with cherry red cushions hung suspended from the porch rafters behind stately columns. A fountain with a very enthusiastic naked couple wrapped around each other burbled in the front yard.

"Is the water coming from his—" Eva pointed.

Bobby glanced at the statue. "Yep. That's his penis."

They mounted the steps, and Eva spied an infinite row of shoes neatly lining the porch. Mrs. Nordemann pushed the door open. Laughter, music, and the smells of potluck beckoned them inside.

A collective squeal went up when Eva stepped barefoot across the threshold.

"The guest of honor has arrived," Mrs. Nordemann announced as her guests flocked into the foyer. "Now, let's give her some breathing room. Enid, would you mind getting Eva —or should I say Ava—a glass of wine?"

A rickety woman who had to be knocking on ninety shoved her way through the crowd of oglers.

"Red or white, Eva?" Mrs. Nordemann asked briskly.

"Uh, red?"

"Red, Enid," Mrs. Nordemann shouted after the woman. "Come on in. We're set up in the parlor," she said, ushering Eva through the grand opening of the front room. It was jammed full of tables, chairs, sofas, and ottomans. Women's purses and dog-earred stacks of Eva's book *Strings of Destiny* rested on every flat surface. Thankfully, given the number of bodies in the room pumping off body heat, the hearth was empty. Even still, it felt like it was eighty degrees in the room.

"She looks flushed," Eden, in leather leggings and a long blood red shirt announced. "Someone fan her."

A dozen hands holding everything from magazines to napkins flashed in front of her face.

"Um, Eden? Ellery? Could I see you two alone for a moment?" Eva asked, staring daggers at her friends.

"Sure!" Ellery led the way through the throng and up the grand staircase to the second floor. She pushed open a nine-foot door that creaked like a haunted house. "This is Jillian's private sitting room."

It was done up in so many pink prints that Eva felt a little dizzy.

"What the hell am I doing here?"

Eden and Ellery shared a glance. "It's Book Club."

"I gathered that from the kidnapping van. Why was I snatched off the street and brought here against my will?"

Eden shot Ellery a look. "I thought you were going to send her the invitation?"

"I'm a bride-to-be! I'm juggling eight thousand details. I thought you were going to send her the invitation."

"Oops," Eden sighed. "Must have got our wires crossed. I blame Uranus."

"So, this was not a kidnapping?"

The women shook their heads. "You're the guest of honor at this month's Book Club. We read your book, and now we want to pick your brain about it. Plus, we thought it would cheer you up after that whole your mom stealing your stuff thing," Ellery announced.

"Do you often accidentally kidnap authors?" Eva asked rubbing her eyes.

"No, of course not!" Ellery said, taking offense.

"Well, there was that one time with—"

"Ixnay on the napkidding-ay," Ellery hissed, making a slashing motion across her throat.

"So, I'm free to leave?" Eva asked. "You're not holding me hostage?"

"Of course, you're free to leave," Eden promised.

"I mean, that would totally devastate your die-hard fans downstairs. Probably damage your readership a bit. Mrs. Nordemann runs a book blog with like fifty-thousand followers. She's like a small-town Oprah. So I wouldn't piss her off if I were you. But you can leave at any time," Ellery said with a diabolical grin.

Eva sighed. "Let's go find my wine."

BOOK CLUB in Blue Moon was an experience. It had the festive feeling of a book signing with the alcohol equivalent of a commercial bar.

They guided Eva to a tufted ottoman in front of the marble fireplace. Her wine glass was magically refilled as the crowd settled itself into the room.

"Attention. Attention." Mrs. Nordemann clapped her hands like a school teacher.

When the chatter failed to die down, Ellery stuck her fingers in her mouth and whistled. "Hey!"

Everyone quieted down.

"Thank you, Ellery," Mrs. Nordemann said. "First I would like to thank you all for being here. I know we're very excited to have tonight's guest author with us. The refreshments for this evening are all available in the formal dining room, and the wine has been generously discounted by Davis Gates at Blue Moon Winery."

Eva spotted Eden off to the side. The woman glared at the wineglass in her hand and put it down on the writing desk next to her and stomped out of the room. She returned a moment later with a beer. Ellery caught Eva's eye and nodded in Eden's direction in a telegraphed *See? I told you so.*

"Now, on to the exciting part of the evening. I'd like you all to welcome our very own Eva Merill who writes under the pen name Ava Franklin. A secret I'm sure that we're all more than happy to keep," she said, giving the audience a steely-eyed look. With no dissenters she smiled sweetly. "Eva is the author of five novels, including my personal favorite *Fated Fools*, which we will be discussing tonight."

There were finger snaps instead of applause, and Eva wondered if it was because most of the audience was busy clutching wine glasses.

"Now without further ado, Eva will read a selection from *Strings of Destiny*."

"I will?" she asked over the finger snapping.

Mrs. Nordemann handed her a paperback with a book mark. "Just the highlighted portion, dear."

She sat on her pink and ivory tufted ottoman and read aloud from an incredibly sexy passage that the group had voted on. She'd never read her own work in front of an audience before.

Sure, during the writing process she'd muttered dialogue out loud, trying out the words, the inflections. But it was a whole different experience to say "rigid length of cock" out loud. Especially when a good portion of the audience was old enough to be her grandparents.

The accolades went straight to her head as did the seemingly bottomless wine. The Blue Moon Book Club was a well-read group. While they preferred romance or erotica, they also dabbled in thrillers, cozy mysteries, and women's fiction. It was refreshing to see a handful of men jumping into the discussion on character motivations and theories on after the epilogue.

This was her first sort-of public event as a writer, and Blue Moon was kind enough to walk her through it while feeding her heart-shaped appetizers. They were as enthusiastic about her stories, her characters, as she was. It was a heady thing to have kept something under wraps for so long only to unveil it to the world and be accepted.

It was the most enjoyable kidnapping Eva had ever experienced. Also the only one. But still.

She answered questions, both the insightful and the ridiculous.

"Who is your favorite hero?"

"What do you read for fun?"

"Do you ever base characters on people you know in real life?"

"How do you research your sex scenes?" That one was asked by the very serious, very interested Mrs. Nordemann.

"What are you working on next?" Eden asked from the back of the room where she was crowded around a table between Fitz and Julia from the juice shop.

"I'm actually working on a small-town series inspired by Blue Moon," Eva told them.

The crowd chatter got louder and more excited. Mrs.

Nordemann fanned herself with a napkin. "I can only assume that our sheriff will play a starring role?"

"He was definitely an inspiration for the main character," Eva admitted. The chatter increased to deafening levels. Titters of laughter erupted.

Oh, hell. Had she just admitted that Blue Moon would have a front row seat to the fictional version of her sex life with Donovan?

"I believe we have time for a few more questions, and then perhaps we could talk Eva into signing just a few books while she's here," Mrs. Nordemann announced.

A hand raised from behind the yellow and purple settee. Eva couldn't see the woman's face.

"Uh, yes. You in the pink?"

"Just how well-endowed would you say Sheriff Cardona is?"

DONOVAN DOUBLE PARKED in front of Mrs. Nordemann's house. Book Club was breaking up and, as usual, had apparently involved a lot of wine. He could tell by the Mooners pouring out of the house. Some of them were stumbling after their designated drivers. He sighed and got out of the car.

Book Club invariably ended in hordes of drunken women, and a handful of men, clogging Mrs. Nordemann's street. There weren't any neighbors left to annoy of course. They were all part of the Book Club. But he still liked to check in every month to make sure everyone got home safely.

"Ladies," he said, greeting the first group of women. They eyed him up starting at the crotch and giggled. He sighed.

It was an odd collection of people, an exact representation of Blue Moon. Nan, the brewery's line cook, was still wearing her John Pierce Brews work shirt, her dark hair hung over her shoulders in braids. She had an arm around Moon Beam Parker, the man-eating good time girl of Blue Moon. Moon Beam had snatched up Beckett Pierce's virginity at sixteen and was currently shopping for husband number three. Willa trailed them in her hot pink cowboy boots, giving Ellery a wide berth. She tried to hide the plastic cup full of God knows what under her poncho when she spotted him.

"Evening, Sheriff," she said with a cheerful wave.

"Evening, Willa. What's in the cup?"

"Just some iced tea for the road," she said innocently.

"It's not that I don't trust you, Willa. It's that I'd hate to pull you and your friends over and find an open container in your car." He twirled his keys around his finger.

She sighed. "Ugh. Fine!"

"You don't have to dump it," he told her with a grin.

"Chug it!" Enid Macklemore, Blue Moon's oldest working dog walker, shouted in her thin old lady voice. She looked like a slight breeze could knock her on her ass, but he'd seen her wrestle dogs the size of Summer's Valentina to the ground if they had the bad manners to ignore her commands.

Willa shot Donovan a coy look.

He rolled his eyes, hands on hips. "Go on. You might as well."

The growing crowd around them cheered as Willa knocked back eighteen ounces of definitely not iced tea. She finished with victory arms and spiked the empty cup on the sidewalk and, with a distinct sway in her step, jogged in a circle high-fiving everyone before picking up the discarded cup again. No one in Blue Moon would ever dare to purposely litter.

"Who's Willa's DD?" Donovan asked the crowd.

"That'd be me," Rob, Julia's husband, ambled up the sidewalk. "I'm taking five of these drunken hippies home." He pointed at the Volkswagen bus behind him.

"Where did you get that thing?" Donovan asked. It was covered in glossy rainbow paint. The interior lights were on, and Donovan could see purple fur covering the interior.

"Ernest Washington loans it out every Book Club. Free advertising for his car lot."

"The Shaggin' Wagon's here!" Julia, several glasses of wine to the wind, announced before planting a sloppy kiss on Rob's chin. "I was aiming for your mouth," she snickered.

"Yes, you were," Rob said affectionately. "Okay, ladies, let's load up. Your sports drinks, aspirin, and greasy veggie burgers are waiting for you in the cup and burger holders."

"You are like the best husband I've ever married," Julia said, batting her baby blues up at him.

"I'm also the only husband you've ever married," he reminded her, giving her a nudge toward the front seat.

"I have such good taste!"

Donovan hid his laugh as Rob proceeded to load four inebriated ladies and one Fitz into the van. They pulled away from the curb, arms waving out of windows. He could hear the giggling even as the van turned the corner.

He turned back to the crowd that was slowly dispersing.

Ellery danced over to him in her Frankenstein boots. "Just so you know. Your girlfriend is amazing." Her thick black eyeliner was smeared into one eyebrow and she had black lipstick on her teeth.

"I am well aware, El," he grinned.

"She's like a legit author, and her characters are so real. I mean, all that stuff lives in her head, and it's like... *wow*!"

"Who's taking you home?" he asked her.

"My Masey just texted and said he was coming to carry me

home. I told him to bring the wheelbarrow because I might fall down," she said, shoving her phone in his face. "See?"

Donovan squinted at the screen that was two inches from his face and burning holes in his retinas. "Actually, you told him to bring your weed whacker because you might have clowns."

Ellery frowned. "Stupid autocorrect." She beamed again when she spotted Mason with a weed whacker slung over his shoulder. She sighed the sigh of a woman head over heels in love. "Do you see how great he is? He listens to everything I say. Even the stupid things!"

She skipped over to her fiancé and laid a kiss on him that was NC-17 at a minimum.

Before Donovan could suggest they take it somewhere else, preferably home, Eva appeared on the porch. Her hair was a wild auburn under the soft glow of the lights. Eyes bright, she grinned at him, and if there had been any questions before about being in love, the hot fist to his gut left no doubt. She was beautiful, she was glowing, and she was his.

Eva jogged down the path, arms open wide for him. She tripped over her own feet. He caught her before she face-planted on the sidewalk.

"Careful there," he said, brushing her hair back from her face.

"Donovan! It was amazing! I said 'cock' *repeatedly* in front of everyone, and no one called me a perv. I signed a whole bunch of books. *And* my wineglass was never empty." She hazarded a glance around before whispering, "It was magical."

"It sounds like your first kidnapping was a positive experience," he teased.

"They treated me like a real writer," she said, eyes shining.

"Baby, you *are* a real writer."

"You're my crazy boyfriend. You're supposed to say that.

Oh!" Her eyes widened. "I almost forgot, I think everyone knows just what kind of weapon you're packing if you know what I mean." She patted him in the crotch and attempted to wink.

"Christ, Eva!" Donovan cringed.

"I didn't mean to tell them. And I didn't get *really* specific, but it's kinda hard not to brag. I mean, you're huge."

Donovan clamped a hand over her mouth. "You are trouble with a capital T, Evangelina."

"And I'm alllllll yours," she said, spreading her arms wide.

The remaining Book Clubbers broke into spontaneous finger snaps around them.

"Eva, just a moment please." Mrs. Nordemann trotted down the walk to them. She was dressed in her traditional black garb. Though, in a nod to the festivity of the occasion, her ankle-length black skirt had a smattering of rhinestones around the hem.

"Thank you again for inviting me tonight," Eva gushed.

"Inviting. Kidnapping. Basically the same thing in Blue Moon," Donovan said under his breath.

"Thank you for joining us. It was a real treat. I just wanted you to know how very proud I am of you," Mrs. Nordemann said, patting Eva's arm. "You're a very talented young woman and so dedicated to your craft. I hope you know how much we all truly enjoy your work. And I hope you can take a moment to step back and really appreciate what you've built."

Eva's hazel eyes glittered with what looked like tears. *Yep. That was a tear that just slid down Eva's cheek. Awh, hell.*

"That's one of the nicest things anyone's ever said to me," Eva sniffled. She wiped her nose on her sleeve.

"My dear, just because you haven't heard the words from someone important doesn't make them less true. I'm, of course, speaking of your mother who, one can only assume, is a real piece of shit."

Donovan swiped a hand over his face. Mrs. Nordemann was throwing around swear words in her front yard. *Fucking Uranus.*

"Eva, I just hope you know how proud we all are of you. And maybe think about naming a character after me." With a wiggle of her fingers, Mrs. Nordemann scurried back up onto her porch. "Enid, let's open the tequila! I feel like celebrating."

Donovan slid an arm around Eva's waist and half carried, half dragged, her to his car.

"Come on, Ava Franklin. Let's get you home to bed."

~

To: Eva Merill

From: Bruce Oakleigh

Subject: Intensive private therapy

Hello, Eva!

Bruce Oakleigh, president of the Beautification Committee here. I spoke to the Berkowiczs this morning and they informed me that you've reached out for help in cementing your relationship with Donovan Cardona.

Rest assured that the Beautification Committee will not abandon you in your time of need. Given your current circumstances (i.e. your mother breaking into your home, the systemic blackmail, and what one can only assume would be a questionable knowledge of healthy relationships), we are tabling all other matching projects for the foreseeable future to help mold you into a healthy, stable significant other.

Please be prepared to meet promptly at 7 p.m. at the police station for your first session. Please bring the following: a box of tissues, an item that brings you comfort, Sheriff Cardona, and a list of your mother's transgressions as you can best recollect.

Yours in matching success,

Bruce Oakleigh, President

P.S. The aforementioned mission has received the code name Project Lazy Parrot. Please reference Project Lazy Parrot in all correspondence.

42

"Ellery had better be planning the most epic thank you in the history of gratitude," Donovan muttered as he held open the door of the police station for Eva.

"Yeah, about that," Eva winced, stepping inside. "I didn't tell her. I didn't want her to know that her former friends were planning to ruin her wedding."

He sighed. "You're a good friend."

"I didn't do it just for her." She winked. "You're the one who would have to get up in the middle of 'does anyone here know any just cause' to arrest a dozen people in a public spectacle."

"A good friend and a thoughtful girlfriend," Donovan amended.

"Just try to keep that in mind during the interrogation," she reminded him. "Hi, Minnie. Heading out?"

Minnie slung her hand crocheted purse over her shoulder. "Mr. Murkle got it into his thick head that we need a date night tonight."

Donovan coughed out the word "Uranus," and Eva elbowed him in his muscled six-pack.

"That sounds like fun," she said brightly.

"It would be if it were a date with someone else," Minnie sighed. "How about you? You doing okay since your mama went all breaking and entering on you?"

Donovan snickered behind Eva, and she shot him a dirty look. "I'm just fine. Thanks, Minnie."

"Well, you all have yourselves a good night while I try not to stab my no-good husband for slurping oysters too loud."

They waved her off, and Donovan towed Eva into his office.

"Since the Oakleighs aren't here yet..." he said, pulling Eva into his lap behind the desk.

The unspoken insinuation had her blood simmering. "You're insatiable," she accused, feeling him harden beneath her.

"You're the one wearing a sexy sweater dress thing that you knew would drive me nuts," he shot back, his big hands cupping her breasts through the soft gray fabric that she'd known would distract him from whatever Bruce had cooked up for them. She looped her arms around his neck.

"I thought we'd already reenacted the sex in the office fantasy," she said lightly.

His hands skimmed around her waist and down to grip her hips and pull her tight against his arousal.

Eva let her eyelids flutter closed.

"I bet I could make you come like this," he said, dragging her over the rigid line of his erection.

She whimpered and went instantaneously wet.

"I'd pull this down," he said, hooking a finger in the deep v of the dress.

Her breath quickened.

"And while you grind yourself against my dick, I'd have my face buried in your beautiful—"

"Well, here you two lovebirds are!" Bruce bustled in with Amethyst on his heels.

Donovan swore quietly under his breath, and Eva jumped out of his lap as if he were on fire. She had to make it look like she needed the Beautification Committee's undivided attention so they wouldn't have time to even think about wrecking Ellery's wedding.

"I'm so glad you're here," she said, her voice overly bright. "We were just... fighting."

"We were?" Donovan frowned.

She kicked him.

"Oh, right. We were. We were definitely fighting," he nodded.

Bruce and Amethyst exchanged knowing glances.

"That's what we're here for," Amethyst said, smiling smugly.

"You fucking owe me," Donovan growled in Eva's ear as he stood. He pulled her in front of him, effectively hiding the tent in his pants. At least she wasn't the only one battling a raging case of lust in the moment.

"We're eager to fix everything that's wrong with Eva," Donovan joked.

Eva reached behind her and palmed his hard-on through his pants, daring him to say more. He hissed out a breath and shut up.

"Well, now. Let's not get ahead of ourselves." Bruce held his palms up. "This could take months. There are a lot of issues that need to be brought to the surface and dealt with."

"Then I guess we'd better get started," Eva sighed. "Shall we sit?"

They gathered around the cramped conference table in the corner of Donovan's office. Donovan's hand immediately clamped onto her thigh beneath the table. When he trailed his fingers higher up her thigh, drawing the hem of the dress with them, she squeezed her legs together.

"We're so excited to have you two with us tonight," Bruce said, rubbing his palms together. "Amethyst and I have been happily married for thirty-four years—"

"Thirty-three," Amethyst corrected him.

Bruce frowned. "I'm quite certain it's thirty-four, my pearl."

Amethyst shook her head, her beehive wobbling precariously. "Thirty-three."

"I have our marriage certificate in our fire safe," Bruce said, his voice rising. "We can settle this easily."

"I can't believe you don't remember how long we've been married," Amethyst pouted. It was the only time Eva had witnessed the woman being disagreeable in any way.

"So far, I think it's going really well," Donovan whispered sarcastically as the Oakleighs' bickering warmed up. Eva's eyes widened as Amethyst shoved out of her chair. Bruce was quick to follow.

"How could you forget our wedding day?" Amethyst demanded.

"How could you accuse me of forgetting our wedding day when you're clearly the one with a deficient memory on the topic?" Bruce argued, tugging at the sides of his beard with both hands.

"It's Uranus," Eva hissed at Donovan.

"Fucking Uranus." He glanced toward the door. "You know, we could probably sneak out of here and break into Gia's studio for some fun..."

"What kind of fun?" Eva asked, suddenly breathy.

"The hot, sweaty kind."

"The *naked* hot sweaty kind, or does she have some evening power class you're trying to con me into?"

"Would I do that to you?" Donovan asked, trailing a finger

down the nape of her neck.

"You absolutely would."

"Probably, but this time I swear it's just sex."

Eva glanced toward Bruce and Amethyst. They were running down a laundry list of complaints against the other. Apparently, Bruce was physically incapable of putting his underwear into the hamper while Amethyst preferred to stock butter pecan ice cream even though Bruce repeatedly reminded her that he preferred brownie batter.

"Let's do it," Eva decided. "Let's go fool around in my sister's yoga studio."

They made it out of Donovan's office and to the front door without the Oakleighs missing a beat in their argument that had apparently been brewing for thirty-three or thirty-four years. When Donovan closed the station door behind them, they were heatedly discussing Amethyst's poor attitude toward Bruce's mother's gravy recipe.

"Who puts bacon in gravy?" Amethyst shouted.

They hustled down the block and ducked into the alley. Donovan already had Eva's dress up around her waist by the time she found the hide-a-key for the back door behind a loose brick in the building wall.

"Does it still count as breaking and entering if we use a key?" Eva asked, slipping it into the lock and opening the door.

"We're only trespassing now," Donovan said. He yanked her back against him and she felt him hard and willing.

"Come on. Let's go in the private studio so no one sees us through the windows," she whispered, grabbing him by the belt buckle and dragging him down the hall. Gia's private studio was a fifteen by fifteen room with a wall of mirrors and a little altar table that held battery-operated candles.

Eva pointed at the stack of mats in the back. "We're going

to need one of those."

Donovan grinned and grabbed one. Eva set to turning on the candles, bathing the room in a soft, flickering glow.

They faced each other from opposite ends of the mat. Donovan's eyes seemed to glow in the candlelight. Eva slipped out of her boots and gestured for him to do the same.

"I think it's time we satisfied one of my fantasies."

"Here?" he grinned, removing his belt.

"That hot yoga class? I started hallucinating that it was just you and me." She worked the buttons free on his shirt and raked her nails over his chest.

"What did we do?"

"Everything," she whispered. She brought his hands to her breasts and moaned when he squeezed.

"There's only so much I can take, Eva," he warned.

She palmed him through his pants and felt him twitch against her. "You seem pretty in control to me."

And then he was dragging her to the ground. He fell on her, yanking her dress open to feed on her breasts. His tongue and lips on the sensitive flesh of her nipple sent a throbbing straight to her empty core. She spread her legs wide for him, and he settled between them. Without releasing her nipple, Donovan slid his free hand down to pull her underwear aside.

"You know these lacy see-through things drive me insane," he murmured against her breast.

"You drive me insane," Eva whispered, arching her back up so he could take more of her. He knew just how to touch, to suck, to drag out the pleasure. He released her breast, gave her nipple another lick with the flat of his tongue, and then moved on to the other one.

She cried out as his teeth grazed her. He drove two fingers into her, and she thought she was going to come apart then and there.

"Did you think about me doing this to you in that class? Did you want to know what it felt like to have me inside you? Because I think about it constantly. Every second of every day, I'm wishing I were inside you, making you come on my cock."

His words had her tightening on his fingers. He crooked them, grazing just the right spot inside her.

"Donovan!" she hissed.

"You're so precious," he growled. "So perfect, and I can't get enough of you." He abandoned her breasts, the tips wet from his mouth, and withdrew his fingers from her.

"Please," she begged. "Please, Donovan."

Without preamble, he brought his head between her legs, swiped his tongue through her slit.

Her hips jacked up off the floor at the sudden, jagged rush of pleasure.

"That's right, baby," he murmured. His fingers were back, gliding into her, brushing across that spot.

Her breath caught, and she felt her body tense.

"I feel it, Eva. Let it happen. Let me make you come." He lathed her aching nub with his tongue while his fingers worked pure magic in her. His hips pistoned against the mat as if to relieve the growing ache in his own cock.

Her moan was breathy. She didn't have to tell him what was happening to her. He had a front row seat to the orgasm that swamped her like a storm. It carried her up and up until it broke and she was hurtling back toward the earth.

He groaned against her slick folds as she came, clenching around his fingers, shivering under him. Her body was alive and not nearly sated enough. Still trembling, Eva grabbed Donovan's hair. "Sit up," she demanded. He sat cross-legged on the mat, and she straddled him.

"I need you in me before I stop coming." The blunt head of

his cock grazed her and it set her off again... or still. She didn't know, and it didn't matter.

"Eva," he rasped brokenly.

She gripped his shaft with her hand and guided it to her opening. She wanted to go slow, to savor, but the need wouldn't allow for that. She lined him up and lowered herself onto him, overfull and aching. Impaled upon him.

"I can feel you still coming," he groaned.

She opened her eyes and found him watching her. Her nipples grazed the hair of his chest as she lifted. She paused at the top and watched him as she lowered onto him. The cords of his neck stood out. His jaw was clenched. And those blue eyes had fire in them.

She shifted her hips, trying to take all of him. And with a look of sheer possession, he gripped her hips and slammed home.

Eva cried out softly. Gripping her hair, Donovan drew her down for a kiss. She began to ride, mimicking the thrusts of his tongue. He set the pace with his hands clamped on her hips, lifting and gripping. Eva watched him, watched his control slip millimeter by millimeter as the thrusts got harder and faster.

They were bound by intimacy, intensity. Joined by the need to fulfill.

He dipped his head and licked at her nipple. She hissed through her teeth and rocked into him. They balanced there, on the knife-edge of desire and ecstasy. His eyes. Those true-blue eyes were dark, half-blind with lust.

"You're mine, Eva. Mine." He gritted out the words as she dug her nails into his shoulders under his shirt.

"And you're mine." It was a promise whether he knew it or not. But it didn't matter because she was quickening around him. The glorious build broke, and then she was fisting around him, drawing his own release out of him whether he was ready or not.

They collapsed, shuddering, in a sweat-slicked heap on top of the mat that smelled like lemons and eucalyptus.

Donovan heaved a sigh. "I think we can work more of your fantasies into our sex life," he breathed, his lips moving against the skin of her neck.

She laughed. "Are you running out already?"

"God no. I've got enough to keep us going to our twentieth anniversary at least."

"And people think I have an active imagination," Eva snickered. "I hope you know that everything we do is fair game for fiction."

"I wouldn't want your sheriff hero falling flat in the moves department. How is the book coming?"

He felt rather than saw the shrug.

"I'm having a little trouble focusing since... the break-in," she admitted.

Donovan lifted himself up on an elbow. "Baby, maybe you should give yourself more than forty-eight hours to process."

"I haven't even gone back in there yet. Not since I walked through with Layla," she confessed. She yawned. Her body was spent, and her brain was ready for bed. Everything had her feeling exhausted lately. She needed to get back into a routine, get her head back in the game.

"You don't have to. Not until you're ready."

"It's embarrassing. I've known since before kindergarten what kind of a person my mother was, and yet I'm surprised that she's found a new way to hurt me. It's pathetic. I'm letting her ruin yet another home for me."

"Well, sooner or later you'll be ballsy enough to stop letting her ruin anything for you," he said.

Eva poked him in the chest. "I know exactly what you're

doing."

He grinned. "You mean enjoying my post-orgasmic bliss?" he asked innocently.

"You're getting me riled up to prove you—and me —wrong."

"Now, why would I go and do a thing like that?"

"Because whining and feeling sorry for myself gets me nowhere. And it's about damn time I take back what's mine."

"You better keep it down. If the B.C. hears you talking like that, they'll be picketing Ellery's wedding tomorrow."

Eva laughed. "Once the wedding is over, I can be cured of all my hang-ups and baggage. And this planetary nonsense will be all over."

He tucked a strand of hair behind her ear. "Maybe then I can take you out on a date?"

She smiled, happiness pooling in her chest. "I'd like that."

He kissed her softly, lips warm and gentle against hers.

Eva pulled back. "Mmm, I can't believe I finally get a date with Sheriff Sexy."

"It's about damn time."

"Hey. Do you want to hear another secret?" she asked. She laughed when he flinched. "It's not mine," she promised. "Emma's pregnant. Sounds like it's going to be a pretty big surprise since they were just starting to talk about kids."

"When are *we* going to start talking about them?" he teased.

Eva snorted. "How about we discuss that sometime after our first date?"

His phone rang from the depths of his discarded pants. "Shit. It's dispatch. Hang on a second. Cardona," he answered.

He tensed. "Uh, you know what. I'm real close to there. Why don't you let me check it out first before you call the fire department?"

Donovan jumped up and made a grab for his pants.

"No, I don't think the neighbor needs to break down the front door. I'm thirty seconds away. I'll check it out and call it in if there's a situation."

Donovan hung up and grabbed Eva's dress.

"We gotta get dressed real fast. Someone just reported a fire hazard at Gia's yoga studio."

"We're in Gia's yoga studio." Eva reminded him.

He pointed at the flickering electric candles. "Neighbors apparently keep an eye on the place, and someone saw candlelight in an empty building. Got someone waiting outside to break down the door and save the day."

Eva yelped and grabbed the dress. She put it on and did a frantic search for her discarded underwear.

"Well, well, well. I guess you owe me an apology, Beckett."

Gia stood in the doorway, arms crossed looking smug. Donovan yanked his pants up over his hips.

Beckett peeked in and grinned. The swelling around his eye had gone down, but the shiner was still prominent.

"This isn't what it looks like," Eva began. "Donovan was showing me some yoga moves."

"Really? Naked ones? Because it looks like you two broke in here to have sex. Also, your dress is on backwards."

Eva looked down and the dress tag tickled her chin. "Crap."

"I hope you were at least going to disinfect that mat," Gia said, pointing with her foot at the mat they'd just sweated all over.

"I'll run it through a car wash," Donovan offered. "Oh, hey. Look at that. I'm getting a call. I should take care of this."

"Don't you dare fake a dispatch call," Eva yelped.

"Sorry, babe. Duty calls. Hello?" he said into the phone.

"You didn't even push Answer," Eva yelled after him.

~

To: Eva Merill

CC: Beautification Committee

From: Bruce Oakleigh

Subject: Lazy Parrot positive affirmations

Dear Eva,

President Bruce Oakleigh here. As part of your rigorous counseling to slay your personal demons, we will be providing you with daily positive affirmations to help guide you toward enlightenment. Please read the affirmation aloud several times a day to really feel the message.

Yours in Successful Matching,

Bruce Oakleigh, President

Beautification Committee

P.S. Amethyst and I would like to apologize for our behavior during last night's counseling session. As it turns out, we were both incorrect. We've been married thirty-five years.

P.P.S. Eva, please reach out to us to reschedule your counseling session ASAP.

P.P.P.S. Eva, we strongly recommend that you suspend sexual relations during Operation Lazy Parrot.

43

Wilson: *Your positive affirmation of the day. Whenever you feel angry, say bubbles.*

~

Eva stared at the front door of her little cottage. She'd felt nauseous this morning, waking up to face what needed to be done. Her stomach had churned at the thought of facing what was within. This house had become the place she'd felt the most at home besides the kitchen of her father's restaurant. And someone had tried to take that from her. Agnes knew how to strike where it hurt the most. But Eva wasn't going to let the woman take one more home from her.

Regardless of whether Agnes was ever caught, her things found, Eva was done with her.

Beckett had already seen to replacing the glass, but inside she could still see the chaos.

"Cleanup crew reporting for duty."

Gia and Emma, in varying degrees of morning chipperness stood behind her, brooms and trash bags at the ready.

"Thank you, guys, for doing this," Eva said, doling out the coffees she'd picked up from Overly Caffeinated.

"Hey! Where are our coffees?"

Summer and Joey sauntered into the backyard. Summer was lugging a carpet steamer while Joey manhandled a drink carrier of what looked like tomato juices.

"Let's get this cleaning party started, bitches," Joey announced. "Julia whipped up some of her famous Bloody Mary mixers, and I've got vodka in my bag."

"You guys don't have to do this," Eva said, feeling insanely lucky and just a little embarrassed that she hadn't thought to ask them. "I mean, my sisters do because it's required by biology. But you two really don't have to spend your Halloween morning cleaning up someone else's mess."

Joey snorted. "That's not what Summer said."

Summer threw an elbow into Joey's ribs. "What Joey means to say is that we're happy that we can help out."

"Who's taking care of the magazine? The horses?" Eva asked.

"Minions," Joey shot back. "Now, if you're done with your 'woe-is-me internal monologue' moment can we go inside and start pouring this vodka?"

They did just that. Until Summer's eagle eye saw Emma passing up the vodka.

"What's this?" Summer demanded, pointing at Emma's straight tomato juice.

"What's what?" Emma asked innocently.

"Holy shit, you're pregnant!" Joey dropped her broom, flipped a barstool upright, and plopped down on it.

"I am neither confirming nor denying until I tell the father of the hypothetical baby," Emma snapped back with a steely-eyed glare. "So, you better keep that trap shut!"

Joey held up her hands in surrender. "My lips are sealed,

but you better make sure no one outside this room catches wind. It'll be another special edition of *The Weekly Monthly Moon*."

"Are you serious, right now? You're going to have a baby?" Summer's high-pitched squeal threatened to rupture ear drums within a one-block radius.

"Geez! Keep it down," Emma said, looking furtively over her shoulder. "I'm going to surprise Niko and not by having my stepsister-in-law shriek it all over town."

"This calls for more booze," Gia said, opening Eva's cabinets.

"Nice try. Our mother took it all," Eva pointed out.

Gia rolled her eyes and whipped out her phone. "I've got it covered."

"The first lady of Blue Moon is having booze delivered," Joey snickered.

"Have you decided how to do it?" Gia demanded, dumping a dust pan of broken glass into the trash bag and snagging her Bloody Mary.

"Well, you know I like to have a plan."

Eva snorted. Emma was nothing if not ruthlessly organized.

"*Anyway*," Emma said, shooting her a dirty look. "I'm having Niko's parents come in from the city for the Halloween Carnival. They're staying at Phoebe and Franklin's so Niko doesn't spot them around town."

"And then, what? Yell 'surprise, we made a baby'?" Summer asked.

Emma gave her a dry look. "No! I've got a plan. A real one."

"I don't know, Em. I mean, he bought you a house and rescued a puppy to propose to you. I hope you're kicking it up a notch," Eva warned her.

Gia snapped her fingers. "Are you telling him with your Halloween costume?"

"Like what? Go as a whale, which is what I'll be next summer?" Emma asked, a soft, dreamy look belying her words.

"Don't be an ass. Pregnancy is beautiful. Even if you're gigantic," Summer interjected.

"I'm just nervous. I don't want to have a conversation about it until I tell Niko. Do you think he'll be happy?"

Eva grinned at her sister. "Niko is going to freak out in the best possible way. Family has gotten a lot more important to him since he met you."

"It's still a big surprise," Emma breathed.

"How about you?" Gia asked. "How do you feel?"

Emma took a breath and stared at the ceiling. "So. Fucking. Excited," she grinned. "I have to get all the f words out now before I have the baby."

Eva hugged her sister. "I'm going to be an aunt again!"

Gia elbowed her way in. "I'm going to be an aunt for the first time!"

Summer joined in. "Our family is growing!"

Eva poked her head up out of the mob. "Get in here, Joey."

Joey rolled her eyes. "I don't know why you guys have to hug about every damn thing."

BECKETT ARRIVED a few minutes later with a pitcher of Long Island iced tea.

"What happened to your eye?" Summer asked, tut tutting over Beckett's bruise.

"Why don't you ask Eva how she got caught breaking and

entering to have sex with her boyfriend last night?" Beckett grinned.

"We had a key! Technically it was only trespassing!"

Joey made a grab for the pitcher and high-fived Eva on her way past. "Nice job on the creative sexing."

"I said I was sorry," Eva reminded Beckett. "We just got... carried away."

Gia swooped in and pressed a kiss to Beckett's mouth. "Thank you for the Beckett Bartended Booze," she said.

He kissed her back. "I'm going to take Lydia to go pick up Aurora from Sanjay's birthday party."

"You're the best husband in the universe," Gia sighed, snuggling against his chest. "I've officially forgiven you for thinking I left a lit candle blazing away in my studio."

Beckett met Eva's gaze over her sister's head, and he winked. It was exactly the kind of thing Gia would do if Beckett hadn't given her battery-operated candles.

The cleanup continued amongst snippets of conversation. Baby names, gossip gleaned from Book Club, and stories about the kids were punctuated by the scrape of broken glass and the rustle of trash bags. The day was sunny enough, warm enough, that Eva opened the windows. The fresh October breeze did its part in sweeping out the bad energy.

It was looking normal again. Sure, there were some new gouges in the hardwood floor, and some things weren't salvageable—like her cracked-in-half mermaid sugar bowl. But overall, Eva felt like she was taking her home back. At least Agnes hadn't gotten into the dishwasher where an entire load of clean dishes waited.

Eva picked up a coffee mug and tucked it into place in the cabinet. The shiny white pack on the shelf caught her attention. Her birth control pills.

It took a full five seconds for her to register the fact that they were in the cabinet and not in her purse. Meaning she hadn't taken one since before the break-in. Shit.

Her stomach did a slow, scary loop-de-loop when she opened the pack. Running the calculations she stopped breathing. She wouldn't have missed this many pills just since the break-in. She'd fucked up at least twice earlier in the month.

Eva snapped the pack shut and closed her eyes. She hadn't taken them with her the night of her first B.C. meeting. The night she and Donovan had made love for the first time. But they'd used a condom. But they hadn't when he'd snuck into her house the night of the Apple Butter Boil. Eva paced the tiny kitchen, nibbling on her thumb nail.

This couldn't be happening. She could not be pregnant to a man she'd been dating for less than a month. Oh, my God. There was a possibility that there was a Baby Cardona inside her at this exact second, and she'd just had a Bloody Mary.

She doubled over and tried desperately to find the oxygen that had gone missing from the room. She needed to buy a pregnancy test. *And just how in the hell was she supposed to do that in Blue Moon without the entire town hearing about it before she'd even peed on the stick?*

"You okay?" Summer asked, bustling back into the kitchen, a laundry basket full of unrolled toilet paper in hand.

Eva straightened quickly and cracked the back of her head off the open cabinet door.

"Ouch!" She grabbed at the back of her head.

Summer dropped the laundry basket and hurried forward. "That looked like it hurt."

"I'm fine!" Eva said, with more panic than necessary. "Everything is fine. Are you hungry? I'm hungry. Maybe I'll run out and get us some lunch since you guys have been so great helping me..." she gestured helplessly around the mostly spotless first floor.

"About damn time," Joey yelled from upstairs.

"I'll get pizza. Or subs. Or pizza and subs," Eva chattered on, wishing she could shut herself up.

"I want chicken fingers," Joey yelled down.

"Let's get something from Dad's restaurant. He'll probably sneak some dessert in with the order," Gia called from upstairs.

"Why don't I go pick it up?" Summer suggested, staring at Eva like she was crazy. "That way if you have, oh, say a concussion, you don't go wandering around downtown all alone."

"No! I mean, no. I don't mind picking up food. It's no problem. I'd be happy to. Otherwise one of you yahoos would try to pay for it, and it's my treat and—"

The knock at the door saved her from herself.

Summer answered it, and Eva glanced back down at the pack of pills in her hand. She was overreacting. There was no way—

Donovan stepped across the threshold carrying pizza boxes balancing a slim wrapped gift box.

In a panic, Eva tossed the pill packet over her shoulder. It landed with a clatter in the sink.

Donovan's gaze met hers from across the room.

"Sheriff Sexy," Eva said in a voice two octaves too high.

"She hit her head on a cabinet door," Summer explained.

"It seems to happen a lot here," he said, winking at Eva. "I'm running delivery. Bobby heard you were handling cleanup today and wanted to aid your effort."

"Did she also send a present?" Joey asked as she and Gia tromped downstairs.

Emma poked her head in from the sunroom. "I smell Peace of Pizza!"

"Present is for Eva from me," Donovan said, handing over the shiny silver box. "It's just a little something I thought you could use," he said quietly to Eva.

Despite the hysterical tremors wracking her fingers, Eva pasted a smile on her face. "Aren't you just the sweetest..." *Boyfriend? Unsuspecting baby daddy? She'd just leave it at sweetest.*

She shimmied off the lid and brushed back the tissue paper.

"Donovan," she gasped. A brand-new laptop, two models newer than the one that had been stolen, was nestled inside the box. She'd been saving up for one, knowing that hers wasn't long for this world. It had purple flower decals on the laptop skin.

"Whoa," Joey said, snooping over her shoulder. "Cardona wins the gift giving category."

"This is the most thoughtful..." Words were failing Eva.

"I'm going to get your old one back," he promised. "But I wanted you to have something that no one else touched."

She dashed around the island and threw her arms around his waist. "Thank you," she whispered against his chest.

"You like it?" he asked gruffly.

She nodded, not trusting her voice.

Donovan tilted her chin up. "Are you okay? Where did you hit your head?"

Eva laughed nervously. "I didn't hit it that hard. So, what do you think of the place?" she asked, sweeping her arm out. She smacked an empty Bloody Mary cup and sent it to the floor.

"Are you sure you're all right? You're clumsier when you're nervous," he asked, picking up the cup.

"What are you nervous about?" Joey asked, with her

mouthful of pizza. "We already went through your nightstand drawers."

Eva's ears turned pink.

"On that note," Donovan said, taking Eva's hand and towing her toward him. "I'd better get out of here so you can discuss my sexual prowess."

To the cat calls of her friends and sisters, Donovan bent Eva over backwards and kissed her until she couldn't breathe. "I'll pick you up tonight."

"Tonight?" she echoed.

"Ellery's wedding? The Halloween Carnival?"

The idea of a Baby Cardona had blanked her memory. "Right. I knew that," she nodded.

He kissed her again and headed toward the door.

"Wedding starts at six. Can one of you remind Eva, please?"

An affirmative chorus rose up from the pizza-eaters.

Six. She could sneak out, drive to Cleary, pee on a stick, and be back in time for the festivities with the peace of mind of not being pregnant.

Easy peasy.

Emma shoved a piece of pizza in her direction. "Here. Eat. You look a little pale. You want some wine or something?"

"No! I mean. No thanks."

44

Ellery's house was a study in the spooktacular. Newcomers might think that the decorative gargoyles and cauldron planters overflowing with orange mums were Halloween decorations. They would be wrong. Ellery's house looked like an homage to Halloween all year-long.

The front yard was filled with black folding chairs all facing the front stoop which was now under the cover of a black and silver tulle arch. Jack-o-lanterns with flickering candles lined the aisle and orange string lights wrapped around tree trunks. Elevated pine coffins were scattered near the sidewalk for the cocktail reception that was to follow, giving the guests the perfect front row seat to the evening's Halloween parade.

Guests, nearly all familiar faces including the entire Pierce family, milled about the yard enjoying the complimentary gin and tonics and corpse revivers from the bar. Everyone was in costume. With the exception of Donovan who donned a Lone Ranger mask with his uniform. It was as in the spirit as he was going to get this year.

The best part? There were no protestors.

Today's therapy session had taken up Eva's entire afternoon, successfully blocking her from driving out of town to procure a certain test to determine her entire future. The therapy session had consisted of a private showing for one of a PowerPoint called "Moms Worse Than Yours" at the movie theater between actual show times.

Mama Fratelli from *The Goonies* was particularly disturbing. However, the only thing Eva could think about during the entire presentation was what kind of mother she might be. It was a waste of time and energy to worry about an unknown—okay, a huge unknown—until it was known.

"You okay?" Donovan asked, nudging her chin up to look at him.

"Me? Sure. Everything is great."

"You've been staring at that gargoyle for a full minute."

Eva blinked. She needed to tuck this worry away. Compartmentalize. Detach. Ellery was getting married. Emma was surprising Niko tonight with their baby news. Donovan was facing a long night managing mischief. The last thing anyone needed was unplanned pregnancy drama.

"I'm just nervous about my costume. I hope it's, uh, Halloween-y enough."

Donovan gave her a long, hard look. "You're dressed like Little Red Riding Hood," he reminded her. "I may not be dressed as the Big, Bad Wolf, but I wouldn't mind eating you."

"Har har." She rolled her eyes.

"Something bothering you?" he pressed, adjusting the ties of her cloak and letting his fingers linger on her neck.

"I'm concerned about something," she admitted.

"Is it something that can be fixed right now?" he asked.

She shook her head. "It's something I'll want to talk to you about if it turns out to be something to worry about. But for now, I'd like to have fun tonight."

He wrapped her in his arms, squeezed. "I'd like that," he told her.

Eva closed her eyes and let herself be held by the man who loved her. Here, in Donovan's arms, she could forget about the rest of the world.

"Two, four, six, eight, who shouldn't be getting married?"

"Ellery! Ellery!"

"Well, fuck," Donovan sighed.

"What in the ever-living hell are they doing here?" Eva groaned. The remaining members of the Beautification Committee were shuffling about in a small circle on the sidewalk in front of Ellery's house. Willa, dressed as what Eva could only assume was a rubber chicken, held a sign that read "Caution: Match Not Approved." Bruce and Amethyst, in matching clown outfits, were lugging around a banner that simply said "SHAME."

Wilson, the diminutive jeweler, carried a sign for his jewelry store. He was dressed as a garden gnome. Or a fairy-tale dwarf. Eva wasn't sure which.

Bobby stood off to the side in her pizza delivery costume, looking first at the protestors and then the gathering wedding guests. Finally, after what looked like monumental inner conflict, she picked up her sign.

I'm not with them. Congratulations, Ellery & Mason.

"This is about to go horribly wrong," Eva whispered.

"Bobby, what exactly do you think you're doing?" Amethyst stormed toward Bobby, her happy clown face hiding her frown. Her clown shoes made squeak noises on the sidewalk.

Ellery's front door flew open, rebounding against the front wall of the house. Ellery, in yards of white lace and an honest-to-goodness veil, stood hands-on-hips, glaring at the uninvited guests.

"Uh-oh," Donovan said under his breath.

The bride stormed down the stairs toward the Beautification Committee.

Donovan gave a warning whistle, and Carter, Beckett, Jax, and Niko arranged themselves between the protestors and the angry bride. It was a dramatic faceoff considering the costumes. Beckett was dressed as George Washington complete with white powder wig. Carter in his crushed velvet pirate overcoat and tricorner hat stood next to Niko Frankenstein.

Jax was decked out as a German beer wench. "What?" he asked, noting the attention. "I lost a bet." He shrugged his bare shoulders and adjusted his sock boobs.

"What do you think you're doing?" Ellery demanded, peering over Jax's shoulder.

"We're protesting an unfit match," Bruce said proudly.

"And I'm protesting their protest," Bobby piped up.

"Oh, this is bad," Eva muttered.

Joey growled at her side. "We're not letting these jackwagons ruin Ellery's wedding." In a nod to the holiday, she'd gone the cowgirl route with an ankle length duster, jeans, and checkered shirt.

"Doesn't Jax have a thing for cowgirls?" Eva asked.

Joey smirked. "Yeah, but unfortunately for him, I don't have a thing for beer wenches. Did you get a load of Emma's outfit?"

Eva grinned. "The mummy?" Emma was wearing a ragged white mini dress that looked like it had been fashioned out of bandages. "Niko's in for one hell of a surprise tonight ."

"Yeah, well, let's try to keep the rest of the freaking to a minimum," Summer said, pointing at Ellery who had her fingers to her temples and was humming as she stared daggers at Bruce.

"I'm not sure if the woman dressed as a bride should be the one to tell the bride to calm down," Gia pointed out.

Summer grimaced and looked down at the crocheted white dress. "I was going for a hippie bride," she said, touching the ring of flowers on her head. "Gotta admit, it never occurred to me that Ellery would actually dress like a traditional bride."

"I don't think anyone saw that coming," Gia agreed.

"Just like no one would *ever* guess you were going as a witch again." Joey rolled her eyes.

"Hey, your guy likes cowgirls. Mine likes witches. Especially since it was Halloween the first time we had sex in his secret passage. So neener." Gia stuck her tongue out.

"Okay, everyone is sexy and creative. Can we please go prevent Ellery from imploding Bruce's brain?" Eva sighed.

While Beckett and Donovan tried to talk sense into the Beautification Committee, Eva and company tried to distract Ellery. Summer pressed a cup of corpse reviver into Ellery's hand before the bride could punch someone on her wedding day.

"So, Ellery. Your dress is beautiful but not at all what I was expecting."

Ellery gave up trying to voodoo Bruce with her eyes. She looked down at her dress, ran black fingernails over the ivory lace. "Do you think Mason will like it? I wanted to wear something that would make him happy."

"I'm pretty sure he loves you exactly the way you are," Emma pointed out. "He's head over heels for you."

"Yeah, but it's our wedding day. The most important day of our lives. I want Mason to look back and see the bride he always wanted."

"See? This drama right here is why Jax was a freaking genius and planned the whole thing without me," Joey said, waving her hand in a circle. "I'd lose my shit."

"I'm about to," Ellery said, narrowing her eyes at the protestors that seemed even louder than before.

Gia and Eva stepped in front of Ellery.

Anthony Berkowicz, camera in hand, popped up next to them like a Whack-A-Mole and fired off several shots. "Dammit, Anthony! I hired you to shoot the wedding, not this!" Ellery moaned.

"Gotta capture the full story! This is news," he said, capturing another dozen stills of Bruce and Beckett arguing.

Niko peeled off from the men and joined their little circle. "That's a nice camera, Anthony. Mind if I take a look?"

"Oh sure," Anthony said eagerly handing it over. "It's a DSLR with twenty-two megapixels—hey!"

Niko gave Anthony a light shove and turned the camera back on Ellery. "Let's see a smile from the gorgeous bride."

Ellery beamed on command, and Niko snapped away.

"Ellery?"

They all turned as one, and Eva heard the quiet click of the shutter as Niko captured Mason's first look at his bride.

"Mason?" Ellery gasped.

Eva slapped a hand over her mouth to hide her completely warranted gasp. Joey was less concerned about filtering her comments. "What the hell is this guy wearing?"

Mason, mild-mannered accountant and general sweetheart, was dressed to the nines in a tux and tails with black tie, black shirt, and precariously perched top hat. All looked as though they'd been rolled in the dirt of a fresh grave. His face was painted like he was a backup member of KISS, ghoulish white with black accents.

Bride and groom floated toward each other as the entire crowd hushed.

"You look—" they both began.

"You don't look like you," Ellery said, running a finger over Mason's face paint.

"I wanted to look good for you," he said, taking her hands in his.

"You did this for me?" Ellery asked, tears filling her eyes.

Emma grabbed Eva's arm and sniffled. "So beautiful," she whispered.

Pregnancy hormones had taken her stalwart sister hostage.

"Keep it together," Eva hissed.

Mason nodded. "And you're wearing this for me?"

Ellery's deep violet lips curved. She wiped a tear away with the lace of her glove. "I thought you'd want a bride on your wedding day."

"I love you just the way you are," Mason said, tenderly brushing another tear off her cheek.

A collective "aww" rose up from the spectators.

"Hang on! Now just hang on one minute." Bruce pushed his way through the crowd. "You mean to tell me that you love this man so much you'd dress up as a *traditional* bride on your favorite day of the year?"

Ellery nodded.

"And you," he pointed a clown finger at Mason's ghoulish face. "You did this... this corpse groom weirdo look for her?"

"Sure did." Mason's head bobbed until Eva thought he might lose his hat. "She deserves a wedding day to remember forever."

"Beautification Committee assemble," Bruce screeched.

Eva and Gia shared a glance and shrugged. The Beautification Committee members huddled up like an offensive line under a tree decked out with fake sparkly tarantulas.

"We may have *slightly* misjudged this relationship," Bruce announced.

"Gee. You think?" Bobby rolled her eyes.

"I'm not afraid to admit when I'm wrong. It's happened once before. I think what we witnessed here really takes us into Article Seventeen, Sub-Section L."

Eva glanced around the circle at the nodding heads. "What's in Sub-Section L?"

"Well, essentially it's an emergency dispensation," Bruce said.

"Meaning?" Gia asked.

"Meaning, the Beautification Committee would grant an immediate, unrescindable approval," Wilson explained through his canary costume beak.

"I second the motion," Eva said quickly.

"Third," Gia jumped in.

"All in favor of granting an emergency dispensation in the matching of Ellery Cozumopolaus and Mason Smith?"

"And reinstating Ellery to the Beautification Committee," Bobby added.

The ayes were unanimous.

45

It was a beautiful ceremony. Ellery's mother and father walked her down the black velvet aisle dressed as werewolves. Her father had to wipe away tears with his furry paws as he handed his daughter over to her corpse groom. Donovan, his arm heavy and firm around her, stroked Eva's shoulder with his thumb during the vows the bride and groom wrote.

Ellery vowed to always keep surprising Mason and learn to golf while he promised that he would buy more black shirts, and not only would he go to Demon Con with her, but he'd let her pick his costume.

They sealed their commitment with a hair-raising, make-up smearing kiss that brought the wedding guests to their feet. While the happy couple posed for pictures with Niko, the guests were free to find their coffins and refill their glasses.

Eva picked up the solar powered calculator at her place. "Looks like Mason had a say in the favors," she noted.

Donovan grinned and settled his hands on her shoulders. "Have I told you that you look good enough to eat?" he whispered in her ear, breath hot on her skin.

"Does the big, bad sheriff have time tonight for a snack?" she asked, turning in his arms. She looped her hands around his neck. "Aren't you on high alert for the worst night of the planetary crossing?"

"I'm hoping that I'll get to undress you tonight in the living room in front of the fire, Red."

"Won't your parents get an eyeful while they're watching TV?" she teased.

"Did I mention that my parents decided it was for the best to rent a cabin at the campground for the foreseeable future?"

"You didn't mention that. You didn't ask them to move out, did you?" Donovan was working his fingers in slow circles on her lower back.

"Yes. That's exactly what I did. 'Mom, Dad, I need more time to get my girlfriend naked on every horizontal surface in my house. Do you mind moving out for a few years?'"

"Halloween makes you a smart ass."

He grinned. "I promise it was their idea, and I pretended to put up a fight about it. But we'll all be happier this way. Especially since I saw they added the Fifty Shades movies to my Netflix queue. I think they want the privacy just as much as we do."

Eva laughed. "Well here's hoping for a quiet, naked night."

Donovan's radio squawked. "Sheriff, we got a problem at the high school."

"Damn it." Donovan raised his middle finger to the sky. "I swear to God. When this is all over and your book is done, you and I are taking a two-week, clothing-optional vacation."

"Count me in," she breathed and grabbed him by the shirt for a short, hard kiss. "Good luck out there, sheriff."

He ran a thumb over her lower lip and shook his head. "Don't walk home alone tonight. I have a feeling the shit might hit the fan."

"I'll be safe," she promised. "Bye, Sheriff."

"Later, Evangelina."

She watched him go, never tiring of the way his uniform pants showcased his ass.

"You got a little something right there, little sister," Gia said poking her finger at the corner of Eva's mouth. "Oh, never mind. Just drool."

"Eva slobbering after her man again?" Emma asked, tugging the hem of her bandage dress down.

"Oh, please. Like I haven't seen you two go all moist in the nether regions over your husbands."

"That's disgusting," Emma wrinkled her nose.

"And true," Gia grinned. "How much time do we have before your surprise? I want to pick up the kids and bring them over for the parade."

"You have until the parade," Emma told her, checking her watch. "Not a word though. Thankfully the wedding pictures are keeping him occupied for now. I'm so nervous I have to pee every four minutes."

"That might not be nerves," Gia pointed out.

"He's looking at us," Emma hissed. "Act natural."

"Laugh like I said something funny," Eva said.

Gia and Emma reacted as if she'd just walked into a plate glass window and fallen on her ass. "Okay, maybe a little less hysterical, guys."

"Great. Now I really have to pee," Emma muttered.

They split up, heading off to bathrooms and kid-gathering, and Eva hung back to watch the wedding revelers enjoy themselves. It was unlike anything she'd ever experienced in her life. This wacky little town and its quirky inhabitants.

"Well, here's to another successful match," Bruce said, off to her right. He handed Amethyst a corpse reviver with a chipper wink. "To the Beautification Committee."

Amethyst raised her glass to his. "To the Beautification Committee and to Ellery and Mason."

"Of course, of course. Them too." His head bobbed in agreement, sending his frizzy red clown ringlets bouncing.

The clowns touched glasses, and Eva hid her laugh. She was surrounded by crazy. Well-meaning, lovable crazy, and she couldn't think of any place she'd rather be. Maybe Blue Moon wasn't the worst place in the world to accidentally change her life.

Donovan: *Crisis averted. Barely. Argument over order of parade floats turned ugly.*

Eva: *All us corpses are behaving perfectly on this end of town.*

Donovan: *I'm going to come through with the parade to keep an eye on things. I'll be the masked sheriff stepping on discarded tootsie rolls.*

Eva: *Try to get close to Phoebe and Franklin so you can see Emma's surprise.*

Donovan: *Will do. Gotta go separate the Girl Scouts from the Boy Scouts. They're either going to start fighting or making out.*

THE WEDDING GUESTS—BUOYED by the flowing alcohol—lined up around their coffin tables to watch the parade. Eva made sure that Emma and Niko had a front row seat. The high school marching band tromped past them playing "The Monster Mash." Evan, sent them a wink over his trumpet, and Aurora jumped up holding Lydia to give him a little sister standing ovation.

The Society for the Preservation of Blue Moon Values was next with their psychedelic herd of VW Buses. They were led by Ernest Washington, who was throwing full-size candy bars from the roof of his rainbow bus.

Sugar stirred the crowd, making them more excitable, and Eva was relieved to see the next float. She brought her fingers to her mouth and watched as Blue Moon's Farming Society rolled up in a hay wagon. Phoebe and Franklin were perched on rocking chairs. Next to them were Vadim and Greta, Niko's father and stepmother.

"What are my parents doing on a float in Blue Moon?" Niko asked, gaping at the wagon. "Am I hallucinating?"

Emma grinned and pointed. "Wait. I think they're trying to tell you something."

Greta and Phoebe were pretending to knit opposite ends of a huge blanket. Vadim and Franklin simultaneously snapped newspapers open. The backs of the newspapers spelled something out. With a wink, Phoebe and Greta held the blanket sideways.

We're going to be grandparents.

"Holy sh— Emma?" Niko was halfway out of his chair. "Oh, my God. Are you? Are we—You're dressed as a *mummy*." The realization hit Niko like a corpse reviver. He was sweeping Emma off her feet and swinging her in a circle as parade participants and spectators cheered.

"Surprise," Emma whispered. "You're going to be a daddy."

Eva felt her eyes go damp at the sweetness of the moment. She spotted Donovan in the center of it all, his attention was on the crowd, but he was grinning. That dimpled smile that melted her every time she saw it. She was looking at her future. And that wasn't Uranus talking.

46

It started innocently enough over a box of Red Hots the fire department flung into the crowd as they inched along in one of their engines. Two kids made a grab for it. And then all hell broke loose. Looking back on it, Donovan had felt the tension in the air as he walked the parade route, vigilant for mischief. It was only a matter of time before it imploded.

The kids scrapped on the sidewalk, and then the parents stepped in. It went downhill quickly from there.

Thanks to the "make love not war" mentality, not many citizens knew how to make a proper fist let alone plow that fist into someone else's face. The fight was more slapping and hair-pulling with some biting thrown in for good measure.

Donovan waded in and dragged two middle-aged fathers apart. "You two need to keep your cool," he ordered. "Now, separate and go on home, or I'm going to have to drag you into the station."

It was right about that time that one of them bit him on the forearm.

"Goddammit," Donovan muttered. "I'm gonna need backup," he said into the radio. He grabbed the bigger of the dads in a headlock.

"Sheriff, we've got problems at the park," Minnie announced from his radio.

"Shit." The melee was spreading. The moms were now shouting insults at each other.

"Meat-eater!"

"Leather-wearer!"

And the kids were running amuck and stealing candy from other spectators. There was another shove down the line, another insulted bellow, and the entire block erupted.

With the man under his arm swinging wildly at the air around them, Donovan whipped out his phone and dialed.

"Mom, I need help. Bring every able-minded adult you can get and split 'em between the park and the parade route."

"On it," Hazel responded before hanging up.

The head-locked dad got in a lucky elbow to Donovan's gut, and the phone went flying into the storm drain.

"All right. You're gonna pay for that one," Donovan gritted out.

By the time Donovan made it to the town square, all hell had broken loose and was barely being contained. He'd managed to break up two more fights, find a lost toddler who had climbed a goddamn tree, and put out an accidental fire that had started with a pile of leaves and a dropped bong on Bruce Oakleigh's lawn.

Deputy Colby had caught up with him a block from the park, and together they'd caught two nursing home escapees as they tried to break into the farm supply store. Mrs. McCafferty had just turned the garden hose on them when Donovan and Colby came on the scene.

In the park, Hazel was showing off her law enforcement background by corralling suspects of full moon rage in the funnel cake stand. "You sit your ass down, Melvin, or I'll kick it," she threatened a middle-aged man dressed as Gandalf.

Donovan's dad was attaching a hose to the fire hydrant to put out a bonfire lit by some enterprising junior high schoolers who were roasting marshmallows on the middle of the sidewalk.

Jax and Carter Pierce were busy breaking up a dance off between the high school football team and the marching band. The crowd parted as Charisma Champion jogged past shouting "Don't worry! The end is near!"

Beckett was performing his mayoral duties by dragging looters out of OJs by Julia. Because Blue Moon was the type of town that stole fresh juice when they rioted.

Joey had confiscated Deputy Layla's bullhorn and was shouting "Calm the fuck down" from the gazebo. He saw her narrow in on a reed-slim hippie working hard to overturn a park bench.

"Oh, shit," Donovan muttered.

Joey dropped the bullhorn and jumped from the gazebo onto the hippie's back. They went down in a tangle of limbs. Donovan reached Joey's side just as she let her hand fly. He'd been hoping to save the guy from a broken nose.

Fortunately, Joey went with the bitch slap instead. "What the fuck is wrong with you, Winston? Go the hell home!" She slapped him again for good measure and then helped him to his feet.

"Hey, Sheriff!" Niko, a sleeve torn off his Frankenstein jacket, held two women by the scruff of their necks. "Funnel cake jail is at capacity. Where do you want these two?"

"Bring 'em over here," Summer called from the knitted sock stand. "I've got room for two more!"

Three buck naked Mooners sprinted past singing a rousing version of "Free Bird."

"Hazel!" Donovan shouted.

"We need a bigger jail," she called back.

He ducked as a woman darted around him wielding a pool noodle like it was a saber. She was chased by Enid the dog walker who held a pair of knitting needles.

Donovan grabbed the needles out of Enid's hands and sent her on her way. He spotted Layla talking two Mooners out of a tree and borrowed her phone.

"Hello?"

"Eva?"

"Donovan, what the hell is going on?"

"I need help. We're out of jail space. Can you find me a place big enough to hold at least fifty people?" A trombone player blasted the quarterback in the ear with a sharp note, and the quarterback retaliated with an epic wedgie. "Shit. Maybe more like sixty."

"Absolutely. I'm on it. I'll call you back at this number."

"What's that noise?" he asked.

"You don't want to know."

DONOVAN'S CALL had caught Eva dragging a wailing Willa out of the Snip Shack. The woman had started proclaiming her need for a perm, and Eva had barely been able to wrestle her out of the stylist's chair. It was definitely Uranus's work that had the salon touting "FREE PERMS AND PIXIE CUTS" at ten o'clock at night on Halloween.

She stuffed Willa in the passenger seat of her Mini and ran around to the driver's side.

"Willa, what place in town could hold sixty or so people?"

"Why won't you let me get beautiful curls?" Willa howled.

"Because you would hate your beautiful curls in the morning. Trust me. Now, focus. Where can we imprison a large chunk of the town's population?"

"The movie theater or the high school, I suppose?"

"Good thinking. Where does the principal or guidance counselor live?"

Willa pointed the way and Eva swung the wheel of the car in the direction. "If you behave yourself, we'll stop and get you hot rollers somewhere."

"So, I can have curls?" Willa asked holding up her curtain of stick-straight hair.

"Yes, the temporary kind that won't make you cry in the morning."

"Okay, turn here."

They found Huckleberry Cullen, dressed as a vampire chasing off a troop of costumed adults who were toilet papering his house and giggling like children.

Eva ordered Willa to stay in the car and jumped out of the car.

"Go home!" she said, shooing the cackling neighbors out of the yard.

"It's the sheriff's girlfriend," one of them giggled.

"5-0! 5-0!"

"Let's go!"

A man who looked to be in his fifties looped a strip of toilet paper around Eva's shoulders before scampering off behind his friends.

"Are you Huckleberry?" Eva asked, crumpling the toilet paper into a ball.

"Huck," he said, scraping a hand through his thick hair. "Thanks for the assist. Usually they're not all insane at the same time."

"Huck, I need access to the school."

His eyes narrowed as he studied her. "Ah, hell. Are you crazy, too? Are you planning to hack the planetarium's computer to phone home?"

Eva rolled her eyes. "No time to convince you of my sanity. I need your keys to the high school."

"Why?"

"I need a bigger jail."

"Maybe I'd better come with you."

"LITTLE RED RIDING HOOD, a rubber chicken, and a vampire are in a Mini Cooper," Huck muttered as they pulled into the high school parking lot.

"I know we sound—and look—like a rolling joke, but if we don't get all the temporary crazies in a safe place, there may not be a Blue Moon standing tomorrow morning," Eva said, yanking the parking brake.

Willa maneuvered herself out of the passenger seat, her rubber chicken head getting stuck on the sun visor. Huck followed, unfolding his long legs and cape from the backseat. He was right around thirty and very good-looking with his angular face, broad shoulders, and friendly smile. "Oh, I get it. Cullen. Vampire," Eva said, pointing at his fake teeth.

He sighed. "When you work with middle schoolers, there's a lot of *Twilight* references. And when your last name is the same as these beloved vampires, you get a lot of attention, especially when they find out that it annoys you. Word of advice, never make a bet with a class of eighth graders. It's not going to work out in your favor." He tapped a finger to the Team Edward badge he wore on his vest.

Huck led them to a side door near the parking lot and fished the keys out of his vampire pants. "This is probably your best bet space-wise," he said, letting them into the gymnasium. "But I don't know how you're going to keep all your inmates separated.

Eva surveyed the cavernous room. It was a typical gym in the shiny floor and bleachers way, but the walls were decked out in a psychedelic rainbow mural. The wall under the digital scoreboard was painted with a depiction of the meeting of the Blue Moon farming community and the wandering hippies that arrived in 1969 after getting lost leaving Woodstock.

"Okay. I think we can make this work. Edward—I mean, Huck—can you get us some tape? And Willa, do you know where the art studio is?"

"Of course, I do. I spent many a happy day molding vegan clay and painting unicorn figurines there."

"Uh, great? Can you go make some signs? Something that will enhance the prison experience?"

"I'd love to!" Willa skipped away, her hair flowing out behind her as her costume made rubber squeak noises.

"Signs to enhance the prison experience?" Huck asked.

"Anything to keep her out of trouble and out of the hair salon," Eva sighed.

"Right, the free perms. I was thinking maybe I should try a new look," he said, shoving his hand through his heart-throb hair.

"Huck—"

"Kidding. Sorry. It's been a long month. Hard not to just give up and join the insanity."

"I know the feeling. Now, go find some colored tape. A lot

of it." She pointed toward the door. Huck swirled off in his cape.

Eva was busy dragging a six-foot folding table in front of the bleachers when her phone rang.

"Hey," she said, breathlessly.

"Please tell me you're safe and have a jail," Donovan said wearily on the other end.

Eva looked up as Huck returned wielding a dozen rolls of painters tape. Willa was behind him holding an oversized poster painted with flowers and butterflies.

Welcome to Blue Moon Jail
We're Happy to Have You

"The new expanded Blue Moon County Jail is ready to accept its first residents. I'm at the high school. Just follow the butterflies and flowers."

"Butterflies?"

"Trust me. You can't miss it," she promised.

"Eva?"

"Yes, sheriff?"

"Thank you."

"It's nice to be needed. Now, get your sexy ass over here so I can help you lock up half the town's population."

47

Donovan marched five suspects into the Blue Moon High School under a sign welcoming them to jail. It had been a tight squeeze in his cruiser. Slim Felderhoff, who had shown the poor judgment to stick a wad of gum in Donovan's hair, had to sit on Kathy Wu's lap in the backseat. Velma Flinthorn, caught egging the police station, rode shotgun. He'd gotten tired of flipping off the lights and sirens that she repeatedly turned on, so they came in hot, lights blazing and tires squealing into the parking lot.

The gym lights were on, and he spotted Eva sitting at a table behind a laptop with Huck Cullen. There was a glittery sign attached to the front of the table that read Processing.

Willa beamed from a second larger table labeled Hospitality. It was stacked with bottles of water, chocolate milk, and snacks that looked as though they had been pilfered from the school's cafeteria.

"Welcome," Willa called out warmly. "Please begin your incarceration journey at Processing and then come see me for your welcome package."

Donovan pinched the bridge of his nose between his

fingers to ward off the headache that was threatening. “You heard the lady, go on,” he said, nudging Rupert the beanpole waiter who had made the poor decision to take up residence on his on-again, off-again girlfriend’s front yard in a tent.

They shuffled forward, lining up in front of Eva and Huck.

“What’s your full name?” Eva asked politely.

“Rupert Meadowlark Shermanski the third.”

“Of course, it is,” Eva said under her breath.

Donovan turned to survey the gym. The entire floor had been cordoned off with tape in six-foot by four-foot blocks. Each block was neatly numbered by a small sign.

“Okay, Kathy,” Huck said. “What’s your offense?”

Kathy shot Donovan a dirty look. “Sheriff Goody Two Shoes over there didn’t think I should be riding a bike in the bike lane. He’s the one who’s gone crazy. He should be getting arrested, not me!”

Donovan sighed. “Kathy, you stole little Casablanca Taylor’s bike.”

Kathy snorted. “So?”

“So, she chased you for six blocks, and you threw all her Halloween candy out of the basket.”

“You have no case! I was riding in the bike lane!”

“On a *stolen* bike!”

Kathy glared at him. “I want a lawyer.”

“I’ll call Beckett,” Eva offered.

Donovan was more than happy to dump Kathy Wu on Beckett. “Sounds great. Next!”

“In the meantime, you’re in meditation spot twenty-five,” Huck said, handing Kathy a sticky note with the number written on it. “You can go on over to Hospitality. We hope you enjoy your stay with us.”

Donovan rolled his eyes. If ever he’d wished for a more normal legal system in Blue Moon, this was the moment.

He ducked behind the table and dropped a kiss on Eva's head. "I owe you so big," he murmured against her hair.

She beamed up at him. "As in 'let me take you on a first date' big?"

"As in, I'm taking you on vacation somewhere tropical where bathing suits are optional."

Her eyes widened.

"Excuse me. I've been waiting at least an hour to be processed," Slim whined. "I want to get my chocolate milk while they still have some." He looked desperately toward the hospitality table.

"Slim, you got here five seconds ago," Donovan reminded him.

"If my blood sugar gets too low, I start to act up."

Donovan pointed at his own head. "You start to act up by putting gum in an officer of the law's hair?"

Eva gasped when he took off his hat.

"Hey, boss. You know you got gum in your hair?" Minnie Murkle bustled in with an overnight bag and a stack of takeout containers.

"Gum?" Willa called from her table. "I can take care of that for you. I'm great at cutting gum out of hair."

"I'd appreciate that," Donovan told her.

"I'll take over processing if Eva can manage the hospitality table," Minnie offered.

"Sold," Eva said. She rose and put her hands on Donovan's chest. "You're sexy even with gum in your hair," she told him.

"I can't wait until tonight is over," he whispered. "I'm going to sleep for a week, make love to you for twenty-four hours straight, and then put us on a plane to anywhere but here."

Eva grinned. "The faster you lock everyone up, the sooner we can get on that plane."

"Willa, can you cut fast?"

THE WOMAN GAVE HIM A MOHAWK. With shears she found in the sheep shearing lab.

And by that point, Donovan didn't even care. As far as he was concerned he'd have his balls waxed if it meant the night would be over. With his deputies and mother working territories around town, they'd managed to round up fifty-seven delinquent weirdos caught red-handed doing mischief.

There were no serious crimes. That wasn't Blue Moon's style. No, rather than a homicide or an assault, Mooners were satisfied breaking into the juice shop, whipping up their own concoctions, and leaving money on the counter for their drinks. Or the spontaneous naked sit-in protesting mainly clothing but also taxes and the town ordinance stipulating the appropriate grass height for lawns.

Nothing, after tonight, would ever surprise him again. Wearily, Donovan opened the gymnasium door for his latest perp, Old Man Carson. The elderly farmer had decided to liberate his neighbor's herd of goats. They hadn't gone far. They'd followed Carson home and into his house where they ate the better part of his couch and the hammock swing on his back porch.

Carson had called the police himself and confessed.

Donovan led the nonagenarian to the processing table.

"Really, Sheriff? Old Man Carson?" Minnie asked in exasperation. "I feel like you're just picking people up out of their beds."

"That's exactly what I'm doing, Minnie. Picking on the innocent citizens of Blue Moon." Donovan shook his head. Eva was staring at him from her spot in the guard section of the bleachers. He raised his hand in an exhausted wave.

She skimmed her hand over her own head and gave him

the thumbs up, mouthing the word "hot." He winked in return. At least his girlfriend wasn't horrified by the chop job Willa had given him.

Beckett was across the aisle from Eva, talking to another client. After Kathy Wu had demanded representation, so had most of the rest of the yahoos he'd dragged in. It was pointless. None of them were going to actual jail, and he doubted that most of them would face any real charges. He just needed to get them off the streets until the sun came up.

Layla, yawning, marched two teenagers covered from head to toe in flour in through the side door toward the processing table.

They just needed to hang in for a few more hours. Then this whole shit-tastic mess would be over.

"No touching!" Eva yelled into the bullhorn at meditation boxes thirteen and fourteen. The two temporary residents stopped their slap fight.

Gia was there, too. She, Phoebe, and Franklin were doling out pillows and blankets to the detainees. Donovan's father was manning the hospitality table and accepting the community donations that were still arriving in the middle of the night.

Michael was deep in conversation with Wallace Wu who had arrived with a toiletry kit, pillow, and lotion-infused socks for his incarcerated wife.

The conversations amongst the detainees and the volunteers were more hushed now at three in the morning than they had been a few hours ago. As the moon sunk lower in the night sky, Donovan began to feel a spark of hope that this could all soon be behind them. He vowed he'd be retired before the next planetary crossing.

His mother ambled up behind him and thumped him on

the shoulder. "Streets are quieting down. I think we're on the downslide."

Donovan put an arm around her shoulders and rubbed the back of his neck. "You ever miss this?" he asked, yawning.

Hazel grinned up at him. "Every damn day. It's nice to spend your days making a difference."

"I feel like today was just chasing my own tail."

"You made a difference," Hazel insisted. "Sure, it looks like a hot mess in here. But nobody's property accidentally burnt down or cars rolled into the pond."

"Did that happen last time?" he asked, guiding her over to the hospitality table for coffee.

"Yep. Lost three cabins over at the campground because some dumb hippie decided to bake pot brownies over an open flame."

"Sheldon Fitzsimmons?" Donovan guessed.

"The one and the same."

"Explains a lot about Fitz," Donovan mused.

"That kid turned out a lot more normal than he had any right to," Hazel agreed.

"You hear about his side job stripping?"

Hazel let out a tired laugh. "Nothing would surprise me about that boy."

"Thanks for being here, Mom."

She rested her head on his shoulder for a moment. "She's a keeper."

Donovan looked up to where Eva was keeping an eagle eye on her detained neighbors. She looked exhausted, and he felt bad that she was wasting writing time helping him babysit an entire town, but he appreciated it more than he could say.

"I plan to keep her," he told his mother.

"She's going to give you trouble," Hazel predicted.

"Oh, I can guarantee that. But if she's willing to stick

through this?" Donovan said, waving his hand at the gymnasium of temporarily impulsive idiots. "She's worth the trouble."

Hazel grinned. "You always did have good sense."

He squeezed her shoulders. "I learned it from you. But I got my sweet dance moves from Dad."

"Hey, boss?" Colby trod over prone Mooners to get to them.

"What you got for me, deputy?"

"I got Agnes Merill in Cleary. Police chief called a few minutes ago. They picked her up when she tried to skip out on her hotel bill."

Donovan swore quietly, his gaze returning to Eva.

"Did they find the stolen property?"

Colby nodded. "All but the booze. Seems she got rid of that evidence."

Donovan sighed and glanced at his watch. "She asked for a lawyer yet?"

"Not as of when the call came in, but I'm sure it's a matter of time. You going?"

"Yeah, I'm going. You two keep a lid on it, okay? I want to talk to her before I tell Eva."

"Sure, boss."

"Why don't you go on and get it over with?" Hazel suggested. "We'll hold down the fort here."

"Keep one actual deputy here at all times. Hopefully the streets are quiet by now, and we won't need the patrols."

"Will do," Colby nodded.

"And keep an eye on Eva for me."

48

The drive to Cleary was blissfully quiet compared to the chaos of the rest of the night. On the way over, he talked to the arresting officer and laid out his plan. Agnes wouldn't walk away from this one, and Donovan was prepared to do whatever it took to make sure that happened.

The Cleary police station was four times the size of Blue Moon's. A new, modern facility with bulletproof glass and an actual waiting area. The desk sergeant saw him coming and buzzed him through the front door.

"Morning," she said. She was young, academy fresh, and wide awake for four a.m. "Coffee?"

"The strongest you've got," Donovan said, taking off his hat.

"Woah. Nice hair," she said, cracking an actual smile. "Have a seat. Officer Lewis will be with you shortly."

She returned with a large mug of steaming coffee which Donovan gratefully accepted.

"Sheriff Cardona?"

The man who approached had dark skin and linebacker

shoulders. His wrist was bandaged, and there was a jagged scratch on his jaw.

"Officer Lewis?"

"Call me Jamal," he insisted. "Come on back. We'll talk before I bring her in."

Jamal led the way to an actual interrogation room. In Blue Moon, they mainly just talked to suspects in the conference room or around the water cooler. "I hear you've been having quite the night over there in Blue Moon."

Donovan took a seat in the metal chair and unfolded his legs. "The grapevine runs pretty far," he said.

"My captain is tight with your mother. She gave him a head's up in case you all needed a hand out there. But it sounds like you had it covered."

Donovan rubbed a hand over his brow. "Barely. I've never seen so many people lose their damn minds at the same time."

Jamal chuckled. "That's some kinda town you've got there. Me and the wife stayed in that B&B last year for our anniversary. Got a kick out of the quirkiness."

Donovan gave a one-sided smile. "Quirkiness. That's a good word for it." He took another sip of coffee. "That scratch looks pretty fresh."

Jamal touched his jaw. "You wouldn't expect it out of the bony-ass woman, but that Merill is stronger than she looks." He held up his wrist. "Nails are pretty sharp, so we'll be keeping her cuffed for your talk."

"I appreciate you letting me have a chat with her."

Jamal shrugged. "She's not the kind of person we need roaming the streets. And not just because she spit on my partner and kicked the hotel desk clerk in the chest. So, let's deliver the DA a nice, airtight case and let the legal system do its job."

"That's the plan."

"I'm gonna let you run the interview, but I'll be in the corner just in case she goes for your neck with those killer claws."

"Appreciate it," Donovan said wryly.

Jamal returned moments later with the spitting-mad Agnes Merill. The jumpsuit bagged on her skinny frame. Her hair was wild, hanging in clumps around her sallow face.

"Record on. Interview of Agnes Merill. Officer Jamal Lewis and Sheriff Donovan Cardona present. Ms. Merill, you've been advised of your rights." Jamal recited by rote.

"Fuck. You." Agnes spat out.

Donovan smiled at Eva's mother. "Ms. Merill. You were found to be in possession of stolen property," he said, flipping through the photos Jamal and his partner had taken of Agnes' car.

"That's my stuff. I didn't steal nothing."

He tossed down another picture in front of her. "So, are you saying this isn't you breaking into your daughter's house and leaving with the items found in your car tonight?"

Agnes picked up the print and sneered. "So I visited my daughter. Who cares? She wanted me to have that stuff. Gave it to me." She gave a one-shoulder shrug. "I want a cigarette."

Donovan glanced at Jamal. "Sorry, ma'am. No smoking indoors."

"Then what the fuck is this for?" she shoved the empty ashtray off the table with her bound hands.

Jamal grinned. "It's for decoration."

"Whatever. I'll be walking out of here before morning."

"Not until you explain what you were doing in Evangelina Merill's house and how you came to be in possession of items that belonged to her that were stolen in a break-in," Donovan said.

"She's my daughter. What's hers is mine."

"Is that why you've blackmailed her out of twenty-six thousand dollars in the past eight years? You feel that you have a right to your daughter's money."

"She could have said no," Agnes pointed out.

"She could have. But you made that a less attractive option didn't you? Threatening her, the rest of the family."

"Threats? That's what she told you? You must be gullible when you got your dick out." She gave him a sharp grin. "Oh, I know you and Eva are fucking. I read all about it in your stupid town's newspaper."

"I'm dating your daughter with plans to marry her," Donovan corrected her evenly.

"Well, she owes me. And if you marry her, you'll owe me too."

"Exactly what does Eva owe you?" Donovan asked.

"She ruined my life. Everything was fine until she was born. Then I got the postpartum and lost everything. Couldn't hold down a job. Frank kicked me out."

"You turned to drugs? Criminal activity?"

"Had to. I had no choice."

Donovan had to tamp down the urge to shove his palm into Agnes' face and shove her backwards out of her chair.

"So, you're saying that twenty-six years ago, you suffered from postpartum depression, and that's why you blackmailed your daughter out of money, broke into her house, and stole personal items?" he clarified.

"I didn't say I stole nothing. She let me take that stuff. And if she says different, she's a liar." Agnes tried to fold her arms over her chest, but her wrists were bound. "And a daughter giving her mother a little loan every once in a while ain't blackmail."

"Loans. So, you were paying her back?" Donovan asked.

Again a shrug from those bony shoulders. "If I ever get

back on my feet. But the depression and all makes it hard. I got an addiction or two. And no one's ever given me a chance to get help."

The perpetual victim.

"Eva owes me. She's got her fancy career with them books, and what do I have? I brought her into this world, and what do I have to show for it? Nothing. She owes me. They *all* owe me."

"Why?" Donovan asked. "Your ex-husband, your daughters, they all worked for what they have. What have you done to earn anything?"

"I gave them life." She spat the words out. "They owe me everything."

"You say no one's ever given you a chance to get help?" Donovan said, shifting gears.

"That's right," Agnes nodded. "Maybe I'd still be married to Frank if he'd given a damn about me."

"And he never tried to get you any help?"

"Never once. Always too busy with his restaurant and the kids." She slouched in the chair like a petulant teenager.

"It sounds like, once again, one of you is lying." Donovan pulled out a neat stack of papers. "This is an affidavit signed by Franklin Merill, your ex-husband, detailing the number of times he tried to get you into therapy. It says here early in your relationship you had issues with recreational drugs. Which leads me to believe that all your issues didn't start with the birth of your daughter."

"Papers don't mean nothing. He's lying. It's all lies."

"Last week, did Eva refuse to give you ten thousand dollars and instead offer you a way into a rehab program for addicts?"

Agnes was looking everywhere but him.

"Agnes, I've got more papers here. An affidavit from Eva detailing every time you shook her down for money. She's a writer. She kept notes, voice mails, texts. It doesn't look good.

Especially since she offered you help right before you broke into her house."

"I needed money, okay? She always gave before. Now she goes and gets some kind of backbone and gets all righteous on me?"

"You needed money, she refused to give it to you, so you took what you could from her house," Donovan spelled it out nice and neat for the record.

"She owes me," Agnes repeated. "It was my right. I needed money. I didn't take everything. I could have."

Donovan turned one of the photos around. "Did you know your grandson took this photo? Got video of you lugging stolen property out of your daughter's house. You ever met him?"

Agnes shrugged and kicked at the table leg with her tennis shoe.

"He's a smart kid. Thanks to him and his recording, we've got you cold on breaking and entering, grand theft, and Officer Lewis just added possession of stolen property."

"What are you smirking at, standing there in the corner judging me?" she asked Jamal. "A big man with a gun. Fuck you both."

"Such anger," Donovan said mildly.

"When I get out of here, I'll come back, and she'll give me what I want this time. She always does."

"There's a difference this time, Agnes. Two actually," Donovan said calmly. "Eva's gotten quite good at saying no. You'll never see a dime out of her again. And if you come within town limits of her, I'll make it my life's work to put you behind bars for the rest of your life."

"You don't scare me. Some sheriff in some pissant town?" she snorted.

"See, here's the thing Agnes. The DA's gonna offer you a

deal. They're gonna say they'll forget all about those blackmail and extortion charges if you plead guilty to breaking and entering, possession of stolen property, and theft. You'll do somewhere around two years, maybe a little less for good behavior."

"I'm not doing time!" She crashed her fisted hand onto the tabletop.

"I was hoping you'd say that," Donovan said, pasting a cocky grin on his face. "Did you know extortion is a Class D felony? That's seven years. Throw in the rest of it, and you could be facing up to ten years in the cage. And if you knew how much I loved your daughter, you'd know how badly I want you to say 'fuck the deal.'"

"I want a lawyer."

"You heard the lady," Donovan said lazily to Jamal.

Jamal hauled Agnes to her feet. "You'd better get real comfortable in a cell," he said cheerfully.

"You'll never lock me up!" she shrieked.

"News for you, lady, you're already locked up," Jamal reminded her.

"Guilty plea, and three years in and out. Or we push for trial. We've already got over a dozen witnesses happy to talk about what kind of person you are," Donovan grinned. "I really hope you don't take that deal."

Jamal half-dragged, half-pushed, Agnes down the hallway. Donovan could hear her yelling the entire way.

"Any new injuries?" he asked when Jamal returned.

"Maybe a ruptured ear drum. Nothing a beer and some aspirin won't fix," the man promised.

There was a knock on the door. The desk sergeant poked her head in. "More coffee?" she asked, holding up two fresh cups.

"God, yes please," Donovan sighed.

They sipped in silence for a moment.

"Think she'll take the deal?" Donovan asked.

"If her lawyer's got any sense, she will. But I don't think she's figured out the rest."

"You mean the part about how, now that she's behind bars, all those other bench warrants will come back to haunt her?

"I may have taken the liberty of alerting a few states to the fact that we've got Ms. Merill in custody," Jamal grinned.

"That must have been satisfying," Donovan guessed.

"Felt pretty damn good," Jamal said, raising his coffee cup.

49

Dawn was breaking when Donovan left the Cleary Police Station. His body was tired, but his mind was revving as he turned onto the town's main drag. He needed to talk to Eva. He reached for his phone before remembering it had gone down a sewer drain about a hundred years ago. He couldn't afford to be without a phone right now.

He spotted a 24-hour pharmacy up ahead and pulled into the parking lot. There was a Mini Cooper just like Eva's parked on the side. He parked next to it just to feel closer to her.

He got out, stretched, and went in through the automatic door.

"Morning," he said, greeting the girl behind the register. "You got prepaid phones here?"

She looked up from her tabloid and cappuccino. "Yep. Aisle Seven."

He headed across the brightly lit store and was halfway to Seven when a flash of red hair caught his eye.

Eva. Every cell in his body sang. It was as if he'd conjured her up out of nowhere.

She was staring at a product display chewing on her lower lip and didn't notice when he strolled down the aisle.

"Well, aren't you a sight for exhausted eyes?"

Eva's eyes widened in shock. Something fell out of her hand onto the floor, and Donovan bent to pick it up.

"What are you doing—"

His question was cut off when he realized what he held in his hand. A generic brand pregnancy test with a man and woman laughing on the box.

She was frozen in place staring in horror at his hand, and the look in her eyes telegraphed everything.

"Are we—"

She snatched the test out of his hand and bolted down the aisle and ran for the front door.

"Hey! You gotta pay for that," the clerk yelled after her.

Eva ran through the front door, and Donovan heard the rev of her engine before he got the feeling back in his body. After last night, he'd thought there was nothing in this world that could surprise him again.

He was wrong. Big time.

His body started responding to his brain, and he jogged to the front of the store, tossing a ten at the woman behind the register.

"It's always the pregnancy tests," she muttered.

Donovan threw his car in gear and peeled out of the parking lot. He could see the blue of her car at the next stop light. There was no way he was letting her get away. He flicked on his lights and siren and took off after her.

~

"OH, MY GOD. OH, MY GOD," Eva chanted to herself. This was the dumbest thing she'd ever done in her entire life.

The knock on her car window startled her even though she expected it.

Looking straight ahead, Eva pushed the power window button.

"Do you know why I pulled you over, ma'am."

She closed her eyes. "Because I might be pregnant with your baby even though we haven't even gone out on a date yet, and I panicked and accidentally shoplifted a pregnancy test because I wanted to be sure before I told you."

"Also, you went through a yellow light while speeding, and if you are carrying my child, I'm going to have to ask you to be more careful in the future."

"How can you even joke at a time like this?"

"A time like what?" he asked, leaning in the window.

"Donovan! We might be having a baby!"

"Do you have to drive with it like that to find out if you're pregnant," he asked, tapping the crumpled box she had clutched between her hand and the wheel. "I thought you just peed on it."

Eva dropped her head onto the steering wheel.

"Don't you think you should lecture me about responsibility and timing and... I don't even know at this point."

"You know what I know?" he asked.

"What?" she asked in a tiny voice.

"I know that last night was the roughest night of my entire career, but I made it through because I had you. You had my back and were there when I needed you most." The woman had set up a prison with twenty minutes' notice, for God's sake.

"You're not mad?" she asked, peeking at him.

"Baby. What have I been saying this entire month?"

"That you're insane and you want to marry me."

"I want kids, Eva. I want kids with you."

"Well, I want them with you, too. But I would have preferred to have a little time with you first—Hey!"

"What?"

"It's November 1."

He looked up at the sky where the sun was breaking over the horizon. "So it is."

"The planetary crossing?" Eva asked.

"We survived it."

"And you still love me?" She felt dazed.

Donovan opened her car door and tugged her out. "I still love the hell out of you, Evangelina."

"Even if I screwed up my pills and we're having a baby?" She needed confirmation.

"Even if we were both irresponsible and we're having a baby a little earlier than we would have planned," he promised, kissing her fingertips.

"I think I need to pee on a stick," she said, staring up into those denim blue eyes.

"I think there's two things that we need to take care of before then."

Eva felt calm and wondered if she was just too tired to worry anymore. She looked up as the cop led Agnes into the room. Her hands were cuffed in front of her. The orange of the jumpsuit made her skin look even more yellow. The bags under her eyes were practically suitcases.

"Your boyfriend talk some sense into you?" Agnes sneered, sinking down into the chair across from her.

"Here." Eva tossed a pack of cigarettes and a lighter across the table. "This is the last thing you're ever getting from me."

Delivering the line had been worth the walk of shame back at the drug store. After running out of the store with a pregnancy test and then returning to buy a pack of cigarettes, Eva had felt the need to blurt out the entire story. For some reason, it felt very important to convince the clerk that she wasn't really a horrible human being.

"Uh-huh," was the woman's only response to Eva's confession.

Greedily, Agnes snatched up the cigarettes. She lit one and blew out a cloud of blue smoke.

"I want you to bail me out," Agnes announced. "And get me a lawyer. Maybe that brother-in-law of yours? If he can dress that well, he's got to be good. I'm gonna sue every last one of these assholes for wrongful imprisonment."

Eva waited for her mother to run out of steam.

"Here's the thing, Agnes. I'm done with you. Prison or no prison, we're done. I don't owe you anything. I've got too much going on right now to pay you another thought. I've got a man out there who wants to marry me."

Agnes snorted. "I don't care what you've got going on. Or how many assholes you marry. You're getting me out of here."

"No." She said it calmly, firmly, feeling the word resonate within her. "I'm not. I let you make me feel guilty for things that weren't my fault. You want someone to blame for how pathetic and shitty your life is? Go look in a mirror." She jerked her chin toward the two-way mirror on the wall. "I'm done with you."

"I'm your mother!"

Eva shook her head. "No, see that's where I was wrong. Just because you gave birth to me doesn't make you my mother. My real mom is Phoebe."

Agnes stubbed out her cigarette, her motions jerky. "Look. Maybe I haven't always been there for you. But—"

"That's just it. You weren't there. And you made me feel like I didn't deserve to have people there for me. You made me feel like if people got to know the real me, they'd find out just how undeserving of their love and attention I was. And you know what? That's on you for the childhood years. But it's on me for not figuring it out sooner. I could have saved myself a lot of time and a lot of money."

"Eva, I need your help," Agnes rasped, desperation etching itself on her face.

"No, Agnes. You need your own help. It took me quite a while to figure out that I'm worthy, and hell, I'm fucking awesome. I don't know what's on the inside of this," she circled her finger in front of her mother's face. "Maybe there's something worthwhile inside. But nobody else is going to see it until you do."

"I need money. I need a lawyer!" Agnes tried to stand, tried to make a grab for Eva, but her hands were cuffed to the desk.

"No, Agnes, you need a lot more than that. And I just don't have the time or inclination to give you anything anymore."

Agnes started to shriek.

Eva got up and knocked on the door. "We're done here," she told the guard.

She walked out into the hallway and into Donovan's arms. The door closed behind her.

"Are you okay? How do you feel?" he asked, running a big hand down her back and pressing her just a little closer.

"I'm good. Really good."

"Good because there's one more thing we need to take care of."

"Two things," she corrected him.

50

Together, they pounded on Beckett and Gia's front door intermittently ringing the bell until they heard footsteps. "Jesus, what the hell are you two doing here?" Becket yawned. He was shirtless and his pajama pants were untied. Gia was behind him wearing one of his law-school t-shirts. Her hair was a crazy snarl of curls.

"We need your help," Eva told them.

"I used up all my lawyering last night into this morning," Beckett grumbled.

"We don't need your lawyering. We need your mayoring," Donovan grinned. "We're getting married."

"Congratulations," Beckett yawned and began to shut the door.

Donovan slapped a hand on the wood. "Today. We're getting married today. You're officiating."

Gia, suddenly awake, launched herself at Eva. "You're getting married?" she squealed.

"What's going on?" Evan grumbled from the foot of the stairs.

"Your Aunt Eva and Donovan are getting married."

"Yippy." Evan yawned and headed for the stairs.

"When and where is the ceremony?" Gia demanded.

"This morning at Donovan's place," Eva announced.

Donovan squeezed her shoulder. "This morning at our place," he corrected.

"Oh, my God! This is so exciting! Wait." Gia froze. "Does this have anything to do with any lingering effects of the planetary crossing?"

Eva grinned up at Donovan. "Even if it does, we'd be crazy not to."

"Ugh, fine. Let's get this over with," Beckett sighed.

Gia slapped him in the chest. "Get excited about this immediately, Beckett, or I won't be having *lunch* with you for the rest of the week."

"Lunch means afternoon delight," Eva translated for Donovan.

"Right now I just want twelve hours of sleep. Is that too much to ask?" Beckett muttered.

Gia stood on tip toe and whispered something in his ear. His eyes opened the whole way. "Okay! Let's get this show on the road!" he announced.

"Dress code is casual," Donovan told him. "But I really need you in at least a shirt."

An hour later, Donovan, in his dress uniform, paced back and forth in front of his own porch steps. His father dropped a hand on his shoulder. "You're wearing ruts in the grass, son."

Donovan stopped and then began fidgeting with his tie. "She's coming out right? She didn't come to her senses and change her mind?"

"She'll be down in a minute. Your mother just texted."

On cue, the front door opened, and Donovan nearly jumped out of his skin. His mother, still in her deputy uniform, and Phoebe, in a dress she threw on after Eva and Donovan woke her and Franklin up, stepped out onto the porch.

"She's ready," Phoebe grinned.

"Places everybody."

They stood in a semicircle facing the house. His friends, his family. People he had known and loved his entire life. They had his back when times were tough and stood up for him during the good.

Carter and Summer, each juggling a twin beamed at him. Jax and Joey stood with arms around Reva and Caleb, a united unit, a family finally. Beckett stood next to Donovan. He was the only one who bothered with a suit. Gia and Emma were anxiously peering over Niko's shoulder trying to give him advice on angles and lighting. "This damn town is turning me into a wedding photographer," Niko complained.

"Shut up and capture my beautiful baby sister on the happiest day of her life," Emma sniffled.

"Anything for the mother of my child," Niko winked.

Evan and Aurora passed their baby sister Lydia back and forth. "Everyone just keeps getting married," Evan rolled his eyes. "Can't anyone just date anymore?"

"I can't wait to get married," Aurora sighed. "I'm going to have a huuuuge dress and a giant cake!"

Niko's parents, still glowing from their impending grandparenthood, held hands and stood close in the morning chill.

The quiet moment was broken by a police cruiser fishtailing up the lane, lights flashing. The car slid to a halt, and Layla hopped out from behind the wheel. "You didn't think you were doing this without us, did you?"

Colby jumped out of the passenger side and opened the

back door. Minnie in her rumpled Sunday best stepped out. “You better not have gotten married yet!” she said, pointing a finger in his direction. “I work for you for five years, and I get a text from your bride-to-be?”

He owed Eva big time. It seemed like his bride was a fast learner when it came to sharing. He never would have heard the end of it from Minnie if he’d neglected to invite her to his wedding.

“I thought you all would be sleeping off last night,” Donovan admitted.

Colby slapped him on the back. “We wouldn’t miss this for anything.”

Layla punched him in the arm. “I promise I won’t spread it all over town if you bawl like a baby,” she said, loyally.

“She won’t, but I will,” Minnie sniffed.

“Thank you for being here,” Donovan said, drawing Minnie in for a hug. “I’m sorry I didn’t insist on it myself.”

“Well, don’t let it happen again,” she said primly.

He would have answered, had intended to, but the front door opened again. Eva in russet red beamed on her father’s arm. Together they descended the front steps stopping in front of him. The morning sun shone like fire on her hair. She was beautiful, glowing. And she was his.

“Family and friends, we are gathered here today to join Eva and Donovan in marriage. Who gives this woman to be married to this man?” Beckett asked.

Franklin held out his free hand to Phoebe who took it and joined them. “Her mother and I do,” Franklin answered.

Emma’s sniffle turned into a wail. “Hormones,” Niko whispered in apology.

Eva’s parents kissed her and hugged her, and Phoebe wiped the single tear that escaped Eva’s eye.

"Good luck," Franklin whispered to Donovan, shaking his hand firmly.

And then he was handing Eva over to him and Beckett was talking again. But all Donovan saw was Eva. His bride was smiling up at him as if he had given her all the happiness in the world. He wasn't even aware that he was moving until he felt her lips under his. He kissed her with everything that he had, everything that he was. Today, on this frosty morning, was the beginning of their lives together. A new chapter.

"Hey, we didn't get to that part yet," Beckett said, prodding Donovan in his shoulder.

"I guess I got carried away."

51

Eva drummed her fingers on the bathroom vanity where she perched nervously. "I never thought I'd be taking a pregnancy test on my wedding day," she hissed.

"Quiet down. They might hear you," Donovan warned her.

The families were in the house arguing about brunch.

"They probably think we're in here having sex."

"What do we do if we're pregnant?"

"Well, we're already married. I guess we go buy a crib and get a dog."

"I mean, do we tell them?"

"Baby, eventually they're going to notice when you balloon up and then when we're lugging a small human being around with us."

She poked him in the leg with her foot. "I mean, do we tell them today?"

"What do you want to do?"

"We already stepped on Emma and Niko's news with this 'I see your baby and raise you a spontaneous wedding.' I'd kind of like to keep this to ourselves for a few weeks. If that's okay with you?"

"Damn. You make it really easy to keep secrets when you say it's for someone else's good," he teased.

"Easily justifiable." She blew out a breath. "How much time do we have left? I am so nervous right now. I don't know if I'm more nervous about maybe being pregnant or maybe not being pregnant."

He ran a hand up her thigh, pushing the hem of her dress higher. "I can distract you in our remaining minutes of not knowing."

She slipped her arms around his neck. "Are you suggesting the first time we have sex as a married couple it's a bathroom quickie?"

He nuzzled her neck, nipping at the flesh just above her collar bone. "I'm saying we've done everything else ass-backwards." He slid his hand higher, finding the edge of her underwear.

She gave a sexy little gasp that had him stone hard in half a second. "You drive me crazy." She spread her legs a little wider, encouraging him. He hooked his finger under the silky material and felt her heat. The alarm on her phone buzzed, and they froze.

"Should we look?" He breathed the question against her lips, his mouth moving over hers.

Eyes wide and glassy, Eva grabbed his other hand and guided it into the deep v of her dress. "I think I can wait a little longer."

~

"WORTH THE WAIT," Eva muttered against his chest. Her dress was wadded up around her middle, her bra draped over the sink. Donovan's pants were around his ankles, his shoes still on.

"We're napping for four hours today, and then I'm giving you candlelight and flowers and clean sheets and the best sex married people have ever had," he promised.

"How about we find out if we're going to be parents first?" she suggested. "Then you can shower me with seduction."

"Deal," he said, sitting up. He reached blindly over his head for the test on the counter. "Are you ready?"

She took a deep breath, and intertwined her fingers through his. "I'm ready if you are."

He held up the test.

"Oh, my God."

"Now you really owe me a first date."

"I'm so happy and so terrified," Eva squealed.

Donovan cupped her face in his hands. "I think we should name him or her Uranus."

Their laughter, bordering on hysteria, was interrupted by a pounding on the bathroom door. The knob jiggled, and Eva tossed the test in the vanity cabinet.

"Hey boss, we got a report of a fire over at the winery. Looks like a stink bombing went wrong."

Eva stiffened. "Oh, shit."

"Eva, what do you know about a stink bombing at the winery?" Donovan growled, pulling his pants back on.

"Well, you see. I signed this non-disclosure agreement—"

"Fucking Beautification Committee," Donovan sighed.

"Boss. Layla and I are going to take this seeing as it's your wedding day and all," Colby said through the closed door.

Donovan paused, his fingers on his zipper. Eva bit her lip.

"That'd be great Colby. If you need any backup... call Hazel or Minnie."

Eva grinned and shoved her husband's pants back down his hips.

EPILOGUE

"I can't believe we're finally doing this," Eva breathed, her hand, sporting her brand new wedding band squeezed Donovan's.

"Right this way." The maître d', a stuffy little man in a starched shirt and slicked back hair, led them into the dining room. It was a glitzy room with its circular shape and decadent finishes. There were actual candlesticks on every white linen wrapped table top. The wallpaper was a ruby red with gold birds and twisting vines. Half a dozen sets of glass doors led out onto a stone terrace. The room smelled like steak and fresh bread.

Donovan's hand rested warmly, solidly at the small of her back. Since they'd been married—all of ten hours ago—Eva didn't think they'd physically separated from each other.

They sat at a cozy corner table on velvet cushioned chairs and Eva eyed Donovan while the maître d' made a show of spreading the snow-white napkin in her lap.

"Is that a rack of lamb?" Eva asked in a whisper, pointing at a diner's platter.

"Why are you whispering?" Donovan whispered back.

"I feel like we're in a library or a museum."

He grinned and Eva sighed resting her chin on her hand. "You are so good looking. It should be illegal."

"And I'm all yours."

What insane twist of fate did she have to thank for that? Eva wondered. "Pregnant, married, and finally going on our first date," she said.

Donovan drew her knuckles to his lips. "Yeah, that sounds about right where you and I are concerned. I know it feels fast. But Eva, I've been waiting a lifetime for this."

"Are we insane? I mean literally insane," Eva asked. "We've done everything backwards and I'm worried you're going to come to your senses."

He rubbed a thumb over her palm, a reassuring pressure. "When are you going to get it through your thick head that I'm here to stay?"

"Maybe by our twentieth anniversary?"

Eva picked up her menu and sneaked a peek at the tables around them. "Is this really where you would have taken me on our first date?"

Her husband gave her a dry look. "Hell no. Do I look like the gold filigree swan type? This is the only place I can guarantee we won't run into a single Mooner. It's twenty miles out of town and there isn't a vegan option on the menu."

"No interruptions." Eva smiled sweetly.

"No interruptions. Just me and my wife on our first official date."

Eva felt the blood drain from her head as reality punched her in the face. "Oh my god. We're married. And I'm having your baby. And I barely know you. Donovan! What were we thinking?"

Donovan leaned in concerned. "Is this hormones?"

"I don't know! Maybe? I've never accidentally gotten pregnant before. Maybe it's just regular, run of the mill insanity? We don't even live together! How did all this happen?" She felt dizzy.

"Here. Drink." Donovan thrust her water glass at her and fanned her with his napkin.

Eva gulped down half of the glass.

"What if I'm terrible at being a wife? What if I'm the worst mother in the history of mothers?"

"Now, listen to me, wife of mine. You are an incredible woman and it's about fucking time you started realizing it. Just by being you, you're going to be great at the whole wife and mother thing. Sure, we're both going to fuck up and repeatedly. But we'll learn together."

"Together." She nodded like a bobble head.

"There is no point panicking over this. We're married. We're having a baby. As we speak, Jax and Carter are moving your things into *our* house. I love you and we're going to live happily ever after."

Eva took a deep breath. She reached for his hand and ran her fingers over the plain gold band on his finger. "Okay." She nodded. "Okay. I can do this. We can do this. I love the hell out of you. I'm sure I'm going to love our baby. You have an amazing kitchen. Yeah. Okay. We can do this."

"I was thinking about turning the loft into your office... if you'd like to work there. I can make you a desk, a big one. And bookshelves. You can put up a big white board on the wall so you can map out your books."

Eva stared at him, wide-eyed and woozy.

"You'll write and cook. We'll raise our daughter or son. Get a dog. It's going to be a good, solid life, Eva. I promise you that."

"I love your faith in us," she whispered.

"I love your worry. It means you care."

"I do, Donovan. More than anything. I just can't believe that this is my life. I don't want to screw it up."

"Baby. We're a team. We'll keep each other from screwing up and if a mistake still slips in, we'll clean it up together."

An invisible weight lifted and Eva gave him a damp-eyed smile. She was one hell of a lucky woman. "Whew. Okay. I'm chalking that one up to hormones. No more freak outs tonight," she promised.

"No freak outs. No interruptions." He raised his water glass to hers.

"To the beginning of a beautiful, *quiet* life together," Eva toasted.

"Excuse me?" A woman in a sequined black cocktail dress approached, a napkin and pen clutched in one hand and reading glasses in the other.

She was staring at Eva with unusual intensity. Eva shifted uncomfortably in her seat.

"Can we help you?" Donovan asked.

"Oh!" The woman leaned in and screeched six inches from Eva's face. "It *is* you! Herbert! This is Ava Franklin." The dining room chatter came to a screeching halt around them.

"Ava what?" Herbert, in a tan suit, harrumphed through his white mustache. He looked like the type of man who'd have a monocle.

"Franklin! You *know*." The woman fluttered her ringed hands like a hummingbird. "The one whose book you found so *instructive*."

Eva choked on her ice water and Donovan coughed into his napkin.

"Oh, I can't tell you how much I love your books! Do you live around here? Are we neighbors?" She slapped her husband in the chest. "Herbert, get my phone. I need a picture. This is the famous author Ava Franklin," the woman announced to the room.

Donovan slumped a little in his seat as women—and a few curious men—started forming a line. His shoulders shook with silent laughter.

Eva held up her menu in front of their faces. "I'm so sorry! I swear after this, no more interruptions. Just hang in there a little longer."

Donovan grinned, that quick, panty-melting smile. "Baby, you're worth the wait."

AUTHOR'S NOTE TO THE READER

Dear Reader,

Only in Blue Moon, am I right? I mean seriously, where else would an astrological apocalypse happen? I couldn't even tell you where the idea came from. It was just there and so insane I had to write it. And thus, Uranus happened.

You know I *love* writing a really, good guy hero. But you may not know that I'm also a sucker for John Wayne movies, especially the non-Westerns. That's where Donovan got his name. *Donovan's Reef* is one of my favorite movies and it only seemed right to name a John Wayne-worthy hero after the character.

What can I tell you about Eva? She and I share a few characteristics including being short romance novelists incapable of opening a cabinet door without whacking body parts. It happens almost weekly for me. On her own, Eva is one bad decision away from making a mess of everything, but with Donovan in her corner she has someone who believes in her and that makes her stronger.

I hope you enjoyed *Holding on to Chaos*. If you did, leave a review or drop me a line. Tell me if you want more Blue Moon! I'd love to hear from you. You can find me on Facebook and Instagram. And don't forget to sign up for my newsletter.

I really, really, really appreciate your readership. Thanks for picking up *Holding on to Chaos*! May your To Be Read list never end and your reading chair get even comfier.

Xoxo,
Lucy

ABOUT THE AUTHOR

Lucy Score is a *Wall Street Journal* and #1 Amazon bestselling author. She grew up in a literary family who insisted that the dinner table was for reading and earned a degree in journalism. She writes full-time from the Pennsylvania home she and Mr. Lucy share with their obnoxious cat, Cleo. When not spending hours crafting heartbreaker heroes and kick-ass heroines, Lucy can be found on the couch, in the kitchen, or at the gym. She hopes to someday write from a sailboat, or oceanfront condo, or tropical island with reliable Wi-Fi.

Sign up for her newsletter and stay up on all the latest Lucy book news.

And follow her on:

Website: Lucyscore.com

Facebook at: lucyscorewrites

Instagram at: scorelucy

Readers Group at: Lucy Score's Binge Readers Anonymous

ACKNOWLEDGMENTS

Kari March Designs for the beautiful cover.

Dirty martinis for making me infinitely more creative.

My ARC team for being some of my biggest cheerleaders.

Torchbearer Sauces for Oh My Garlic.

My editing team (Dawn, Amanda, and Mr. Lucy) for being really good at stuff that I'm really bad at.

Mr. Lucy for always cleaning up after I cook.

Public libraries for supporting the reading community.

Bacon.

Dan for doing that research thing that I needed that time.

LUCY'S TITLES

Standalone Titles

Undercover Love

Pretend You're Mine

Finally Mine

Protecting What's Mine

Mr. Fixer Upper

The Christmas Fix

Heart of Hope

The Worst Best Man

Rock Bottom Girl

The Price of Scandal

By a Thread

Forever Never

Things We Never Got Over

Riley Thorn

Riley Thorn and the Dead Guy Next Door

Riley Thorn and the Corpse in the Closet

Riley Thorn and the Blast from the Past

The Blue Moon Small Town Romance Series

No More Secrets

Fall into Temptation

The Last Second Chance

Not Part of the Plan

Holding on to Chaos

The Fine Art of Faking It

Where It All Began

The Mistletoe Kisser

Bootleg Springs Series

Whiskey Chaser

Sidecar Crush

Moonshine Kiss

Bourbon Bliss

Gin Fling

Highball Rush

Sinner and Saint

Crossing the Line

Breaking the Rules

Printed in the USA
CPSIA information can be obtained
at www.ICGtesting.com
CBHW021307190924
14681CB00004B/25